The Boy Who Danced with Rabbits

J.R. Collins

W & B Publishing
USA

W & B Publishers

For information:
W & B Publishers
9001 Ridge Hill Street
Kernersville, NC 27284

www.a-argusbooks.com

ISBN: 9781942981718

Book Cover designed by
Capsaicin eXtreme Marketing

Printed in the United States of America

Acknowledgements and Thank You

A desire for my children to respect their ancestor's heritage spawned this book from one who has never written down the stories of his imagination. I had no intention of sending the words I'd written any further than to my own family living room. I want to thank my wonderful wife, Colleen, for all she has done to make this book happen as well as my son Alex for his support. But, it was my daughter Emma, with her enthusiasm for the first of my stories and her love of history, that kept me writing until my simple bits of historical fiction became a novel. Thank you, Emma, for giving me the confidence to finish something I never would've thought was possible.

To my new friend, Shawn Jarrard. A graduate of the University of Georgia with a degree in Journalism. Thank you for your guidance and patience. You did a great job helping prepare my manuscript. Your edits were insightful and inspiring. Good luck my friend.

To my agent, Mrs. Jeanie Loiacono. How can I ever thank you enough for believing in me? A true novice. Your encouragement kept me going when things seemed way too big for my little world. Thank you ever so much. I am so glad that the word "can't" is not in your vocabulary!

But most of all, I thank God for giving me the desire and the words that made this book a reality. To him belongs all the glory. He is the Great Spirit. A true friend, and He loves us all.

Prologue

I am the last of my time and kind. I have walked what my
Indian brethren call Mother Earth for some ninety years and
have seen many changes. Buried many friends. My family
were among the original settlers to what is now called the
Appalachian Mountains. We knew them as home. The
Cherokee Indians were native to the land where we settled
and my best friend all my growing up years was a full blood.
His family became my family and mine his. We learned from
each other. It was the way.

I have seen things. I have done things. Many different
things that no human will ever have the opportunity to do
again because of the changes. We were spiritual. We
depended on God to provide our needs. Our toil was that of
survival. We made what we wore. We grew or killed what
we ate. We lived during a time that was proper before God;
the Great Spirit. Life was lived according to what was known
to be right and we respected that there is right and there is
wrong throughout the whole of our beings. Duty to family
and the people we shared life with was a dependency that all
accepted. A person's actions affected all and we cared about
how what we did made others' life change. Responsibility to
our neighbors, to treat them the way we wished to be treated,
was the rule. Not only because we believed the Bible, but
because it was right. Both settler and Indian knew the way.

I tell this story because I need for those coming on
behind me to know what it took for their ancestors to
survive. For my children to know that how they live and how
they treat others is important. I want folks to know that
trusting God should be first in their life, and to guarantee
they see their loved ones across the Great River, is only by

accepting the love Jesus leaked out on the cross. I have buried many and soon I will join them, but I will see them because He died for me and I accept Him as the Life. That is also the way.

I need to tell my story. I need for folks to hear it. I am the last of my kind, and I am willing to share the adventures of my youth to bring benefit to those I will leave behind. So, if you desire to hear then take a seat and listen. I will fire my pipe and commence. I hope my story will find favor with you.

Chapter One

Ain't What Jesus Would've Done

My name is Jebediah Collins, but folks always called me Jeb. I was born on a cold and snowy night, late in the winter of 1815, at the base of Ben's Knob Mountain, on the southern end of the Appalachian in a valley called Choestoe; this is a Cherokee name and you say it the way the Indians do, Cho-E-Sto-E. My parents' names were Thompson and Celia Collins. Our folks come from Ireland. I picked a terrible time to be born. It weren't just any kinda snow that night. It was what my dad, 'Thompie,' called a 'mule-stoppin' snow.' He know'd all there was to know about mules 'cause he raised 'em to trade, just as my granddad before him.

The old Cherokee woman that helped our women birth children couldn't make it to our home that night, so my sister Anne, who was only six-years-old at the time, had to help me be born. She was a wonderful sister to me. I would grow to love her almost as much as I did my future beloved, Elizabeth.

I was born too early. Momma had a tough time with me. It must've been a scary sight when I showed up. Anne told me later that Momma cried and Dad just kinda looked at me like he couldn't make out what I was. She told me that I looked like one of them baby rats we'd find in the corncrib durin' rat-killin' time. I had no hair and I was blue like the mountains on a clear winter evenin'.

As Anne would tell it, "We all thought you dead, Jeb. I cleaned you up, then Dad put you in a flour sack and was plannin' to bury you the next morning. The ground was so froze that we was gonna have to boil water and pour it out on the grave site just to dig a hole. So, since it was late and for some reason he never could explain, he put the sack under the cook stove for the night."

I'm sure glad he put that sack under there. By the next mornin' when he come in to get it, so he could put my body in the ground, that sack was movin' when he slid it out from between the legs of our stove. He allowed a rat got in over night and was feedin' on my body. Dogged if he weren't about to smash it right there with his boot. Thankfully he decided that since it would make a bloody mess on the floor, and blood was hard to clean up, he'd let the critter out on the porch boards and then smash it. He carried me outside, poured me out on the wood plank porch, and raised his foot to smash whatever was in there with me…and near did, till he realized it weren't no rat at all. It was me a-movin' 'round in that sack.

He shouted out, "Anne, come quick, this young'un ain't dead. He's movin'."

Anne come runnin' to see what he was hollerin' 'bout, and there I lay, wigglin' like a red worm. She screamed when she come out the door and saw me, wakin' Momma up.

Momma made her way out to the porch. When she saw me, she hollered at Dad, "Thompie, you're awful mean for spilling our boy out on the porch like that. What in the good Lord's name was you thinking? Now, get him up and fetch him in the warm before he dies again, this time from the cold."

My folks was real religious. They thought a lot of Jesus and his bunch. I got a gash on my knee from a nail he poured me out on that morning. I still have that scar to this day. It reminds me that God was lookin' out for me. You see, my dad was a big man. If he'd 'a-smashed me with his boot, I surely would've been kilt'.

That was the second time in my young life that I'd escaped the Death Angel. It would not be the last.

The old Cherokee medicine woman finally made it to our place a couple days after I was born. It was a good thing, too. My momma was bad off. She'd turned white. Follks said her skin looked like the underside of a rabbit's belly till that old woman started doctorin' her up. The Cherokee was respected for their healers, and she was the best in the clan.

That Indian woman know'd all the plants in the woods and could brew up a tea or salve that would right almost anything. Her hair was as silver as moonlight and long, reachin' all the way near to her knees. She kept it tied with old leather straps, a single beaded feather woven in the bindings.

My first memory of her scared the life outa me. I used to have nightmares about her and the things she'd talk about, like spirits and haints, painter cats and all that spooky mountain lore. She looked scary, too. She wore old beads and claws draped 'round her neck with some woven into her hair and more hangin' off her skins. The skin on her hands looked like the skin on the back of a horny toad, rough, and her fingernails were long and black like the coals you find in the fireplace when you cleaned it out. Her voice was loud, so when she hollered it could be heard all over. She hollered a lot, too. I guess it scared the bad spirits away. I didn't cotton to all that spirit stuff, but somehow she know'd things. Like when it was time to go and help some poor woman have a baby or if somebody got hurt, she'd just show up. Maybe there was somethin' to what she believed. Fortunately for us, she wanted my sister Anne to be her second, so that old woman got to teachin' Anne all she know'd. Come in handy, too, the day my dad got struck by that rattle maker. Anne saved his life, but I will talk about that later.

Turns out that old woman was Wolf's grandmother on his dad's side. I got to know her as I got older. She was as kind as any woman could be, but as tough as a pine knot if she needed. I saw her catch a copper backed snake one time with her bare hand and squeeze its head flat. She caught 'em that way so's to use their venom in some kinda stuff that helped with snakebite. When she was done with 'em, she'd give 'em to Wolf. Him and me would make things outa their hides, like belts and pouches for bead and tobacco carryin'. Wolf and me got real fond of smokin' tobacco. We had a pipe in our 'possibles bag' most all the time when we was old enough. My dad didn't like for me to smoke; said I was too young. Wolf's brothers and his dad would sit around the fire and smoke. Me and Wolf would smoke with 'em, too, if my dad weren't around. But that was when we was older, maybe twelve or better.

***

My folks weren't the only ones birthin' babies on that cold and snowy night. The boy who would become my best friend and blood brother was born in what the Cherokee called Panther Cave. It was in a rock cliff on the west side of Blood Mountain and, as I would learn later, it was a good place to be in bad weather. His folks, Dancing Bear and A-Ga-Li-Ha, named him Wolf. He was a full-blooded Cherokee Indian. To this day, I ain't never met but one soul as brave and courageous as him. He near got me killed and saved my hide more than once. I will always remember our growin' up years in the Choestoe Valley.

His folks had a log home on Slaughter Mountain, just west of the gap, but bein' Cherokee, they had their own way 'a doin' things. Seems to me it would've been better to be born in their log home in front of a big fire, like I was. But as I would learn time and again, them Indians had their own way of seein' things, and weren't no changin' their thinkin' once their minds got set.

Panther Cave was a special place for Wolf and his family. They would go there often. Maybe him bein' born in that cave on such a cold night was for the best. Since after that, Wolf never did mind the cold. He could bathe in Wolf Creek in the middle of winter and it not bother him at all. I tried it once and my privates seemed to shrink up to nothin'. That scared me so that ever since that day, I would warm my washin' water with a fire when it was cold weather. Dad built Momma an oak tub with a fire pit above it and a iron tub to heat water in. We had hot water in the winter to bathe. That was nice.

Wolf's momma was one of the prettiest women you'd ever meet. She just moved in a way that sang to your soul. His dad sure was lucky to be hitched to such a grand woman. My momma was pretty, too, but not like her. Her skin was golden and her hair shined like that of a black bear during the time of fallin' leaves. I saw her bathin' herself in the falls at their place one time when Wolf and me come from huntin'. I never will forget how pretty she looked. It weren't such a big deal that I saw her; them Indians did a lot of things with just their moccasins on.

I got to be part of their family. Wolf and me would get near naked and run in the woods when we wanted. You just had to be careful of the briars and tree limbs. I never did tell Momma that we did that. She'd 'a-took a plow strap to my backside if she'd found out. One afternoon I even got Anne to strip down and run with us. She loved it, too, but she had a bad time with a copper backed snake that crossed her trail, so she never did it again.

Wolf and his family made almost all the things they owned. By watching and doin', I got to learn how to make stuff the way they did. My momma sure liked what I made. She'd fuss over them things like they was sacred. I once made her a bracelet outa some bone beads that I carved and colored red and blue, the Cherokee way. She wore it for the rest of her days. She even wore it to her grave the day we buried her. It made me awful proud that she cared for that bracelet as much as she did. I was many years older when she died, but that bracelet still looked like it did the day I give it to her. It had main beads that were blue, her favorite color, made of deer antler. The rest was smaller that I carved outa rabbit hipbones, they was red.

A-Ga-Li-Ha, or Sunshine as her name meant in her native Cherokee, bragged on my work, sayin', "That bracelet is as fine as any I've ever made, Jeb; as good a job as most Cherokee could do."

That set well with me. I figured if she thought that much of it, then it should be fine for my momma.

My folks always liked me spendin' time with Wolf and his family. He had an older sister named Rose, and two older brothers named Fox Running and Moon Shadow, who taught Wolf how to hunt. His sister was pretty like her mother. I always liked it when I would come around and she was doin' chores with just her moccasins on. She would dress herself when she knew I was comin', but sometimes I would forget to holler out and I'd walk in unexpected-like. I never told Momma that, neither. Indians liked doin' things in the near raw and went mostly naked a good part of the time, 'cept in front of folks other than family. I could never bring myself to strip down in front of any of 'em except Wolf, his brothers and Anne, once.

My older brother, Cain, was fond of Wolf's sister. They ended up runnin' off in later years. I can't blame 'em for doin' that 'cause of what happened against all the Indians when that awful President Jackson took charge. Them government men ought'ta been mule-whipped for what they done to the Mountain Cherokee. They weren't smart enough to get 'em all, though. Several of the Cherokee families hid in the mountains and never come out till the craziness was all over. Wolf's bunch was one of those families, even though their land was safe.

Cain was older than Anne. He weren't born to my momma and dad, but he was theirs all the same. Folks could tell, too. He looked different than we did. I guess he came from a different place, 'cause he had the yellowest hair you'd ever see. The color reminded you of the yellow sweet corn we grow'd in our garden; his eyes as blue as a clear sky at noon. The old Indian woman said he had a tender spirit due to the way he was colored, but I reasoned she must've never seen him once he got riled up.

He had a temper that would scare the devil away. He weren't afraid of nothin'. I once saw him grab a big wounded buck by the antlers and break its neck with his bare hands. He said the gun he was usin' didn't shoot straight, and that was how come he missed its vitals. I believe it was his shootin' that did that. Dad could hit a rabbit in the ear at thirty paces with it. It was a small bore rifle. He just didn't hit that deer good and had to finish it off somehow. My dad know'd he couldn't shoot straight, so he only gave him a couple of loads at a time to hunt with; helped save on powder. I think that set him off most. Wolf's dad taught Cain later on how to use a bow for huntin'. After that, he never picked up a gun again. That is not till him and Rose had their trouble with the clan from Yonah.

Cain was always kind to me and we got along, but Wolf's brothers, Fox Running and Moon Shadow, didn't care for him and they'd fight. Cain had a couple years on Moon Shadow and three on Fox Running , so he whooped 'em every time. It didn't matter if it was one-on-one or one-on-two. Finally, after a time, them boys got tired of bein' beat so bad and they all become the best of friends. Them and Cain would run the mountains together and hunt. The brothers figured out it was best to be friends and not enemies. When Cain got to fightin', his temper would spark and the blood would start runnin' outa whoever it was he was fightin'. He once got into a fight at the church house with one of the deacons and near killed the man. That deacon was even bleedin' from his eye. It was bad, but Cain didn't care.

Momma had a fit, but Dad just reasoned it away. "He had it comin', Celia, 'cause of the way he was actin' toward the Indians." Cain had grown to like the Indians, with that special likin' to Wolf's sister, but fightin' deacons was bad business. Folks didn't take to what he'd done for a while. Near got Cain put upon by the church; that was bad if that happened. I think Dad got him outa that.

There was another time when Cain's takin' up for folks near got him the what for. He ended up whoopin' three full-grow'd Cherokee while saving Fox Running's hide.

Fox Running was gentle and kind; had a way about him that folks would cotton to. He was more of a softer Indian than most you'd find in the mountains, but could be hard when needed; liked bein' around the women folk more than the warriors. Cain sorta took it on himself, since he was older, after they became friends, to try and look out for him. Moon Shadow was tough and kept to himself mostly, bein' gone a lot huntin' and doin' only God know'd what, so Cain and Fox spent a good deal of time campin' and huntin' and goin' on walks. Cain grow'd real fond of Fox Running, like an older brother, kinda. One walk ended up near costin' Fox his very life. Cain earned his keep that night. Fox told me about it later on 'fore all the Yonah trouble started.

"We were on a walk, Jeb," Fox Running began. "We'd been gone three suns. As the fourth sun was settling, we crossed paths with three Cherokee men traveling. They had their pouches and weapons, so I didn't know if they were hunting or just goin' to another place. Cain paid them little mind and passed on without so much as looking in their direction, but I hesitated and looked at them. They were bandits. Cain knew it by simply looking at them as he walked. That is why he did not stop and visit. Unfortunately, I did not see them for what they were. That night at camp he let me know how I had done wrong."

"Those was slave bandits today, Fox," Cain had said to me. "And now they know you know who they are. They come and take folks and sell them to the big boats to take away. They would love nothin' better than to take your young carcass and trade it for some common goods or hard coin. So you best be on the watch tonight. I will stand guard as well."

"Sleep would not come for me that night," said Fox Running. "I felt weak and small at not knowing those evil doers' aim. Cain knew what was gonna happen, and when it did, he was ready. The tug on my blanket was enough to wake me; the gag they stuck in my mouth was nasty. It hid my screams. I was so scared. I looked for Cain, but he was nowhere that I could see. I did not know if that was good or bad. Turns out it all worked for the good, really."

"'Where is your friend, little one?' the biggest of the three men asked me," said Fox Running. "Before I could think how to answer, I heard a dull thud and the Indian let go of me, falling to the ground. He'd found out where Cain was.

"The second Cherokee was on Cain like a cat, but he was ready. He slung his club and took that one out cold with a blow to the side of his head. Blood flew from the man's mouth and nose. The third jerked his knife and poked it toward Cain with a hard jab, who stepped to his left and brought the club down hard on the knife arm of that Indian. I heard the bones break as the knife hit the ground along with its owner. In less than a minute, Cain had whooped all three of them boat rats and saved my hide from becoming a slave. I owe my life to Cain. He is my brother."

Cain always figured it that way, too, and made sure Fox Running was never bothered for nothin'. He was as nice a body as you'd ever meet. Him and Cain stayed friends their whole lives. Brothers to the end.

We had neighbors, too. They was several folks that lived in the valley, but the ones I liked best was the Weaver family. They lived in Hog Pen Cove, which was a couple of miles to the east of our place as the crow flies, and weren't hard to get to. They was a good bunch of folks and had many kids. They was true farmers; chose their place where the ground was flat and rich and had good water all around. They grow'd all sorts of good stuff like vegetables, tobacco, fruits, nuts and such, with everybody bein' real fond of their tobacco. The Indians thought it was the best in the mountains. They would come from all over to trade for it. Wolf and me liked it, too. It made a body feel good. You had to be careful of it, though. Too much would make you near lazy.

All the neighbors was good and worked hard to provide, 'cept a certain bunch that lived down off the River Notla. Folks would say they was bad; that everybody ought to leave 'em be, but my dad saw it different. He allowed, "That ain't what Jesus would've done", so that ain't the way he was gonna act. He'd go down and visit them folks ever so often and help 'em out with things best he could. I was nine, about to be ten, when he decided he'd take me with him, though he usually took Cain. I ended up wishin' Cain had gone over me, all things figured.

I ain't to this day ever seen such a place. The cabin was made outa logs and looked like the gray you see on a fish when it's been outa the water too long and is startin' to rot. The roof was a sight! You could tell that the rain would run through it like when one of our wooden buckets cracked and took to leakin', lettin' the water run out.

Their old dog come out from under the porch and it stunk. With its eyes sunk back in its head and its ribs all showin', that dog looked like it just crawled outa its own grave. But it was a friendly dog. For some reason it had a piece of old rope around its neck, like it'd broke loose from its confines. Come right up and licked my hand. I figured it was hungry. Probably had worms, too, so I wiped my hand off on my pants leg. Wolf's grandma could fix that 'cause she know'd how to doctor animals as well as folks.

The door to the place was crooked and needed fixin', with a crack down low where a pair of eyes was lookin' out. I figured it for a child. My dad walked right up and knocked on that old door. I was scared tight of what might come out. Wolf and me talked about that later and come up with all sorts of things that might've showed when it did open. Turned out it was a woman that opened the door. She and the young'un was dirty, just like that old dog. They smelled bad. I wondered why, with all that river water runnin' back of their place, they didn't wash.

The child was a boy. I thought it strange that he looked so much like Cain. He had them blue eyes like his, and you could tell he had yellow hair even though it was real dirty. I wanted to show him how to strip down and wash in the river like Wolf and me did, but I thought better of it. It was early fall and the water was most likely cold by now, but he really needed to wash, so did his momma.

The house stunk, too. You could smell the stink when she opened the door. Smelled like old rotten cabbage that had soured in winter storage 'cause the hay hadn't been laid over deep enough. I could hear things movin' around in there, but it weren't people. It sounded like critters of some sort. We never did see any menfolk, so I guessed they was off doin' stuff. Dad said they was hardly ever around when he went there.

Dad and I worked till dark that day, fixin' broke things around that old smelly house. When we got thirsty we had to drink outa the river. There weren't no bucket about the place to lower into the well. Come to notice, they had no rope neither, 'cept the short piece tied around the dog's neck.

The woman never offered to supply us with food, so we ate walnuts off the tree in back by the river. I never cared for walnuts much, but I was hungry, so I ate a few. I wished we'd 'a-stopped and picked up some of those big sweet chestnuts that lay on the ground between our place and that old stinky place. I loved them big old nuts. Wolf and me would eat 'em till our gut was pokin' out, then eat some more later on. We could hardly get our fill once they started fallin'.

That boy that was there would slip around the house while we was workin' on different things. I'd know when he was spyin' on us 'cause you could smell him. That old dog followed him around; hardly left his side, too. I'm sure he growled at me once when I got too close to the young'un. I kept thinkin' it was curious how that boy looked a lot like Cain.

It was near dark when Dad loaded up Big Jim, our lead mule, and we headed home. Dad led the way, letting me ride Jim with what tools we'd carried to use that day hung over his shoulders; his huntin' knife strapped under Jim's neck. We just had cleared the last gap before home and was followin' the trail through a deep ivy thicket when we heard it. A low, throaty growl that made the hair rise up on the back of my neck and stopped Jim dead in his tracks.

Dad know'd right off what it was, freezing hard with Jim and said, "Be quiet as a church mouse, boy, they's a cat close by. Don't want to get Jim stirred up. Something is wrong. That cat ain't right. Might be sick or could be he's guardin' a kill. Most likely he ain't hungry, but it just ain't right he didn't run off or stay hid till we passed."

He didn't need to tell me to be quiet. I couldn't 'a-made a sound if I'd 'a-wanted to. The stories about spirits and haints and mountain cats that Wolf's grandmother had told me come back. I was near shakin' to death.

Jim could tell that I was nervous, which made him edgy, too. He started to get skittish. His ears perked up and I felt his back muscles tighten like a fiddle string. I know'd he'd run if he got any more scared.

It didn't take long for that to happen.

The big cat came from thin air and landed on Jim's rump, makin' him strike outa there like he was shot out of a gun, takin' me and the cat with him. The cat's landin' near knocked me off Jim's back. And as I was tryin' to get turned back front ways, I saw the cat's snout covered in blood. Dad was right, it was guardin' a fresh kill.

"Whoa, Jim," Dad hollered. "Stop, mule."

But that did no good at all 'cause there was a huge bobcat on Jim's haunches. Me and that cat was goin' for a ride whether we liked it or not! It was 'bout all I could do to just hang on.

Ole Jim was runnin' for all he was worth, while that cat was makin' its way toward me one claw at a time. It was screamin' and I was screamin', and Jim must've thought the devil was on him, I never know'd a mule could run so. I don't know to this day how I stayed on his back, but I did, and so did that cat.

I finally gathered my mind enough to remember that Dad strapped his huntin' knife under Jim's neck, so I bent to try and reach it. Big Jim was runnin' and I was holdin' on, tryin' to watch the cat and reach for the knife all at the same time, when all hell broke loose. The cat had reached my head and was bearin' down on me for the love of blood, when my hand felt the leather that was wrapped around the handle of that knife. Somehow, I got the blade loose with my right hand just as I felt the claws sink deep in my left shoulder. Pain shot through me like hell's fire as the cat's other claw grabbed the back of my head. At the same time, his back claws locked into Jim's rump, makin' the mule run even faster. I was prayin' that he'd keep runnin' 'cause he was headed straight for home. I had no idea where Dad was, but I know'd there was no way he could run as fast as Jim, he would be way back.

I began to figure that Jim was leavin' it up to me to rid us of this cat. As the fear I felt turned to anger, I jerked the knife free and swung it as hard as I could around toward that cat. I felt the blade hit somethin' hard as its claws tore my head and shoulder open even more, causin' me to scream out louder in pain. I pulled the knife back and struck again. This time it sunk to the hilt. I felt the warmth of the cat's blood as the knife sliced through meat and bone and tore into the cat's heart. I must've hit it clean. It was deadn'r dried leather britches as we ran full on into the barnyard of our home.

Anne heard the commotion and ran outa the house with Cain to see what I was screamin' about. What a sight they saw! That cat died so quick that it was still stuck to me and Jim like a bobcat blanket.

Anne screamed, "Momma come quick! Jeb's been hurt bad by some kinda' critter, and it's still gotta hold on him."

Cain know'd what it was; could see Dad's knife sunk in its side. He jerked the knife clean and ripped that cat off me so fast I didn't know it was gone till I looked up to see Momma. I guess what I was feelin' was all the pain I could stand, 'cause I fell from off of Jim's back into her arms. She held my head back to make sure I was still breathin' and the last thing I remember was Momma's tears as they fell onto my face. I was alive, but for how long only God could say. I was hurt bad and bleedin' like a stuck pig.

The old medicine woman was at our place before the sun was up. She know'd somethin' had happened and that we needed her. She came with her medicines and took charge of my wellbein' the very moment she arrived. Anne had cleaned my wounds and done all a body in her position could, but it still weren't enough to keep the evil spirits from comin' on me.

Wolf's grandmother had much experience with deep meat cuts. She praised Anne, sayin', "You've done a fine thing, girl, cleaning this boy up the way you did. Now, boil me up some honey and inside hickory bark, then let's open up these wounds and get that claw dirt outa there. If we don't, the wounds will get festered up. A cat's claws have bad spirits trailing them."

Anne and the Indian woman stayed with me till I come awake the next day. Havin' that old woman in your room when you wake up is not somethin' I would wish on a body at all. I thought for a minute that she was the devil and I hadn't made it. She was scary enough when she was outside in the open.

The Cherokee Indians fought many battles in the old woman's life. Tendin' this type of hurt was natural to her; she did it well. She said things I didn't understand, and there was smoke in the room that had an odor I'd never smelled before. I was sittin' up when I come to. The poultice she was a puttin' on me stunk like burnt lard. I didn't mind, though. It made the pain go away.

I remember Anne givin' me a cup of a bittersweet brew at some point, which made me feel warm all over. I sure liked it a lot. It made my body feel good. The poultice they was puttin' on my cuts burned a little. But if it would save my life, then I weren't gonna say a word. That cat had torn me apart. I could tell my life was hangin' 'cause of somethin' Momma called infection. The old medicine woman was gonna keep me alive, though, that much I believed. Sleep soon had me again.

That's when the dream started.

It began with me standin' on a cliff overlookin' the Choestoe Valley. A huge black bear come to me and started talkin'. He called himself Freedom. I tried to speak back, but I couldn't.

The Indians would call him Old Man Bear. He said to me, "I have come to make you understand the way of the future for the Cherokee in this land."

I weren't scared so I just sat down with him and listened. He spoke of Wolf's folks and how they'd lived in Choestoe for a long time. But that time would end soon, strangers were comin' to the valley to look for the yellow rock.

"Wolf and his family will be in danger. You must tell them of this vision when you return from the spirit world," said Freedom.

He spoke of Panther Cave and how it would save them from the trouble ahead; that no one should know of its secret location inside.

"You can go there if you want, but never take anyone else. Only you and Wolf's clan should know where it is," commanded Old Man Bear.

He warned that I couldn't tell anyone else about the cave. This was strange to me since the only thing I'd learned of it was that my friend had been born there. I'd never been to the cave, but when Freedom spoke of it, I saw it clearly. I know'd from that exact moment that I could walk to Panther Cave without ever havin' been there. It was on the west side of Blood Mountain, behind a sheer rock cliff—the very cliff I was sittin' on now.

Freedom led me to the cave and showed me a secret room in the back that couldn't be seen from inside. You had to crawl over a tall boulder to see where to enter the room. This is where he said Wolf and his family would be safe when the time came.

Old Man Bear said, "You will survive your wounds. Your sister will learn the ways of the old medicine woman. It was the mountain spirits that led Old Man Bobcat to you that night, and now I have brought you the words you needed to hear. This cost a mountain critter its life, so hear my words and remember, young one."

It all made sense to me when I woke the followin' morning, in a Cherokee sorta way. This was a lot for a boy of ten years to settle on, but it was all clear in my young mind what I must do. From that night on, I began to understand the Indian way better than any white man I would ever meet 'cept my dad and Mr. Boone, the son of the great Daniel Boone from Kentuck.

Chapter Two

People Come to Visit

The mountain folk loved to go and visit. There was no better reason than the birth of a new baby. That winter of my birth saw almost everybody in Choestoe comin' to our home to visit. It didn't take long for news to travel from one family to another when need be. They brought gifts, too, just like when Jesus was born in the *Bible*. It was the better part of two months 'fore everybody made the rounds, with folks comin' and goin' for the longest time that cold winter in 1815. Even the Indians come to see the baby that survived the Blue Death...and the rat stompin'. Them kinda things was spiritual to the Indians; most important to their way of thinkin'.

Wolf's dad and the old medicine woman were the first folks to come 'round. My dad sure was pleased to see 'em. He met 'em as they were comin' across the pasture above our home, saying to the old woman, "It is an honor to me that you have made time for a visit. I wish to thank you for all you have done for my wife and my family. My home is your home for as long as you walk the earth." This was the way my dad felt. He owed that woman much and more, and not just on account of my birth.

The old woman was touched by what my dad had said. She almost cried as she introduced her son, "Thompie Collins, this is my youngest son, Dancing Bear. He and his wife also share a new baby boy, born on the same winter's night as Jebediah. The child is back home with his mother, A-Ga-Li-Ha, on Slaughter Mountain, but my son wanted to see this child who survived the blue skin birth. To my people, this is strong medicine. Your boy has been touched by the spirit of the mountains."

My dad was amazed with this new Indian, as he said, "Welcome, Dancing Bear. It is an honor to meet family of your mother. You and your family are welcome here. You may come and stay as you please. My fire will always welcome you and your family."

Dancing Bear was touched by my dad's respect, as he spoke, "Thank you for your words, Thompie Collins. You and your family will be welcome at our home as well. Bring your son. He and my son will become friends and hunt the mountains together. I know this in my heart."

My dad told me later that he felt they would become good friends in time; that both our families would someday come together. He could not have been more insightful.

Dancing Bear and the old medicine woman stayed at our place for several days. Durin' that time, everybody got to know him. He was a big man like my dad, smart and strong, too, and had a keen sense of humor.

He brought me a gift that must've been hard to tote all the way to our home from their place on Slaughter. It was a new bear hide blanket he'd just finished that fall. The bear that gave it up had'ta been huge. I spent most of my baby years sleepin' on it. I loved that bear hide. In later years I carried it with me when we camped on trips durin' cold weather. I slept many a cold night away in the mountains on that bearskin. It kept me warm even without a fire.

Dad and our family owed that old Indian woman more than we could ever return. As they was leavin' to return to Slaughter Mountain, my dad stopped 'em and made her a gift of one of his best young mules.

"I would like to honor you and your family with a gift of this mule for all your mother has done for us; to honor your new son as well," he told Dancing Bear. "It is a good mule and will serve your family well. It would please me for you to have it. He can log, plow and ride, so it will be good for your mother."

Dancing Bear was stunned. "I will take your gift with great pride and use it to help my family. My mother will ride and ease her old bones on the long walks she makes through the mountains. My family says thank you, Thompie Collins."

The look that my dad and Dancing Bear shared that mornin' as they locked forearms and said goodbye was a look into one another's soul. From then on, they know'd they could count on each other to be there when the other needed. It was a good thing, too, 'cause that bond would come in handy more times than they realized that morning.

Dancing Bear and his family favored that mule Dad give 'em; the gift brought honor to Wolf and his family. No other Indian family in Choestoe had a mule as big and as high quality as they did to help with their work and travel. That was big medicine for Dancing Bear and his family. My dad's mules were bigger than the normal-sized mule. He sired 'em from Belgian Draft horse mares while usin' Mammoth Jacks bought from actual stock of George Washington himself. Made their feet bigger, too. They could hold a trail better than a horse and not slip. They cost twenty dollars gold each. Most Cherokee would not part with their gold for a mule.

When folks would come for a visit, they'd stay a while; travelin' in the mountains weren't easy; it took some time to get anywhere. They brought their own truck and camped out in the woods around our place. They had to stay in the woods; no fires were allowed in the barn and our log home was too small for everybody at once.

Dad liked it that all them folks come 'round 'cause he was good at fixin' things. They would bring their broke tools and such for him to mend. In return, they'd trade him goods for his effort. You didn't have to worry 'bout anything bein' stole. If a thief was found out in the mountains, he was tarred and feathered before he know'd it. Mountain justice was swift and common.

There weren't much coin money to be had, but folks always had somethin' to trade with. Knives, lead, powder, beads, flour, sugar, food, hides, tobacco and handmade stuff was what most had to trade 'stead of money. Everybody had a gold piece or two, but those were put up and kept for tradin' in the spring or Killin' Time in the fall. Gold was used for buyin' things that couldn't be made, like new guns, or in Dad's case, horses and Jacks for breedin'. They kept his mule business goin'. That's how he'd make any gold coin he ever got. Tradin' was the way most mountain folk got what they needed. It took a lot of trade to get one of Dad's mules.

Since my birth was in wintertime, there weren't much to do in the way of work 'round their homes, so most folks saw my birth as a way to get together. Everybody that know'd how to make music brought their fiddles, guitars and banjos when they visited us that winter. Whisky was popular in the mountains, too; most everybody could make it. Problem was, when the music got to goin' and the jugs got to bein' passed around, trouble could follow. That's exactly what happened one night while folks was at our place visitin' for my birth. Two rough-lookin' tramps come callin' and said they'd heard about my dad's big mules and how fine they was; said they was stock traders from down south.

As them traders got to our home, one of 'em asked my dad, "Are you Thompie Collins?"

"Who wants to know?" my dad asked.

"My name is Dallas Jarvis. I trade stock for the Allison Company from down south of here. We ran into some folks on the Keowee Path who told us 'bout your mules. I was wonderin' if you had any you was ready to sale. I would pay your price if you do."

"You got any gold coin?" asked Dad, not knowin' these two. "That's the only way I trade with stock folks."

"'Course we got coin."

"Let me see it then."

"Well, we ain't carryin' it with us," Jarvis explained. "We hid it on our way into the valley and we'll need to go and fetch it. We don't like travelin' around with a bait of gold in our truck and possible bandits about. Uh, no disrespect intended of course."

My dad could tell them varmints weren't no good 'cause of the way they was, so he told 'em, "I got no mules to trade till I see gold. Hard gold coin. Lay it on the barrel head, then we can trade."

That kinda made them scoundrels mad, so they set to makin' excuses.

"Okay, but like I said, we'll have to go and fetch it, and it's grown late. Can we camp in your woods tonight then leave out at first light?" asked Dallas.

"I reckon that'll be fine. Just y'all mind your manners. I got guests about the place visitin' us for a special occasion. Y'all can camp on the head of the creek that runs down behind the barn to the west," Dad replied, turned and walked away.

The folks that was there to visit learned about the traders and kept a watch on 'em but treated 'em with kindness. They let 'em come in when the music got to goin', even passed the jug to 'em a few times. It was late when the whisky got the better of 'em, and they wandered off toward their camp.

Nobody allowed the devil was fixin' to show up.

The scream was frightful and distant, makin' the night seem haunted. Dad couldn't figure what in the world had happened till Wayman Bryson hollered, "Mary! Where you at Mary? Mary! Mary!"

It was her that let out that scream and it didn't take long for folks to figure out what'd happened. Them tramps done snatched the girl and run off with her. Dad feared the worst. When he went to check on his mules, they was two young ones missin'.

Every man there gathered at the fire and made plans to go and fetch Mary back. Three of the Cherokee warriors that were there visitin' had already took to the trail. Dad know'd it was just a matter of time 'fore them Indians tracked 'em down. He also figured it would not be good for those two when they were found, neither.

Them warriors was part of the Cherokee Winter Guard that patrolled the boundaries of the Cherokee Nation durin' the cold time, watchin' for hostile folk. They had much experience trackin' men; this was one thing they lived for. They'd heard of me on the trail and were at our place to pay their respects, which was unlucky for them outlaws.

As the sun rose, the mule tracks was clear where the traders had made off with Dad's mules and Mary. By the looks of the tracks you could tell they was ridin' them mules, 'cause the only human footprints visible was the moccasin tracks of the warriors.

Dad told Wayman, "Them Indians will be on 'em soon. You'll have your daughter *and* your vengeance. Just pray they ain't hurt her. I hate I let them stay near our place last night. I ask your forgiveness, Wayman."

He replied, "It weren't your fault, Thompie. Mary wandered off with them rascals while I was makin' music. I should've been wiser than to take my eyes off her. She's just comin' into womanhood and she's feelin' her oats. I know'd to watch her more close and I didn't."

"I still feel bad. When we find 'em, we'll make it right," swore my dad.

It was around noon the next day when they heard them Indians let out a cry that could've been heard throughout the valley and up to the ridge tops. Nobody know'd what it meant...except my dad. He had a good idea.

"I think they've found her, Wayman. They wouldn't yell like that unless they'd closed in on them rascals. I believe that was a war cry. I've heard it before. That'll get 'em worried. Lets the enemy know your close, gets 'em scared. That tells me them 'coons is treed."

The Indians left signs along the trail. Before long, there were three sets of mule tracks. My dad know'd when he saw that third set of tracks that Dancing Bear had joined the hunt. That got Dad a sight more excited. He know'd it would be a short time now till Mary was back and on her way home. He just hoped she was still alive, and herself.

Sure enough, it weren't long till they saw Mary hobblin' back up the trail they was followin'. She was bruised and bloody and walkin' funny, but she was alive. She began to tell Wayman what happened.

"The Cherokee caught up to us and they were gettin' close when those two vermin threw me off and started high tailin' it up the mountain," Mary told him. "I landed hard on my head and the blood started to flow, but other than that I'm fine, mostly. I hope they catch 'em and make 'em pay for what they've done. God forgive me, I do. I'm so sorry for wanderin' off, Dad, but I didn't think they was bad. Dallas seemed real nice when he asked me to walk in the moonlight with him. Please forgive me for causin' all this fuss."

Wayman was holdin' back tears when she finished talkin'. He grabbed her up and hugged her so hard it made her feet come off the ground. He pulled a rag from his pocket and began to wipe the blood off her face as he said, "Mary, forgive me for not takin' better care of you. I knew them tramps was no good and I let this happen. It's my fault. You ain't old enough to judge folks good or bad for yourself. I should've watched better. I promise you that I will make this right."

With that said, a look of killin' come over Wayman's face.

Them outlaws dumped her off and headed south for fear of bein' caught. I guess when they figured out the Cherokee was near they know'd their lives was now in danger. Dad and Wayman weren't gonna let this pass. They kept to the trail while the rest of the men took Mary back to our place.

It weren't long before they met up with Dancing Bear and the Indian warriors. They were waitin' near the base of a steep ridge. They had Dad's mules and were lookin' up the mountain like they was watchin' somethin'. When Dad saw that Dancing Bear and the other Cherokee was stopped, he know'd justice would soon be had for Mary.

"How'd you know we needed you?" Dad asked Dancing Bear.

"One of the warriors came to my home during the night and told me what happened. I have been with them since. We got close to catching them and they dropped the girl and started running the mules. I know the way they went and it is an unlucky way for them to go. They can no longer ride. The girl's father will soon know their fate," replied Dancing Bear, smilin'.

The Indians had stopped and waited. They know'd Wayman and Dad would be comin' on after the girl went back. They would've been pleased to capture them varmints and make things square, but they know'd that vengeance was due the girl's family. Indians was big on settlin' things proper. They know'd them outlaws was treed and weren't gonna get away.

The Cherokee that tracked Mary was restless and sweaty. They'd been runnin' the trail most all night, smellin' blood. Their eyes were like a wolf's eyes. You could tell they was ready to end this chase and have at them tramps. Cherokee didn't take to hurtin' the young ones. If Wayman had wanted them to, they would've tore on up the ridge, and all you would've heard was screamin' as they done justice. But Wayman and Dad needed to finish this. Them Indians understood when Wayman simply nodded his thanks and set out up the ridge.

The ground was rocky and steep, no problem for the Indians to move up. Within a short time the traders was close to bein' trapped, with Dancing Bear takin' the high ground. He got ahead of the two varmints and worked his way on above to let himself be seen, as he figured to turn 'em toward Wayman. It worked, too. They turned and started headin' back the way they'd come. This was an old Indian trick they'd use when huntin' deer. The two Indian warriors dropped back and let Dad and Wayman keep on. They know'd who deserved this due.

Dad was leadin' as he stopped a little ways up the ridge, turned to Wayman, whisperin', "You go on to the south and I will move 'round to the west and try and get 'em between us."

Wayman nodded.

After climbin' a few more minutes, Dad saw the traders. They was hidin' just below a stand of huge oaks, in amongst a bunch of boulders and rocks that looked like they was scattered about by God Himself, as if He'd pulled 'em outa His pocket and throw'd 'em down.

Dad was close when he'd spotted the two. He slowed some, but kept on movin' up the ridge while tryin' to be quiet and keep an eye on the traders at the same time. The goin' was steep. He was workin' his way through the rock bed, steppin' from rock to rock and tryin' to keep quiet, when he lost his footin' on a moss covered rock and fell, droppin' his gun. He landed on his back on the rock below, where he slipped. That shot him down the mountain like he was slung out of a slingshot. He rolled over a couple of times on his way down the steep, and ended up in some sharp rocks that were near the edge of the rock bed. His left leg snapped with an awful sound as it wound up between a big boulder and a smaller one makin' Dad scream out in pain. The fall broke both bones just below his knee. Pinned and caught up, he know'd the outlaws would be movin' on him now for sure.

By the time Dad fell, Wayman had made it up the mountain a little and had stopped above 'em some. He had a good view of where they was and could see 'em closin' in on Dad. Dancing Bear could tell there was trouble, so he turned down the mountain and come on a dead run to help. The warriors had heard it all and started up to where Dad was pinned. They told Dancing Bear later they thought the sound of Dad's leg breakin' was from his .52 caliber smoke-pole.

The trader was on my Dad before he could get free, was fixin' to plunge a knife into his chest, but Dad saw him just in time and rolled to the side, loosin' his leg and endin' him up in a kinda sittin' position. The blade missed him by inches. Dad's anger stoked as he and the stock man was dead face-to-face. He hit that tramp in the back of the head with an apple-sized rock his hand had landed on when he dodged the knife. The trader let out a grunt as Dad kept fightin'. He held him off with his left arm while he jerked his own knife free. Dad jabbed out as hard as he could muster and sliced the man's thigh through just above the knee. The blade sank plumb to the bone and tore out the side, cripplin' him up somthin' terrible. Dad shifted his weight to his left side and was able to roll and kick with his right leg, sendin' the trader down the mountain screamin' to beat all and bleedin' from his head and leg.

Dallas saw what happened and let out a holler as he ran for my Dad with murder in his mind, sayin', "You say you ain't got no mules to trade me lest I got me some gold, huh? Well, I got some lead for you. How will that do?"

He turned sharp and swung his musket at Dad. But just as he was 'bout to pull the trigger, an explosion rang out. Dallas Jarvis' face turned to mush as he slammed face down on the ground dead. Wayman had drawed a bead on the man as he turned toward Dad. He put a .69 caliber lead ball through the back of Dallas' head, landin' him square face down on the ground. Dad said later it was a sickenin' sight, as the tramp's head exploded—brains, bone and meat flew all over—with Dallas' ear, nose and part of his jaw landin' in Dad's lap; the rotten teeth grinnin' up kinda evil like.

The trader who was still alive was tryin' to crawl away just as Dancing Bear got to the fight. He and the other

Cherokee came 'round in front of the man and stopped him from crawlin' away—the Indians know'd Wayman wanted justice. Wayman walked up to the man and asked him his name as he lifted him in one clean motion and propped him against a big white oak. The man moaned in agony.

"Simmons, Luke Simmons," he replied.

"Well, Luke Simmons, you like carryin' off little girls, huh? Folks 'round here don't cotton to trash like you. My friends here will show you just what happens when mountain justice is deserved." And with that, he gave them Cherokee guardsmen a slight nod, turned his back and walked away.

All that blood got to them Indians. They left that man in pieces for the critters to finish. It took 'em three days.

Dallas Jarvis was left hangin' by the side of the Keowee Path with a note tied to his leg written in English, which spelled out what happened for all who passed by. Their kinda behavior would not be tolerated in Choestoe.

***

It was hard goin' for Dad on the trip home. Dancing Bear put him on one of the mules and they rode together back to his place on Slaughter Mountain, where the old medicine woman was. Dancing Bear figured it best for Dad to stay so she could care for him and set the bones in his broke leg. Wayman rode the other mule back to our place to let everybody know what'd happened to Jarvis and Simmons. He kindly left out the details about Luke Simmons.

Anne and Cain left for Slaughter Gap as soon as they heard from Wayman about Dad. It was good for Anne to go. She learned a lot about healin' folks with broke bones over the next few days. Dad went through some *serious* pain, but they looked after him, and he come home soon enough. Some of the neighbors stayed and looked after Momma and me while Dad was mendin' at Slaughter, so he didn't have to worry. That's the way it was in Choestoe. Folks looked after one another when they was needed.

Dad didn't mind that them tramps got what they deserved. He never told a soul about what happened to

Simmons, neither. It was Dancing Bear that told me the story long after them men rotted away. Dad said he never know'd anybody from the Allison Stock Company to come lookin' for 'em, so he figured he was right about them bein' outlaws. Mary got over the shock of what happened and got on with her life. She married one of the Weaver boys, and they settled down close to where we lived near Ben's Knob. I would go to their place often. She became one of the best women in the valley when it come to watchin' over kids, teachin'em readin' and writin' and math and such. Strange how God works sometimes.

Chapter Three

First Memories

My first memory as a boy was of my dad. Him and Cain were
buildin' a new mule barn. They was half through with it when I
come to my reckonin'. My very first memory was helpin' Dad
carry the auger all over the place so him and Cain could drill
holes where the doors and windows was to go. My dad had a
fine hand with workin' wood; built his stuff right when he
fashioned somethin'. He always said if it was worth doin', it
was worth doin' proper.

My dad was a wise man.

I'll never forget how big I thought he was. He was a big
man, but he seemed like a mountain to me. His boots made me
think of a big piece of chestnut firewood, like the ones we used
in the main fireplace. He was kind and always gentle with me. I
loved him beyond words. He taught me stuff through the years,
too; grew up knowin' things other folks didn't. He could handle
an axe better than most when it come to carvin' logs for a
cabin, working for folks quite a bit. He taught me all he know'd
'bout cabin and barn buildin'. I even built my own little cabin
when I got older, with Wolf's help. Me and Wolf spent much of
our time in that cabin. It and Panther Cave kinda became our
base for all the stuff we was mixed up in through the years.

That mule barn Dad and Cain was buildin' had some
size. It was three full logs across the back and two long logs
down the side. It had a big door in the front and another in the
back. Each side had a window for light, and there was a loft
you could stand up in with a ladder reachin' to the ground you
could climb up on.

Below the loft, right in the middle, was a work area
where we could tie up a mule and store our tools and mule gear
for work. Saved my hide a couple of times, too, when an old

mule got ill at me. They're smart animals, but I believe they hold a grudge. The cantankerous ole critters will bite the fire outa your person if they decide to. Mules can be as good to a body as they will, then one day you do somethin' wrong, and *BANG*! They'll draw blood off some part of your body, and it don't matter which part neither. I met old timers who'd lost the tops of their ears to bad mules, and fingers, too. I remember thinkin' how awful it would be to have a part bit off by one them big mules of my dad's.

It was around noon when I first ever remember seein' Wolf. He and his dad come to our place one day while they was on a walk. They walked a lot, stayin' gone for days at a time. They liked to get out and see places. They weren't a stream in the Choestoe Valley that Dancing Bear didn't know, but that didn't stop him. They just got out and went from time-to-time. It was an Indian thing. Wolf would do it some when we got older. Just when you need a body, they run off on some spirit trip or just take off for no reason that one could really know. Troubled me to no end.

Wolf and me had just turned six over the winter. His dad was takin' Wolf on his first walk. They was a day or two into it, when Dancing Bear wanted to come and visit with my dad. Wolf told me later that he didn't remember me 'fore that day, neither, even though they'd come round to visit many times.

We were workin' on the mule barn. I felt 'em before I saw 'em. It was like a warm breath across the back of my neck. When I looked up, I was spooked to see 'em standin' in the edge of the woods, still as oaks. It was a most handsome sight seein'em froze in the woods like that. They looked alike, 'cept Wolf was 'bout three feet shorter than his dad.

Me and him both had big dads. They would arm wrestle, 'specially after the jug got passed a time or two. One never did beat the other. I've seen 'em locked up for over a half hour till they both were so numb they'd have to quit. They was usually great amounts of gruntin' to get 'em through that time. Wolf and me would laugh out loud at 'em. They couldn't do nothin' to us for laughin', 'cause they was all locked up and wouldn't let go.

I went out to meet 'em with Dad. Wolf and me just looked at each other like the other was a ghost or somethin'. It was a strange happenin', but I felt really calm. It was like I know'd 'em already; had know'd 'em for a while.

My dad introduced us. "Jeb, do you remember our friends from over on Slaughter Mountain? Dancing Bear and his son, Wolf. You and Wolf were born on the same night durin' that awful snowstorm. Y'all share a birthday. They honor us with a visit, so be polite."

Standin' before me was a boy my age, but a bit shorter than me. He had long black hair with beads woven in, with more hangin' around his neck. He was some kinda handsome. He and his dad looked like brothers instead of father and child. They were both muscular and smelled like the woods after a cool spring rain...and they was naked from the waist up. They had on pants that was kinda like my homespun, but they was made outa skin and didn't have any pockets.

He carried his possibles in a leather pouch slung over his shoulder. It didn't look uncomfortable at all, movin' with him smoothly as he walked. Soft, like deer hide, it had red paw prints on the flap with beads. There was also a knife in its sheath slung 'round his waist and tied onto his leg that had beads swingin' from it, too. It weren't real obvious, but you would see it if you looked. His hair was tied with a leather strap, with a magnificent feather woven into the leather just below his ear, hangin' to the middle of his back.

I remember askin' Wolf one day how he come by that feather, 'cause it was a fine feather. Turns out, his dad pulled them feathers out of an eagle's tail up in the rock cliffs on Rattlesnake Mountain. I never will forget that story. I would hear Dancing Bear tell it many times. He gave me permission to pass it on. The Cherokee had to say 'fore you could tell stories about what they'd done.

***

Dancing Bear had a need. He wanted the perfect gift to give a young maiden he intended to marry, A-Ga-Li-Ha. He decided that takin' a feather from the tail of a live eagle would be one true way he could show her how much he loved her. He thought it out careful, and finally come up with a savvy way to do it.

He built a blind with a top and four walls out of oak poles he could just stand up in, then lowered himself inside. He'd caught a squirrel a couple of days before and was usin' it as bait, tied on a leash that he held from underneath the top of the blind. He could make that critter bark when he needed just by pullin' on the leash a certain way. Once he was set, all he had to do was wait for morning, for Old Man Sun to wake and light the day, so the eagle would start his hunt.

The top of the blind was hinged with strips of hickory bark on both sides and would open in the middle. There was a hole in the top for him to poke the squirrel through when the time was proper. He hoped it would run around on the roof of the blind and catch the eagle's eye. When the eagle come for the squirrel, Dancing Bear would throw open the blind and grab the eagle's tail feathers. It was a good plan—he just forgot to tell the eagle.

It was late in the mornin'. Old Man Sun was shinin' bright 'fore he ever saw the bird soarin' low overhead and around and behind the ridge he'd set up his ambush on. The bird's path circled back behind the top, disappearing for just a few seconds on each trip. He decided to release the squirrel as soon as the eagle made it behind the top of the mountain on the very next pass. So as the eagle disappeared behind the ridge, Dancing Bear said a short prayer and poked the squirrel through the hole, a leather leash tied tight to its foot. It just had cleared the openin' when it commenced to jumpin' and hollerin' without him ever pullin' on the leash. It was bouncin' around on top of his blind as mad as it could be. That critter didn't like bein' carried up a steep mountain in a leather pouch in the dark, no water or food for two days, and now its foot was all tied up. It was mad, makin' all kinds of noise, grabbing the eagle's attention as it cleared the top of the mountain. The eagle quickly changed his path to move out and over the noisy squirrel. Dancing Bear know'd then it was fixin' to happen. That squirrel had just made its life very short.

The eagle come back around and made a short circle above the trap where the squirrel was dancin', to kinda look things over and get his aim, when all of a sudden he folded his wings and dropped in a straight dive right at Dancing Bear and his squirrel. The closer he got the bigger he got. Dancing Bear know'd fast he'd picked a fight with the king of the roost in those parts. *I will have some good feathers*, he thought, as he watched it dive right at his trap, and him.

The bird was huge, headin' toward that squirrel with no hint of slowin' down. Less than twenty paces from the trap, the eagle spread his wings to slow the dive, but it still hit that squirrel so hard that it shattered Dancing Bear's blind top, leavin' him little room to reach and grab the tail feathers. The force of the bird carried it into the blind. There he was, face-to-face with one mad eagle. The blind was small, with little room for both of 'em. One of 'em had to get out. That eagle had it in mind it was gonna be *him*.

The eagle's path had slammed him against the far wall of the blind opposite of where Dancing Bear was standin', reacting with such speed that Dancing Bear barely had time to raise his arms to protect his eyes. He heard the talons rippin' flesh before he felt the searing pain, as the bird was usin' him as a way out, the claws slashin' Dancing Bear's body with every step up and out toward freedom.

Dancing Bear knew he was screamin', but the eagle was screamin' louder, so he couldn't hear himself. He lashed out at the bird with rage in his heart; felt as though he was trapped in battle again. He instinctively reached for his knife, but then remembered what he was there for. He needed at least three tail feathers from a live eagle, and he was gonna get 'em if there was any way. The knife would only hinder his ability to grab the feathers, so he left it where it was and set on that winged devil with his bare hands.

Dancing Bear know'd the bird was headed for the sky and would be outa the blind and gone in a matter of a few breaths. He reacted fast, while the eagle kept tryin' to use his body like a ladder. As the bird's head passed in front of his face, he grabbed its body in a bear hug and held on for life *and* feathers. The beak made a thud as it ripped a gash in the top of

Dancing Bear's head. He felt himself scream again as the eagle's talons found muscle on top of his chest just below his throat, the warmth now runnin' down. Dancing Bear moved his right hand to the rear of the eagle and wrapped his fist around a bunch of tail feathers as he released the bear hug he'd fought so painfully for. The beast screeched, but no tail feathers would come loose. The top of the eagle had cleared the trap and it was beatin' its wings harder and harder, tryin' to reach the sky above. It was startin' to pull out from the blind, and since Dancing Bear refused to let go of the feathers he'd latched on to, he was gettin' lifted into the air, too.

This is impossible, he thought, but it was happenin'. He know'd it was now or never. As his feet started to leave the floor of the trap, he gave a mighty pull. Four big, beautiful feathers remained behind as the eagle flew for his nest. He was aimin' to hide from whatever stinkin' thing it was that he'd just fought with, his tail stingin' and feelin' quite a bit lighter than when the day had started. The squirrel was nowhere to be seen, or heard.

Dancing Bear received four beautiful feathers from the eagle, and had in mind exactly what he'd do with 'em. Of the four, two were almost identical; the other two were different but still beautiful. The twins would be for him and his future bride, and the other two for his family. Wolf got one of those later on after it had guided his brothers to manhood. It was a great gift. His grandmother got the other, which she cherished as bein' very powerful. When it came time for her to cross the Great River, she would pass it on to Wolf's sister, Rose.

***

I put my hand out and said my very first words ever to Wolf, "Nice to meet ya. Wanna wrestle?"

He grabbed me so fast I barely had time to breathe, sayin', "I will wrestle any time you wish, Jeb Collins of Choestoe." And with that, we were on the ground locked in a two-sided bear hug. There weren't no way either one of us was gonna break free, so we rolled around till we got tired.

Wolf sat up and looked at me and said, "That was fun, Jeb Collins. You would do well among my friends on the wrestling ground at Big Camp. You will go with us when we are older, then we will wrestle the Creek and Choctaw and show them how strong we are."

It weren't no question. He was tellin' me what we was gonna do, which sounded right by me.

I asked him, "Do you really think I could hold up with all them Indians? What is Big Camp, anyway?"

"It's a place south of here where we go when the leaves begin to come back in the spring. Many Indians go there. We trade and dance between the tribes. It's a time of peace between us so we can trade and have games. I will take you, and you will have a place at our fire. You will wrestle against all the others and me. The best boy wins a full set of skins made of soft doe hide, finished the Cherokee way. I plan to have those skins," declared Wolf. I had no doubt that he just might have 'em.

I learned later that the word skins meant clothes to these Cherokee. Language differed from valley to valley in the Cherokee Nation dependin' on how much influence the missionaries had on the Indians that lived there. Skins meant to Wolf and his family a full outfit of clothing: pants, shirt, belt and foot skins. I sure wanted them skins myself. I wasn't plannin' on finishin' second, neither, if my dad would let me go. Maybe he'd want to come with me?

***

Wolf and me spent the rest of the day scoutin' out the farm and the woods around our place. He was as much at home in the woods as I was on the farm. He could move like the wolf he was named for; a sight to watch. One might've thought they'd seen a ghost if they saw him on the move. His dad taught him to be quiet and to listen to the natural sounds. The Cherokee, as well as other folks, still had to be careful of rogue Indians and outlaws in the valley. They weren't messin' with regular folks much, but sure was botherin' the local Cherokee at times. Every winter, the clan had to post warriors to guard against intruders. Usually, it was some bad Creek braves that still held a family grudge, or maybe a Choctaw out on his manhood journey or those who wanted to steal the yellow rock. They'd be watched from the point where they crossed the Cherokee boundary. If they appeared threatenin', it was quite possible they would never leave the valley. 'Better safe than sorry,' I think was the way the Cherokee figured it. They was Indians that died in fights most every winter in the mountains, but usually not Cherokee.

***

I followed Wolf down to the creek to begin my journey into the Indian way of lookin' at things. It would become an education no book could teach, but an education all the same. Wolf would teach me the ways of the mountains as his father taught him. I soaked up everything he ever told me. You never could know when a little knowledge might save your life in the woods. The woods was dangerous. Folks died in there.

Chapter Four

Our Adventure Begins

The leaves had fallen and the winter cold had begun before I saw my new friend again. He was comin' outa the woods on the trail above our barn, and he was not alone. There was an old woman and a young girl ridin' a big mule while Wolf and another woman walked. They all had pouches on their backs. I somehow know'd those was their possibles. I began to think of all the wonderful things that Wolf might have in his pack as I ran up the hill to meet 'em—stuff I knew would lead us to the woods.

I stopped dead in front of Wolf and just looked him in the eye. No words was spoke for a minute, then he placed his hand on my shoulder and politely said, "Jeb Collins, my friend, this is my momma A-Ga-Li-Ha, my sister Rose, and as your family knows, this is my grandmother. We call her Owl the Wise One because she is very cunning with her medicines."

I turned and squared my shoulders like my folks had shown me to do, made a slight bow in their direction, and in my best English said, "It is my happiness to meet you good folks and welcome y'all to our kind home."

I think I might've got my words mixed, but it seemed to be all right. My dad and momma were born in the mountains of North Carolina, but their folks came direct from the 'motherland', Ireland, so they talk different than most folks born in the mountains. Confuses a body sometimes, 'specially when you're just a kid. They can both tell you the same thing, but it sounds like it ought to mean somethin' different, dependin' on which direction their face is pointed.

Strung across the mule's back was a fresh skin full of deer meat and some folded up skins. Wolf's momma just smiled when she saw me lookin' at the bloody hide. Since she was the one with the gun, I figured she was the one who shot it. I couldn't wait to sink my teeth into some of that ham meat. Made my mouth water just thinkin' on it.

I looked at the gun she was totin' and saw that it was different from Dad's. It had a shorter, more silver-like barrel and a long wood stock that appeared to fit her just right. Wolf explained later that it was a gift from a young British cavalry officer before he left to go home after bein' wounded in the war.

I asked him about it later in the day and he told me about it. "My mother won't speak of the soldier or the gun anymore— it is forbidden. I know he was shot and she helped heal him. If she had been caught helping him, she could have been burned and her family banished since the Red Backs lied to us. We don't speak of it, so don't tell anyone. My dad likes for her to carry the gun. She can shoot better than any of us. She killed that deer this morning with a single shot behind the ear as it slipped through the woods. That shot saves much meat and kills quickly."

I was in a daze lookin' at the gun, when I was shocked back to life by a voice that sounded like angels in harmony.

"Will you help Wolf wash and clean our meat, young Jeb?" asked A-Ga-Li- Ha. "Then will you help stretch the skin for drying?"

I nearly fainted from her voice. One minute I'm carryin' in wood for the stove, the next I am face-to-face with people of the woods; 'cept for the old woman, a most handsome folk. It was the first time I'd ever met Wolf's mom. I'd never forget it. She seemed to be the queen of the forest, and the girl on the mule was her twin. It was downright spooky to me. What was I supposed to say to the most beautiful people I'd ever seen? I froze and simply nodded.

I couldn't help but watch her lead the mule Dad had give 'em down the valley and to our barn. She moved like a panther and had eyes like a hawk. They reminded you of the yellow petals on the Brown-Eyed Susie flowers that grow'd in the lower meadow on our farm; a yellow-gold color that would shine in the dark like the eyes of a mountain cat. That is where her father and mother got her name, A-Ga-Li-Ha, which meant sunshine. That sure fit her.

Her arms were long and muscular. She was strong, I could tell. Her stride was long and powerful and she covered a lot of ground when she walked. Her hair was the color of night and it flowed as she moved, but it was truly her gaze that drawed folks so. Everything about her was as it should be; you could tell that just by watchin' her. Her movement was in perfect stride with the motion of nature; never did her sharp eyes miss anything. She always had the simple fix for any problem me and Wolf ever faced, was as carin' as a body could be. I would grow to love her like a mother, and Rose like a true sister.

When the Dancing Bear family came for a visit, they stayed a while. Their visit lasted for more than a month. I loved every minute of it. Our families became one durin' their stay. I will remember their first visit as long as I live, mostly because of all the gifts they brought us, the gifts that changed my life.

We had plenty of room. Granddad had built a seven-room house with a huge loft for us to live in. It was one of the biggest homes in the valley. He and Grandma had hoped for more children, but that was just not God's plan. So whenever important people visited the valley, they always made their way to our house for keep. It had the most rooms of any place around for miles. I got to meet some very interestin' folk in my growin'-up time there.

Wolf and his family all worked while they was there. It was like we was all kin and worked right along with each other like we'd been doin' it for years. Wolf and me helped my dad and Cain on the farm. We had the biggest time! Dad spent much of his time with his mules in the winter. Wolf and me learned a lot about mule keepin'. Dad was very patient with us that winter. We both profited from the time, learning what to look for if a mule gets sick or ornery, how to tie different knots in the ropes to make 'em work one way or another, how to string up gear to use on the mule if you're gonna plow or log, and what kinda shoes work best on which type of mule for whatever it is they are workin' at. We learned how to mix up concoctions to help them feel better if they got the colic or foundered on somethin' they ate, and how to care for the hooves, which is very important to a mule, 'cause if his feet hurt, he won't work. Everybody know'd that when a mule sets his mind to somethin', it's hard to change.

Wolf's momma, A-ga-li-s-gv, 'Sunshine' in Cherokee, which I think is much easier to say, taught my momma many things in how to prepare food and preserve meat and vegetables the Cherokee way. In turn, my momma taught her things as well, like cake bakin', clothes tendin', readyin' a garden spot for vegetables to plant in the spring, pie bakin', quilitin' and just plain old rockin' on the porch while listenin' to the night sounds or the smooth music my folks made.

Momma had a "store-bought stove" in her cook room that you could fry and bake at the same time with. You never tasted any better biscuits in your life than what my momma made in that oven. Apple pie almost too sweet to eat and more stew than a good rain barrel could hold had been cooked on that stove. It was my mom's pride and joy, right behind the family *Bible*.

Sushine never did get the idea of the stove for fixin' food. She was used to open flame and could lay out a spread when it came to hangin' cook pots and smoked fish and meat.

Momma taught her how to spin yarn and make cloth on a loom. She got very good at it. She actually made a homespun shirt for Dancing Bear outa cloth she wove while stayin' at our place that winter. Later on, the Government gave the Cherokee Indian women spinning wheels and looms in order to improve their quality of life, to try and make 'em more comfortable with white man ways. They turned out some pretty stuff; learning to wear homespun in the spring and summer, then add a layer over their skins in fall and winter for extra warmth. Sure was comfortable.

The old medicine woman, Owl the Wise One, spent the whole month showin' my sister how to make medicine and doctor wounds. She taught her what types of things she could gather in the winter to make potions or rubs. She showed her the herbs and roots and flowers that healed cuts, burns and small wounds so they wouldn't become festered. Anne learned how to brew tea both for healin' and for pleasure. It was a learnin' time for both families that bonded us. I didn't realize how much until Wolf brought it to my attention one cold afternoon just before dark.

"Have you seen Cain?" he asked.

"I haven't seen him since supper. Why?"

"Rose has not been seen since then, either. Have you not noticed that they are both gone at the same time every evening?"

"No, not really. I kinda did but haven't spent much time thinkin' on it. He always goes out in the woods in the evenin'. I just didn't realize that Rose was gone, too."

And then it hit me like a fist to the middle—him and Rose. The thought of Cain courtin' Wolf's sister was very worrisome; made me shake my head. I wondered if Momma know'd, then I remembered that Momma know'd most everything. I'd ask her about this. If it was fine with her, then it was fine with me. After all, they was near the same age, with Cain bein' a little older. It just made sense with how close our families was and all. It's just he weren't Cherokee. I saw her as more of a sister than a possible wife for Cain, but I would have to admit, she was real pretty for sure.

"Let's go and find them and see what things they are doing," said Wolf. "I would like to see where it is they go and what it is they have found there."

I was always ready for a trail, so I said, "That sounds like fun. I'll follow you."

Wolf found her tracks on the trail above the barn. We didn't get far before there was sign of two sets of footprints, then followed the trail they'd took. It was strange how they'd circled through the woods like they was lost or somethin'. I began to wonder if Wolf had found their trail, but then I remembered who he was.

They'd wondered all over the farm, near walked us to death till they got down by the creek. Dad had built a small pond from a good sized fresh flow of water at the lower end of the cornfield, with some rock seats built into the side of the dam at the far end of the pond. At the bottom of the dam he'd built a very large and very tight wooden tub for bathin' or soakin'. Water would run from the pond into the tub by removin' a plug from a wooden gate he'd dug into the side of the dam above and off to the side of the stone seats. A wooden trough connected the gate to the tub. When you had all the water you needed, you simply put the plug back in the gate and the water would stop flowin'. It was big enough for our whole family, and often times Indians would come 'round durin' the cold time to soak in it.

A large iron kettle with a fire pit beneath was next to the rock seats; another wooden trough that split off from the main pond trough went over to it. There was a smaller bamboo trough then from the kettle to the tub. If you wanted warm water for bathin', you would just build a fire under the kettle and heat the water, then use a gourd to scoop the hot water into the bamboo trough which carried it into the tub. It didn't take much boilin' water to heat the tub, which would stay hot for the longest time. The tub was made outa hemlock, which would hold heat and never rot or be eaten by bugs. It was here we found 'em, the end of the trail, and Cain already had the water boilin' in the kettle by the time we got there.

There was no wind blowin' at all, a perfect winter night to be in the tub, clear with stars shinin' bright overhead. I'd been in it with my family plenty over the last several weeks. The hot water feels great when the outside air is cold. Dad had fashioned some steps to walk down and some seats on the inside so all you had to do was step down, sit and soak. It was great. I remember bein' in that tub on several snowy nights with a hot fire by the side and steamin' water up to your ears. There must be a tub like that in Heaven, 'cause there is little else that could be that pleasurable, though Cain seemed to be havin' a real nice time with Rose just then.

The top of the tub was level with the bottom of the fire, so you could step into the tub from where you sat in the rock seats. That is where Cain and Rose were now. She with her back against the stone and her legs pulled to her chest as her arms wrapped around her shins. He was sittin' across from her on a small wooden bench just lookin' at her. They weren't sayin' much; they simply sat and stared at one another.

It all didn't make a bit of sense to us what Cain was thinkin'. Why in the whole put-together would you want to take a bath with some girl on a perfectly good coon huntin' night? The dogs were hungry and ready to run, but here he was wastin' time bathin'. I just couldn't wrap my mind around all of it.

The whole thing got real curious when Cain started dippin' hot water from the kettle into the bamboo trough. A huge bullfrog jumped up in my throat as Cain finished with the hot water and Rose stood. I could hardly believe what I was seein' as she slipped off her foot skins, then walked over to the tub. After touchin' the water with her toe, she turned like creek water rollin' smooth around a large round rock and stared straight at Cain. With a simple lift of her slender arms to the back of her neck, her heavy winter buckskins fell to the stone landing. The cold air was shocking to her skin; her body shinin' from the reflection of the moon. What I saw has been in my mind since that night. I will never forget how it felt to be in the presence of such a perfect creature as God had made in her. The flow of her step as she entered the tub was as smooth as the smoke risin' off your pipe early in the mornin'. Without a movement wasted, she turned and sat in the tub facin' the moon.

Cain seemed to be in shock at what had just happened, as Wolf brought reality back to my world.

"Did you see them?" Wolf whispered into my left ear after Cain had stripped down and entered the tub. "How could he think my sister is pretty? She looks like a hellbender water dog with long black hair. How could he stand to wash with her?"

I just shook my head. He had no clue that his sister, who moved like a young doe, would be desirable among the young bucks in the valley.

It now made sense to me, but I still had rather been in the tub with Wolf. We would play with small ships Dad had carved for us when we was in it, but what could Cain and Rose play? I guess they'd just sit and enjoy the hot water and look at the moon and talk. That sounds pretty good, too, but still not as good as coon huntin'.

***

In all the excitement from their first visit to our place, the thing I remember best is the gifts that A-Ga-Li-Ha, Owl and Rose had made for us. Cain, Anne and me all received our first full set of winter skins with the fur turned in. I can't tell you how comfortable and warm they was; how the rain would just run off and not soak through. You could walk through briars and not get a single scratch.

They made us each a coat with a collar that had a leather cord at the neck so you could open and close it at the throat, a pair of heavy pants with a belt sewn into the waist, and a set of foot skins that rose all the way to your knee like soldier boots with beaver tail coverin' the soles. We also got gloves that had a trigger finger, along with a beaver hat that tied under your chin to keep your face warm. No other sets of clothes was more suited to mountain livin' in the wintertime than the skins they made for us that winter. We all liked 'em very much. Thankfully, they taught Momma how to cure and sew skins. She would keep us in homespun clothes and skins just like the ones they'd made from then on.

Dad's gift was a new pipe that Dancing Bear carved for him durin' the summer outa the huge antler base of a big buck he killed the winter before. The bottom had been flattened and the pipe was big. It would sit up by itself. You could put the tobacco in it without ever liftin' it off the table. It had a bamboo stem that had been scorched just right to make the taste of the pipe better.

On it was carved the figure of a rabbit's head with the ears fanned back and its paws out front like it was runnin' for its life. The bowl for the tobacco was between the rabbit's ears, and you could see the top of its front paws under its chin. It was really well done. Dad said it smoked as smooth as the coolness of the early mornin' air off a cold winter night's snow. I saw my dad smoke that pipe many times and it never failed him. He enjoyed his smoke almost all of his ninety years on this earth.

Mom's gift was well thought out and could not have been better. They made her five pairs of foot skins and two leather aprons. My mother broke down in tears as she accepted the shoes from Rose and her mother.

"These are an answer to a prayer I've been praying for a long time," said Momma. "I've been in need of proper cold weather shoes, and now I have some. They are just exactly what I need. Thank you so, so very much."

She turned to the old woman, who simply raised her hand and dropped her eyes. Celia then figured out that the old woman had known what she needed. She chose to believe that God had instructed her. The way she believed, they was an answer to her prayer.

When it came time for them to leave, we all cried 'cept Dad and Cain. It was like there was gonna be a death in the family and we couldn't do anything about it. It was a strange thing, the feelin' on that day. I felt it many times later as Wolf and I grow'd up. It felt as though a part of you was tearin' itself away; they was takin' it with 'em, and you wouldn't be whole again until you was back together. You pray that the people are well while they are away, so the part of you they took will come back. You are weakened by the leavin' of your friends so much, you want to see them again soon. I swear it felt like death.

This is how it was with our friends from Slaughter Mountain. They was truly missed. Without tellin' me, Dad made plans for our first trail together. It would be to visit their place as soon as the leaves started to return and the plowin' was done. Wolf and me would've turned eight by then. They weren't no tellin' what we could get into.

Chapter Five

Lucky

The mountains was just startin' to turn a light shade of green when Dad and Cain finished turnin' the cornfield and layin' in the garden. Plowin' that field weren't no small task, neither. The cornfield was so long you couldn't hear a body holler from one end to the other, even on a day with no wind. Took 'em most of three days to get it all done, with two of Dad's best plowin' mules, but it sure looked fine when they finished. The rows were gun barrel straight, which would be a big help with hoein' and totin' corn out. Them mules sure know'd what they was doin'. Dad set 'em straight soon after they was born, so they loved to plow. That pair of mules went everywhere together; you never saw one without the other. They ate at the same time, they went to water at the same time and they even made piles at the same time. Wolf saw it as somethin' spiritual, but I knew it was just the way Dad had trained 'em. They learned to do everything together, so when it come time to plow, they moved as one. My dad could speak mule, I was sure of that.

It was a little while passed breakfast the day after they finished the cornfield when Dad asked me, "How 'bout you and me takin' a couple of mules and goin' over to Slaughter for a visit. Cain can take care of the place. Anyways the field needs to settle for a while before we plant. Could do some early season fishin' on the way. How would that be?"

My world got foggy when my dad asked me that. A trip to see my best friend, time with my dad in the woods, mules to ride and tote our stuff, trout fishin', explorin', sleepin' out in the woods with fresh meat on the spit—and he'd asked me how'd that be?

How would one answer Jesus if He asked you to make a trip to Heaven with Him and stay for a while, then come on back home to your family? What do you say to the perfect time of your life when it's starin' you in the face? Are there words in an eight-year-old's vocabulary to describe the word 'yes' in its purest sense to answer his question? Could I make him understand just how important my first ever trail with him would be?

The offer stunned me, so I could only smile and nod my head. The words just weren't there for me at that moment. I would find those words later, as we roasted fresh mountain trout for supper in the valley of Upper Wolf Creek near the base of Slaughter Mountain.

Dad chose Jim, our lead mule, and a couple of younger mules for the trip. They weren't completely trained for a trail like this, so that was a concern for me. Dad's mules were really big 'cause they come from Belgian Draft horse mares. Most of 'em were as good as could be, but some of 'em was just plain mean. The ill ones respected him, but they would take a notion at times and catch hold of you if you was near when they got riled. You had to watch yourself or suffer from not. One pinched Dad on the shoulder once. I swear he knocked it plumb out. He balled up his fist and hit that mule in the side of the head, it hit the ground like you'd just cut its feet out from under it. Laid there a while, too, 'fore it stirred around later in the day. That mule never offered to bite nobody else for the rest of its time at our place. He traded that "old bastard," as he called him, to an Irish man Dad had traded with and made friends with years before from up north.

The day he traded that mule was the first time I remember ever meetin' another true Irishman from the home country other than my granddad and the owner of the Souther Mill. He was as nice and polite as a person could be, and he sang like nobody I'd ever heard. I loved to hear him sing them old songs from the 'motherland', even though I didn't understand a word of it. He could speak clear enough to be understood, but with lots of Irish in his wordin'. He would stay at our house while he was in the valley tradin'; told me stories about the people who lived where he did, in some place called

Boston. I know'd *that* name. I remembered Dad talkin' about a really big tea party they had up there once. I never did like tea, so it didn't matter much to me, but I remembered it. I preferred coffee, the blacker the better. Made my pipe taste good in the mornin'.

He lived near the sea and owned a freight haulin' business. They would unload ships from across the ocean and haul the goods to stores and people's homes, as well as to other towns. That's how come he needed my dad's mules. He got to where he would trade for six or seven every year. Kept my dad busy for sure. Dad looked forward to his visits. I think he made good money at that haulin' trade, 'cause he always paid in gold coin. My dad got to callin' him Lucky. Well, it kinda stuck. We all called him that till the day he died.

He was due to be at our place just before Thanksgiving a few years after Dad had first traded with him, but he never showed. His luck had run out late one evenin' as he made camp in the east end of Calf Stomp Gap just west of the Duncan Ridge. A few Cherokee out huntin' found him tied to a tree with his heart cut out. Someone had murdered that poor man and tried to make it look like an Indian did it, but it weren't no Indian that done that work. They brought the body to our place. Dad saw right off that it was the act of a white man. The white man cuts with a knife different from an Indian.

"Only rogue Indians would do somethin' like this. They would've yanked the heart out with their bare hands instead of cuttin' it out with a knife. They'd 'a-sliced him open, then used their hands to take the heart. They like to feel it beat its last," Dad explained.

What is really strange, when that happens—and all mountain folk know'd the story—the person dyin' is made to watch their heart beat its last beat, since they stay alive for a breath or two 'fore death dulls their eyes. A few outlaw Indians gave other Indians a bad reputation and caused the death of many innocent Cherokee at the hands of ignorant folk.

My dad sent Cain and me to get Dancing Bear. We was to ask him to come and sit with him a while, if he could spare the time. At the same time, he hired the Indians who'd found Lucky to track down his killers, then let him know their trail.

There weren't a trail these Cherokees could lose. Those murderin' outlaws were simply on a long lead that would get short in a hurry over the next few days.

As Cain and I rode Big Jim up the main trail in a hurry, into the gap near where Wolf lived, we couldn't help but be in awe of how grand everything was. It made me think Heaven would probably be like that when we "walk through the Pearly Gates," as Dad always said. The white oaks were huge! We stopped to eat dinner next to a branch in amongst some Chestnut trees that was bigger than we could reach around together, then headed on.

Dancing Bear was the only livin' soul home when we arrived near dark. He was glad to see us 'cause he'd been alone for several days. His family was gone to Yonah with Owl to trade for supplies and to visit with A-Ga-Li-Ha's folks that lived there.

Dancing Bear waved as he saw us come down the ridge and into the flats surroundin' his place. His voice was loud as he called out, "Welcome. Come and sit and we will smoke and talk. Is everything well back home?"

"No," said Cain. "My father asked us to ride here and invite you to come and sit with him a while, if you can spare the time."

"What made Thompie ask such a thing as this?" asked Dancing Bear.

"A man who is his friend has been found murdered over in Calf Stomp Gap. The Indians that found him brought him to our home. My dad says that white men did this. He is very angry and sad. This man was a close friend to our dad," replied Cain.

"Come and let us sit by the fire and smoke," said Dancing Bear. "I will then make ready to leave and we will start back with Old Man Sun's first light."

Dancing Bear then filled his pipe with some Weaver tobacco and offered it to Cain. I was too young to smoke then, so he didn't offer it to me.

"Have you ever talked to the Spirit of the Pipe, Cain?" asked Dancing Bear.

"No, I haven't had the honor, sir," said Cain. "I am only fourteen. My dad thinks me too young for spirit talk tobacco. I have my own pouch, though, with some good barn cured burly."

Indians were big on respect. Sayin' somethin' important the wrong way could get you in trouble as far as proper Cherokee talk went. It was also very important to the Cherokee that young men respect and obey their fathers and honor their authority.

"Around my fire, you are old enough to walk with the spirits. It is time you were learning the importance of the pipe. I will tell Thompie. He will agree. For the Cherokee, it is a way to aid our prayers or to celebrate good fortune. It is a cleansing influence in a dangerous world. Tobacco is a gift from God. It was meant to be sacred and enjoyed," declared Dancing Bear, as he showed Cain how to light the pipe and draw air through the hand-carved stem to taste the tobacco.

Dancing Bear had carved the stem to look like an eagle's head—the eyes of the eagle locked on unsupectin' prey—and it was made from the heart of an old white oak. Cain had never tasted better.

What better way to learn how to smoke than from a true Cherokee warrior, I remembered thinkin'. Maybe that is why I grew to like good Weaver tobacco and a fine white oak-heart pipe. In my young mind, I was sure that God Himself must enjoy a fine pipe of some kinda good tobacco. I know'd I sure did.

Dancing Bear spoke very little for the rest of the night. I could tell he was troubled. He'd moved to an open place that overlooked the Choestoe Valley and sat there, starin' out over the tops of the trees below him. Cain stayed by the fire, just starin' into the coals, like he was watchin'em change colors— red to orange and white or gray—not sayin' a word. He was near in a trance, so I didn't bother him and walked to where Dancing Bear was sitting.

"What do you see?" I asked.

"I see everything, little one. The hawk that soars overhead and the bear that is downwind of us. The fading of the sun as the mountains block her light and put her to bed. I see the rising of the moon and the lighting of the stars, and the coyote as he sings his song to the moon and asks it to shine. I see it all, little one, but mostly I see my friend as he grieves death and I sit here," said Dancing Bear.

Murder was not acceptable in the mountains; for sure not in Choestoe. Killin' for a reason could be tolerated if the reason was good, like justice for murder or stealin' or insultin' a body's family. Mountain folk took care of their own and didn't have no formal law. We all know'd murder was spoke of in the *Bible* as sin, yet them Israelites kilt' many in their time. But in 1822, murder was rare in Choestoe. It got to be more common after the gold was found. Some of them Indians didn't take kindly to greedy folks comin' in and messin' in the streams and crowdin' up the valley. It all settled down, though, when the gold miners moved west.

***

We left at first light the next mornin'. It was rainin'. I'd worn my skins and the rain didn't bother me, 'cept for the place where it ran down between the back of my neck and my shirt collar. I'd took to wearin' a hat, but some way the wet still found its way in. It was a chillin' rain, too. Cold weather hadn't all gone yet, even though we was already into early spring.

Dancing Bear was in a hurry, the rain was runnin' down his bare back. He was leadin' the way on foot; seemed to feel a need to get to our place as soon as we could. The trip was about half done when he stopped and knelt to the ground.

"A mule came through recently," said Dancing Bear. "Three men walking. The mule is packed very heavy. Two Cherokee trail them."

I couldn't help but ask, "How do you know that when it has been rainin' all mornin'?"

"The rain has not washed away all there is to see, young one. You must know how to read what is there even though it cannot be seen."

"Do you know who they are?" asked Cain.

"These could be men looking for gold in the waters of Choestoe or bandits. I wish they would go away," replied

Dancing Bear. "They are not yet close to finding our gold, but I fear that one day they will. The Cherokee do not talk of it."

"Why do they want the gold?" I asked.

"To trade for the gold coins. That is gold that has been heated and made into a circle like the sun," Cain answered.

"Oh, like the ones Dad keeps hid?" I asked Cain. "You mean gold is the stuff like we find in Wolf Creek under the waterfalls?"

"Yep, the very same stuff, only a lot more than what little we find," said Cain.

"We need to make us some of them gold coins, then Dad wouldn't have to sell our mules to get some," I near shouted.

"No!" came a loud yell from up ahead. Dancing Bear sounded angry. "Your elders create the coins the gold is used for, so men want it. That is why strangers come here and ask questions. They want the Cherokee land for the gold to make the coins of which you speak."

He said no more until my dad met him at the front door of our house at high noon. We'd made good time. Dad figured almost to the minute when we would arrive. Momma had made a huge pot of wild hog stew and a large skillet of cornbread for our return. It made me realize just how hungry I was. I ate two bowls full and a large piece of her cornbread with some melted butter and honeycomb on top.

"It's always good to see you, Dancing Bear. I am glad you had time to come and help me in this matter," said my dad, as they grabbed one another's forearms in a sign of friendship.

You could tell Dad was sad. Dancing Bear showed he understood this in his reply.

"I am sorry for the loss of your friend, Thompie Collins. It saddens my spirit to see you grieve. I would like to help you settle this debt. Maybe you will feel better when there is justice."

The people who did that to Lucky were bad people; their actions would call for proper punishment. It was understood, even among the Indians, that God is not in favor of killin', but sometimes folks reckon they become the tool God would use to reap vengeance. Right or wrong, I believed that to be what my dad was feelin' then. He'd grown to be good friends with

Lucky, had even gone to Boston with him for a while one spring. He'd met his family and had grown close to them while he was there. He took his killin' personal. With the help of the Cherokee, Lucky would find his peace.

After dinner, Dad said to Dancing Bear, "I asked the Cherokee that found Lucky to track down them murdin' varmints. One came back here this mornin'. He said they are camped on the River Notla, 'bout two miles below the mill. There are three men with long beards and a pack mule—the mule wears my brand; it belonged to Lucky."

Dad made it a habit of brandin' his mules so he could keep up with them better; had his own custom brandin' iron that he'd made himself. You'd find no other iron that could make that same mark, Dad was certain of that. The Indians told what it looked like, so he was sure it was the exact mule he'd give Lucky.

After speakin' with the Cherokee, Dancing Bear was more than positive that those were the thieves who murdered Lucky.

"The trail says these three men are guilty. The sign does not speak falsely, Thompie," said Dancing Bear. "These are the people who took the life of your friend. We must sit and smoke about this. Killing white men requires much thought."

Plannin' what to do with them skunks was a tender matter. Neither my dad nor Dancing Bear liked the idea, but both knew it meant justice for Lucky; would probably save the life of someone just like him on down the road, too. These men were what people called "trail bandits". At one time they'd been a problem in the valley, but problems like Lucky's was rare these days. These three would be a warning to other bandits that decided to hurt folks in our valley.

Choestoe would have its justice.

***

These bad men had crossed the river and were camped in a sharp bend just below the mouth of Wolf Creek. They must've thought they was in the clear, 'cause it was a terrible place for outlaws to make camp. It made it easy for Dancing

Bear and the Cherokee to slip in and have at them rascals. They never made a sound movin' through that water. Within a few minutes, a blood-freezin' scream broke the silence of the night.

Dad crossed the stream to an unforgettable sight. Two of the men had been dragged from their beds and were face down on the edge of the fire pit; a wet, dirty foot and knee of a Cherokee Indian planted heavily atop their backs, their heads pulled back by the hair. Each Cherokee held a knife to a man's throat. Small streaks of crimson had begun to run across the shiny blades into the dirt and ash at the edge of the fire. One of 'em was a little too close to the flames. Dad said he remembered smellin' his meat burnin'. Any more pressure from the Indians and the outlaws' throats would pop open like a ripe watermelon from the sharp edges of their knives.

The third bandit had been tied to an oak tree with both of his arms pulled tight to the back of the tree, not a stitch of clothing coverin' his body. It looked as though his shoulders were outa joint and his mouth was full of dirt. You couldn't hear the screams.

"This is the one who cut the heart out of your friend. He is the one who stole the mule and told the others what to do. These two told us. My brothers saw him wash the blood off in the creek," said Dancing Bear, slowly carvin' a deep cross on the outlaw's chest.

Dad watched the blood rise up behind the tip of the sharp blade as it moved across the man's skin. He would surely die, but not right away.

His body jerked and twisted, but he made very little noise, as his mouth was still full of dirt. Dad walked straight up to the man till he was near nose-to-nose with him.

"You and your friends are fixin' to die. There ain't nothin' you can do about it. I want you to feel the way my friend did when you cut out his heart," Dad said, while the other two men begged for their lives.

The Indians built up the fire and tortured the vermin all the rest of the night, cuttin' off bits and pieces and burnin'em with hot coals. Murder was not gonna be tolerated in Choestoe. These men were to be a testament to what happened to outlaws who enter the valley to kill and rob. The men were hung by the neck above the only trail into the valley, a wood board nailed to a tree beside'em, read, "Murderers Beware," stood as a warnin' to others.

Word quickly spread of the hangin' men. There was never any more trouble from bandits in the Choestoe Valley after that. Dad and his friends had reached their need of protectin' their families and all the other families in Choestoe, from the evil of murderers and bandits who would dare lay a spiteful hand on a friend of Thompie Collins.

Chapter Six

Crawdads and Spring Lizards

Dad and I left around noon the day after he and Cain finished the plowin'. I could tell that Dad was in no hurry as we packed; that let me know that we'd be takin' our sweet time goin' to Slaughter Mountain.

We loaded the mules and made sure we had all our possibles in place, includin' two guns, powder and ball. Momma let Dad take her gun, even though he knew she weren't fond of not havin' it around. It was a small bore rifle and fit her just right. I got excited 'bout havin' that gun with us, 'cause a boy my size could handle it. I'd only turned eight a few weeks earlier; hadn't ever shot a gun. I hoped silently that my dad had that in mind for me on this trip, bein' that we brought Mom's gun and all. It weren't safe to be home unarmed. Dad had a few guns he'd got in mule trades, so he left Momma and Cain two long guns, a side-by-side shotgun and a pistol, though she still liked hers best.

Dad kept our guns in oiled beaver pelt scabbards. They were in near perfect condition. He was always real particular when it came to his guns, sayin' how a gun could mean life or death in the woods. Most everybody carried 'em. A lot of women had guns, too. They hid them in their clothes and other places, like even their hair, for safe carryin'. Dad said he saw a lady down at the mill once that was bein' harassed by this gentleman, and when she'd had all she could stand, she fetched a small handgun from behind her back slick as butter slidin' off hot corn. He said she laid that cold steel barrel right between the eyes of her violator and explained his disrespect. She gave him a proper learnin'. I always found that story to be funny 'cause I thought everybody know'd that women from the Choestoe Valley was tough and respectable.

We packed our clothes on the mule I was leadin', but there was still enough room for me to ride when I needed. Dad would most likely walk the whole way, but I didn't know if I could make it. I wanted to show my dad that I was strong, so I was gonna try my best to keep up. The bearskin blanket that Dancing Bear had given me as a gift at my birth was laid across the mule's back, and our blankets were tied across it with leather straps. Atop the blankets were some small loggin' straps that dad would use to drag firewood down to our camp. I now realized that we'd be spendin' some time in the woods. It was no more than a whole day's walk to Wolf's place, if you traveled the main trail, and there was no need to camp. My heart started to pound as I realized we really was gonna be takin' a few days to get there. It made me feel alive. We was takin' the long trail to Slaughter Mountain. I'd been to their place before, but me and Cain took the main route and it come in from a different direction all together than the backwood trails. The long trail worked the ridges.

On the other mule was packed some gifts for Dancing Bear and his family, along with our possibles, like the fryin' pan and cookin' truck, a coffee pot, a rod for turnin' meat on the spit, a poleax, three short pieces of rope, blankets and a piece of canvas to sleep under. We tied the guns on top of all that, makin' sure the butts was showin' so Dad could grab one if he needed—they were both loaded. It would've all fit on two mules, but we were takin' three: Big Jim and the two younger ones. My dad had his reasons for doin' all he did, so I let it go at that.

As we started to leave, Dad went over to Momma and gave her a big hug and a kiss that lasted longer than usual. It must have hurt. They was tears in her eyes by the time they come apart. I couldn't figure why Dad would hurt Momma like that. Grown folks always did do things in a strange way; this was just one of them ways. After Dad was done with his huggin', I moved in for mine, but that kissin' stuff weren't due me. I would have no part of it. I liked huggin' Momma, though. She was good at it and she always smelled so nice and clean.

As I squeezed Momma, I asked her why she cried. "Did Dad hug you too tight or tell you somethin' sad?"

That made her smile, as she replied, "No, son, he didn't hurt me. It's just sad for me. I know your trip will take several days. I just...worry about your well-bein'. I know the good Lord is with you and will bring you home safe, but I will still miss my man and my big little boy until you return."

"Ah, mom, we'll only be gone a short while. You know Dad can take care of us. He knows the long trail to Wolf's place like he knows the way to the outhouse. We got good mules and plenty of provisions, so there ain't nothin' to worry 'over.'" It was my way of tryin' to comfort her.

"Enough about me. You go and visit your friend and enjoy your time on the trail with your dad. Tell Wolf and his family hello from me, Cain and Anne. And you be respectful of Dancing Bear and his family, they're our friends." She snatched me up and wet my cheek with a sweet 'momma kiss,' then turned toward Dad and dried her tears on her apron. We were down the trail a ways when I figured out what them tears was about. I began to miss my momma.

Dad was followin' the long trail to Slaughter. I know'd from listenin' to him and Cain talk that it would take us a few days to get to Wolf's. If we stopped to hunt or fish, then it would take longer. My dad never shared his travel plan with me, so I just tried not to lag behind.

He made me ride 'cause I walked so slow, but it weren't slow to me. I felt like I was near runnin' to match my dad's long legs. Near killed me with fright when he did it, too. He'd caught on that I was strugglin', fallin' behind, so he snatched me up by my arms so fast the world spun. He threw me in the air and over one of them young mule's backs 'fore I know'd what'd happened. It took me a second to realize just what had happened. When it hit me, I froze. He'd throw'd me over the back 'a one of the young mules, not Jim. I trusted my dad, though. After ridin' that mule for a spell, I figured exactly how God must get around in the mountains of Heaven—He rides a good mule. I think even Jesus rode one, too, or maybe a Jack, into Jerusalem 'fore they killed Him, sheddin' His blood for our salvation.

My whole world changed when Dad did that. Sittin' on the back of that mule was like havin' a set of big long legs connected to your rump and coverin' the ground smoothly like an early mornin' breeze. It was like floatin' along the trail without your legs even movin', with your eyes way up off the forest floor.

As I rode, I could feel the muscles in the mule's back, the up and down of his shoulders as he surefooted it down the trail and through several small creeks and branches. His breaths were even, could smell and feel the heat from each exhale he gave, yet he never broke a sweat or seem to struggle. He just moved along at a steady pace, stoppin' ever so often to shift his load when it got outa balance. I swear he'd look back at me from time to time, like he wanted to understand this strange thing on his back and why it was not tied down. The next time I caught him lookin' back, I gave him a little squeeze with my knees. He turned his ears to me and raised his head like he know'd I'd done that, but just what it was I did must've not worried him, 'cause he never broke his pace.

His back felt good to me, my legs wrappin' perfectly around the bearskin that molded itself to his curves. I felt like I was a part of his effort as he moved us to our camp on the banks of Wolf Creek in the upper part of the Choestoe valley. I was growin' fond of this young mule. I think he liked me, too.

Dad picked a great place to camp. I couldn't 'a-been more excited than I was. This was my first night in the woods, camped on the banks of Wolf Creek with my dad as we traveled to see my friend and his family even deeper in the woods. I didn't have a thought that life could get any better for a boy like me, till Dad strung his river cane with fishin' line and a hook. Visions began to form in my head of huge trout and other unknown critters that might be in the creek. I could hardly wait to get goin'.

I'd been wonderin' why he cut that cane 'fore we left the river to turn up Wolf Creek. Now I had the answer. I'd never been fishin' or really even heard anyone speak of it much, 'cept Wolf and his dad. I knew in my soul that this was gonna be fun. I think that, of all the things I did and would do in my life, this trip with my dad was probably as good a time as I ever had in my whole put-together. The only thing that might've made it better was if Momma had 'a-been there. I was missin' her somethin' awful.

Most folks didn't fish with cane poles and hooks, mainly 'cause there was an art to weavin' horsehair fishin' line and carvin' bone hooks. Both required what my dad called "the patience of Job." I didn't know this man Job, but I remember thinkin' that he probably carved some really good fish hooks.

"We need to find us some bait for this hook. We'll look up in the creek branches for somethin' a big trout would want for supper, then we'll see what's hungry down in the big bend."

"What would a big trout want for supper, Dad?" I asked.

"Spring lizards, son, and crawdads. You turn over the rocks in the middle of the branches and get what's crawlin' underneath. That's what big trout like for supper."

God help me, I prayed. *What in the world was a crawdad? Why would it live under rocks, and did it bite your fingers when you caught hold of it? And spring lizards, did they jump on you when you turned the rock over? What would want to eat a nasty ole lizard anyhow? Was I supposed to eat somethin' that would eat that critter? If we didn't catch any fish, did we have to eat the lizards and crawdads for supper?* I was really glad Dad was there to take care of all the strange things I was runnin' up on. I couldn't get comfortable with this huge world I'd just entered, with its weird critters and lonesome trails.

We started up the nearest small creek we found after makin' camp. We didn't turn over many rocks 'fore Dad started grabbin' some of the God-awfulest lookin' things I'd ever laid eyes on. I know'd sorta what spring lizards was gonna look like 'fore we caught any, but those crawdad things was a different critter all together. I weren't expectin' the likes of them.

Dad told me to hold open the leather pouch we brought to tote bait and, as he was droppin' 'em in, I got a good close look at them critters. They was fearful. The smallest one was half as big as my hand, with a pincher that grow'd where the front legs was supposed to be that looked as though it could take my finger clean off. I weren't gonna let Dad know I was scared of them rascals, but I was. Their beady little eyes were evil lookin' in a sad sorta way. They *looked* mean. Them pincher things were vicious. I weren't gonna put my hand in that bag for nothin'. Dad would have to fetch his own bait outa that bag.

We filled our poke with eight of them crawdads and a half dozen spring lizards. I liked them spring lizards. They was fun to catch. I must've caught at least a dozen 'fore Dad had a few good ones to fish with. I still hadn't touched one of them crawdad devils. I weren't makin' no plans to have at 'em, neither.

"Look here, son," said Dad, as he took the opportunity to teach me which lizards were best for trout.

"If the lizard is too big, then you'll miss some hungry, smaller trout. They eat good, too, and most of 'em are small kinda. It's better to use one a good size, but not too big, 'cause when you're fishin' for food, most fish are good. You sure don't want to scare any of 'em off."

"What place in the creek are we gonna fish, Dad?"

"I wanna make it down to the big bend, 'bout a quarter mile below our camp. I've done good there before, and know some good fish hunt that hole at supper time."

My curiosity was stirred, so I wondered aloud, "What kinda fish have you caught outa Wolf Creek?"

"Well, let's see...I've caught brook trout, catfish, carp and horny heads, but the trout are the best to eat. I tried to eat a carp once, but it was not to my likin'. It was bad, tasted like mud. Your momma knows how to do it right. They are good when she cooks 'em, but lest I'm starvin', I ain't eatin' one outside 'a her fixin'."

He grabbed his fishin' truck and we headed down stream to the big bend he wanted to fish. A quarter mile don't seem very far, but when you're eight-years-old and headed for your first ever fishin' hole, it's a long way.

Just bein' near the water and tryin' to stay hid was a chore for me. I wanted to look in every hole and see what was there. This was all new and I meant to get the whole of it, but Dad kept pullin' me away from the edge of the creek bank. We crept through the woods as quiet as we could, makin' sure we didn't let our feet hit the trail too hard. Dad said the fish could feel us walkin' if we stepped too hard.

We stopped several yards shy of the big bend. Dad got down and looked me right in the eye and said, "Jeb Collins, you can't swim. Promise me that you will be careful around the edge of this creek and not let yourself end up in the water. It's a huge hole for a creek, and it will swallow you up if you fall in, so keep your feet under you at all times and stay close to me. Do you hear me, Jeb?"

I know'd what swimmin' was, but I couldn't do it yet. We all went to the swimmin' hole down on the river in the summer. Everybody could swim but me. I could float, but that was it. Momma was a good swimmer. She was helpin' me to learn, but I just hadn't caught on yet.

The look in my dad's face let me know that he was very serious, so I squared up and said right to him, "I will be careful. You do not have to worry about me." He nodded and turned down the trail so fast that it kinda seemed like he hadn't even been squatted there—my dad was at home in the woods.

You could hear the water 'fore we got there. It was a small waterfall no higher than I was tall, which began at the head of the bend Dad wanted to fish. The air, damp and cool in the woods surroundin' the creek, fell on your skin like a fresh cool sheet as you moved. Clean and refreshin' as it flowed into your lungs, it tasted like fresh spring water. The moisture made the forest floor quiet so that we moved through the woods like ghosts. I became one with the woods; could feel the flow of the creek in my heart. It was what my friend would call spiritual.

The noise from the waterfall was calmin', soundin' like a church choir singin' mixed with a soft summer rain. Comin' on it from the north, I could see the water as it broke over the top rocks of the falls long before I could see the creek bend. Dad made us almost crawl the last twenty paces or so. He didn't want to spook the fish, and I'm sure glad we didn't. The sight that awaited us on that day burned into my brain. I will never forget it. I felt like the water was a whole other world, with the trees its keeper. It truly set you in awe of our Maker.

The first thing I noticed was how big the bend was to the size of the creek flow. It was a place where the water seemed to turn around and head back to where it came from. A switchback, Dad called it, it scared the devil outa me. I know'd then why he had been so serious about me not fallin' in. The creek was so big here that it could really swallow me. I was sure I couldn't throw a rock across it to the other side. I think maybe Cain could've, but not me.

The water was deep and the current slow, as it made the lazy turn to the south before headin' back north again. You could tell by lookin' that some big fish could grow here. I was glad Dad had a long and solid river cane to use fishin' this hole. He might need the strength. I sure hoped he did, anyway.

It was a while 'fore dark. Him and me, we just lay there on our bellies at the top of the creek bank, watchin' the water, when he pointed at the far side of the pool. Some trout was feedin' on the bugs that was landin' on top of the water and couldn't fly away.

"Now, ain't that somethin'," I said to nobody in particular. "Them fish lay around in there, and God just sends 'em their supper. All they got to do is rise up and eat it. He must think a lot of them fish. He sure makes it easy for 'em."

Dad smiled as he listened to me ramble. Everything I was seein' was new to me, makin' me feel lost and small. I guess I needed my dad to hear my thoughts, 'cause I know'd very little about the world out here. He was my rock. I was sure he had all the answers, which gave me the courage to observe and notice the things that were important. I would watch him so I wouldn't miss the things he saw, which helped me to learn. I followed his path to the creek and did exactly as he did, not near as good as him, but I was there and I was tryin'. It was the most excitement I'd ever had in my life. I would feel guilty askin' God for more.

We was just startin' to move to a good spot to fish when Dad caught my arm and froze. I followed his gaze into the water and could see a dark form movin' under the surface. The form was in no hurry. It turned up under the white water at the base of the falls and came out on the side nearest to us. I watched as it went a little deeper and near disappeared from sight, when all of a sudden, it broke the water dead in front of me to snag a bug from off the surface. I saw it plain as it splashed the water and returned to its home.

I'd never seen a trout feedin' in the creek 'fore that day. It was somethin' that made my trip even more of a keepin' memory. That fish was beautiful, with bright red fins and a dark green back covered with small black and red and orange spots. It looked like one solid muscle, never slowin' down as it hit the bug and dove to the bottom to finish its meal. This was a huge fish, even I could see that. Dad got really quiet after we saw that fish.

"We need to catch that fish. It's so big that it's probably eatin' all the little trout. I'm surprised the Cherokee ain't caught it 'fore now. That is a wise fish to have made it to this size, but we are gonna get him outa there and have him for supper. I'm gonna do my best to see to that for sure. Hand me one of them crawdads, Jeb," he said, stretchin' out his hand toward me.

My blood turned cold and my vision grew dark as I heard those words. I couldn't find the strength to reach into the pitch black of the bait pouch and pull out one of those little demons for him. I'd just as soon take a whoopin' with a saw briar as to handle one. I couldn't help it. What was I gonna do?

Tears of fear slipped into my eyes, cloudin' my vision even more, as Dad kept his hand back toward me, waitin', watchin' for the trout. I guess he wondered why there weren't no crawdad in his hand after a minute, 'cause he looked back and started to ask me if I'd heard him. He saw my eyes was wet. The look on his face was confusion till he saw the pouch on the ground. It didn't take him long to understand my problem. He reached and picked up the pouch, stuck his hand in and felt around till he fetched out the ugliest of all them critters he'd caught earlier.

"Hold out your hand, boy, and take hold of this crawdad."

"I can't...I'm scared."

"Agh, there ain't nothin' to be feared of from this little critter. You're a lot bigger than he is. Don't you think that he's more scared of you, seein' how you're so much bigger?"

"No," I said, as I crossed my arms behind my back. "I think he wants to eat one of my fingers. I ain't gonna let that happen, even if you whoop me. I swear I ain't."

"Agh, come on now. Bein' scared of somethin' don't call for no whoopin', you know that. You're a good boy. I'm as proud of you as I can be, whether you cotton to nasty ole crawdads or not, but he ain't nothin' to be scared of. It don't hurt when they get them pinchers in ya."

"I'm sorry, Dad, but I can't believe that. Look at that thing stickin' off him—looks like the hand of the devil. I ain't never seen it, but if he had one, I know it would look like that thing," I said, as I pointed at its pinchers. "I told you, I ain't touchin' that devil, whoopin' or no whoopin."

Dad could tell that my back was up and that I meant to stand my ground. He was an understandin' man, so what he did next weren't no big shock to me. He opened his mouth up wide and laid that crawdad right on his tongue. Then he slowly closed his mouth and stared me right in the eye. I didn't hear a crunch and he never swallowed, so I know'd it was still in his mouth. I almost feinted as he put my hands together, leaned over and spit that critter out into my right hand palm, then closed my left over top of it and held it there. My world stopped dead still; breath was hard to come by. My dad was tryin' to kill me.

Chapter Seven

Watching the Brookies Dance

That crawdad was the most horrible thing I'd ever had a hold of in my life. I could barely breathe. It felt like the devil himself diggin' into the palm of my hand. I just know'd it was gonna rip the skin loose from my bones. It moved in a way that let me know it was wantin' out from between my hands; its pinchers was goin' to a lot of trouble. I was nearly able to breathe again when the pain come.

Somehow, that ugly thing had found some skin at the base of my middle finger with one of them pinchers. It latched on for what I'm sure it felt like was a fight for its life. The warmth of my blood trickled out from between the fingers of my right hand, but I never moved one bit as it dripped onto my foot. Dad saw the blood and just smiled as he looked down, seein' that my hands were still cupped over the little red demon, my eyes locked on him. He gently opened my hands. There that thing was, lickin' its little red lips and lookin' all proud at what it'd done.

My hand weren't hurt none, it just stung somethin' fierce, but right then and there I learned that if you're gonna handle wild critters, you'd better do it proper or they'd damage your person. I bet Momma would've been proud if she'd 'a-seen me stand up to that little red heathen. I wondered what she'd be doin' about now. She seemed so far away.

I never liked crawdads from then on, but I never had no problems with 'em, neither. I could snatch 'em out from under rocks and pick 'em up and run a hook through their back without no worry. I learned it from Dad that day. He took that critter outa my hand and put the hook through it without so much as a second thought. He did it in such a way as to keep the beast alive, too. He also taught me that trout don't like dead food; always need to fish with somethin' fresh. I got to where I'd rather have a good-sized spring lizard or night-crawler over anything else.

It was still early in the evenin' when Dad baited his hook. We slipped through the woods and eased up on the first part of the bend, still crawlin' on our hands and knees, makin' it a chore keepin' the bait in the pouch. We stopped a few feet short 'a the edge of the creek and peeked over into the water. You couldn't see the bottom like you near could earlier in the day, when the sun was straight up overhead. The water was a dark green in color, like the dark stripe of a watermelon. The current moved with a motion that felt alive, first turnin' one direction, then back another, with a main whirlpool right out in the middle. It had a center swirl that looked like an eye starin' out as it kept the water movin' through the bend and on its path north. The water flowed north in the Choestoe Valley.

I caught myself day dreamin' as my dad was loudly whisperin' to me, "Jeb! Jeb! Hey, Jeb!"

I looked over at him and nodded slightly. This place had me in a trance, same as when we was up all night helpin' one of our mares have a young'un, and didn't get any sleep by the time morning come.

"Take this above the falls and throw it in the creek just a few feet out from the bank. I want it to float over the falls and downstream to where we're fishin'. Jeb. Do you hear me, Jeb?"

I hadn't heard it all, but I'd heard enough. I looked at the piece of old bark he held in his hand— a little longer than my arm and wide as my leg. He wanted me to go above the falls and throw it in the creek. That was curious to me.

I had no idea why he wanted me to do that, so I looked at him and had to ask, "Won't that scare the fish?"

"No, toss it gently out in the middle, a little ways above the falls. Don't make a big splash. It'll wash over the falls natural-like, just the way any other piece of wood floatin' in the creek would. Once you've done that, slip around down here and watch. You may see somethin' you're gonna need to remember."

I stood the bait pouch against a tree and went and did as he said. I near crawled back below the falls to where he was squatted now, ready to set that crawdad into the water. This was my first ever honest-to-goodness fishin' trip. I was so excited that my knees was shakin'. I couldn't wait for Dad to get his line in the water and catch a big'un, but there was a problem— he weren't movin'. He simply sat there and watched, like he was lookin' for some kinda sign from God to tell him it was time to fish. I didn't understand, so I just watched. This was my dad's world. I allowed he was handlin' things the way he chose to. I waited, but he still weren't movin'.

It was a few minutes 'fore he whispered his first words since I'd returned from above the falls. "Be still and quiet, boy, I'm puttin' the bait to 'em."

His gaze was intent on somethin' in the water. I followed his eyes until I saw the piece of bark I'd tossed in the creek above the falls. He watched as it made its way over the short falls and started turnin' with the flow toward us. He made ready to move as it turned gently in our direction.

Dad grabbed the line just above the crawdad with his left hand, the pole in his other. He raised up on one knee and turned toward the creek where he'd have room to move, stayin' hid behind the base of a poplar tree. He held the tip of the pole high over the water and let the crawdad swing out and land perfectly on the back of that piece of bark. It looked natural as it rode the wood on past us and around the whirlpool toward the central eye, and all the while Dad kept turnin' the cane to let the line out.

It made its way around the eye of the bend until it crossed over the spot where him and me first saw the big trout earlier in the day. Dad made a short, soft jerk on the line as the piece of bark turned long ways away from us, and that crawdad slid off and into the water like it was of its own desire. I watched as the critter's hellfire-colored back had no more than disappeared below the surface of the swirlin' green water when the end of Dad's pole bent straight down and the line went banjo string tight. Somethin' had snatched that crawdad the second it got down in the water good. Dad had a fight on his hands! I was so excited I nearly screamed at the wonder of what was on the end of his line. I'd never seen a fish caught before, or at least I didn't remember ever seein' it done, so this was a first for me. I didn't know what was comin'.

"This is a good trout I got here, son. I'm gonna try and work it toward the bank close to where you are. When I pull it outa the water, make sure you don't grab the line or it'll break. If it gets off the hook, then fight to keep it from goin' back into the water. Do you hear me?" Dad's voice was calm but excited as he fought the fish.

I still hadn't seen the thing 'cept for a flash of redish orange as it got close to the surface, then it hadn't stayed there very long before divin' to the bottom. Dad just kept handlin' the pole as the fish directed, till all of a sudden it broke water and started dancin' across the surface on its tail before losin' speed and fallin' headfirst back into the green, murky depths. It was probably the most beautiful thing I'd ever seen in the woods that lasted but a few seconds. It come clean outa the water several more times, but that horsehair line held strong, as did the bone hook Dancing Bear had carved.

Dad eased the tip of the pole to an openin' next to me, stood and got ready. On the fish's next jump, he gave a solid but very smooth whip in my direction. The trout came flyin' through the air and landed at my feet. It was simply amazin' how he worked that pole and brought the trout to land.

"Catch hold of that trout and don't let it back toward the creek!" hollered Dad, as I jumped back from the madness that was floppin' at my feet, covered in old dead leaves from the forest floor.

"What do I catch hold of?" I hollered back.

"Just grab him behind the head where his neck outa be with both hands and hang on. He'll be easy to hold with all them pieces of leaves on him. Put your body between him and the creek in case he gets away and tries for the water. Fall on him if you have to. That's our supper for tonight! You might get hungry 'fore breakfast time comes if you let him back in the creek." Dad was funnin' with me as I tried to catch hold of the thick wad of muscle that had been pulled from the creek and slung at me.

I was really hungry, so I took Dad's advice and fell on the fish. He was a good-sized trout, near as long as my forearm, but not as big as the one we saw earlier. Still, he put up a good fight, but I won in the end.

Dad slid a small leather strap through its mouth and out the gill hole, then we walked above the bend a ways. He made a loop around his wrist and put the fish back into the water to clean it for supper. The cold creek water runnin' through its gills got it to goin' and it started movin' its tail like it was gonna swim off. He grabbed its head and rolled it over in the water and washed it of all the trash on its skin. He reached and got his small knife from his side belt and slit its belly front to tail in one easy motion to get the guts out. That trout did not like that at all and commenced to floppin' even harder in the water, the leather strap holdin' firm. I could see now why he'd tied that strap on his arm, 'cause of how hard it went to floppin' when he gutted it. It was a big fish, strong.

"Why did you gut that fish before it died, Dad?" I asked in a stunned sorta way. I swear that thing was still floppin' after all its insides was gone.

"Makes the meat sweeter. Get the insides out first, then the meat is much better. Keeps the bad flavor of death from soakin' in."

Once he said that, I know'd that was a Cherokee thing. There weren't no disputin' it was proper, so I had to ask, "You learned that from the Indians, didn't you?"

"Yep. It's believed among Indians that you should clean your fish before it dies. They begin to rot quick once they're outa the water," he explained. That made sense to me.

I didn't want rotten insides touchin' that sweet trout meat before I could eat it. I'd only tasted it a few times, but I really liked it. My mouth was waterin' just thinkin' about this big'un smokin' on the spit.

It was a big fish and would've probably fed us both if we'd needed, but that was not the way of this trip. We were on a journey to visit friends, and we was gonna enjoy God's bounty as we went. Tonight would require a good brookie for each of us, so we hung that trout in a tree by the trail and headed back to the fishin' hole as dark was slowly approachin'.

"Get into that bag and fetch me another crawdad, Jeb. I think the fish are hungry this evenin'," he said with a troubled look on his face.

"What's wrong?" I asked, as I saw his concern.

"Nothin'," he replied, but I could see somethin' was on his mind, which concerned me some, but I would worry over that later.

This time I was ready as I brought out a big'un from the bottom of the bag. Somethin' didn't look right when I handed it to Dad, so he raised it up to take a closer look. Right there in its pincher was a fat night-crawler he had found under a dead tree log on our way to the bend earlier. It had eaten about half of it and was preparin' to eat the rest when Dad put the hook through its back. All its legs and even its pinchers shot straight out to the sides. Makin' the thing look like it was flyin'. The half worm dropped to the ground 'fore Dad flung the line into the water just below the eye of the whirlpool. Together, we watched as the water moved the limp line in circles 'round and 'round.

It was worrisome for me to watch the line, hopin' it would snap straight and start movin' against the motion of the water's flow. I saw it in my mind several times as the line moved its way around the bend and started to follow the current north, leavin' the good fishin' waters. Dad felt a slight tug but nothin' serious so he pulled in the line. The back half of the crawdad was gone. Somethin' had taken interest, so he was gonna try again. I fetched him another one outa the bottom of the bait pouch.

He moved to a spot some twenty feet closer to the falls and eased the crawdad into the water up close to the bank. He let it kinda wander down to the bottom and into the current on its own. The line started to move out into the creek as Dad dropped the end of the cane pole and let the line lay on top of the surface, followin' the currents path. It lay in circles that slowly unwound like a coiled rope as the water pulled the bait out into the whirlpool. The line picked up speed as it moved through the eye of the bend and out the far edge of the hole. The creek got to pullin' so, I couldn't tell if Dad had a fish or not.

I was eyein' the point where the line entered the water, watchin' how the current would move faster than the crawdad that was on the line. It made it seem like somethin' was under the water, movin' the line back upstream. That's why when it actually happened, it took me a second to realize just what was goin' on.

The line suddenly cut upstream through the water like a knife, as another big trout broke the creek's surface and did that amazin' trout dance across the whirlpool, disappearin' headfirst below the surface. I was near shakin' from all the excitement.

"Yah-hoo," I screamed at the top of my lungs. I couldn't help it. I had to scream or bust. It felt so good, I did it again, which rewarded me with a scowl from Dad.

"Don't be hollerin' so, boy," he said in a very serious tone. "We don't know if anyone is around here or not. We ain't got but two fish!" Then he started laughin' hard as he hauled in the one I would eat for supper.

My dad had a good sense of humor and he enjoyed life by usin' it quite often. He could drive my momma plumb crazy with his goin' on, but she loved him all the same. Momma was tough; she'd give him the what-for ever now and again. They made bein' a family fun.

Dad got a good cookin' fire goin' soon after we returned to camp. It was a good-sized fire, so I knew it would serve as our campfire for the night as well. It was longer than it was wide. When the coals got just right, he pierced them fish and laid 'em on the spit to cook.

"You watch them fish and don't let 'em burn. Grab the end of the cookin' rod and turn 'em ever so often. I'm gonna fetch some of that young poke salad we saw on the trail comin' in earlier. We'll boil it up with some of those onions your momma packed for us. Keep an eye out and mind them fish," ordered Dad. He grabbed mom's gun and a leather pouch and headed back up the trail on foot. He didn't make a sound as he disappeared, which left me feelin' very small in some really big woods.

I was now all by myself, which scared me some. I felt comfort knowin' the Lord was with me, though; that He'd provided me with some good mules to keep me company.

Nothin' gets by a mule and their senses. It really is helpful how they can let you know things is stirrin' near by. Dad hadn't been gone but a few minutes when all three of them mules started gettin' restless. Somethin' was closin' in on our camp. They could sense it.

They were lookin' downwind of the camp, so it made me think some critter had smelled the fish. I was hopin' it would just move on, but the mules didn't act like it was. They was gettin' more spirited by the minute. I feared they might break the leather straps tied to their halters and run off, so I turned the fish and wandered on over to where they was tethered. I stood on my toes and whispered to the mules that everything was all right, but the streak of black I saw just as I finished talkin' changed my mind about that. I feared I had to do somethin'.

I eased around to the side of the mules and grabbed Dad's gun from off the bearskin. I held it the way I'd seen him do several times, tryin' to line up the sights. I remembered from bein' with him many times how to shoot it—I'd just never done it.

It was hard to get a feel for the gun since it weighed so much; it was one of Dad's bigger guns, way too big for me. I feared I might not hit that critter, but I was sure gonna put the fear of God in it if I missed.

The weight of the gun gave me the courage I was gonna need it to protect our truck. I know'd I'd only have the one shot, a fact that held my courage some. I wished really hard that Momma was with me. She'd drop the flint on that critter, no worries at all.

I checked the flint and primed the charge like I'd done many times, then replaced the small pouch of powder into the leather pocket of the gun slip. I moved around to the front of the mules and raised the gun to my shoulder and waited. It wasn't long before it got too heavy for me to hold up, so I dropped it down to hip level and held it there with both hands. I watched for any sign that the danger had moved on, but the mules was still nervous. They had wide eyes, which meant that the black critter was even closer now. I said a little prayer and stood my ground.

The groan I heard was more than I could stand. My legs began to shake like I had the fever. I could feel it was close and the mules was nervous, but there was no sign of whatever it was that was sneakin' up on us. Dad should be back soon. I sure was wishin' he'd hurry.

I could hear the leaves and sticks crunchin' on the forest floor as the critter was closin' in on our camp. It sounded big. I was holdin' the gun so tight I could feel my heart beatin' in my fingers, but I never took my eyes off the woods ahead of me. That thing was there; felt as though I'd be meetin' it face to face soon. Braced for the worse, I didn't have to wait long.

I caught a flash of black to my left toward the fire; couldn't believe my eyes as I looked in that direction. Standin' as tall as a mountain was the first bear I'd ever seen in the woods. It weren't twenty of Dad's paces away and lookin' straight at me, with its head cocked to one side like it was tryin' to figure out just what it had come up on. The black of its fur was shiny, like when the sun shines on water, as dark a black as I'd ever seen. It had a white star like a cross on its chest. I remember thinkin' that would be a good target if I had to shoot. Its front feet were hangin' down to its sides and its ears were standin' straight up and cupped toward the mules and me. I was really scared of this bear bein' so close.

The mules had steadied. The whole world seemed to stop as the bear and I stared at each other. I tried to raise the gun to my shoulder, but it wouldn't move. I thought about a shot from the hip like my dad does sometimes, but somethin' about the way this bear was actin' caused me to take notice. It seemed more curious than threatened, so I just stood my ground. If it made a move in our direction, then I would fire, but as of right then, it was just standin' there watchin'.

It looked at me; raised its left front leg in a type of wave that left me in wonder. The white star on its chest looked even more like the cross Jesus died on with its leg up like it was. Its head raised and straightened as it let out several bellows that curled the hairs on the back of my neck and made the mules freeze. It looked like it was tryin' to tell me somethin', but I didn't speak bear, so the message never got through my understandin'. The question entered my mind whether or not to shoot, but I felt somethin' about this bear; know'd to just stand still even though I was near scared to death.

The hand that grabbed my shoulder made me jump the same time the bear hit the ground and run off. "Are you well, little one?" came the question from behind me.

As I turned to reply, I know'd surely who it was.

"Yes, Dancing Bear, I am fine."

"You were very brave, young Jeb. I will tell this story around the fires at night during the long winters that come to the mountains. You will be honored for your bravery in our songs. Yours will be a name many will know because of your courage. Now, come and let's see to those fish at the fire before they get like jerky. I am hungry."

"Why did the bear not attack?"

"It is not for me to say why Brother Bear did not come at you, for he is his own spirit. I believe he respected you for your courage. He would not disrespect that courage. I have been here a while; was ready to shoot if he had charged, but in some way I knew he would not. You must think on this as time goes on. Soon you will understand why he came to you. That is what I think."

"Did you see how beautiful he was; how he stood and looked at me?"

"I saw how you honored him with your respect. He will remember your scent. You now have a spirit friend in the woods, but use caution near all bears. Not all are good in spirit like your new brother. Even he is still a bear of the woods."

I was stunned that Dancing Bear called the bear my brother. It gave me a new way to think on things. Dad would be back soon. I couldn't wait to tell him what happened while we sat around the fire and ate the smoked fish. It would be a good night in Choestoe, as there was a new story to hear. I could hardly wait for Momma to hear Dancing Bear tell it, but that would happen in its own time.

Chapter Eight

Wolf Creek

Wolf Creek is the biggest creek that runs through the Choestoe Valley, but it's a sight smaller than the Notla River. It was real special that me and Dad camped on the creek for my first ever overnight camp. That time is burned into my memory, somethin' I will never forget. The bear visit made it that much better, but it still would've been a most favorite time, even if I hadn't got the scare of my life.

Supper was so good I can hardly describe it. Dad found some young poke salad back down the trail. Since it was early spring, the leaves were small and tender. He boiled 'em up with some of the dried onions and salt Momma sent along, addin' a few mushrooms he'd collected on his salad run. The boilin' greens made the air around the fire sweet. You could taste the onions in your mouth as you got close to the fire. It was the size of the poke leaves that required him to be gone longer than he'd wanted to be, but it also made the taste that much better.

I guess bein' scared half to death makes a body hungry, 'cause I was sure ready to eat by the time Dad got the greens ready. The smell of those big trout smokin' over the fire, mixed with the boilin' greens, set my mouth to waterin' so that it hurt down in my jaw. The fire under the crispy brown skin of the trout would jump and sizzle as the juices from the fish dripped into the coals. It would just sing of what we were fixin' to eat. It sure was somethin' for a hungry body to have to wait for. That waitin' made me kinda dizzy with want, too.

We invited Dancing Bear to have supper with us. Them trout was plenty big for us all. He accepted, and we had us a little feast after Dad bowed his head and said the blessin'. Dancing Bear bowed his head, too, as he and his family had a cause for the *Bible* just like us. Christian Indians was spread throughout Choestoe on account of all the missionaries and their *Bible* teachin'. Dancing Bear and his kin were real spiritual. They reasoned they was part of the earth; that God made everything, them included. Says so right there in the front of that big ole' *Bible* book back home. Them missionaries, the ones that traveled through the valley, taught the Cherokee and many settlers to Choestoe the Christian way. Folks was strong in their faith. They depended on God for all they had or ever got, which was food mostly, and health and healin'.

I wondered what the folks back home was eatin'. I felt for 'em. They was missin' out on a tasty supper. Fish cooked over an open fire and smoke fillin' the cool night air, mixed up with the calmin' sound from the waters flowin' in Wolf Creek—I'm positive this was a lot like Heaven. Mom's cookin' was real good, but this was special. I made the most of it by takin' in things that I can still remember, like how bright the stars was against a deep black sky, and the chill of the night air as it surrounded our camp. You could feel it in your lungs when you took a breath. It made you feel fresh and clean.

Dad didn't know we had company till he got back from collectin' poke. Dancing Bear had been back in the woods watchin' my back when the bear was there, but I didn't know it. I'm glad he let me stand my ground. That helped teach me to be brave and not fear the critters of the woods. He stayed the night since he was on a walk, which is what the Indians called it when they went out into the woods for a few days and not exactly on a hunt. It was just a walk. Wolf and me would have our share as time went on. They carried their weapons and took game to eat, but nothin' they would have to tote while they was travelin'. I think sometimes a body just needs to be alone in the woods to think and soak up the beauty of the Great Creation. I know'd plenty of folks like my granddad that would go out into the woods to pray. Sometimes he'd take me with him to his special prayin' place, and me and him would get on our knees and have a talk with God.

A walk was a time of reflection and thought. The Cherokee believed spirits lived in the woods; would converse with 'em just like they was a real somebody. They called many of 'em ancestors, but I had a hard time with that way 'a thinkin'. The *Good Book* says we go to Heaven when we die as long as we know Jesus. I'd never met Him in person, face-to-face, but I know'd he was always with me; the *Book* says so right there in the *Gospels*. Maybe that's why I felt safe around that bear.

It would've been a bad time if the bear had charged, since it turned out I hadn't got Dad's gun ready correctly. It wouldn't 'a fired even if I had needed to pull the trigger. Fortunately, there was no reason to shoot that bear. All went well even though I was scared to death at the first sight of that big ole thing. I learned that some critters respect a brave soul who shows no fear. Dancing Bear added that to his story, which made me proud. I'd now discovered that crawdads and bears were not somethin' to fear, but somethin' to respect, even though you still had to use caution when a body got near 'em. The cut on my hand was proof of that, as I remembered how that little red devil licked my blood off its little red-devil lips.

Dancing Bear started his story 'bout me and the bear's visit as we all settled down for a good smoke. Dad said I was still too young to try tobacco; there weren't no way he was gonna let me sample what he'd brought in the jug he and Bear was passin' back and forth. It must've been strong. It made their faces look funny every time they took a swig. I didn't care. I was too busy studyin' on how my story would tell, anyway. I loved to hear the Cherokee tell their stories, and now my story had become one of theirs. It was almost too much for a boy my age to take in.

Dancing Bear began by letting us know how he come to be in our camp earlier in the day.

"I left Slaughter Gap two suns ago for a walk. It was time to wash, so I headed for the creek where the Wolves gather. The big bend is a spiritual place for the Cherokee. Its swirling waters speak to the Great Father for us as it cleans our bodies. I had just crossed the main ridge between the creek and our home when I heard a loud cry in the valley, so I came to see who had entered here."

At this point, Dad gave me a hard look as though to say, "See, I told you. You must be careful when travelin' through the woods. You can never know for sure who might be out and about."

"It wasn't long until I smelled the fire from your camp and followed the scent. I could see from the ridge that the bears had circled young Jeb; that he'd made his stand near the mules. I knew the gun he held only had the one shot, so I ran as hard as I could to the rise behind the camp. There I saw the bravery this young one showed our Brother Bear."

I looked across the fire at my dad; could see that he was starin at me with a very serious look. I'd only told him about the one bear, but not of the others. I couldn't 'cause I never saw 'em. I now realized for the first time that there was more than one. I was shocked by this. The fear I felt earlier in the day suddenly come back. My skin grew cold even though the fire was warm.

With a quiver in my voice, I asked Dancing Bear about the others. "You mean to say there was more than one bear here? I only saw the one."

"That is the way of the bear, young one. You will only see the one they wish for you to see, while the others circle and scent for food. You were surrounded by four bears, but only the big male showed himself to you," Dancing Bear explained.

My heart skipped a beat as I shook to think that there were four bears around our camp. I never would've dreamed that bear had his clan with him. Now I know'd why the mules went steady and didn't make a sound once the big male made itself known. They could sense them other bears behind 'em, so they froze. I should've figured out what was goin' on, but I had no thought about them bein' more than the one. I would never let that happen again, when critters like them bears come around.

"The big female was very close to you, coming in on the trail that you and Thompie traveled to get to this place," Dancing Bear continued. "She was close enough to charge, but for some reason the big male stood and challenged you first. You were very brave and stood your ground, so he did not know what to do bein' that you showed no fear. If you had run, you would have crossed paths with his mate. That would've been a bad thing since the other two bears were near grown as well. The big male's look was that of confusion as he tilted his head and lifted his front paw to send his mate away. He respected you because you were small in size, but big in courage. I think he will remember you, if you ever meet him again. That is the way I saw this thing that happened here today. I will remember the courage of such a young boy, as will my story of your bravery, young Jeb."

Well, you could've heard my heart beatin' as I sat there and pondered all that Indian told about my meetin' that bear. I was absolutely without words, could only stare into the fire as Dad and Dancing Bear passed the jug another time and smoked over the story we was just told. I declare to this day that it weren't 'cause I was brave that I stood my ground, but that I was just too scared to move. If Dancing Bear saw it as courage, then that's what it shall be, but my knees was shakin' so bad that I couldn't 'a-run if I'd 'a had to. That's all that were. Far as I could figure, I was just lucky I didn't wet my britches.

Although, I do remember feelin' kinda calm when that ole bear stood up and squared off at me. Somethin' about the way he looked let me know that he would stand his ground and not charge at me. Maybe it was courage or maybe I simply cotton to critters that way. I'm just glad I didn't run, 'cause that other bear weren't far away. I could see the brown in the big male's eyes he was so close, and I could smell him, too. Smelled like one of our coon dogs after it'd run through the river chasin' a big 'coon. I would have to study on this later. All that food and the goin' on of the day made me real sleepy; my thinkin' got slow beside the warmth of the fire and the soft sounds of the creek waters rollin' by.

***

I woke the next mornin' to the smell of somethin' cookin' on the spit. I couldn't for the life of me figure out what was smellin' so tasty. I got up and put on my foot skins, grabbed my possibles bag and headed out to see what was cookin'. I nearly screamed when I walked out and come face-to-face with the biggest Indian I'd ever seen. I was used to seein' Indians in the Choestoe Valley, but none this big. He was standin' with his bare back to me. When he heard me open the flap, he turned his head and stared at me. He brought to life the image of the bear I'd seen standin' the night before, he was so big. I froze where I stood. It was mornin' and I was in need of a tree to go behind, but I nearly let it go right there at the sight of this huge Indian who had the hardest, most intense eyes I'd ever looked into.

His hair was long and mostly braided, with a red hawk feather on each side of his head. His skin was dark and kinda red lookin', near the same color as the hawk feather. His legs was really big, as were his hands and his head. He wore skins like Dad's and mine, with foot skin boots that rose to just below his knees. I could see a small knife handle kinda hid in a sheath built into his right boot. This Indian wore beads, but not as many as most Cherokee. The only Cherokee I know'd wore less was Wolf and his clan. Around each wrist he had leather straps. It looked like he'd been wearin' those for quite a while. I knew by the look of those straps that he most likely used 'em to help catch or skin his game meat.

His jaw was square and his forehead was high; looked like he could wrestle a bear. There were several scars on his arms, back and chest, and his face looked like he'd fought a mountain cat. This was a man you wanted as a friend, not an enemy, this much was certain.

He had a look of surprise mixed with glare that turned me to stone. He was naked from the waist up, and his long knife hung at his side in a skin sheath that was tied around his middle hangin' from a leather belt. He wore a necklace of what looked like carved bones, with some dark beads and a round gold piece right in the center at the bottom. He had a long scar across his middle that was a different color than the rest of his skin, which ran from his left rib to just above his right hipbone. The scar looked to be fresh. I remember thinkin' how it still needed tendin' to. He looked very strong, with muscles pokin' out all over his upper body like the bark on a maple tree, smooth and rigid with fine lines between each muscle under his skin. He was a sight to behold and smelled like a rotten apple, kinda sweet with a little nasty mixed in. I recognized that smell, but couldn't remember from where.

I was 'bout to do my mornin' normal where I stood, so I decided I had to do somethin'. He was just standin' there with his head turned, lookin' at me, not sayin' a word, so I raised my hand a little and said, "Mornin', my name is Jeb Collins. I don't know who you are or why you're here, but I got to go to the woods, so don't come at me when I turn to leave. If I don't go now, I'm gonna wet my skins, which'd be a problem for me as I do not have another pair."

He studied me for a second, then tilted his head back and laughed so loud I felt the ground shake. I took this to mean it was okay, so I turned and ran to the nearest big tree I come to back in the woods. What a relief to feel myself let go! I know what I'd said sounded stupid, but it was the best I could come up with considerin' my trouble. It come to me while I was doin' my private that I saw nobody else in camp; that me and him was the only folks around. *Where was Dad and Dancing Bear, and why was this big Cherokee here in camp cookin' breakfast?*

I eased myself back down toward the fire. As I got close, I could see he was squatted with his back to me. He was so big that his back completely hid the fire. I still hadn't figured out what was cookin. I didn't want to startle him, so I moved around behind our tent and came back into camp from his right side. He caught my movement outa the corner of his eye and swung his big ole head to look straight at me. I still weren't used to him bein' there, so I didn't dare look him in the eye.

As he reached out and turned the handle of the spit, for the first time I realized that it was rabbit that was cookin'. He had three of 'em on the rod, tendin' to 'em like he know'd what he was doin'. I carefully slipped up to the fire and squatted like he was. He never let on I was around, other than when he looked at me comin' back from the woods. It was really strange the way the mornin' was shapin' up.

Neither one of us spoke for a while, until the worry got the better of me and I asked about my dad and Dancing Bear.

He never said a word and just kept turnin' the spit rod. I figured he must not hear too good, so I said it a little louder.

"Excuse me, but could you tell me where my dad, Thompie Collins is, and if Dancing Bear is still around?"

He finally lifted his head and nodded toward the creek, like maybe they'd gone off in that direction. I wondered if he could even talk, when all of a sudden he said, "I watched them leave just before Old Man Sun woke this morning. They will return soon."

His voice was deep and clear, a strange kinda talk that was different than any other I'd heard. After he spoke, he rose, grabbin' a leather pouch I hadn't noticed, and headed for the big bend in the creek. I was curious so I followed him to see what it was that he had in mind.

He stopped on the edge of the creek and stripped down to nothin'. Then he reached into his pouch and pulled out a bar of what looked like soap. He dove into the middle of the whirlpool headfirst, never lettin' on that the water was cold, even though I could see my breath as it left my body. It was cold around the creek, but if it bothered him, you could not tell it.

His big ole head popped up right out in the middle of the eye of that whirlpool, and even though he was a tall man, he had to tread water just to keep from sinkin'. That's how deep the pool was. He commenced to washin' himself, so I headed back to the fire to get warm. Just the thought of him in that water made me shiver.

I could tell that the meat was near done when I got back to the fire, so I raised the spit rod up to the highest level on the cookin' post so it would stay warm. I figured he'd collected them rabbits and it was his meat, but if I'd left them on the lowest rung, they would've burnt. I weren't about to eat his food if he didn't offer it to me. That would've been disrespectful of me. Besides that, he could tear my head right off of my body if he'd 'a wanted too. *Where in the world is my dad?*

The big Indian came back to the fire soakin' wet and naked as the day he was born. His hair was no longer braided, lookin' slick in the mornin' light. He stood by the fire turnin' front to back till he was dry. I couldn't help but see that he was big all over. His arms and hands were huge, and his feet were as long as stove wood. Once he'd dried he got dressed again, still not sayin' a word about nothin', but I could smell that he was clean. I saw him look at the rabbits, then at me. Then a look come across his face.

"You are wise, little one, to raise the meat. I thought you might be." And that was all he said as he handed me a whole rabbit while takin' the other two off the spit.

He laid his pouch on the ground in front of himself and placed his meat on it, as he again squatted and bowed his head. He began speakin' like he was prayin', so I bowed my head with him, but I never took my eyes off him. I hoped God would forgive me for not closin' my eyes during the blessin', but I still didn't know who this strange Indian was. *Why is my dad not here?*

We ate in silence. He finished both of his rabbits before I'd finished the one I had. He then cleaned the bones of any remainin' meat and placed some of 'em in his pouch, throwin' the rest into the fire. I figured he'd use them later for whatever it was he was needin' 'em for. When I was done with my rabbit, I handed him the bones and he nodded, cleanin'em just like he'd done his, after which he handed 'em back to me. I, too, placed some in my possibles bag, while tossin' the rest into the fire like he'd done, though not havin' a clue what I was to use 'em for. This made him smile, yet not until all was done and the cookin' truck was clean and put away did he begin to speak. Most Cherokee were tidy that way.

"I am Black Oak. That is what the Cherokee call me. I like to be called George because my ancestors fought alongside the Great Father of this land, George Washington. He and my grandfather were friends. They fought the red backs that were from the land across the big water. That was many years ago. I do not like those men and am glad they are gone. They fooled many Cherokee into fightin' for them, but not my clan. The Choestoe clan fought with General Washington and the warriors of America. We are better for it. I will be here with you until your father returns. He has gone to help a family up the creek that lost their man to some bears late last night. He asked me to stay with you while he is there."

Bears?! Hearin' of the bear attack sent a chill down my spine and made my stomach tighten up. Could that have been the bunch that came to our camp, or was it another bear all together? I had to know, even though there was part of me that didn't want to.

"Black Oak, how many bears were in the bunch what killed this man?" My voice quivered slightly.

"I found four sets of tracks that led to their farm. It was a big sow that killed the man. She is dead by my blade. The others ran into the night. I stay with this family often and was camped near their home when the noise from the barn woke me. The bears killed two big hogs and a half grown calf before the father ran them away. The sow was a bad bear and turned on him, breaking his neck with a swipe of her paw. He was a friend of mine and had been for many years. I am very sad, but I know I will see him again in The Land Across the Great River where Jesus is. Her front paw did this to me," Black Oak said as he drew his right hand across the cut. I could tell he was holdin' back much pain.

A chillin' thought rose that the big male bear had stopped the sow from attackin' the mules and me. *Could that be true?* I realized then how close I was to endin' up like the friend of Black Oak. I jumped from my squattin' position, fell to my knees and thanked God for what Dancing Bear had called my brother, the bear. Somehow the spirits used this bear to protect me. From now on I would be wise to show more respect to the critters in Choestoe Valley.

George saw I was prayin' and commenced to chant a very sorrowful Indian song that I knew was partly for me, but mostly for himself and his friends who had lost their father and husband. That was a spiritual time, one that brought the big Indian and me together in a kinda spirit bond. It would not be the last time we shared a special moment that only we would understand.

Chapter Nine

The Bluest Eyes in Choestoe

It was late in the night before Dad returned from the Englands' place, so I was already bedded down and asleep. That's the name of folks what lost their loved one—Zebediah England who it was. We go to Killin' Time down near his place in the fall to butcher winter meat.

George and me didn't do much all that day while waitin' on Dad to come back. He showed me his whetstone and the way he uses it to keep his knife sharp, includin' all the possibles in his bag. He didn't have much with him, but then I remembered he was camped near the Englands' place when the bears come, so I figured he was travelin' light. He'd be goin' to collect his truck when Dad got back.

I was tired from all the happenin's and restless sleep durin' the night, so I slept durin' the heat of the day while waitin'. I didn't realize how tired I was until I laid down beside the creek after midday. This adventure life sure tired a body out; bein' half scared to death two or three times made it even worse. I realized real quick that I was gonna have to get tough to live out on the trail in the mountains. That thinkin' come in real handy when Wolf and me got out and about later on. I think it probably saved his life and mine, too, a couple of times. That's the way I see it.

George was a gentle man. He seemed like one on those that thought the best in folks until he saw worse. I could tell by the way he was on guard all the time that he'd seen battle and had probably taken life. Most of the Cherokee men in the mountains had, so that really didn't bother me much. I felt like I wanted to be friends with this man; was already hopin' I would run into him again. Little did I know that I would see this man often through the rest of my years. He liked my mule, so we had that in common.

The handle on his knife was from the base of a huge, dark deer antler, which hung to his left side. By the look of his massive right hand, I know'd he could wrap his huge grip around that handle in one easy motion when he needed. I learned later that he'd made this knife. It fit him custom. He let me hold it; took both my hands and arms just to lift. The thing was nearly as long as my leg, but it fit him perfect. The smaller knife in his boot was similar, but he never took it out for nothin', so I didn't trouble him about it. He may have used the smaller knife on the rabbits, but I was asleep while he got 'em ready for cookin'. You gotta remember that Indians are Indians. You don't study on the whys of what they do. They're all the same, while at the same time they're as different as night and day. I learned early on to leave 'em be on many things. They wouldn't stand for no disrespect.

***

It was early in the afternoon when I started wakin' from sleep. The air comin' off the creek was cool and felt crisp on my skin. You could taste the soul of the forest in that moist air; the richness made a body feel free. The smells were so intense that it almost made your eyes water. The earthy odor of the decay on the forest floor mingled with the young green plants fightin' for precious sunlight through the shadows of the trees. The birch and the maple strugglin' to get their sap up mixed with the evergreens and the chestnut, providin' rich smells that put you at one with the Creator. At times, even in my young life, I would border on what the Cherokee called the Spirit World. The closeness I found in the woods provoked that.

I'd just begun to wake, or I was still dreamin', but one thing was for sure, I was flyin' through the air. Not until the freezin' cold water hit me did I know for sure which world I was wakin' in. Turns out, I was in the present, and the present was cold and wet.

I broke water with my head and looked back at where I'd been layin' a few seconds earlier. There stood a grinnin'

George, holdin' a bar of his soap. I was treadin' water and tryin' to float when he threw it at me, nearly hittin' me in the head. As I stretched to dodge the bar of soap, my legs went straight and my feet found the sand and gravel on the bottom of the creek. He'd throw'd me in a shallow spot that only came up to my shoulders. This fact made it even more amusin' to him.

"If you are going to share a camp with me, young Jeb, you must be clean. Now wash yourself, then come join me by the fire when you are done."

I had been given an order from the biggest Indian a body would ever see. What else could I do but wash?

The water was cold but bearable for cleanin'. I stripped naked and took the soap to my skins, scrubbin' them as well as myself. I washed my hair and all over my body. The soap smelled of wild flowers and made my skin feel good. And then it come to me that I'd used this kinda soap before. It was some Momma had made. She must've gifted it to George.

When the washin' was done, I put my foot skins on and walked back to the fire as he had, naked as the day I was born. He didn't pay me no mind, just told me to get dry and comb my hair, as he handed me a hand-carved bone comb with a thick handle. I returned Momma's soap. Indians take care of their hair. Mine was startin' to get some length, but it weren't straight like theirs was; rabbit thick and looked more like the ripples you see when you dropped a stone into a calm spot in the creek, kinda floated like that.

I carried my skins over and laid 'em on some ivy bushes to dry in the sun. I could feel the heat on my naked body; a relief after bein' throw'd in the cold water of the creek. I took the comb and began to work my hair back across the top of my head. It felt good goin' through, so I spent a good while usin' it. So long, in fact, that my clothes were dry when I finished combin', and I was able to get dressed again. I didn't get a chance to be in the raw very much. I liked it, but it weren't nothin' to an Indian. It was the way we crossed into this world, which held proper with the Cherokee.

When I was clean and dressed, George called me over to the fire. He had some thick-cut jerky that he said we could eat for supper. It was from the big brown deer that use to frequent the valley durin' the time of the chestnuts fallin'. Them deer weren't comin' as much now as they had before, but some of 'em would come close down on occasion. They liked them chestnuts. I'd seen their antlers from before, when folks had killed some, but I'd never seen the true thing. They were really long and much bigger than the deer with the white tail. That's what we ate most here in the mountains. And even those seem to be goin' away, many killed them only for their hide.

From the first bite I favored that meat. It was rich and sweet with a soft texture that made for easy chewin'. The Indians dried it outside, givin' the meat an open air kinda flavor. The sun made meat taste good. You could also flavor it with a hint of smoke. I know'd some Indians like to finish off the sun curin' process like that; made for a perfect meat taste. George could tell I liked it, so he told me how he come by it.

"I took this deer three-days walk north of here during the cold time. He was big and fighting for his females against another big brown deer. This one lost the fight, so he was no good for the herd anymore. I shot him with my bow. He gave up his meat for us. I thanked the Father for it," he said, as he raised a piece toward the sky. I did likewise.

"What did you do with his skin and the antlers?"

He proudly pulled his knife from its leather sheath and smiled as he showed me the handle, the base of one of the brown deer's big antlers.

"I made this handle from one and I gave the other to my uncle. He makes knives; needs bone such as this for the handles. I made this one. He has taught me to work the metal and fashion the bone. I can teach you if you would like."

"I don't know if I am big enough, but I sure am willin'," I said, but right then, I was studyin' on his knife. "Do you make all your knives or does your uncle make some?"

"I make some and he makes some," he replied.

And with that he pulled out two more knives from his pouch and one from his hair. They were beautiful, but he still never pulled the one in his boot.

"I made the two larger knives, but he made this smaller knife," said George, showin' me the hidden knife he had woven into his hair.

I looked close and saw the sheath, but you'd a not see it if you didn't know it was there. It was made of tightly woven horsehair that mixed in with his own hair, makin' it hard to see. I didn't hold on to that thought long, one of the two knives he'd had in his possibles pouch got my attention.

They were both solid lookin' blades. Their steel danced like somethin' alive as he slid them from their sheaths. The shorter of the two really caught my eye. The color would change when turned. It was a real work of art to me. You could tell that someone spent many a concerned hour over its makin'. I, for one, was amazed.

It almost seemed like it was my own when I first saw it; felt like my knife lyin' there on his pouch. I couldn't take my eyes off it. Somethin' inside me seemed to growl as he removed his hand, leavin' it lyin' there on his buckskin pouch. He then leaned back on his heels, lookin' at me. Old Man Sun's light shone from its blade, whose build was unbelievable. I remember thinkin' that I'd sure like to learn how to make such a fine but deadly blade; that I would enjoy workin' with Black Oak and follow his teachin' to make my own, one day.

He picked it up and held it out to me. I took it. It was like the most handsome object I'd ever had in my hands. The handle was bone, dark and shiny. It had a solid steel guard between the top of the handle and the end of the blade. The edge shown and had been recently worked. I knew by lookin' at it that if I even barely touched the edge, the blood would run, but I couldn't help it. I drug my thumb across the blade. The rich, red crimson ran before I felt any pain. I removed the blade and examined the slice in my left thumb, a mark for me to remember the blade by. I felt bonded with the knife in that instant; held it for several minutes before I returned it to him. I swear that knife felt like a part of me. I just couldn't explain it. It was torture for me to watch him put it to bed in its soft leather home, only to store it away with the rest of his possibles and away from me.

He looked at me as he finished with his pouch. "You like that knife, young one?"

"I do, very much. It's handsome, a fine piece of work with a sharp blade," I replied, holdin' up my thumb and grinnin'.

He laughed out loud at the sight of my bleedin' thumb, then said, "You must be very careful with a knife, young Jeb. My blades are always very sharp or else they are no good to me. Do you remember how I showed you to keep a knife sharp with the stone? You can hurt yourself if you are not careful. One simple slice to a bad place on your body and you will bleed out, like a stuck hog after the kill, so be careful if anyone ever gives you a knife. Do you understand me, young one?"

I felt kinda scolded, but I knew he was just worried for me.

"I couldn't help feelin' the blade when you showed it to me. It felt like it was a part of me. The blood runnin' felt good, but I will honor your desire and be very careful with any knife I might ever own." I wanted him to understand how much I respected him.

He smiled at my fondness of the knife. I learned later that in the Indian world, oftentimes a weapon chooses the warrior. Maybe that is why he placed it in my tent when he left the followin' mornin'. When I woke and found it lyin' on the edge of the bearskin, I cried.

He was gone so early, I didn't get a chance to thank him. I went to bed shortly after dark and Dad came in sometime after that. He told me him and George talked about it and decided I needed a good knife to carry into the mountains with me, so he let Black Oak, the Cherokee, give me a rare and special gift. My dad was one who could always see reason in a good thought. A good knife, indeed. I would cherish it for a long, long time.

***

Dad got me up early so we could get a move on. He wanted to take the trail back by the Englands' place for the night, then hit the long trail again to Wolf's the next day. We soon had all our truck on the mules and was movin' on, when I started to wonder about these folks we'd be stayin' the night with. I'd never visited for an all-night stay with folks before. I figured it was just natural curiosity for a boy, but I should've studied it a sight more.

I rode the mule most of that day. Dad fixed a place to tie my knife to the mule, hangin' over the animal's left shoulder. I could easily grab it, pull it, when I wanted. I must've pulled that thing two dozen times or more. The weight felt good in my hand. That knife quickly became my most prized earthly possession. Now, I was just bustin' to ask Dad for the mule I was ridin', but the time needed to be right for that.

"You be careful with that knife up there, boy. You slip and split that mule's ear and he ain't gonna like it," scolded my dad. "And make sure you don't slice your own person swingin' that thing around. Be careful playin' with somethin' dangerous like that, boy."

It might've looked like I was bein' careless, but I know'd exactly what I was doin'. I gave him the only reply I could, sayin', "Yes, sir, I'll pay more mind to that."

He looked up at me and grinned. My dad was the best—right up there with my mom, of course.

This would be an afternoon that changed my life. I know God has a sense of humor. I saw it firsthand that evenin'. I'd just turned eight recent, and it worried a boy to have the type of run-in that was comin' my way.

Later in life, I considered it a gift from God that we arrived at the England place late in the afternoon, to be met by the widow England and her brood that flocked out to meet us—eleven in all. Looked like some fool left the chicken coop gate open and all the chicks had got out. They was kids everywhere, goin' in all directions. I was tryin' to follow 'em this way and that till my eyes locked on one of the most beautiful sights a body could ever see. She was even more handsome than my knife, or my mule.

She stood about four foot tall and had hair of the prettiest color. It was a mix of red and brown. What first come to mind for me was the brown of a chestnut hull. Her eyes were a hauntin' blue, like the sky on a clear day. They locked onto mine with the force of a north wind in January. Her face was like that of a fawn just learnin' to walk, perfectly innocent with a hint of mischief 'round the edges. I can't say what happened inside me, but somethin' first exploded, then the world went still. The only thing movin' was this vision. I could barely breathe. This feelin' was much too much for a kid my age. I did not understand this at all. I lost sight of her and the world began to move again, but all was very strange. I suddenly started missin' Momma, who I know'd could explain this.

Dad had decided to stop by and collect some of the meat that was now on hand at the England place because of the bears. We took several pieces of beef and quite a bit of hog, since they lost two at once. We would end up leavin' some of it with Wolf and his clan, but still had a lot to cure once we got home. Mrs. England took all she could keep and let the rest go to us and some of her neighbors who'd come by. Even the bear got took, as I got to use my new knife to help cut her up. The meat weren't hard to get at 'cause the hide was already gone and she was hangin'. I had an idea who took that judgin' by how good the skinnin' job was. I felt certain we would find a fresh bear skin hangin' at Wolf's when we got there.

I never did see the chestnut-haired girl again on that visit, but her face was in my memory along with the color of her hair. There was no room in the main house, so we stayed in the barn with the mules. We preferred fresh air, so we pitched a little camp in one of the overhangs off the wood shed outside of the main part of the barn. We needed a little fire to cook some beef strips over since we had some fresh. You don't build fires inside a barn as a rule. Made me proud when Dad used my knife to cut some thin beef strips 'cause it was so sharp. He really liked my new treasure. I still couldn't believe it was mine.

The England's rooster woke us 'fore daylight. We got packed and left real quiet-like. We didn't even rouse their ole hound dogs laid out on the porch. A couple of the black-and-tans raised their heads, but didn't care nothin' much about us. They weren't here earlier. Somebody'd been huntin' them dogs most of the night, and they was tired.

My dad could slip around Indian-like when he needed. This was one time we both just wanted to leave without a big doin'.

"Women make a big deal out of a body leavin', but we just want to slip away without no fuss," Dad warned me.

I liked it like this way. We'd already thanked dear Mrs. England. She'd said her goodbyes the night before, knowin' we'd want to leave early. I said a little prayer for her as we were leavin', as I turned around for a last look. Maybe I just wanted to remember the way things looked, or maybe I had a strong hurt for the widow and her kids. I know'd folks close by would look in on 'em till she got her a new man. I bet she married Indian, but nobody probably thought that 'cept me.

That last look back on that chilly spring mornin' is one I will never forget. I liked bein' there. But unknown to me, there was someone who was curious about my bein' there as well. I couldn't see 'em, but there was a small set of blue eyes shinin' down from one of the oaks behind the main house, watchin' us leave. I remember thinkin', as we moved down the trail and deeper into the woods, that the blue-eyed girl was without her father now. I felt very sad for her.

***

We stayed the trail for over two hours 'fore Dad ever spoke about what exactly happened to the father. But as we stopped to water, he felt obliged to tell me. It was somethin' he had to say just to get it out, more than it was to tell me. What happened to that man bothered him greatly. That was a rare sight; one I weren't use to.

He spoke in a humble way when he told the details of the bear killin'.

"I ain't one to judge a man's thinkin', especially when life is at stake, but that man should not be dead. He did not show that bear the respect it deserved, and he paid with his life. Don't you ever catch yourself in a bad way with a bear, Jeb. They can kill you with a slap of their paw. The sign showin' at the killin' site said Mr. England must've got mad and ran at that sow with a pitchfork. He got way to close to her for his own good. She flipped that fork from his hand with one paw and broke his neck with the other. By the time Black Oak got there, it was too late."

"George said he killed her with his own knife. Is that so?"

"Oh yes, that *is* true. The sow had stab wounds on her right side, almost exactly where the heart is. I suspect he came up from behind, and with a warrior's cry and a long sharp blade, ended her murderin' life. He ain't told me much about it yet. I only saw him for a little while before Dancing Bear and me left early the next mornin', and for a time last night, but I was tired. He was headed to our place to check on us when he found our camp. He backtracked the bears downstream. They worried him. He is somethin' else, son. He is a good man."

"I ain't never seen a body so big. Is he Cherokee?"

"Far as I know, he claims to be the genuine thing. He looks like 'em and acts like 'em, so I reckon he is." He shrugged his shoulder indicatin' it didn't really matter to him, so I let it go.

My thoughts turned to George's huge knife and what it must've looked like as he jumped that bear with a yell and a stab. I bet that bear thought the devil his own self had come on her. That blade most likely split that bear's heart and lungs in about three hard jabs. No wonder he stunk the mornin' I first met him—he was covered in bear blood. Had to be with the size of blade he killed that critter with.

There weren't much conversation as we traveled, yet there was somethin' in me that was just bustin' to get out. So after a couple of hours on the trail, and hardly a word said, and without really thinkin' things through, it was outa my mouth. I froze when it slipped my lips. I was scared to draw a breath. I was gonna mention this at a better time, but I'd spoken. It was out and I would have to live with it. I'd put Dad on a short leash. He'd have to say yes or no now. It just didn't happen the way I'd planned on askin'.

"Dad, can this mule be mine? Me and him talk to each other and he likes me," I nearly shouted.

Dad never broke stride as he replied, "What makes you think he wants you?"

His answer caught me off guard, but I reasoned it out. "Well, he responds to me. He looks at me when I'm talkin' to him. He'll gee and haw for me when I press my knees to his sides. Don't that mean he's smart? 'Cause I don't want no dumb mule."

"If he was yours, what would you name him? Mules have to have a name or they don't come when you holler for 'em."

I had to give that some thought. It was a while on down the trail 'fore I told him that I would name him Peter.

He studied on that for over an hour before we stopped to adjust the loads on the mule's backs. Packs tend to shift when travelin' over mountain trails. The trail to slaughter was tough in places, both for the mules and their loads. My tail would've been raw from all the shiftin' if it weren't for the bearskin I was sittin' on. That thing was sure handy. I was ever so proud Dancing Bear give it to me as a gift when I was born.

"I think I got it figured out as to why you'd name that mule Peter," Dad said. "It would be after Peter in the New Testament. You figure ol' Peter was tough and ornery, which makes him a lot like a mule. Do things the hard way 'cause that's the way you like it, *I'm* kinda thinkin', huh? Got a temper, but mostly tame till somethin' gets 'em riled up. Brave and near fearless, and can stand in the face of death. That's the way *you're* thinkin', ain't it?"

"Yes, sir. Jim and this mule let me know there was somethin' on the prowl when they started actin' restless shortly after you left camp for poke salad. Then he stood right there and didn't make a sound when the big male bear stood and let himself be known. Both of them mules acted brave, but I was standin' at his shoulder and I could hear him breathin'. He never quivered at the site of that bear standin' there so close."

"I understand your wants and will study on what you're askin'. You take care of him on this trip, and I will settle on it soon." And that was all that was said as we headed off to Wolf's.

I wanted the mule because of all the freedom it would give me. Wolf and I could ride it together. I could even haul our truck on nights we camped and hunted. But mostly, I just felt like a body needed a good mule. After all, I had a new knife, so now I needed a mule. Made sense to me, but I'm sure Dad saw it more straight than that. A mule could hurt a body if they tend to get mean and hateful. I know'd this one was okay, but he didn't have that feelin' yet. He would watch us and see. I had a feelin' Peter would be mine soon enough. We belonged together, I was sure of that. Me, him and my gift from Black Oak. Life was grand, and I thanked God.

Chapter Ten

A Warrior's Welcome

We left the valley and headed for the high country on the South Highland Trail. Most folks used the trail to travel into the mountains from Wolf Creek, seein' as it was the easiest and less steep. You could even pull a small wagon on it, but Dad said you hardly ever saw anybody, not even Indians. They weren't too keen on bein' seen, so they'd hide before you ever got to 'em. Indians, just like other folks, had to be careful out on the main trails.

The trail seemed alive as it guided us up the north side of Blood Mountain and around to the top. A thought came to me that this must've been absolutely one of the freest places in my entire world. Once we hit the top, we found the leaves were still small; in many places there weren't any at all. If you stopped in the right spot, you could see for miles. Several places I saw the Notla River and a cornfield or two. You could spot the houses from the fireplaces and cookfires burnin'. I could even make out a team of two mules plowin' and the farmer behind 'em. It was nearin' midday when he would stop soon for dinner. I bet his house was gonna have somethin' good to eat—no doubt, grow'd or got from the woods.

Just off the top of the Blood, Dad stopped and tied the mules to a small tree, which meant I was to get off the back of my mule and let him rest. We'd been goin' for a while and we all needed a stop, but Dad didn't sit to rest. Instead, he walked off into the woods. I didn't know what to do. He was movin' farther away by the second, so I took off runnin' after him. When he stopped suddenly, I ran right into the side of his leg as he turned to scold me for runnin'. Nearly made my nose bleed.

"Don't be runnin' in the woods, Jeb," he said scoldin' me. "Only run if you absolutely have to. The sight of someone runnin' puts everything in the woods on alert and makes you stand out among the cover. Be careful about that. It might save your life someday, you understand?"

He always got my attention with that save your life stuff. I was learnin' full well the dangers in the woods. I'd been hearin' stories all my young life. Several about panthers and bears and other dangerous critters, but it was the ones about Indian spirits that got me stirred up most. I could just see them ghosts wanderin' around among the trees, watchin' me.

"Yes, sir," was all I could say.

He stopped on a flat at the bottom of a small cliff, around the west side of the mountain, and began kickin' back leaves like some sorta crazy man. For nearly an hour, he moved the cover from the forest floor, stoppin' every once in a while to get close and look at somethin' or another. I watched as he kicked and kicked until he had a big spot uncovered, then he stilled, stared and directly he let out a grunt like a dyin' bear.

He leaned down for a close look, then stood and said back toward me, "I been huntin' this flat a long time. This could be the one I've been lookin' for. Come and see, Jeb, you won't believe it."

I hurried over to him. Lookin' down, I saw lyin' at his feet was a curious charcoal-colored piece that looked like pottery. It was partially covered in dark earth, but I could tell it was Indian-made, the way it was shaped and all. Most of it was still buried, so it was hard to tell if it was whole. I'd seen old Indian stuff that the old-timers had found from the battles between the Creek and Cherokee. I'd seen broke pieces throw'd around barns and yards without much worry, but they kept the whole pieces inside around their hearths and fireplaces; would tell stories about 'em since every piece had one. I'd even seen some who smoked outa real Indian pipes they'd found or been gifted through the years. Some, I'd learned, made it to the family as gifts from actual warriors who they fed or helped durin' the Great Struggle, as they called it. Some was found just like my dad was hopin' for. Made sense to think smokin' out of an Indian pipe would be better.

I always loved those stories, tales of Cherokee bravery and courage, of why their spirits still roam the earth. The older folks seemed to hold many of the same beliefs as the Cherokee. It was kinda spooky listenin' to 'em talk.

The war ended when the Creek moved outa the mountains and went south and west. Neither tribe won, really. Occasionally, some rogue Creek would sneak back in to the valley for revenge or to cause trouble, but those things would grow less and less as time went on.

Dad was froze to the spot, not takin' his eyes off that piece for nothin'. He'd uncovered several adl-adl points and arrowheads just lyin' there for the takin', but he didn't care about those. It was the pipe he was after.

I know'd he had some broken ones in the barn, but I never know'd he actually got out and looked for 'em. Some of the ones he'd found were really nice, but all were broken. Only the whole ones held much value to the folks in Choestoe. You'd only want to smoke from a whole one. They could find broken stuff anywhere, but to find somethin' like a pipe or a knife, or bead necklaces and wraps that was whole, then you had somethin'. If you found a knife blade or a pipe that wasn't broken, then you had a nice piece that'd been dropped in battle or lost by a warrior somehow. The fact that it might have belonged to a Cherokee warrior was what got my dad excited.

He reached down and gently brushed away at the earth. I held my breath, as I'm sure he was holdin' his. The edges of the pipe started to show, was beginnin' to look whole, when he paused and looked at me.

"This is a nice-lookin' find. It's been made by Cherokee and was probably lost in the battle they had here. It was a very important battle involvin' over half the warriors in Choestoe. Many died, leavin' families to be provided for. Your grandfather was one of those who tended to the widows of some Cherokee friends he lost to the war. Dancing Bear's father was among those who joined the ancestors durin' the Great Battle, as it became known among the folks in Choestoe."

He held out his hand toward the flat where he'd been searchin'.

"This flat was the location of a huge battle near the end of the fightin'. Many beautiful pieces have been found here, but some have been lost to outsiders. The folks here want to keep the pieces in Choestoe. This is a way to honor the lost ones of the war. There are more places such as this all over, many on Blood Mountain."

When he'd finished tellin' me what he thought I should know, he got back to uncoverin' the charcoal-colored pipe. Brushin' away the soil and rotted leaves revealed that a large portion of the stem was missin'. The rest of it was there 'cept for the part that stuck out from the bowl and held the stem. The pipe would've been a great find if it'd been whole.

Dad may not've cared about all them points he'd left, but I did. I filled a small pouch that Momma sent with me for just such as this. I'd picked up fifty or more when I spotted a curious piece of black, shiny stone that looked kinda like the back of a baby snappin' turtle. I called Dad over and he came to see what it was.

"That's a knife blade, son. It's made outa trade flint and was either carried here by an Indian, or a Cherokee traded for the stock and made the blade. If it's whole, then you'll really have somethin'. I wish you better luck than I had."

I began to slowly brush the black earth away from the edges. Everything was lookin' good as I exposed the point and worked down toward where the handle would've been strapped on. It was a nice piece to me, whatever the outcome. I was startin' to get excited. But of all of a sudden, things didn't look exactly right. Somethin' was missin'. There was no black color where there should've been some. My heart sank as I realized the bottom was broke clean off right where the handle should've started. The blade was whole 'cept for the very bottom of the piece, right where the leather would've tied it to the handle. I looked all around by kickin' the dirt away and diggin' under, but there was no more to be found.

The blade looked to have been broke when it hit somethin' solid; broke clean across right where the handle would've been.

Dad sighed and said, "It's gettin' harder and harder to find whole pieces up here anymore. This blade is still a good find, because you can tell it was most likely broke durin' battle. That is somethin' that makes these finds very important. It saves our history, keeps the memories alive for the Cherokee and their friends."

Dad cleaned the piece and wrapped it in cloth as we loaded up and headed off for Wolf's. I would be back here again. I could just feel it. It made one think, wonderin' on how the Indian that owned a certain piece had ended up. Had he met death, or had he walked away from battle with the livin'? You could never know by simply holdin' a find in your hands. The desire to know was hauntin'; made a body want to look for answers. I guess that kinda made you want to keep searchin'. I'd seen some knife finds in the old folks' homes that still had part of the bone handle attached to the blade. Now, those pieces could really talk.

My mom's dad even had a nice pipe that belonged to a dyin' Cherokee warrior. He was shot through with an arrow, was near death when Granddad ran up on him. He crossed his blood trail and followed him to a lay of rock just south of Wolf Pen Gap, west of Wolf's home. He was in a great deal of pain, and my granddad sat with him for several hours as he died. He took the dead warrior home to his family. They actually gave him the warrior's pipe as a way to say thank you, as well as his medicine pouch, which held important spiritual things a Cherokee warrior would want to have along when goin' into battle. My granddad never opened that pouch.

His family buried him on top of Duncan Ridge, close to where he'd been wounded. Some say you can see that warrior's spirit on full moon nights, still watchin' out for enemy souls tryin' to enter the Choestoe Valley. That gives me comfort knowin' he's up there protectin' us. I planned on seein' that with the naked eye someday. The thought made me wonder if he was there now, so I turned and looked at the top of the mountain just in case. 'Course, I didn't see anything, it was the middle of the day. The legend clearly says that you can only see him on full moon nights. I just shook my head when the thought made me feel stupid.

I'd get Wolf, then him and me would trail up there and find out sometime, 'bout mid-dark when the moon is so full it looks like daylight in the woods. You can hunt when the moon is that bright. I've done it. You can see things clear. I could just imagine that Cherokee spirit movin' from tree-to-tree in the light of the moon. I thought to find out his name in case we ever got to talk to him.

***

Dad stopped the mules late in the afternoon, then climbed up and sat down on a chestnut log that'd been blown down by the wind. That ole log was so big I could hardly get up to sit by him, but after some struggle I made it. I just had to walk the log before I could sit down. It was like walkin' a trail to me. The tree was beautiful. I was sad that it had fallen as I wandered up into the limbs near its top, but I was makin' the best of it. I'd been ridin' the mule the whole time and was needin' to stretch my legs, whereas Dad had been walkin' and needed to rest his.

Dad pulled out his pipe, loaded it, then commenced to tellin' me our plan as we sat at the base of the ridge that leads from the Blood to Slaughter Gap.

"We'll be at Wolf's place soon. The next gap we come to will be Slaughter. We'll take a hard-to-find trail outa there and head up Slaughter Mountain a bit, then turn north on a small trail that will take us to Wolf's home at the head of a long ridge, just off the east side of the mountain. It's a perfect place to live; was given to Dancing Bear's father by the great General George Washington himself. It was his private land. He gave it to Dancing Bear's father as gratitude for his service to the country and his bravery under fire. General Washington came and visited in his later years; gave them a *Bible*. It's a great story that Dancing Bear tells about his father fightin' for General Washington. I've heard it many times. They have other things the General gave his father, too."

Dad sat for a while smokin' his pipe. I went back to playin' on top of the log. The bark was thick and it was easy to walk on. I got comfortable with it and started to run its length from where my dad sat at the stump all the way back up to the limbs, which still had the makin's of leaves from the early spring we were havin'. Dad didn't say a word, he just smoked and looked down the ridge toward the way we'd be travelin', wonderin' about somethin'. I could tell. He most always let me be a boy, was very understandin' of a boy's curious ways.

"Dad? Why don't we just stay the night here by this big ole chestnut log? We could move on in the mornin' and make it to Wolf's."

"Nah. We need to go on in there 'fore dark. Dancing Bear is expectin' us. He'll worry if we don't show. Pay mind, we didn't tote enough water to spend the night here. There's few streams this high up. The closest is a ways to the south. There's a springhead at Wolf's that comes out of a rock cliff. Wait till you see it. There is so much water flowin' that you can stand under it to wash."

"How much land does Dancing Bear own?" I asked, curiosity settin' in.

"He got the land way back before the treaty, so I don't really know, but I'm sure it's a lot. Land was given to the Cherokee in blocks of 640 acres not too long ago in the Treaty of 1817, but General Washington deeded their land to 'em before then, so they ain't no tellin' how much he's got. Some of Daniel Boone's folks was part of the survey company that laid the blocks out and made record. All I know is, his place runs from ridge top to ridge top across a nice little valley. Their home is located in the back of the property to the west, with all the rest lyin' in front toward the valley floor. Dancing Bear and his clan grow some fine crops in the low lands. His home is higher up on a nice level ridge that is hard for anyone to find unless one knows it's there. Slaughter Mountain is steep directly behind their place comin' in. It's hard for a body to travel that way, makin' 'em safe from strangers and bad storms. They see and kill a fair many bears near in, so be on the lookout as we go."

Well, it didn't take long for us to make it to Slaughter Gap. I saw our trail as good and bad, felt a kinda sadness that our trip up to Wolf's was almost over, but I couldn't wait to see his place again, this time with him here. I didn't really realize it or think on it then, but I would come to spend a large amount of time at his place, and he at ours. We would have many walks that led down the very trail I was on now. Wolf and I would meet possible death at times, as we set out on walks that Wolf said would "form our beings for the spirit world." I didn't see it his way on some things.

When Dad started on the trail to Slaughter, we made a turn through some hangin' hemlocks instead of stayin' to the main trail. I *swear* you could not tell it was a trail. The limbs hid the entrance like a hangin' quilt. It plumb hurt to ride through with those limbs knockin' me sideways. I near fell to the ground headfirst till I felt my mule adjust to the rough goin'.

We had to venture through hemlocks for a while until we popped out on this ridge top, which was unlike anything most folks outside of Indians ever saw, a place where only a few had passed. Many Indians know'd this trail, but folks like us did not. This trip was settin' the way for my upbringin'. I could feel it in my guts, but just didn't know what it was yet.

The oaks were huge, spaced like they'd been planted there. Seein' more than a couple hundred feet in most places was hard since they was so close and so big. Their bark was gray and slick, like wood Dad had rubbed with creek sand. There was a few smaller trees, and the ground was covered with old acorns and chestnut burs. In the mix were a few of the granddaddies of them all, that wonderful nut-bearin' chestnut. Later on, when I would study the *Bible* with Momma, I would see this place when she spoke of Heaven. It seemed perfect.

The trail was faint as we moved outa the hemlocks and farther down the ridge. You had to know where you were headed to make your way in a certain direction. I could tell that when the trees filled with leaves, it would be hard to see the sun; everything was flat so there was no left and right. Dad weaved through them trees like he was bein' pulled on a rope. He made every turn required to stay the track. I be dogged if Big Jim didn't know right where to go.

We were travelin' on what the old-timers called a ridge-a-hidin', as in, 'They's a ridge-a-hidin' behind that big top yonder,' or, 'If we can get to that ridge-a-hidin' behind ole Bald, we'll be safe.' Most were flat and easy for travel and stocked full of game to hunt.

Them kinda ridge tops was different, in that you couldn't usually see 'em. They was hid between two other big ridges, makin' for a perfect place to live. The only way you find 'em is if you climb a mountain that is taller than the two ridges that are a-hidin' the other, or stumble over 'em when you're huntin' or on a walk. Them big ridges keep the bad weather away, too, a big concern for the Indians livin' in the woods, Wolf's family included.

A half hour after we cleared the hemlocks, we changed directions and started movin' due west. The trees began to get smaller and grow'd thicker, with the bigger trees becomin' more sparse. The trail got more worn as we went, so that even I could tell where to go. Dad stopped short, come back and lifted me off the mule, directin' me to a spot on the ground. As I sat, I leaned up against one of them smooth oak trees, usin' the bark edges to scratch my back. I could tell me and Dad was fixin' to have a little talk.

He came and sat beside me. "Jeb, this is your first visit away from home, and you got to understand how to act when you visit folks. You never, ever show disrespect. Dancing Bear and his family are our friends. You respect your friends' ways, how they live; you watch their backs. You and Wolf will spend many hours in these woods as you grow older. You gotta learn how to survive. These Indian friends of ours have been in these mountains for many generations. Their ways are their ways. You don't ask many questions. Never touch anything of theirs unless you ask first. Things have different meanin' to different people. You never know what a thing might mean to an Indian. Keep your eyes open and your mouth shut. That way you'll leave this place with plenty of new knowledge. Trust me when I tell you these things. I have been amongst Indians the better part of my years."

Once he finished what he had to say, we left. He'd no more'n got the words out from his mouth when he jumped up and started down the trail toward Wolf's. These kinda talks weren't custom to his way, but when he called 'em, you'd better be listenin', 'cause he had somethin' important to say that just might keep a body from gettin' hurt, lost or dead. Death could always be found in the big woods if one didn't follow the rules.

He took off without puttin' me on the mule's back, so I started walkin' as well. I could tell we must be gettin' close. The trail looked used more. Every so often you'd see a side trail comin' into the main trail. It weren't near as hard to find as it was back in the huge stand of oaks; White Oaks, Dad called 'em later. I caught myself wonderin' where them faint little trails might lead. I had a hankerin' to walk 'em and find out. Probably Indian trails, a thought that caused me to want to go even more.

We hadn't traveled very far before I caught the faint hint of wood smoke; know'd without a doubt we would soon be at my new friend's home. I certainly didn't think on it at the time, but this would be like a second home to me for much of my life. I would grow to manhood with my friend and his family, come to love them as my own blood. You form bonds with folks. The one with Dancing Bear and his family would prove unbreakable time and time again.

The last thing I remember before the world went dark was the sea of bronze skin I saw as we rounded the final curve before Wolf's home. Half naked Indians from my left to my right, and all looked ready to kill, all wearin' paint. If I've ever been near scared to death in my life, it was then.

I was comfortable around most Indians, but there was always the fear of what they would do if they turned uncomfortable with you. No encounter in my young life prepared me for the war cry of nearly a hundred battle-hardened Cherokee as they announced our comin' before Dancing Bear and his clan. My visit to Wolf's place was gonna have to wait, as the world turned black and I fell to the ground. I never expected such a welcome. It showed. Wolf would never let me forget that day. He found the story quite amusin'. Indians are funny that way. I never thought it to be funny.

Chapter Eleven

My First Run with Wolf

It was dark when I woke. I looked around and could see the glow of a fire off to my left, could hear the soft sounds of someone sleepin' from somewhere in the place where I was. But where was I? I remembered that I was at Wolf's, but where was Dad, and who was everybody I could feel in the room? I stayed quiet so as not to wake anybody. I felt lonely and thought about Momma. I really missed her, though I was more comfortable now than when we'd left.

It was a soft touch that raised the hair on the back of my neck. A sudden whisper and a pull on my arm, and I was outside the place I woke in. We slipped through a slit in the back of what felt like a skin house and out into the woods so fast that I almost forgot to breathe. It was Wolf that was doin' the pullin', know'd we was headed into the woods, but I couldn't think of no reason for it. All I could figure was he must have somethin' he wanted to do. He was in a mighty hurry. My feet was barely touchin' the ground as we ran, but it didn't take many steps for me to realize I was barefooted.

We stopped so fast that I plumb ran by him and had to turn around as he grabbed my arm to stop me. I'd never seen such a pure expression as he had when I turned face-to-face with him in the near darkness, as he held out my foot skins. The night was dark, couldn't make him out clear, but the visible part was just as I remembered him—slightly shorter than me with much longer hair. Many of the Cherokee wore their hair short since the Creek went away, but Wolf and his clan kept their hair long like their ancestors. George wore his hair long, too, as did many of the warriors that lived in Choestoe. I liked Indians havin' long hair. Just seemed right to me, natural.

Wolf spoke first. I was calmed by his voice as he said, "My friend, I am so glad that you have come to visit my home. I have been waiting for you to wake so we could travel the woods together this great night. Now, lace your foot skins and catch up with me if you can."

He was gone so fast I hardly had time to tie the leathers that held my foot skins tight. I could hear the way he was travelin' since the leaves were dry, but if the forest floor had been wet, he would've been lost to me. I realized right then that I would have to work on my nighttime woods travel. He ran like he was part of the woods, almost like he could see in the dark. I was startin' to understand what Dad was talkin' about when he said to pay attention to how they did things. Wolf was at home movin' through the woods. It was obvious he'd done this nighttime travelin' before.

We come to rest a while later, much higher up the mountain on a flat ridge that lay above his home. Dad was right again. It was steeper than a mule's face up to the top of that ridge. No one would want to work this ridge unless he had purpose. As we walked ahead, I watched as Wolf's purpose was startin' to spread out in front of me.

We perched on a small cliff overlookin' Choestoe Valley in all its glory. It weren't quite full daylight yet, but Old Man Sun was wakin', just south of the Big Bald. As I looked down into the valley, I could see the Notla as it slithered its way to the north. My gut began to growl as the day aged and my mind wandered to the trout we'd cooked outa Wolf Creek. The hunger caught me, made me realize I hadn't eaten in a while. I must've slept through most of the night. I felt a dizzy spell hit me as I remembered the war cry that put me out. I felt my face turn red as the thought of fallin' out in front of so many embarrassed me considerable, but I never expected such a welcome as that. I remembered not havin' no idea what that was all about. *Why was they there anyway, and where was they now?*

The cliff we were sittin' on dropped straight down for several feet, with big rocks scattered about below. I reasoned it would most likely kill me if I fell, so I was a little slow in takin' my seat along the edge. Wolf had no such fear of fallin'. He walked straightaway to his chosen seat and planted himself without concern.

We was seated on a smooth stone that lay at the top of the cliff with a small shelf just below it for our feet. It turned out to be a real nice place to watch the sunrise. I could tell others had sat where I was, the place where your feet settled was bare dirt with not a piece of rock or sticks or leaves on it. Indians believed that sunrise was a spiritual time. I was sure many had sat right where I was sittin'. Somehow, I felt it would not be my last time sittin' in this seat. Wolf was as spiritual as any Cherokee I ever met. His whole family was special that way.

The valley laid out before us as the sun rose in the east. It reminded me of the bowl of apples Momma kept on the table back home after most had been eaten and just a few were left in the bottom—big tall ridges around the edge, with smaller mountaintops spread out on both sides of the river connected by smaller ridges with some tops standin' alone. The Frozen Top was the biggest and steepest I could see from where we were. I'd been up there with Dad to get some late season apples from the folks who lived up there. It was just an old man and his kids; weren't no woman about. It was strange to me thinkin' on how they'd have to tote their water up from a ways below, but they always had plenty of apples for folks willin' to make the climb up there to get 'em. I think Dad went for the brandy. He could grow apples as good as any.

The light started at the end of the valley and slowly worked its way south as the sun rose over the ridge tops to our right. It was as if the whole thing was comin' alive. You could feel the warmth as it got closer and closer. The mornin' was chilly. I was lookin' forward to gettin' warmed up. Folks below was wakin', too, as roosters was sure to be crowin' to let folks know that dawn was breakin'. You could see blue smoke risin' straight up from the chimneys of homes what were visible, as cookin' fires and heatin' fires was bein' lit all over the valley. The valley was still and not a breeze was movin'—yet.

Most of Old Man Sun had cleared the ridge when Wolf jumped up from his seat, raised his arms and began to holler. He 'bout scared me to death as I jerked spooked and nearly fell off the cliff in fright. I would learn to watch for things like that as I grew to understand the Cherokee and their beliefs. They would do things all of a sudden like, and you was hardly ever ready for it, even if you know'd it was comin'.

"Thank you, Old Man Sun, for your life-giving heat and for the light you give us each day. I thank the Great Creator for you and ask that you touch the things that grow so all here can eat and live. Mother Earth is your child. Through you she will be kept alive for all who live and walk her trails," he said, then sat back down and bowed his head.

That prayer was strange to my ears then, but one I would learn to speak on many occasions. It was not all Christian nor all Indian, but it said what all folks that depended on gardens and crops took to heart. The sun made things grow. Without it, we would all surely die, the critters, too. I never really thought about it till he said that Mornin' Prayer, but it was somethin' I would never forget.

Wolf finished his prayer and raised his head. Lookin' over at me, he smiled. I smiled back. No words were said as me and him turned to watch the sunrise. It was a moment in time, one in which I'd just learned my first lesson of many about bein' Cherokee. I would learn so much more from Wolf and his family. I bowed my head and said my own little prayer of thanksgivin'.

When I'd finished, I looked up to see if my new friend approved, but the look on his face was that of a hunter, not lookin' at me but at the floor of the forest, directly in front of us. As I followed his stare to the ground, my heart sank. Chills ran up my back; the fear I'd had on my first night at Wolf Creek returned. Three bears were makin' their way toward the rock cliff and were only steps away. I was sure proud to be sittin' up high where I hoped they couldn't get. It was not until the biggest of the three stood on his back legs and sniffed the air did I know it was the bear I'd seen several nights before. This was spooky.

"Wolf, I think that's the bear I saw my first night on Wolf Creek. The same bear your father saw as well. The bear that killed poor Mr. England and his stock was with this bunch. What do we do?"

"I know of this bear, Jeb. Father told me the story by the fire the night he returned from his walk. It was the night I learned you and Thompie were on your way to visit. Sit very still and let us watch and listen."

As we sat in silence and watched, the bear walked even closer to the cliff. Again, he stood on his back legs and stuck his nose straight up to the sky. I could hear the air goin' in its huge nostrils as it drew in a hard breath, searchin' for smells. I could see the shine on its nose and watched as the whiskers on the side of its snout moved back and forth, partly showin' his yellow teeth. I was sure then that it was the same bear. There, clear as day, I saw the star on its chest. I would never forget what that star looked like after I ran into it that first night. A four-point star with a white like none I would ever see on any other bear alive or dead. That star was tall and had a point on top. The sides were long and reached from leg to leg, the single point on the bottom reachin' almost all the way to the bottom of its chest. It was the Cross of Christ planted right there on that bear's chest that Dancing Bear had said was my brother. I nearly shouted as the spirit took over my body, standin' to let myself be known. Wolf stood, too.

"I am here, Brother Bear. I mean you no harm. I am glad you've come to visit me on this fine morning," I said, as the other two bears took off with a grunt, rumps turned under. "This is my friend, Wolf. I am with him as family. You honor him as you do me with this visit." It was strange to me, soundin' like an Indian.

The bear stretched out his front feet and let out a huge roar that bounced off the sides of the mountains, echoin' through the forest. His lips were curled back and his tongue stuck straight outa his mouth, bouncin' up and down and side-to-side as he kept roarin'. He hit the ground and covered the remainin' distance to the cliff in one big jump, puttin' his front paws just below where I was standin'. His paws were hittin' only a few feet below me; looked like he was tryin' to push the cliff away so he could get to us. His nose was stretchin' to where I was, tryin' to figure out if we was danger. I got down on my knees and reached my hand toward his snout, stoppin' a few inches from his face. He sniffed and sniffed, tryin' to sort out if he was okay with all that was happenin'.

Bears ain't got too good 'a eyesight no how, they depend on their noses, so Wolf began a soft chant. The bear shifted and walked off a little ways from where we stood on top of the small cliff. It was amazin' to watch as the bear stood and turned a circle, while Wolf kept chantin'. He slapped the air above his head, turnin' and gruntin' several times. As Wolf stopped his chant, the bear raised his legs into the air again and let out another of those big lip-curlin' roars. He stopped and lowered his left paw while his right stayed in the air. It looked as though he was wavin'. He fell to all fours and turned to follow the two bears that had run off earlier. He didn't run, though, just simply walked away, stoppin' to look back a couple of times as he went. I sat down feelin' a little dizzy. Wolf sat, too. It was several minutes before either of us spoke. The look on his face was one of wonder.

He finally broke the silence. "This bear knows you and will find you again, you must know that. He is a spirit bear, of that I am sure. I believe none will ever kill this bear. Bears cannot be trusted, my friend, so be careful when you see him again. He is still a bear and knows only what it takes to survive, unless the spirit is in him. I don't understand all that he did, but my grandmother will. We will sing songs about this in times to come. The elders will want to honor you. Of these things I am sure."

I couldn't speak, simply lowered my head, feelin' kinda sick deep down in my gut. It was an unnatural thing to me, but common among the Cherokee, as many stories were told of critters visitin' folks. I didn't want this bear to be my brother. I certainly didn't want folks to make a fuss over me, but Wolf would see to it that everyone heard. To the Indian folk, this was special and must be remembered. I just didn't know how to act now. It weren't such a big deal to me. When I got older, though, it *became* a big deal. Me and this bear would meet again. Wolf called that for sure, and he was right.

The sky had become gray as me and Wolf left the cliff and headed back into the woods. The clear mornin' was gone. In its place was what looked like rain. We slipped back across the ridge top and worked our way south to a huge white oak that had a place 'bout half way up where we both could sit. There were hand holds cut into the bark, so it weren't nothin' for us to climb up. Wolf went up it like a squirrel and me like a possum. It would be a while, but I would learn to travel like he did. The sittin' place had turkey feathers and squirrel tails hangin' in it right next to a small bow and several arrows. I know'd right off that this was a place where Wolf came to hunt. I felt outa place not knowin' how, but that was fixin' to change.

Wolf took up the bow and got one of the arrows outa its hidin' place. It had a small point that was just right for small critters, drew it and fired so fast I didn't have time to watch how he did it. The arrow hit solid in a white pine tree some twenty paces away, right in the middle of many other marks where arrows had hit before. He grunted a little after his shot, then handed me the bow. He fitted another arrow into the string and placed my hands just right so that the first three fingers on my right hand held the tip of the shaft against the string. My left hand held the bow; the arrow shaft sat just above my first finger on the left side of the bow handle. He showed me where to pull the string to so that it would rest against my cheek and how to tilt the bow just a bit to help hold the arrow.

He pointed to the tree and said, "Pull the string back while you take a deep breath and let it out. Look down the shaft of the arrow and let go of the string in your fingertips smoothly. Try to hit the arrow I just shot. Hold the bow still and don't let it move while you are lettin' the arrow go. Keep your eye on the place where you want the point to hit and think of nothin' else. Feel the shot and don't worry if you miss."

I had no feelin' that I would even come close to hittin' the tree, but I did as I was told. I drew the bow like he showed me and concentrated on nothin' else but where I wanted the point to hit, all the while lookin' down the shaft. I never felt the arrow leave the bow. The next thing I heard was the solid hit of the point right next to his. The scream he let out near made me fall outa the tree. I could not help but scream as well when I realized there were now two arrows stickin' outa that big ole white pine. I quickly pulled another arrow from its pouch and notched it just like he'd done. I let it fly just as I had before, and although it didn't hit as close to the first as I wanted, it was still close. Wolf called both of my efforts killin' shots. From then on I trusted myself as a fair shot. I would get better as time went on and I shot more. I wanted a bow of my own, but Dad would have to be in charge of that.

We were so caught up in shootin' that we didn't notice that the air had become cooler and the wind was pickin' up. The woods had grow'd dark, and there was a strange feelin' all about us. Wolf had a look of worry as he studied the sky. Even I could tell somethin' was startin' that weren't right. When we got down outa the tree, Wolf guided us back to the cliff where we was before. This time we went around the east side and crawled up under a rock overhang as the winds got to goin' for sure. I never would've found the overhang. You woulda had to know it was there, but thanks to Wolf knowin' of it, we were safe as the storm found its way across the ridges and into the valley. I prayed my family was safe, as it looked to me like it was headed right at our place. I worried for Momma, Anne and Cain. Surely they'd be alright. It weren't but a bad storm.

Chapter Twelve

Cain Takes a Lick

There was a hot fire in the cook stove when Anne woke on the first Sunday after Dad and me had left. Cain was makin' to cook the mornin' meal, then he'd be out in the barn tendin' to the mules. He was keepin' things up while we was gone. It was a fine spring mornin', and Wolf and me was up in a big white oak, but they didn't know that back home. Momma had gone to the Weavers.

Anne had been gone for a few days, helpin' Owl tend to some hurt kids whose home had caught fire and burned up down in the lower part of the valley. Dad always said they was a lot of folks what never raised much of a sweat down in those parts, but I guess if there was a town in Choestoe, it was probably as much of one as they could be, the way folks was scattered around the mountains.

The road what led into the valley was steep, bottomed out in the lower lands near the cool waters of the Notla, and a ways north of there was a kinda tradin' post with a horse barn, mill and blacksmith forge, but that was 'bout all. The mill ran from a huge waterwheel next to a dam the old-timers'd built to move wagons and such. The man who bought the mill, Jepson "Jep" Souther, made it better; his saw could really turn.

He ground meal, too. Dad would take us with him when he went to get the corn ground for the stock, as well as Momma's cornmeal. I loved her cornbread growin' up, 'cept for her cracklin. Hog guts in cornbread weren't desirable to me, but some folks liked it.

The church was there, too. Most folks would go there from time-to-time. They only had preachin' the first Sunday after the full moon; that's when the Baptist preacher came. He'd call revival two times a year that'd last a week or more; always depended on what my dad called the "movin' of the Spirit," as it went. You should've seen the way some of them folks took on when that happened.

They was missionaries about, who worked mostly with the Indians. They'd been in the mountains since way 'fore I was born, had been teachin' Indian folk to read and write and all 'bout Jesus. The Indians had their own language and ways of talkin', yet most got religion, so they learned to speak the language of the *Bible*. The Cherokee language was beautiful, but you could barely understand a word when they was carryin' on a conversation, never if it was a heated conversation.

"Good mornin'! How'd things go in the valley last night, Anne?" asked Cain, as he came through the back door with an armload of stove wood. He'd noticed the worry in her face.

"It was an awful sight when we got there, Cain. The mother was burnt near as bad as the kids. Nobody knew where the father was. I'm not sure he was ever there, really. Old Mother never said she saw him. She spent most of her honey salve on the kids, 'cause the momma wouldn't let us touch her till the kids were cared for. You could tell it sickened her to see her kids hurtin' like they were, like they still are," she said, her eyes waterin' up.

"How on earth did it get started?"

"Neighbors said nobody knew. The woman was too shook to say much. The whole thing burned to nothin', was just a bed of ashes by the time it started to smolder. It was just terrible."

"Well, thank goodness they're all safe. It could've been worse."

"It was worse, Cain. Two little girls never came out, four-year-old twins who the neighbors said liked to play with dolls and go fishin'. It couldn't hardly have gotten any sadder."

Cain had to reach and catch her from fallin'. She took death mighty serious. Those little girls had burned to death 'fore life ever got real good for 'em. I reckon the Good Lord is givin' 'em comfort now. Youngens like that don't know how to sin.

The Old Mother—a new name Anne had started callin' the old medicine woman, Owl the Wise One—was on her way back to Slaughter, so me and Dad would soon hear from home. It was bad why she was in the valley, though.

Cain finished breakfast and went back to the barn to feed the stock and continue workin' on forgin' some heavy mule shoes for fall plowin'. Dad liked to use a heavier shoe at that time. The mules was always havin' to pull plows over old corn stalks or other plant stalks, like beans, taters and peas. Made pullin' hard, so the mules did better with a heavier shoe. Cain was good at makin'em. Dad told him to make several dozen 'fore we got back. I reckon he wanted to keep him busy. He'd formed a bad habit of sneakin' off. I think Dad know'd where he'd go. Didn't 'cause Dad no trouble other than he missed his chores a time or two, but I always covered for him when I could. That way Dad never said much.

It was a couple hours after daylight, and me and Wolf was still up in the big white oak, talkin'. Cain was poundin' in a short mule shoe curve with a two-pounder when the first crack of thunder and lightnin' shot through the mountains, rattlin' the windows of the barn. It was strange to hear, seein' as they weren't hardly a cloud around. Things changed in a hurry, though, as we realized a rogue spring storm was workin' its way over the ridges, meetin' the heat from the valley below. Cain know'd it sounded serious, so he stepped out the big door in the front of the barn and looked toward the south. He realized real quick things was foul, as his breath was near sucked from his lungs. The clouds was turnin'!

The day turned black as night as the storm covered the early mornin' sun and moved across the ridges to the south, startin' its fall into the valley floor. Rarely did a storm this size make it across the back of Big Bald, but Dad would tell us later that every once in a while, one would muster up the strength to do it. It could get bad if that happened. Them storms would bounce off the sides of the mountains that formed the valley and ricochet back and forth across its floor, causin' all sorts of mischief. He said it sometimes killed folks, too.

Anne was in bed, catchin' up on her missed sleep. Momma was over to the Weavers to pick the last of some winter turnips. We needed the food or she wouldn't 'a-made the half-day trip to the Weavers' place, but we was sure glad when she did. It was a trip she'd make every year in the late spring, stayin' a few days before makin' her way back. It was a trip her and Anne would look forward to doin' together, but not this year.

Food, other than meat, ran scarce in the late spring, and winter vegetables was 'bout all they was left to gather. Mr. Weaver always grew much more turnips and salad than he could use. He know'd folks'd need it come spring. Momma would bring Dad home some cured Weaver tobacco when she went, kept her a little poke as well.

Cain know'd by lookin' that this storm could be dangerous, and so did we. We could see the roll of the thunderheads. Bein' up in a tree durin' a storm like what was brewin' was never somethin' a body wanted to do. Wolf hurried us back to the cliff where we'd watched the mornin' start our day. He led us to the rock overhang to take shelter under and wait out the storm. I wondered at how I'd 'a-never found that space if I was alone.

Cain would be fine, too, if he could make it to the root cellar before the fury of the storm rolled by, but the problem was Anne. She was upstairs in her bed, asleep. He'd just checked on her shortly after breakfast, dead to the world asleep, she was. I guess makin' people better was hard work. She was plumb wore out. No wonder God had to rest every seven days.

Cain hit the front door on a run and never slowed up as he took the stairs to the loft two at a time, hollerin' for Anne to wake. The storm had already traveled the distance it needed to center itself right over their part of the valley, and it was mad.

"Anne," screamed Cain, bustin' into the loft with terror in his eyes. A horrible roar got to blowin' outside that swallowed his words.

"What is it, Cain?" Anne woke, strugglin' to get the words out. She was exhausted, hardly slept for three days tendin' to them kids that was hurt.

"Tornado's got in the valley and it's bearin' down on us. Get your bones movin'! Let's get to the cellar!" He jerked Anne up from her half-sittin' position just as one of the upstairs windows blowed out.

The fear in Cain's voice got her awake; know'd quick it was time to move. When you live in the mountains, you learn to pay attention to what's around you.

"No time to grab nothin', just follow me," yelled Cain, as they ran back down the stairs that centered our log home. "We got to get outside to the cellar before the wind gets too strong. Keep your hands at the level of your eyes once we break through the door so nothin' gets stuck in 'em. Don't talk, and keep your mouth shut and your head down so the wind don't blow in and take your breath."

The roar from the wind was deafenin' as they broke out the backdoor and headed for the flat doors of the cellar. Trees up on the side of the mountain were breakin', the tops bein' carried away, as Cain struggled to pull himself and Anne to safety. Tornadoes was rare in these parts, but this one was here and nothin' was gonna stop it now. The damage would be done.

The root cellar was a hole in the ground where we kept our food, or most of it, anyway. Dad built a plank roof over the top and covered it with more than two feet of dirt. He let Big Jim stomp it down every so often. It never fell in from his weight, so it would hold up to a storm like this. The door was made of heavy wood that'd been milled and nailed together with spikes Dad'd forged. He drove them clean through and bent 'em over to hold tight. The thought'd made me shiver as I thought of how they did the Lord when they nailed him to the cross.

The cellar was a place where the family would be safe if things got nasty out, but mostly it kept our food from turnin' bad, kept the cheese and fruit cool. Dad would get on to me for goin' in there in the summer. I let the hot air in, but it was always cool in the back where the food was stored. Made a body feel good when it was hot outside and you couldn't go to the creek.

The vegetables were kept in a dug-out pit layered in hay. Each piece was kept from the other and not allowed to touch. This kept it all mostly fresh for as long as possible. Still, a lot would spoil by late spring, thus sendin' Momma and Anne to the see the Weavers for late winter greens.

It was nice inside. Dad and Grandad had worked for a long time diggin' it out. The cellar had plenty of room for us and the things we would need for a stay if that was required. Food, of course, and chairs, blankets, water, lanterns and weapons—guns and bows, arrows, knives, adl-adls, powder, lead and dynamite. Dad salt-cured his hams in the cellar, too.

Momma kept her flour, meal and salt sacks in there, but she had to keep 'em near the front so they would stay dry. She also kept our stores of grain in barrels Dad and Cain built durin' the winter months. I wanted to learn how to do that. There was a way it had to be done or they would leak.

Barrel makers stayed busy gettin' ready for fall harvest and all the whisky work folks done durin' the winter. Corn whiskey was the only way some folks had of makin' any coin. There was gold for those who could sell their barrels south. Folks could sell that stuff when nobody'd buy their corn for grain. Most preferred the brandy from apples and peaches over corn whiskey. Apple would become my favorite later on.

The cellar was on the side of the hill behind our house. Anne and Cain had to work their way up the hill while keepin' an eye on what the wind was blowin' loose, which was already blowin' hard enough to push the rockers off the back porch and out into the yard. All but three of the chickens had taken cover under the porch up near the base log of the house. Cain and Anne know'd three hadn't made it. They were plastered against the logs on the south side of the house. Anne said they looked like Dad had nailed 'em there.

The mules took to the barn and were raisin' a ruckus, scared of the wind and noise. There was a white pine top layin' in the creek behind the house that just missed the barn after bein' ripped from its stump and flown down from the side of Ben's Knob.

"Keep movin', Anne," hollered Cain, as he pulled himself and Anne up the hill to safety. "Don't let go of my arm. We gotta get to the doors and get 'em open. If we can get there and get inside, we'll be fine. Hang on and lean into the wind as much as you can."

Hail was splatterin' the ground. They felt the sting of the tiny ice bullets as they ran. A large piece hit Anne on the side of her head and blood began to flow. She staggered some but kept her feet as they drawed near the cellar. Hay and grain along with leaves and limbs were flyin' through the air, makin' it a real tough time gettin' to the doors. Once there, it took both their strengths to pull just one of them doors open. Anne was just about to stumble down the steps into the cellar when she turned and saw it.

"Cain, look out," she screamed, pointin' to his left.

Cain turned just in time to see the wooden bucket flyin' at 'em like it'd been shot out of a cannon. His quick turn probably saved his life, but it didn't keep him from sufferin' a terrible blow to the ribcage. The two small cracks he heard and felt at the same time would prove to be misery for him and Anne after the storm died down.

"Are you okay?" yelled Anne over the storm as she pulled a stagerin' Cain on in and let the door slam.

She was not strong enough to lift the oak beams needed to seal the entrance, so she and Cain stumbled their way through the pitch black darkness to the back of the room and prayed for the best. Her cut would have to wait for now, as she realized Cain was growin' weak.

"Hard...to breathe, Anne," Cain whispered. "Hurts...to suck in air. Feels like Big Jim is...on my chest. Need to lay down."

She guided their way through the darkness until she felt her hand bump against the cool, flat surface of the Georgia clay wall in the back. She leaned him gently against the side wall of the cellar and held him in a standin' position with his knees locked and his back against the clay. She didn't want him lyin' flat, knew if blood was gettin' into his lungs it would block his air if he tilted forward. The room was cool, which would help with slowin' the blood flow, but it was still gonna be a struggle. Lung wounds tended to be deadly in the mountains. Pneumonia was the 'old man's friend', I remember my granddad sayin', as he held my grandmother's hand and watched her fade away. She couldn't fight it. She was *so* old. He cried.

A sudden coughin' fit minutes later told her all she needed to know. Cain sent warm blood splatterin' to the clay floor and onto her hands. It stunk, she know'd it was dark and thick. She remembered the smell and feel of fresh blood right off. He had a hole in one or both of his lungs. She would need to act fast and proper to save his life, but that was gonna remain between her and God. She would not tell Cain. She hoped Momma would be home soon, or maybe Old Mother would sense her need. Not surprisin'ly, both would be the case

***

Old Mother found a safe refuge up on the west side of a short top less than a mile from our home. It was a small cave she actually shared with a young raccoon while the storm blew over. She sat and talked to the 'coon, gave it some cornbread Cain sent with her for supper. She made a friend of that critter, who came to visit her often thereafter. She named her Sassy 'cause she liked sassafras tea with honey and mushrooms. I liked it, too.

She told me once that it was God's own angels that talked to her when folks was in need, but Dad said they didn't converse with common folk, so it must've been the Holy Spirit. That made more sense to me. Whatever it was, she was feelin' like she ought to turn around and go back to check on Anne and Cain. The feelin' was strong, so she minded soon as the storm mostly passed.

Momma stayed safe at the Weavers' place, as the worse part of the storm was west of their farm. After it passed, she felt the need to get home and check on things, had that 'mother feelin' knowin' the storm moved close to her home and her children. She loaded her mule with the greens she'd picked and left for home even though it was now late afternoon. She'd be pushin' dark and would need to be careful. Remember, me and Dad had her gun.

Back home, Anne was gettin' more worried about Cain. He was strugglin' to breathe and stay awake. If he slipped into sleep, he could drown in his own blood. Right now, he was able to cough up most of what was leakin' into his lung from his standin' position. She tried talkin' to him, which worked for a while, but he was gettin' mixed up in the head. He weren't movin' the blood through his body proper, makin' what he was sayin' a struggle.

"Cain! Cain!" she hollered into his ear. "It's Anne. You gotta stay awake, Cain! You gotta stay awake! Talk to me, Cain! Tell me your secret to trickin' them bees outa their honey. You know, you get it for me and Jeb all the time. Cain! I want some honey. You stay awake and we'll go and get us some; take some sweet comb to chew, too. We'll mix it with some of Momma's hot pepper cornbread, wash it down with some cool sweet buttermilk. We'll climb the Knob and take us a young doe, fry up some backstrap with Momma's biscuits and butter. Cover it all with your honey. Cain! CAIN!"

***

Wolf and me, we headed for his place as soon as the winds died down. There weren't too much damage up high where we was, but I figured the lower lands might've got it worse. You could hear the roar of the wind as it raced down the valley. I felt terrible for the folks in its path. Made me wonder even more about how Momma, Anne and Cain made it. That storm went near our home.

We had to walk careful-like. The strong winds had blown the whole first layer of old leaves away, chestnut burrs was everywhere and, worst of all, they weren't all rotted soft as of yet. Many still had good firm stickers. They would lay into the soles of your feet, even through foot skins. Somehow they could find the smallest of holes to poke you through. The storm weren't no more trouble than that for those up high.

We'd traveled for a while when we stopped at a point in the trail where a small spring crossed and bent to drink.

Wolf stood when he'd finished and faced me. "Have a drink, Jeb. It is the last water we will have between here and my father's home. That is where I live, where you are now going to be our guest. Anything you need is there, just ask. I hope you will be able to stay with us for some time. I liked it at your home, your farm, with your folks and all the mules. I learned many things while we were there. My sister talks of our visit often, reminds us that is where she met Cain. I like it when he visits our home to see Rose now."

I didn't really know what to say back. A simple thank you and a nod was all I could do. He looked at me curious, then nodded back and headed on down the trail. I stood there and watched him go, stayed a while for some reason, didn't feel the urge to follow right off. He'd just told me that Cain was slippin' up here when he went off. Dad know'd it, I was sure, and now I did, too. Cain was a sly one when he wanted to be. Me and him was always close, but he never said nothin' about likin' Wolf's sister enough to slip off.

***

Cain was in bad shape. Death was not at the door for him, but it soon could be if they didn't get him in and seen to. Anne was afraid to move him for fear of makin' things worse; Cain really didn't feel like it, anyhow. For the time bein' they would just stay put, wait and pray.

It was gettin' colder and time seemed to crawl by. He'd slept some, but mostly worked to breathe. Anne would describe it later as one of the worst sounds she'd ever heard. Teeth chatterin' and air suckin', a terrible mix of sufferin' noises. But as bad as they were, it was better than no noises. He was still alive; gettin' weaker, but alive.

Twice she'd tried to get outa the cellar and down to the house where it was warm, but Anne found the doors leadin' to freedom to be heavier than she remembered. Cain had no strength to help and she couldn't budge them by herself. She got scared even more as she realized they was trapped and the air was gettin' thin.

A little while 'fore dark, Old Mother topped the last little ridge before hittin' the creek that runs behind our house. The damage she found was much less than she thought there might be. She offered up a whisper of a prayer as she dropped into the holler above our home.

She could feel the pull of need and stepped up her pace. She was wishin' she'd brought the mule, but it was gone when she'd needed to leave. Dancing Bear had rode it to Camp Town for tribal elections. He was well respected among his people; was most likely gonna get some kinda council position.

A tribal leader can't just walk into a gatherin' like that, he had to have his fine mule with him to make that trip. It was a sense of honor that he owned such a powerful gift. That kinda stuff held weight among the Cherokee, meant the Creator smiled on him and in turn would smile on his people. How could one go wrong?

Old Woman was a small person, but strong in spirit. She took it all in as she made her way to the cellar, knowin' full well that was where she'd find 'em. The ground around the house was littered with boards off the sides and roof of the barn, as well as limbs from higher up on the mountain. There was a wooden bucket layin' strange, kinda flat-lookin' on one side;no longer round, like it hit somethin' hard.

Several of the mules were just walkin' around smellin' things and lookin' forever like they was tryin' to figure out what happened. It was odd to them. The older mules wouldn't leave the barn unless they was led, but some of the younger ones had made their way out to the cornfield and were playin' around with their short time of freedom. Cain would've had 'em back and the corral fixed in no time, if he were able.

The tree top coverin' the cellar doors was no surprise to her. It was small to most, but it still had enough size that she would need some help movin' it.

Cain and Anne might be in a bad way if they're in there, she thought, as she started tappin' on the doors.

Anne could hear the tappin' and prayed it was help.

"We are in here and Cain is hurt," Anne hollered. "I can't move him."

"Be calm, my child. Are you hurt?" called a faint voice. Anne recognized her at once.

"I am fine, but Cain needs you. Open the doors so we can get out. We need fresh air, too," said Anne.

There was no return voice. Anne couldn't understand what Old Mother was doin'. "Why is she not openin' the doors?" Anne whispered to herself, absently. "Did she hear what I said? Maybe I should scream louder. Maybe she didn't hear me."

Anne got set to yell as loud as she could, even if it meant poppin' a lung of her own. She was gonna *make sure* Old Mother heard her cries. She straightened up from where they was standin', leaned against the wall, and just as she was fixin' to let'er go—

Tap. Tap. Tap.

She thought Old Mother was back at the door.

"Anne," came the voice from the other side. It was not Old Mother. It was—

"Momma!" she screamed, and then to God, "Thank you for bringin' my momma to me in my hour of need. You are so kind to answer my prayers this way."

Anne began to kinda half laugh and half cry. She was scared for Cain, but she was happy they were gonna get out and into the warmth of their log home.

Cain was strugglin', and Momma arrived in the short time he was gonna have left if somebody hadn't showed.

Momma had them out with her mule and a rope in just a minute. She and Anne helped Cain into the warm, layin' him out on the supper table like he was a cooked hog, blood and all, bare from the waist up.

"We must move him to where his head is hanging off the edge of the table. I need to find out if both lungs are hurt or just one," said Old Mother as she paid mind to the wound.

She took three smooth reeds from a leather sleeve in her medicine pouch. They were hollow, burnt smooth on the inside and worn smooth like butter on the outside.

Old Mother had treated many wounded warriors in the last war with the Creek, many of which were lung wounds, most ended in death.

It worried Anne studyin' on what them sticks was for, as well as how they got that smoothness and odd dark color.

Old Mother began rubbin' them with some type of ointment that looked like squirrel gravy, 'cept it was more dark and not near as runny. Smelled like somethin' the mules leave in the barn that I have to shovel up and take to the compost pile. Dad puts that on our garden, after it turns, of course. He knows it's good when the smell is right and the worms are a certain color.

"Anne, when we get started, you will need to gently hold his head still while I find out how bad this is. Celia, you hold him steady, because this may hurt. Cain, if you can hear what I'm saying, hold still and try not to move. We must roll you on your front side with your head over the edge. I have to check your lungs, but I will be quick," said Old Mother as she and Momma rolled him over.

She stuck one reed into the other. They each had a small end and a big end. She covered them again with the smelly stuff.

Anne suddenly figured out what was fixin' to happen, and caught herself almost gaspin'. It was only Old Mother's trainin' that kept her from openin' her mouth. She was taught better than to worry someone who is hurt, and the blood that poured outa Cain's mouth when they rolled him over was proof enough he was hurt bad.

Old Mother raised Cain's forehead and made Anne grab his hair and hold it off the table. This made his windpipe straight. She started runnin' the reeds down his throat while carefully guidin' the point into his airway. Findin' the windpipe runnin' to his right lung, she eased it forward until she reached the inside of the lung. She gently blew a small amount of air into the reed, then put her cheek near the hole. After a couple of seconds, air came outa the tube, but no blood.

She eased the reed out and cleaned it off with a strip of homespun soaked in hot water from a kettle Momma always kept on the cook stove. She put more of that stinky stuff all over it and loaded the end with some type of white powder she fetched from a small pouch, then covered the end hole with her finger.

When she slid those reeds down Cain's throat the next time, it was much more aggressive. She knew it was his left lung that had been poked by at least one broke rib since the right one held her air.

She slid the reeds in so fast Cain couldn't have felt it. She moved them in as far as she wanted, then bent, slid her finger outa the way, placed her mouth over the end and blew a strong breath of air through the tube. Cain's body jerked rigid as he moaned a deep gurglin' groan. He would say later that the blast hurt a right smart; that he felt what Old Mother was doin' most of the time she was workin' on him. He never mentioned the mouthful of blood she spit out after she jerked them reeds from his lung.

They sat him up and he came more awake. He was in pain and wanted to lay down to rest, but Old Mother would have none of that. They moved him to a rocker on the front porch, where he sat, leanin' back with a gentle sigh of relief and pain. A sharp grimace come over his face every time he was required to draw a breath.

Old Mother gave him some pain-killin' herb tea, which would help him soon enough. They would let him rest tied by the head and shoulders in an old rocker to keep him from leanin' over and smotherin' while asleep. That let him rest better, as rest was what would heal his wounds. That, and Old Mother's powder.

The ordeal would soon be over. He was at death's door. Because of this, his life would change, as his thinkin' would change. He was becomin' a man. The little Cherokee girl up on Slaughter became much more important to my brother after that. Things between them would get more serious once he healed.

Chapter Thirteen

Bear Meat and Dried Peaches

I finally took a notion I should go on down toward Wolf's. I got up and started walkin', hopin' I could keep to the trail. The woods were lit up with bright daylight. All the bad clouds had moved on, so it was easy to spot where the trail ran. The path was covered in old leaves with just a faint hint of a worn place leadin' you. Tree roots were a problem. You could easily catch your toes on 'em, makin' you stumble and fall or leave your toe hurtin'. The maples were the most troublin'. Them roots seemed to grow right on top of the ground. Footin' this trail of a night would be tricky at best, but only if you knew the way. Not knowin' would make the goin' impossible.

I walked only a short way when I found Wolf sittin' on a log fell some twenty yards off to the north of the trail. He was leaned up against a big limb, rubbin' his knife blade on the soft leather of his skin leggin's, waitin' on me. I was sure glad he took thought and stayed. I walked to where he was sittin', put my hands up on the log, jumped up to where I was kinda layin' across it, spun myself around and sat down on the rough bark of the old chestnut tree top. It'd been hit by lightnin' and cut plumb in two. There was a split that ran down the west side of the log. Then there was the stump still stickin' outa the ground that was the base of the tree 'fore it got struck. These chestnut trees were big and tall. You could stand right under the big'uns and look straight up and not see one top limb. Some took three or more men to circle around the base, hand to hand.

"Are you okay to leave now, Jeb? Have you settled on what was keepin' you up there? Do you want to leave for home now or stay a while longer? If this be between you and the Creator, then you must do what your heart feels."

"I am good, now. I felt a want to just sit a while and study on things, that's all. Thanks for waitin' on me. I'm not sure I could've found my way back," I said, all the while tryin' not to act too concerned.

"You are a stranger here and have not traveled these trails as I have during my growing up time. We walk this trail at all times during the seasons. I would not leave anyone alone here who did not know his way. For you, it could be dangerous. Our men have seen strangers on this trail. Father says it is wise to be careful along any trail one travels in the mountains."

When we started out the trail was noticeable where we was, but a little way on Wolf turned on a barely-there trail, which led us to another even less visible trail, neither I would have known to take. The last turn carried us to a small hilltop about a quarter mile from Wolf's home.

The place was called Little Rock Top by his family, 'cause that's exactly what it was. Granite, my dad called the rocks. The Indians had many different titles for the place. Wolf called it home; the old medicine woman called it sacred. Wolf showed me a smooth place in one of the flat boulders just off the top to the east where Old Mother would come and sit and pray, sometimes from moon-to-moon. That woman had the gift for sure.

We walked on till we came to a place where there was nothin' growin' but the big trees. You could see Dancing Bear's home clear as day. For some reason, it was a most comfortin' sight. The closer we got, the more it felt strangely like home—a log buildin' carved from some of the best pine logs ever put to a mule. I knew my granddad had a hand in workin' this place out since the logs were just the right size for a mule to move; straight and notched just fine to seal it tight against the hard freezes that hit Choestoe without fail each winter. The house faced east so the sun would hit it early, helpin' to warm the place up when it was cold and the leaves had fallen. There was no glass in the window holes, only little door-lookin' boards that a body could close over the openin's with a pull from the inside.

Near the home was a log barn, not too big, but good for a couple of mules. A smokehouse stood close by with two stacks pokin' out the roof and a woodshed off to the side. There was a second log home, smaller than the main house, and a springhouse hid in a thick stand of laurel, its logs near covered in thick green moss. None of the log structures were real big, but the logs were straight and tight so that one could keep safe inside if need be. With a close look, you'd see small round holes where lead balls had hit. They'd been dug out and most likely melted and used to shoot back with or kill game for food. Cherokee wasted nothin'.

A good-sized root cellar finished off the place. No sweeter water was found in the mountains than right there at Dancing Bear's home. The water come from a sure-enough waterfall that was a little ways from the back door of the smokehouse, makin' a year-round spring that shot straight out of a rock face. It was mighty handy for Wolf's family to have.

Though somethin' seemed to me missin', I wondered where the skin house was that I woke up in this mornin', where all my possibles was. I kinda figured it was around somewhere, so I didn't give it much mind. Besides, that waterfall had my attention.

It weren't no natural fallin' spring. It was a waterfall that shot outa the rocks higher up. Wolf saw me starin' at it, so he explained that when his clan first came to the area, it was nothin' like what it was now. Wolf's folks had moved all the rocks from way back under the hole where the water comes out. Now you could stand and wash under it or sit and cool-in behind the water, which was real nice. Made it easy to wash and clean things. Later on, we washed meat there when we killed it, when I was older, about eleven or twelve, I guess. That was when we started huntin' critters bigger than rabbit or squirrel by ourselves.

I stood and wondered at how the water landed on the surface of the smooth, flat rocks laid at the base of the fall. It was where you'd stand and let it hit you when washin'. The pressure was hard under the center of the falls. Wolf said it would sting bare skin; that you'd do best to stand on the edge of where the water hit when you washed yourself.

There was a wooden barrel full of water just on the edge of the fall of water with a river cane stickin' out near the bottom. The water was shootin' outa it in a steady stream that reached out some before fillin' another wooden barrel on down below where the falls hit. Everybody know'd it wise to keep a store of fresh water for times of need. It was real handy to have a place to rinse things as the cane stickin' out from the lower barrel was just behind the backdoor of the smokehouse; its water went back into the branch from the spring that formed the water fall. I got too close while walkin' behind the water and the splash from the main fall hittin' the stone got me. It was cold! I would learn that it was cold any time of the year.

The base of the fall overlooked a big holler that spread out in two directions. The ridge tops to the north and south were tall, so you felt no danger. Rogue storms could and did hit, but most of the time things stayed fairly calm. In the wintertime, you could see a long way down the valley and up toward the top of the leads across the way. The woods there had a lot of boulders and chestnut trees, and you could see in all directions. It was spooky sometimes late in the evenin' or early in the mornin', when the shadows played tricks on the eyes. Many times, Dancing Bear talked of battles fought there and of the Cherokee who had been killed. Wolf said deer and bear moved through all the time. I did not doubt that one bit.

We entered the main yard, hopin' to see my dad. I figured he had my knife and pouches, but there weren't nobody there at all 'cept me and Wolf. There was some ash smokin' in the burn pit, and our mules was still at the barn, so where was everybody?

"Are you hungry, Jeb? Would you like some food? We have many different things, but I don't know what you eat. I will get a few sundried beans and peaches and see if you like that," he said, walkin' into their log home.

The thought dawned on me that I'd been without decent food for a while. I started thinkin' I'd need more than that little bit of sundried stuff—I needed meat. Good, juicy, tender, bloody meat, and my stomach said soon. It was hurtin'. Them Indians a-hollerin' like that sure upset my world. I got kinda ill 'bout it. I was too young to have to put up with such as that.

I needed my momma in a bad way; not really feelin' scared of anything, just small and wantin' somethin' big to help me hide. Momma was always good for hidin' behind. She always smelled good, too. You could taste it, kinda like chicken fryin' in the pan for supper. I could almost eat a whole one if it was small. Dad would let me kill the small ones. I could pop their necks in one good whip. Way it was, boys learned to survive at a young age, and my dad was a good teacher. He was patient and kind, but hard as a tree when need be. I was doin' a day's work 'fore I ever turned nine.

The sound of a heavy door openin' made me turn to look back at a sight that stopped me for a second. I'd never forgotten their first visit to our home, but only bein' young, I did almost forget just how beautiful Wolf's mother was.

When you first lay eyes on her, everything else is just a blur. Her hair was shiny and moved when she walked, and her muscles would show themselves when she lifted somethin' or pulled back a bowstring. She made things seem in their place, as to the talent and worth of the beauty God created. She was fun to talk to; just made ya' feel great. I grew to love her as I did my own family; never feared to talk to her about things. I learned much of their ways durin' my growin' up years by stayin' with 'em in their home many times.

Her name was A-Ga-Li-Ha. It meant sunshine to the Cherokee, which was a perfect way to describe how you felt around her. I wondered if she was named later in life since the name fit so well.

Unlike many of the Cherokee who used an English name instead of their native name around folks who weren't Indian, she went by her Indian name most all the time. If she did go by her English name, it was just Sunshine for what it meant. Dancing Bear always said she married him because she was wise. Her father was a war chief durin' the Great Struggle, an honored man among her people. She had to stay whole Cherokee to honor him. But like many of the Indians, she liked her English name, too. She liked many things English, like looms and certain dyes, but she valued the books most. Her dad taught her to read and would bring books to her from trips he made to the English towns. She came from a different branch of the Cherokee Nation, south of Choestoe, called Yonah, but she was whole mountain Cherokee. All you had to do was look at her and you could tell that. God made her extra perfect for a reason only He could know. I was sure of that. Her beauty was considered spiritual. Rose's, too.

She weren't the only one from over that way to look like that, though. Me and Wolf went with her once on a visit. They was many among her folks. Dad always said it was somethin' in their breedin'; kinda like puttin' a certain Jack in with a certain mare to get a certain kinda mule, the way he told it. I guess I understood that. The mothers were pretty, so then the daughters was pretty. That was like puttin' a long-legged Jack in with a high-rump'd mare so you get a mule who can pull logs better than one with level hips. Anybody know'd that, so I learned about breedin' a little bit.

Their kids was good wrestlers, too. Me and Wolf both got whooped a couple different times. We fought a couple of 'em for cheatin', but they whooped us, too. Had 'em beat till their friends jumped in and give us a good one. We left walkin', but there was a few of them groanin' a lot more than us. Wolf managed to steal one of their knives durin' all the fightin'. We laughed about that many times.

A-Ga-Li-Ha's voice was smooth and she spoke with much authority, almost like you couldn't help but mind what she said and had to listen. When folks was near, they would pay her mind when she spoke. It was nice to be around her. She respected everyone until she got a reason not to trust a body. She knew her way in the world, havin' grown up with her father leadin' people; took to it natural. I liked that. She reminded me of my momma.

"Welcome to our home, Jeb Collins. It is good to see you again. I am very happy that you and your father are here. I hope you will stay for a while and be at home here the same as you are down below."

"Thank you, ma'am," I said, mindin' to be as proper as I could. "Do you know where my dad is?"

"Do not worry," she said, calmly. "He has gone with several of the men to meet Dancing Bear and his party on Blood Mountain as they return from Camp Town. They will meet at the top and escort them back into the valley. Runners arrived a few days ago and declared his election to the council.

It is a great honor for a warrior from this region, means a great deal to our family. My father will be proud to know this has happened. We will have a come-together and eat and dance, honor the Creator for his choice."

"I am very happy for Dancing Bear and look forward to that, but do you think you might have a bite to eat that I could have now? I am mighty weak. I hate to trouble you, but my stomach is mad and wants food," I said, as I was runnin' close to desperate.

She smiled at me and said, "We have food and you are welcome to what we have. Come and let us find you something to fill that empty place inside you. You and Wolf should go sit by the fire. I will fill a bowl for you both."

I'd forgotten about Wolf, but there he was, big as day. We sat by the fire and it made me feel sleepy. His momma brought us a flat bowl of smoked venison and bear with some dried peaches. I thought I'd died and gone to Heaven. That meat made the inside of my mouth shoot water out, it hurt so. I never minded it and got to indulgin' myself.

It weren't long till we'd eaten all the slices she'd carved for us, with a good chunk of bear meat still left. I wanted more, but didn't have anything to cut with, so I decided I would just pull off a chunk and moved to grab it. Wolf stopped me. He pulled a small carvin' knife from a hidden space behind his back and sliced off a half-dozen small pieces. I felt without as I studied how he had a knife and I didn't. My knife was with my stuff, wherever that was. I would need to find that soon, but I still hadn't seen the skin house I woke up in.

It was already past midday, so Wolf and me didn't eat our fill. We wanted to leave room for what was comin' later. I didn't know what was fixin' to happen, but I was gonna watch and learn. It sounded excitin'! I could hardly wait, but for now I wanted to find my stuff and maybe wash in the falls after Old Man Sun warmed the day up. I hadn't got to wash since George throw'd me in Wolf Creek. Dad had cut me a new piece of black gum 'fore we left home, but I'd only had a chance to use it once on my teeth. Momma was always makin' sure we stayed clean all over. She said it kept us from gettin' sick. I think it worked 'cause we hardly ever got sick.

It was near dark when Dad showed back up at Wolf's place. He was with a few other Cherokee, one of which could not 'a-been confused with any other Indian in the mountains. George had a form all his own, walkin' in tall over all the other folks. My dad sometimes called him the Gentle Giant.

Dancing Bear and his clan showed soon after. Everybody was happy for him. He was now a full member of the main Cherokee council. Dad always said the Cherokee ought to make him chief over all the nation, but doubted he would accept. Takes a lot of time to be a main chief, and Dancing Bear liked to go on long walks and hunts many times a year.

He was chosen several days before he arrived home, but it takes a while for Indians to make things official, so he'd just made it back. The runners were sent from council a few days before to carry the word. The men made ready to gather much meat while the women made food in preparation for the thanksgivin' they meant to have. It weren't like our Thanksgivin', when we celebrate and give thanks to God for our folks comin' over and settlin' the country, but it was an honored time to show respect to one who deserved it. They trusted Dancing Bear, who loved his people in a mighty way. He told Dad that the people was the main reason he even went to Camp Town for the decision time. The Cherokee in the mountains of Choestoe were a tight clan. I felt honored later in life to be a part of their culture as it lived out its last days in the North Georgia mountains, the home of the Choestoe Valley, the land where the rabbits dance—my home.

Chapter Fourteen

The Secret Told

It was still dark when me and George left Wolf's the next mornin'. The old medicine woman made it back sometime in the middle of the night, way after sleep took me. She described to Dad in sharp memory what she'd found when she went back to our farm to check on Cain and Anne; what'd happened to Cain and our home when the storm hit. He and Dancing Bear left on foot right then for our place.

George was to wait till daylight and fetch me and the mules back, but he couldn't wait that long and got me up to leave way before then. Old Man Sun weren't showin' down in the valley yet, so you couldn't see the ground where your feet was hittin', but you could feel the heat was comin'. You could see Old Man Sun'd woke, as the light drawed an outline of the bigger ridges surroundin' the valley, makin' a body feel small. It was dark as dark gets where we was, but somehow George could see the trail and led the mules like it weren't nothin'.

He tied a leather cord to the tail of the last mule and looped a handhold in it so I could hold on and know where to walk. The cord really helped about fallin', and bein' led by the mule kept me on the trail. But gracious, there was bad, too. The air trailin' them mules weren't real fresh at times. Mules is terrible stinkers in the mornin's. Many times I'd have to move off left or right of the trail when a stink pile come on me from up front. I'd know they was comin'. I could hear the stinkin' things as they landed in the trail, could smell 'em, too. George wouldn't let me ride 'cause it was still too dark to see the limbs hangin' over the trail in places that would've put a good sized knot on my head or worse. I finally got to ride on Big Jim once daylight come. He was next in line behind George.

"How long does it take to get home goin' this way, George?" I asked, as Old Man Sun rose slowly over the ridgetop to our right.

"We should be to your home a while before supper, little one," said George, stoppin' to look at me. "Now, you pay mind. Don't fall from old Jim's back, or you will be a hurt body, too."

With that, George jerked his head back front real quick, knowin' he'd just slipped up.

"Too?" I asked, worried. I didn't know much about what'd happened. "Who else got hurt, George? What's happened? You gotta tell me, George. The cat's outa the bag and I'm gonna chase it till I know what's goin' on."

George then realized for sure I was ignorant of the whole matter and tried to work it out for me.

"Has no one told you of the damage to your farm from the angry skies day before the last? Have you not wondered about why your father and Dancing Bear left on foot during the night?"

"No. Dad woke me late, but only said he needed to get back and tend to the mules and check on Momma. He said the storm had hurt our place some; that it would be good if he went on back and you and me would bring the mules back at daylight."

He stopped the mules and come back to where I was sittin' on Jim. He looked up at me as he put his hand on my knee sayin', "Jeb, I do not want you to worry. Owl has said things will be good."

He looked down, then away, and then back at me as he struggled with what to say next. It was gettin' me anxious.

"Well...let me see...it's just...well, you know...the wind was strong...and...there was this bucket, now...and the bucket got loose...and...well...it got loose...and the spirit of the wind made it fly, close the ground, see...like the eagle taking the slow rabbit, only this eagle was blind and it did not see Cain. Do you hear me, Jeb?"

He took his big hand off my knee and made the sign of an eagle flyin', then looked up at me again in a hurt kinda way and told it sure.

"He got hit by this eagle bucket flying through the air. It's hurt him on the inside some. Owl was able to settle in on him. They believe he will be fine, but it's still in the Great Spirit's hands. Your father is worried about him, so he left to go find out for himself. Nothing short of what any true father would do. Think on it. I hate you had to hear it now, from me."

Cain was hurt and may die is all I got from what George was sayin'. I started to tear up just a little as he went back to leadin' the mules. I suddenly felt all alone again, with my thoughts turned to Cain.

I'd never thought about death in my family before, became all empty inside at the thought of Cain bein' gone. He couldn't die. That just could not happen. I decided to have a little talk with Jesus. Dad always said if you were at the end of all you could do, then ask Him for help, but not to bother Him unless it was important.

It weren't an easy thing to do, but right there straddlin' one of the biggest, toughest mules in the mountains, I bowed my head to beg God to take care of Cain. I was lost in a deep cave of sorrow and it hurt somethin' awful, but 'the peace that surpasses all understandin' descended on me like somebody pourin' water out of a bucket. I searched my heart for an answer. It didn't take long, as my prayer was returned.

The Voice was as clear as if I was standin' with the Master Himself. "Cain is in My hands and will be fine."

I opened my eyes. George had stopped the mules and was starin' up at me with a very curious look. Even Jim turned his ear toward me. I was talkin', but not in any word they could understand.

"Cain's gonna be fine, George, just you wait and see," I said. "The Spirit has told me so, I know it to be true. Jesus is with him and he is fine."

George jumped to the side of the trail and hit his knees with one quick move. He looked me right in the eye and said, "What is it that has told you this, and how do you know it to be true? I will trust you, Jeb, if you believe it is from the Great Spirit. The words you spoke are none I have ever heard."

"I heard the Voice in my Heart, George. It was clear, just like me and you are talkin' and listenin'. Cain is gonna be fine, I know it. He told me. I believe Him."

"Yeee-Ai," hollered George. It were a mountain-shakin' scream from the pit of his bein'. That scream sent Jim into a startled jump, which nearly caused me to be throw'd off the back of his rump to the ground.

"I am so glad that he will be made whole again. Cain is a friend. I would miss him if he went across the river. I am glad he has decided to stay. Praise be to the Creator, because I know what He spoke to you will be. You are the child that survived the blue death. You are chosen among others and can speak the word of the ancestors. That is an honor and holds much truth with me."

Again I was confused, on account of him sayin' he and Cain was friends. That meant Cain know'd George way before I ever met him on Wolf Creek. Maybe I'd met him and just didn't remember since I was so young, but I reasoned it was just another thing I would have to figure out later—that particular bunch of stuff was growin' almost every day now. I would have to talk to Dad about this when I got the chance.

***

Cain was propped up in his rocker asleep when Dad and Dancing Bear got to our place shortly after daylight. Momma gave Dad a hug that made his neck hurt, but he didn't say a word, just hugged her back, breathin' in her sweet scent. She always kept herself clean and smellin' good. He loved my momma. Sometimes, if he'd been gone a while, he'd hug her for a minute or two. It was always the first thing he'd do when he saw her whether he was clean or not. I liked watchin'em, too. It made Momma happy. Most times, she would cry a little. She was lonesome when he went away for any time at all, and happy when he'd come home safe and not hurt. Sometimes he wouldn't be in too good 'a-shape when he got home, which made her terrible restless till he come back from bein' gone any time.

He could tell she was shaken up by the goin's on, but Cain was now restin' and it all seemed to be okay. Anne began to cry when Dad came through the door. She'd missed him so with the storm and all, but she never took her eyes off Cain as she stretched out her arms to draw him near. He'd just finished a coughin' fit, and Owl had told her to keep a close eye on him and watch to see if the coughin' made any blood come out his mouth. Fortunately, there was none. Owl told Dad when she'd got back to Wolf's that she'd mended the hole in his lung. Dad sensed time for healin' was all he needed now. There was no doubt in his mind that Celia would see to that.

***

The trail off the mountain was steep in places, but George's big feet never slipped once as he led the mules and me down. The ground was still soft and quiet from the storm; even my feet would dig in as I had to walk on the steeper places. Fact was, George's feet was so big they made places for me and the mules' hooves to settle as we went.

We hit the main path a couple of hours after daylight, then travel became much easier. The only problem with the main path was that other people used it. You could cross up with gold-lookers or rogue Indians, or just plain ole bad folk, so you had to be on the watch when you traveled it. That main path was the fastest way down outa the mountains, and we was ready to be home.

I studied George from the back of big Jim as we traveled. Although it was kinda cool, he wore no shirt. The scars on his back were like ghosts from the past, tellin' about the life he'd followed. Gouges and slices and burned places found their home on his back and shoulders, makin' a body wonder how he got so marked up. No tellin' how many died makin' them marks while they was tryin' to kill him. I was sure he was one warrior an enemy did not want to face when the battle was ragin'.

We stopped to water the mules and eat a bite around midday where a creek crossed the path, still a few miles from home. The creek was small here, as we were near the headwaters of Wolf Creek. They couldn't 'a-been but a few small branches emptied into the main flow by the time it made it to where we was. George got me down. I was stretchin' my legs by the creek with my left hand on Jim's shoulder, who had his nose down to the water fetchin' himself a drink. The rest of the mules was stretched out down the holler drinkin' when I felt him tighten as his head jerked up and he spun on his hooves to face back down the path. The breeze had brought him up a scent of warnin' that he answered on the quick. He held his head high and made not a sound as he trotted forward a few feet and stood his ground. His muscles made sharp outlines beneath his skin, and his nostrils flared as he breathed in deep, desperately searchin'.

George responded by slippin' quietly up the creek and disappearin' into the ivy that grow'd on both sides. He was only a few feet away, yet he was impossible to see. The only hint of his bein' there was the shine of his huge blade as he slid it from its leather bed and prepared to face a possible threat.

His actions left me standin' in the middle of the path without any mind for what to do. Fear was again risin' up my back, just like it did when it was me and the mules facin' a curious bear on the main creek a mile on down. Jim was tied then, never made hardly a sound, but he was loose now. He meant business for sure. I felt an urge to run, as I had no gun to stand behind this time. I know'd George was close by, so I just stood there wonderin' what, but still knowin' somethin' was there.

"What do you want me to do?" I whispered to George. I strained to see back down the trail for what made Jim jump so.

"Stay very still, little one, and make no sounds," he said, his voice barely a whisper. "Do not be afraid. Do not move until we see what has found us. It could be trouble, so stay very quiet."

"Trouble? Huh? What kinda trouble, George?" I whispered, loud as I could while starin' back down the trail, feelin' quite lonesome out in the open. "Why am I out here and you get the hidin' place?"

The question jumped loose from my mouth without as much as a thought. The way things was had me near tremblin' in my foot skins. This didn't sit right with me. I was just a pup.

"I said be quiet, little one. We need to see what this is," George said.

"Okay, okay. Quiet, I got it," I said. I could now only squeak like a mouse as I tried to whisper.

The woods got real quiet. I could hear most everythin' 'cept the sound of what was on our trail; loud like it was screamin' at me. I could hear the roar of the water as it crossed over the path and ran on down the valley. I heard Jim's tail swishin' like a bull-whip through the air, nervous-like, and his iron shoes grindin' as he strained against the grit and gravel of the path. He was workin' hard, tryin' to lift his massive head and nose as high as he could into the breeze, still not findin' the scent.

My eyes were dry and stingin' in the corners, I had 'em so wide. I strained to hear so hard my ears hurt. The breeze reminded me of the winds off that rogue storm a few days back, could feel the depth of the woods as all my senses reached for the source of my sudden fear. I sneaked a slight peek at George and got a shock—he was nowhere to be seen. My world had just become too big for my little body.

I felt like cryin' out for Momma, but know'd I couldn't. Our folks had taught us kids that it was important to show no fear when faced with these kinda problems, so I tried my best to not move or make any sounds, just as George told me to do. The continuous prayer passin' my lips was nothin' but a whisper, yet I figured God had good ears and that He could hear me. It was really all I could do, so I settled on that as a dark, black shine started edgin' out from behind a huge poplar tree back up the path a ways. That sight made certain I didn't move. If I had, I would've wet my skins right there, which was for sure somethin' I did not want to do, but that Indian I was lookin' at was pushin' me to start leakin'. Lookin' at a person in the woods when critters was all I was used to seein' felt strange.

The movement was slight and the vision appeared slowly—black, slick hair and a slender brown arm just easin' out from behind that tree like molasses pourin' in winter. I was ready to scream for George, but held my voice as I realized that the arm I was lookin' at could not be that of any warrior. I reasoned in a minute who it was after she cleared the tree and made her way to the path above us. The look on her face was of worry. I felt an instant sorrow for her as I now realized what was happenin'. Rose was goin' to see Cain, and she was trailin' us to get there.

She walked on down to where I was standin', and without takin' her eyes off me, she said, "Come on out, Black Oak. I know you can see me. I am going to the Collins' home to see Cain. I want to go with you and Jeb."

George appeared beside her.

"Why is it you want to do this, Rose?" he asked, not understandin' what all this was about. It was odd to hear him called by his Indian name. I liked it better than George.

"I heard the talk when Owl returned last night. I know he has been hurt, so I must go to him. He is my friend and I am worried," she said, still not takin' her eyes off me.

"Friend?" asked George.

"Yes, a very good friend." There seemed a slight twinkle in her eye.

"I do not understand, Rose," said George, in a deep voice. "What is this of you, and why would you travel alone in these mountains without family? Does Sunshine know of your actions, young one, because I will have to answer for this if she does not?"

"I have not been alone, Black Oak. I have been close to you all the time you have been traveling this morning. I did not let you know because I was scared you would send me back if I made my presence known before you arrived at this creek. We are now too far from Slaughter for you to make me return alone. I am going to see Cain. You will not stop me," she said, then she took her eyes off me and stared at him.

It was like a ray of sunshine cuttin' through a rain cloud as George's face lit up with the knowledge of her concern. He understood now; that she was more than just friends with my brother. This was not a surprise for me, nor for Dad, neither.

"Again I ask, does your family know you are here, young maiden?" George said a second time, much more direct.

Askin' a question twice was not somethin' a Cherokee warrior would usually do, but this was Rose. She was the eldest daughter of Dancing Bear, a tribal leader elected at Camp Town. George could be punished for takin' chances with a respected leader's daughter. As an elder's daughter, the Cherokee rules was clear.

I know'd the rules, as did most folks. She was puttin' George in a bad way. She was just as beautiful as her Momma. It was then that I realized Cain was gonna be a lucky man someday, that this was serious. Her leavin' home by herself to go and visit Cain was kinda her way of lettin' folks know how she felt, whether that was her plan or not. She was gonna check on her loved one no matter the chore. That's how it come to George that Cain and Rose was close. I nearly laughed out loud, but know'd not to outa respect when George had turned so serious.

"My mother knows that I have come. She will explain to my father. He is with Thompie so I was not able to speak with him before I left. Mother will make it right for me. My hope is that Father will understand."

"You are a brave child, but you are foolish traveling behind like that. Get up here on this mule and ride so I don't lose you in these woods. You can never know who is watching and waiting for a chance to attack. You were careless in your actions to follow us," said George, as he grabbed her up and threw her on Jim's back, then turned to me with a slight grin on his face.

"I am so glad to see you, Rose," I said, after George lifted me up behind her. I wrapped my arms 'round her slim waist. "The Great Spirit has told me Cain will be fine, so don't worry."

She turned to me with a tear in her eye.

"I am glad He has told you this, young Jeb, but I need to see him with my own eyes, as I am very worried. I need to go to him, comfort him, help care for him...and nobody will stop me." With that, she faced forward again to look on down the path.

If there were any doubt on how she felt, she cleared that up the moment she stepped from behind that tree and let us know how worried she was for Cain. It made me feel a little weird that Cain had been slippin' around seein' her, and hadn't told Dad or me. That was just Cain, who had his own way 'a doin' things, kinda like Indians. I guess maybe now he was lookin' at things a little more like a Cherokee, but I felt in some way left out. It was alright, though. I was thinkin' he still couldn't shoot a gun no better. He was deadly with a bow and adl-adl, but not a smoke pole, as the Cherokee called the white man's gun (although, he had been practicin' and doin' better of late). His last couple kills was with one of Dad's favorite guns.

Like it or not, she was comin' with us. That was now truth. The more I thought on it, the more it seemed right. George never said anymore about it, but went on and finished waterin' the mules. It was not in his or Dad's plan to take her on this trip home, but take her we would. The Cherokee was loyal to their clan, and she was most certainly a part of his people, born to these mountains. The Choestoe Valley was full of Cherokee, a mighty tight bunch. It was gonna be an interestin' homecomin'. Cain would have some serious explainin' to do when he could. The important thing was that he get healed. I know'd the sight of Rose at the door would go a long way in helpin' him down that trail. Yep, it was sure gonna be interestin' when we got home, there was little doubt in that.

Chapter Fifteen

Rose Tells a Story

Me and Rose talked all the way home, which was real nice since she spoke perfect English. Them missionary folk spent a lot of time with the Cherokee teachin'em to speak right and read the *Bible*. I come not to trust them preachers much. They dressed funny and they couldn't afford no mule to ride. Some of 'em got run out on account of the way they'd treated certain folk. They tried to work us, but Dad would have none of that. Said the Lord washed him in the blood; that he had no time to listen to a bunch of Morvians—that's what folks called 'em. But mostly they done good by the Indians, what with learnin'em stuff and givin'em spinnin' wheels and washboards and cookin' truck. Dad always said it made their lives better; they had better food cookin' and clothes like the homespun we wore mostly. Turns out the government was gettin' that stuff and usin' the missionaries and their schools to get it to 'em. I guess at one time the American Government liked the Indians.

Rose told me about how she thought Cain had first took a shine to her when he'd come and go huntin' with her brothers, Fox Running and Moon Shadow. I didn't tell her it was most likely 'fore that, back home when her family come to our place that time. She told how he just started showin' up to go huntin'. That's when he got busy courtin' her. Said Dad thought he was out huntin'. He was a good hunter, too. Now it was clear why he hardly ever come home with any meat no more. He must've never hunted much on them trips. The way she told things, huntin' was not first on his mind. It would've been near impossible to spend time tryin' to kill somethin' when you was courtin' like they was. You gotta be quiet when you're slippin' around lookin' for game. There was no way, by what she was tellin', that there was time for any of that. The times he did bring in a deer or such had to be the times he really hunted. He was struck by this girl. 'Fore we ever got home, I saw what made Cain like her. She was tough like most Cherokee women, could hunt, skin and run the woods as good as any accordin' to Wolf, but she was sweeter than a hound pup. She had a firm middle where my arms wrapped around, but the skin on her arms was soft. I had to hold on to her 'cause there weren't none of Jim's mane that I could reach since we was ridin' with her in front and me in back. I liked ridin' behind her. It made me feel important, like I was keepin' her safe. She smelled good, too. I would catch her scent as the breeze would blow her long black hair back in my face when Jim got to goin' a little. The Cherokee could make some fine smellin' soap. They washed a lot, too.

We'd left the main path shortly after the creek and had been ridin' the trail for home a while when Black Oak, as she favored callin' him, decided we needed to rest the mules some. A couple of 'em weren't shod yet, and he was mindin' their hooves. We stopped in a holler a couple of ridges short of home, where a small branch near-covered in ivy ran over the trail. It weren't big enough for nothin' but gettin' a drink or washin' some. The next two gaps we had to cross, bein' Six Drops of Blood and Quiverin' Antler Flats, was tall and kinda steep, so he thought it best to be fresh 'fore we started up. I was glad, too. My belly was talkin'. Jerky was all we had, but it had been a while since midday and it tasted real good. I weren't too fond of jerked meat 'cause there was very little salt on it, but this had salt and it was good. Some meat was smoke jerked and some was sundried jerked, which usually had more flavor since it was easier to add a touch of salt and dried pepper. Momma always had an herb garden, with peppers bein' a part of it. She would dry 'em real good and ground 'em into powder, which made the flavorin's easy to work with. I didn't like the hot much, but the sweet peppers was just right to me. Dad and Cain liked the hot best, but not me and Anne or Momma.

The jerky got Rose to thinkin' on things, so she started tellin' me a story that was on her mind. A story about one of the first times her and Cain slipped off into the mountains, why they was bonded so. They was on a walk. All he'd packed to eat was jerked venison. Things got bad after they stopped to eat, and I found out somethin' serious 'bout my brother I never really figured him for. Black Oak grunted a warnin' about tellin' this story, but it didn't stop her. Women in the Cherokee clan made many of the decisions when it come to home matters; the men was expected to pay mind. He was probably settled on that, so she kept talkin'. Turned out the story was already bein' told around the Cherokee fires late in the night when only the men are listenin'. I think she know'd it was bein' told and wanted me to hear it right. Sittin' there restin' must've provoked her. It was a good time for a story. Release us from worryin' on Cain.

"It was on one of his later visits to see me and not to hunt with my brothers. We took off without telling my father. We knew it was not proper, but we just wanted to be alone for a while...talk. We hadn't planned on being gone very long, just for a while. I enjoyed being out in the woods with him just walking the trails and talking. We would search the mountains for special places and were having a great time, but the time turned bad when Cain had to fight for what turned out to be our lives. Maybe I should not tell you this, Jeb, but I know Cain might never and you're gonna hear it told soon enough, so it's best you hear it from me. But, you must swear to not tell a living person that I told you," Rose near demanded.

I just stared at her and nodded.

She continued, her face somethin' serious. "Cain took life on that walk. He had no choice. He also saved my life by nearly giving up his. I realized that day that I loved his soul more than my own life; that I would love him forever. Not even death can change that," she said, her face now lit up like daylight as tears wetted the corners of her eyes.

The chills ran down my back as I turned to look at George, but all he did was nod a little and drop his head. He know'd what'd happened and just how Cain felt, as I would learn in years to come. It bothered a body to take life from a person. Right or wrong, it bothered a soul for sure. Poor Cain had learned to live with the thought. I know'd it must tear at him somethin' awful from time to time. It explained a lot of his behavior to me that I'd never been able to figure out till now. I never asked, but I hoped Momma never found out. I was wishin' I'd not learned it, but I did.

Cain got to her place a little 'fore daylight, and they left without tellin' anybody. That was the first thing Cain did wrong. Dancing Bear near made him stop comin' around to visit Rose 'cause of all that went on durin' that walk. Everything worked out in the end, so things were back right soon after, but it was bad what happened. Love must worry a body. Why else would he follow strange tracks with a girl along in the mountains? That was just dangerous. He should've turned back and got her home instead've searchin' out trouble. Still, Cain was tough. He probably thought he could handle whatever they found. Fortunately, it finished up he could, but it was near death for both of 'em in what turned out to be a couple of ways.

She sat down on the bank of the branch, took off her foot skins and rolled up her britches some to cool her feet in the water. She put her toes in the edge and gently rubbed each one with the tips of her fingers. It was cool for this part of spring, but the water must've felt good, 'cause she let out a little sigh. I had my foot skins off in a couple of seconds. Our feet shared a small little pond of water at the bottom of a tiny waterfall. Dad could've stepped across the whole place with his long legs; the water weren't but a few inches deep. It was a small branch, but the water was clean and cool and tasted like cold sweet milk in the middle of winter. She smiled as the cold hit my feet and I flinched. She pulled her long hair back and kinda twisted it into a knot, gettin' this faraway stare in her eyes as she looked into the water, like she was dreamin'.

She reached down with a cupped brown hand circled in beads and scooped up a little water. The beaded jewelry on her arm reflectin' off the ripples as she moved her arm over and let the water run out her fingers and over her lower legs. She started softly hummin' a song, ever so quiet and under her breath, all the while enjoyin' the cool water. I didn't make a sound as I listened to her.

She finished her hummin' and looked up at me, kinda worried-like.

"I will finish the story if you promise not to let one living person know that I have told you, ever. Not even Cain." Her words sounded like an order. She looked at Black Oak as well.

"I will never tell one livin' soul, even if my life depended on it," I said, tryin' to show her I was just as brave as Cain. Black Oak nodded in agreement and dropped his head again. He was not comfortable with this.

The seriousness seemed to disappear, as she laughed a tiny little ole laugh and said, "Then we are agreed. Listen closely and you will learn."

Before she could begin, Black Oak went to tend to the mules. He'd heard this story from before, when he saw the truck Cain brought back. Rose stared into the water again for what seemed like forever, then took her feet out and put them on top of her foot skins to dry. She scooted herself back until her legs were straight, leanin' back against the base of the huge poplar we was sittin' under. She crossed her long arms over her middle like she was tryin' to keep warm and began her story.

"We left my home just after daylight. As I told you, we were not planning on being gone very long. Cain just happened to think to put a small poke of jerky in his pouch for if we got hungry before returning. It was good he did, because that was all we had to eat that day. We climbed the high ridge that runs behind our place and worked our way to the cliff where the ridge ends."

I know'd right where she was talkin' about. That's where Wolf and me watched the sun come up the day before.

"From there, we turned west to a place where Cain and Fox Running would stop to camp during their hunts. It is a nice flat gap between two rounded tops with a small stream and a clear view of the mountains to the east. He knew of a cave farther west of the gap that he wanted to show me, so we stopped by the water to rest and eat a bite of jerky, much like we just ate. We sat for a good while, talking and enjoying the perfect, clear weather and the view that showed us the majesty of the mountains that surrounded us. The day was growing older, so we thought to leave for the cave and then on home.

"Cain became very bold as we stood to leave. He reached out and drew me so close our bodies pressed together. With a touch like a gentle breeze, he placed my face in his hands. I found myself staring deep into his sky-blue eyes, his warm breath on my lips. I could hear my heart pounding in my chest, my breath got hard to draw and my knees grew weak. His scent strong and fresh like the woods after a hard summer rain.

"I had never been with anyone like this before. I was unsure of how to act. I tried pulling away, wanting to resist his notion, but I could not. I did not have the strength because my knees were so weak. My breath refused to come as his face slowly moved toward mine, all the while his eyes searched deep inside what felt like my soul. I could feel the warmth of his body as he wrapped his arms tightly around me and kissed me for the first time, for what seemed like forever. I nearly fainted as the touch of our lips set my world to spinning. I wanted to sit, but his embrace was strong and kept me standing. We drew apart and held each other's eyes until desire brought our lips together once again. After that, we lay down side-by-side in a sunny spot on the east side of the mountain. The air was cool as I lay over his chest with my head on his shoulder, wrapped up in his closeness, not saying any words, just enjoying our time together.

"I still remember the quiet sounds of the woods as we lay still following our embrace—the soft trickle of the water as it ran south, the searching tap, tap, tap of a woodpecker off in the distance, grubbin' out a hole of what must've been a hard tree. There came the crisp crunch in the leaves of a hungry squirrel as he moved from spot-to-spot huntin' the buried treasures he'd hid in the fall, and a distant call reached us as a lonely dove sang its mourning song, which reminded me how lucky I was this spring. The chipmunk chirped his nervous little mating call...but the thing I heard best, that I remember most, was the beating of a heart that I never wanted to be away from again. My love for Cain had just become who I was.

"There was no breeze, just the warmth of Old Man Sun. The peace we were feeling relaxed us, so we fell into a deep sleep. That is why we were gone longer than we should have been. It was one of those moments when you wish time could just stop for a while. That was a time my soul can never forget."

It was an interestin' story so far, but I was gettin' kinda bored with all that kissin' and holdin' talk. I could understand the sleepin' part. Old Man Sun can make you real lazy once you start gettin' warmed up on a cool day, but that lyin' side-by-side in the sun stuff was to juicy for me to get. I was beginnin' to wonder if they ever made it to the cave, as I was lookin' forward to hearin' about that. I'd only ever been in one, a cave Cain showed me near our farm. It weren't a big cave, but it was fun for me and Wolf to explore in.

"Cain and I were lying there, in what is now our favorite place in the mountains, asleep," Rose continued. "I had no thought about anything except this wonderful creature God had put in my life. And the best part was, I knew he felt the same. Somehow, we had just become one, so when the dog began his bark on the west side of the gap, it was a shock. We both jumped awake at the same time from the sound of its deep voice. It was close."

A barkin' dog in the mountains can only mean one of two things: they's critters about or trouble about. Either way, it was somethin' that got Cain's attention. He know'd what strangers in the valley could mean. They would not be Indian folk, as Cherokee dogs would never bark in the woods unless they was told. If they was told, they would be barkin' trail or treed. All mountain folk could tell the difference between a dog's trail bark, its treed bark and its danger bark. This sounded to me like it must've been a danger bark, 'cause Cain paid it mind. He wouldn't have if it had been a trail bark. I couldn't help but think this was gonna be the part of the story that proved what he'd done wrong, if anything.

"Cain jumped to his feet, lifted me to mine, and took off on a run to the south side of the mountain with me following. The dog was close. As soon as he heard it clear, he knew we had to move, at least till we figured out what was happening.

"It came on after us like it had purpose. Cain moved us on toward the top of the mountain and across several large boulders that ran along the edge of the ridge, then back down to the head of the spring where we had eaten our jerky. We halted under a wide bottomed hemlock and hid in the low branches to catch our breath. The barking stopped as the dog lost our trail in the boulders. Cain laughed at such a stupid dog.

"We were trailing the water flow back down toward the gap, trying to slip away behind the dog, when we crossed the tracks of visitors—two men on foot, a horse and what had to be a big dog with a pad missing from his right rear paw. They were wearing boots that made tracks like the ones the red devils wore in the last war with England. I knew to be wary, as did Cain. It became clear that we needed to get back to the main trail and head for home, leaving these fools and their now quiet dog to the Cherokee Guard. It would not be pleasant for these men who would dare wear such boots," she said, growin' near to anger.

Even I understood at my young age how most all mountain folk felt about the English; how they'd treated the Cherokee and the Creek durin' the war that would be the final war the Cherokee fought for any white man other than the Americans. Sadly, in the end, the Americans did 'em wrong as well. Dad always felt real bad about all that. He tried to help the Indians, "but the government has a strong arm," he would say, "and is very deceitful in its doin's."

I was taught at an early age to never trust any soldier that wore red, to be on guard if around any folk who worked for the government. White men discoverin' gold didn't help the Cherokee none, neither. President Jackson and his lyin' bunch only made it worse.

She started back to tellin' the story.

"Cain would not let it go and started following the tracks, even though he knew better. He felt as though these men were a threat to folks, wanted to see who they were before we left for home. I knew it was foolish of him and feared for us both. The only weapon we had was his knife. But he is very stubborn when he thinks himself right, so I followed him. After all, I was loving him more than life.

"With Cain in the lead, our trail had completely circled in behind the two until we knew they were upwind of us. We could smell their stink long before we ever saw their disgusting hides. Cain froze when he caught their scent. We both knew only bad folk could smell that dirty. We were right.

"He squeezed my hand tight, motioned me to stay still, then crept forward crouched nearly to the ground. He had not gone far when he stopped and settled on one knee, his eyes locked on something ahead. He never turned his head, but simply slipped his hand behind his back and held up two fingers, followed by a slight flip of his forefinger to motion me to come forward, quietly. As I eased up behind him, my blood went cold as I peeked over his shoulder. The most horrible thing I had ever seen in my life was standing not forty paces dead in front of us: two bearded, long-haired, grimy, dirty, filthy white men trailing a near-dead horse had stopped and were looking up toward the top of the mountain, after where their dog had gone, no doubt. Their heads bobbed up and down like turkeys, not paying any mind to what was behind. No wonder we could smell those rascals, we had slipped in close.

"They were bandits for sure. You could tell by the look of their possibles. They probably killed the men who owned the boots, because the rest of their truck was unfit to own. Their clothes were nothing but patched-up, worn-out homespun, and the brown of their dirty white skin showed in the rips and tears. They wore no hats to cover their dirty long hair, but simply strapped it and their beards with nasty looking leather cords, their hair matted like long-haired dogs' tails.

"Each had a long gun and a knife, and they looked hungry. But the thing that was the worst, the most unbelievable, was the Indian hair hanging from the saddle horn of their near-starved horse. Fresh blood stains down the horse's front leg from the recent scalping. I had to hold Cain and quiet him after he saw that.

"I feared the two had heard us, as they became quiet and turned to look our way. I waited for the dog to bark, but no sound came. A true fear gathered in my heart, because I didn't know what Cain was gonna to do. I was truly scared now, as I felt his body tense and a soft, growl-like sound came from his throat."

I'd heard that sound outa Cain before. It meant he'd just got mean in his thoughts. You'd hear it clear when he'd get nasty with the mules after they'd act up and he lost his temper. I'd heard it when he missed a deer and had no powder to make another shot. I'd heard it once or twice when he got into fights. He liked fightin', which rarely made him mad, but he sounded mad now. He was gonna do somethin' for sure, and in this story it might not be good for him and Rose, I was sure of that. Them scalps meant murder—Cherokee murder—and although it rarely happened anymore, some folks still paid a price for an Indian scalp. Murder weren't to be tolerated, and scalpin' had to be revenged. Cain saw it just so.

"We backed out of there as quiet as cats and turned back up the way we had come. I hoped Cain knew what he was doing, because we were headed right back toward where the dog had been. But a sudden turn to the west and we were far enough away so they could not hear us. We stopped behind the base of a huge pine. He turned to face me while sneaking peeks back the way we had just come," Rose said.

"'We need to get you away from here, Rose,'" said Cain, still crouched as he spun to face down the mountain. 'They's just too much wrong with all this. We'll turn south and go down in the valley a ways, then head back east and skirt these devils. Our families will hunt this trash and make things square. Hell's fixin' to gain two new souls when Black Oak finds their trail.'

"He turned to face me and got even more serious than he had been, saying, 'I gotta go and fetch somethin' we'll need, now, since we're goin' the long way back to your place. You gotta stay right here. Don't make any noise, and don't move and they won't see ya'. I won't be gone long.' Before leaving, he looked into my eyes, then pulled me to him with a strong arm. Our lips pressed together, firmly, passionately. I did not feel that it would be our last kiss ever, but I knew it could be.

"I did not want to stay there without him, but he felt he had to go. I wanted to trust him, so I said I would not move unless I had to. He smiled and took off with a simple turn, his leather foot skins silent as he left. I could not know what it was that could be so important that he would leave me there, but I trusted him; watched him disappear heading west away from me. I forced myself to stay calm.

"I had all but dozed off when the soft stir in the leaves made me believe he had returned. I raised my head to look around and quickly realized it was not my beloved that had returned to me—it was the dog. He was big and ugly, staring right at me. The stuff dripping from its mouth looked like sap dripping from the maple in the cold time. The beast was terrible-looking, its mouth full of dirty black teeth, rotted and bared for me to see. A deep rumbling growl came from its face and made me shake with fear. I had never been as scared as I was right then. It looked like hell's own hound, and it was hungry. It was coming for me, was goin' to eat me; and there was nothing to stop it. I knew then that death was at my door.

"Each time it would growl, it would take a step forward. Not big steps, just easy steps, but each step drew a long hairy foot and its master closer. It walked in a way that made its shoulders rise and its head move up and down, a lazy kind of step where its claws dug into the earth each time they found the ground. They were long and filthy and deadly. I could just feel them tearing into my flesh. I was quiverin' with fear.

"The dog was moving in on me. There was but one thing I could do—fight back with all I had. I raised up on my legs and looked around for something to fight with, but there was nothing. My only hope lay not more than three or four good leaps to my left, where I saw a chestnut log I could jump behind, but I knew that cover would be short-lived, and would still mean certain death. I began to hum my death song.

"There is a certain look when a beast is ready to pounce. It had that look. It was farther away from me than a cat would have been, so at least I had a little more time to find cover. The thought entered my mind that I may even have time to run once I hit the ground on the other side of the log, but come what may, it was getting ready to happen.

"The dog's back legs got low to the ground, its mouth snapped shut with a growl and its tail started slapping side-to-side. The front paws dug in, as it went into a full crouch. Like a huge cat, it made its killing lunge at me. I heard a strange grunt and a thump as I turned left and leaped toward the chestnut log, just clearing the top and landing on my back, too stunned just then to get up and run. I rolled onto my front and waited for the dog to make its first blood-thirsty rip into my back or legs, but it never came. In fact, nothing came at all. There was no noise, no growl, no dog trying to kill me. When I rose from behind the black coarse bark of the chestnut log, all I could see was Cain's bare back and a quiver of arrows, his long, light-colored hair now tied with a dark leather cord. A hawk feather hung loose, a single gold bead woven into the tie. He held a short, dark bow, pointed right at where the dog had been, with his drawing arm held at shoulder height and the elbow pointed straight at me.

"I rose to my knees and placed my hands on the log to steady myself, then got a clear look at what the strange thumping noise had to have been. Standing between me and the now dying demon dog was Cain. That dog was finished, lying not three steps in front of Cain, a black flint arrowhead covered in blood poking through the back of its head, the fletching sticking out its mouth.

"The arrow had gone nearly straight through its filthy head. Life took on new meaning as I realized that had Cain's arrow missed its mark, the dog would have probably killed us both. I now owed him my life, but as far as I was concerned, he already had it. Though, my life would not be the only life Cain would claim that day.

"Cain knew the outlaws would hear the noise killing the dog made and would come in search of what caused it. They would be tracking us and would follow us to our homes, which would cause risk to our families. He had no choice but to defend our lives and the lives of our people. His instructions for me were to stay still, and if he was not back soon, to go get our fathers. I protested, but Cain would have none of it. He said it was fine and he would be back. I could only pray that God would protect his foolish hide. I knew now, for sure, that I was deeply in love with him from the center of my soul; that we were created for one another. There was not, nor would there ever be, someone who would replace him or take his place in my heart, of that I knew.

"He turned to leave but stopped, put his bow on the ground, turned back to me and got down on his knees. He took me by the shoulders and looked me right in the eyes, saying, 'I will be fine. I have to do this or they may catch up to us. I'm just gonna slow 'em down, that's all, so don't worry. I will be careful, but these varmints deserve more than what I can do now. Slowin' 'em down some will give us plenty of time to get home without them comin' on us to do harm. Our fathers and Black Oak will hunt them down. You stay right here. I promise I'll be back d'rectly.'

"He was right. It was not very long before he came back. The only problems bein' he had blood running from a dark bruise on the right side of his face, and a cut above his left eye with a small trail of blood coming from it. He walked back to me like he was on a simple walk through the woods, bow in hand and arrow fletchings showing over his right shoulder. I had seen him walk just this way many times, except that he now led the half-dead horse with the two Indian scalps hanging from the saddle horn. As he came closer, I saw something trailing from the horse that was not there before. Two more scalps had been tied to the animal with a bloody leather cord. The scalps were dripping fresh blood and the matted hair was full of dead leaves. They were bein' dragged a few feet behind the horse's backend. That was the purest form of Cherokee insult Cain could think of. I knew then that those two were across the river; that times had just gotten bad for them. I never said a word as I tended Cain's wounds.

"Cain would not tell me what happened. As far as I know, only Black Oak knows the truth. If that is the way Cain handles what happened, so be it. He will tell me one day if he feels I should know, but I do not really care. He saved us that day from three very bad spirits. We should have gone home, but then those murderers might have killed again. It is very likely that Cain saved more than our lives by settling with those evildoers. Dancing Bear felt the same way after we were given the chance to tell the story and he heard what the dog did. Our friendship was allowed. Cain was accepted to be a part of our family," Rose said.

I studied on what it meant that Cain was now part of her family. I was lost in her words, tryin' to put it all together with what I know'd about Cain. My mind was now set different 'cause I thought of him different. I weren't exactly sure how he killed that scum, but he did. I didn't know that, if it came down to it and I was his age, if I could've done what he did. I wondered if it made him feel like the Cain in the *Bible* what did the killin'. Dad would say that ours was the 'Good Cain' whenever anybody said anything.

One thing was for sure, from the wounds he come back with, he left Rose meanin' to kill them rats, whether he told her or not. He most likely did it up close, too. If she'd 'a-looked at his knife, I reckon she'd 'a-found fresh, dark blood and folk meat, but no hair. No, sir, he'd 'a-used one of their own knives for the scalpin'. He sure didn't want no bad spirits on his own blade. He could've shot one of 'em with an arrow, but he'd 'a-give the other a fair shake while his friend died. He couldn't 'a-not. They'd done murder. It was the way mountain folk lived. Justice had to be paid for fair. Cain was now a man, and a man protects his family. To mountain folk, it's the way of honorin' how they lived their lives. Gettin' rid of outlaws like that kept the valley safe. Folks depended on one another for that kinda watch. Folks looked out for others the way Jesus told 'em to do. Sometimes that meant handin' out justice. Eye-for-an-eye, tooth-for-a-tooth. That's the way folks saw it in Choestoe. Cain made us all proud.

Chapter Sixteen

Back Home with Cain

It was late in the afternoon when I first smelled smoke from the chimney of our log home. We were close now; wouldn't be long until I could hug my momma and Anne and see Cain. It seemed so long since I'd seen 'em. I was gonna give Momma the longest, tightest hug I could. Jim could feel we was close, too. He was startin' to do some high-steppin', ready to get back to his barn for some fresh oats and shelter. Black Oak was havin' to hold him back some, which worried Rose a little, but I'd rode ole Jim enough that I weren't troubled by it.

The trip had been a long one, but the comin' home part was made shorter by the fact that Rose was travelin' with us. I couldn't help but wonder what Momma was gonna think. I could guess what Dad would be thinkin', but Momma was different. She was more showin' in how she felt about what folks said and did. Cain was near grown, so they weren't much she could say. And knowin' the way Rose felt, it would likely do more harm than good. It was still worryin' to me how Momma would feel 'bout all of it. She loved Wolf's family and felt them a part of our family, too, so I was hopin' that all would be good. If it weren't known 'bout Cain and Rose yet, it would be truth soon enough. Her showin' up would add a little season to our comin' home gatherin'. I was sure of that. I was hopin' Cain was awake and could know she'd come. I figured he'd likely feel better if he saw her.

That rogue storm had caused a lot of damage about the place; made me mad. This was my home. It pained me to see it like this. Boards was gone from the barn and there was holes in its roof. The well house was blowed over, and the oak spindle that worked the water bucket up and down was cracked near in two and layin' off to the side with the bucket rope coiled up and laid on what was left of it. The bucket was plumb gone. There were tree tops lyin' all over, and some of the big trees around the place was blowed down. They'd make easy firewood, but ole Jim would earn his oats pullin' them stumps. It was strange, but there were chicken feathers stuck by somethin' on the side of the house. I got to wonderin' if the chickens was still in them feathers when they hit the logs. That must've been a strong wind to work things up the way it'd done. I got to hopin' our bathin' tub was still standin' and no trees had fell on it. I really missed it while we was gone; hoped to be in it soon, soakin' in hot water and dreamin'.

Jim was tight as we rode through what was left of the back gate and into our mule yard. Things weren't right and he know'd it. The horses and mules was in their pens. Some of the mares actually cried to him as he come down. Rose was near in tears as she looked all about the place. It stood to reason from the looks of the damage that Cain or Anne could've been killed. It had to trouble her. She'd be seein' to him soon, but for right now she was very quiet. I felt for her bein' here and what she was facin'. Black Oak led us through the mess and stopped in a clear spot a little ways short of the back door. No one know'd we was back yet.

Black Oak came around and lifted me off Jim's back, set my feet on the ground. Rose just threw her leg across and slid down beside me in one easy motion.

I reached up, grabbed her hand and smiled as we turned to walk toward the back door.

"You can hold on to me when we go in," I said. "Just lean on me if you feel the need to."

She looked down, the corners of her mouth risin' some, and smiled back.

"You are more like your brother than you know, young Jeb. I feel much better having you walk in with me. I trust what the Great Spirit told you, all will be fine."

She bent and gave me a short hug, which made me feel really good all over. I wanted to hug a while longer, but it was time to go in the house. I prayed it wouldn't be too hard for her to see Cain.

We kept holdin' hands until we opened the back door and walked right into the kitchen. It was a site to behold as everybody turned to look at everybody else, realizin' who was who and such. Not one person said a single word. It was like a haint opened the door and not a body could see us—it was an uncomfortable time for sure. Black Oak walked in behind us. I know they saw *him*. But still, not one word from one soul and there bein' seven in all. Dancing Bear and Momma had the two most wonderin' faces in the room. Cain lit up like a streak of lightnin' on a hot summer night. I felt Rose shiver as her hand tightened around mine. Still, not one word from nobody. It made me feel strange.

"Rose!" Momma cried. Everybody in the room jumped a little, not expectin' that.

I didn't know if she was glad or feared. I was hopin' for the best, but I'd learned 'bout female folk from hearin' Dad talk. He'd mumble 'bout 'em that nothin' doin' is for sure. He'd say, 'They do what you can't reason they'd do, then they surprise ya' and do somethin' normal. Can't figure 'em out sometimes. Make you think they want one thing and really want another. Confusin' to a body for sure, near frustratin'.'

Momma's hollerin' took us all by surprise. Not a word was said again, all wonderin' what she was about. Momma could make you wonder with the way she done things sometimes, but the wonderin' soon come to a stop.

"Rose, child, what are you doin' travelin' with the likes of these two? Don't you know you'll get a reputation? You don't want folks to talk," she said, then moved to grab me by my neck and commenced to huggin' me somethin' fierce.

She kissed me on top of my head and buried my face in her chest as I threw my arms around her middle. She felt oh so good. I was squeezin' her back and rubbin' the soft homespun she wore, but I don't know if she even know'd it. Her hair smelled like spring flowers. I found out then why Dad held her so long when he got off the trail. She was very nice to come home to. She opened up a little, but kept her left arm around my neck while her right arm waved Rose over to join the huggin'. She was cryin' and I was cryin' and Momma was cryin', a movin' sight to the rest of the folks in the room.

My thoughts quickly turned to Cain after I'd seen how Momma was gonna take things. My heart sank as I turned to look at him. I weren't ready for how he looked.

I'd never seen one, but I reckoned he favored a dead person. He was near white in color, 'cept he looked more gray, with purple lips and dark veins stickin' outa his neck and forehead. His eyes were sunk back in their holes; they was gray-lookin', too. His arms was folded across his lap, the hands that laid off the ends were black with white in the fingernails. He was freshly washed, with his hair combed back slick. You could see his ears, which were usually covered with his long hair. He was bare from the waist up. They had him tied to a rockin' chair to help hold him straight. His feet laid in a steamin' wooden washtub of water. Grandma was sittin' beside him with a rag, wipin' the sweat away. Fever was on him awful. He and the rocker was covered with my bear skin Dancing Bear had gifted me. He was bad off. The cook room stove was near red hot. It was kinda warm as spring was comin' on, but he was shakin' with cold. Fever was 'a-beaten on him. By the looks of things, he was barely makin' it. Somebody was gonna have to get this right. It would be time for plantin' soon, and Cain weren't lookin' too good.

Rose never let out a noise as she walked to where he was sittin' and faced him. She leaned down, placed his hands inside her long fingers, wrappin' em plumb up, then looked him straight in his eyes that were so weak. As her mouth moved to his ear, she said in a kinda whisper, "I am here. I will not leave you until you are well. I will help take care of you. Together you will mend. The Great Spirit is watching over you. I am praying for you. Grandmother told me of your wound; has said you will heal. She has seen this hurt many times during the wars. She can sense these things. I trust her. But if nothing else, my spirit will love your spirit back to this life." She then kissed him on his ole sweaty forehead.

Cain could barely make a sound, only squeaked out a simple thank you with a slight nod. He was weak. You could tell this thing was near whoopin' him. That was scary to me. Cain was tough as any folk in the mountains. I could only have faith what I'd heard in my heart was gonna be true. He looked like he was dyin'. I just weren't set for it. I walked back outside before havin' to talk to anybody. George come out with me. He had to finish puttin' the mules away anyhow. Jim was sure to be growin' restless. Nobody could hold him if he wanted to go, he just let folks know what he wanted, and right now he'd be wantin' his barn. He was such a good mule. My thoughts turned to Peter for some reason, as I followed George out to the barn. I wanted to make sure my mule got put away proper, too.

I watched as George tied each of the mules we'd brought back to a steel tie what was drove into the logs of the side wall of the barn. He moved to each one and pulled up their legs to check the hooves. Mules' feet had to be kept proper or they'd not pull. He had a small steel hook with a flat scrape on one end that he scraped all the dirt, rock, mud and old leaves from the bottom of their feet with, while watchin' for cuts or hurt places. Findin' none on any of 'em, he took off their rope halters and set 'em free. It was a big welcome home for all the mules, Jacks and horses. They all took to kickin' up their heels and swingin' their heads side to side, just playin' and havin' a good ole time. Our herd needed big Jim. They was awful glad he was back. He was the king of the stock that was for sure.

It was now just me and George. It didn't seem like neither one of us wanted to go back into the house. We looked at each other, walked to the front door of the barn and stopped in the openin', where the doors was swung back.

He leaned against the door with an eye toward the house.

"Cain does not look good. I will trust what the Great Spirit has told you, but I have seen this look on many brave warriors who crossed the Great River. I am troubled for him. He is strong, but I know fever is a great enemy. We must build a fire tonight and pray. Dancing Bear and I will smoke and dance to the spirits, for them to walk this way and do the Great Creator's will. They will hear our prayers on the smoke and they will listen. Dancing Bear is a great man. His father was an elder in our tribe. They will listen to him as he prays to Great Father and his Son Jesus for the healing spirit to come."

It was the first time I'd heard George use the Lord's *Bible*-given name. It didn't sound just right, but it did prove he knew the real God. I'd not thought on that before, but it made sense he would know. Indians were real tight in their thoughts over the spirit world. God didn't have a place for some Indians when they entered that world, but for Dancing Bear and his clan, they understood God was first. They still had the very first *Bible* the clan ever got. George Washington, the father of this great land, had given it to Water Runs Deep, Dancing Bear's father, after he'd fought so bravely and been of great purpose for the General durin' the war with the red backs. Many Cherokee had sided with the outsiders, but most of the Choestoe Cherokee were hogtied with ole General Washington. He later got to be the first president of our nation. Waters Run Deep got to go to his home not long before I was born. They built a new one shortly after he went there since the red soldiers burned the first one. I later heard through stories it was a big white house with lots of people livin' in it. I never saw it myself, so I don't really know for sure.

I studied on what he'd said, and kinda felt the same way.

"I know what you're sayin', George, 'cause I'm thinkin' the same thing. You reckon he's gonna die. Was I wrong about the hearin' in my heart, George? He don't look like life, that's for sure. He looks poorly and he looks like he will be that way for a spell. It worries me, too, George. I reckon y'all need to pray real hard tonight."

I looked up at his face as I was done talkin'. His eyes were kinda red and they was water in 'em. If I didn't know him better, I would've thought he was cryin'. Weren't no tears fallin', but he sure was sad. He had a soft spot for Cain, which had mostly grown softer since he'd come to realize that Cain was gonna be family. That could cause a body to change his thinkin'.

He looked down at me and said, "You will come and pray, too, little one. You are a part of us. You must grow in your prayers. Your brother needs you to pray. You are a part of him. God will listen to you just as he does to us. Now, you must go in and be with your family. I will ready the fire so we can smoke and pray when the darkness comes."

He reached and gave me a little shove, which was small for him but strong for me. I nearly fell over.

"Go on. They are worrying for you. Stay with Cain and talk to him. Tell him of the things that happened on your first trail with Thompie to Slaughter. He will listen and it will make him feel better. Go on, little one." He gave me another little push toward the back door. I had no choice but to go.

I stood in front of the back door. The latch string was out. All I had to do was pull on it and the thick huge oak door would near open by itself. Dad did his door-hangin' work right. The doors on our house had stopped .69 caliber lead balls, yet could still be opened by a simple pull on a string. Their balance was just right the way he built and hung 'em. I was reachin' to pull the latch string, when the door started openin' on its own from the inside.

The hand that pulled the door open was not the small hand of a woman, but the strong fingers of my dad. He stepped out on the porch and closed the door behind him. He reached down and picked me plumb off the plank porch, haulin' me up face-to-face. I sat in the elbow of his arm, wrapped my arms around his neck and looked him in the eye. But 'fore I could say a word, I started to cry. He drew me near in a hug I didn't want to get loose from. Somehow, he know'd I was in need of his attention, so he'd come to find me. I thanked God near every day for my folks back then; still do to this day.

His voice made things square, as he said, "It's gonna be fine with Cain, son, you don't need to worry. He looks poorly, but he's as tough as they come. He'll be up and goin' in a few days. His body has to fight the evil that's got in there. We have to stand with him and pray. He needs you to be strong now and brave, like he knows you are."

I pushed back from his hug and he looked into my leakin' eyes as I tried to explain how I was scared.

"Cain looks like somethin' near dead, and it's a worry to me. He just can't go away, Dad. He has to stay and help with the plowin' and the mules. I ain't big enough to be good help. He has to be here," I said, latchin' on to his neck as the tears fell again. I couldn't help it.

"Here, here, listen," he said, as he put me back down on the porch and got down on his knee, his eyes level with mine. "Cain ain't goin' nowhere. He's bad sick right now, but he ain't gonna die, son. Your momma won't let him go. That ain't gonna happen, I know. She's said he'd be fine, so we need to put stock in what she says. Let's not worry no more about it. He's gonna whoop this thing what's got a hold on him, hear?"

He weren't scoldin' me, he was just explainin' how things really was. He believed Cain was gonna be fine; he was just tryin' to get me to understand. I understood, all right, but I weren't swallerin'. They was worry in his eyes, I could see it. I felt like tellin' him what the Lord spoke to me, but I thought better of it. I figured if the Lord wanted Dad to know, He'd talk to him His own Self. Weren't up to no young'un like me to be stirrin' in the Blood.

Dad stood, looked down at me and wiped the tears off my face with his thumb.

"You can go in now, or you can wait a bit and go in when you're ready. I'm out to the barn to see to the stock. I'll be in after a while. Go talk to your momma, she missed ya' a sight. She wants to catch up on your trip to Wolf's and back home." Without a glance, he turned and left for the barn.

Facing' the door, I stopped again. Cain had a long row to hoe. It was gonna be days 'fore we'd know for sure 'bout him. Knowin' the way Momma handled things gave me good hope. Cain was strong, so I knew the favor was his. The old medicine woman had worked him over good. Anne was here to watch out for things, too, so he was as good off as one could be. Rose bein' there would help a sight. I was so proud Momma welcomed her. I still wondered if Momma knew exactly why she come.

I finished the tear-wipin' chore after Dad went to the barn. It was time for me to go in and sit with Cain and Momma. Anne and Rose were good friends, so I know'd things were good with them. Rose was stayin' since Cain was in a fight. Momma and Anne needed Grandma and Rose's help—it would give him a better chance to live through this. I'd done worried Momma enough 'cause she couldn't leave Cain's side and come look for me bein' out too long. I reached for the latch string and pulled it. The door quietly swung open and I walked in. It was a moment froze in my memory. The kitchen was empty.

Chapter Seventeen

Rose Gets a Gift

Not a soul was in sight. The rockin' chair was gone and the washtub had been moved out. The little potbellied stove in the center of the room had its damper closed; the lamps was all turned down. They was still some rags on the Lazy Susan where Grandma had been wipin' Cain's face, but nothin' else. I would have to open one more pass-through, as I'd stayed out so long they'd moved Cain to the main room.

Dark was near on and haintful shadows wandered around the cook room. I moved toward the quilt that covered the main room openin'. We didn't have a heavy wood door splittin' the two rooms, a body just had to walk through. Momma would hang a quilt when it turned cold to keep the fireplace heat in the front part of the house. I was scared to death of that ole heavy thing. It was made by a bunch of old ladies Dad called 'aunts'. He said they'd haunt me if I was bad. I believed him, too. It was real old and worn. Them aunts had nothin' on Momma. She could throw a quilt better'n any folks ever 'cept Grandma. Momma learned all she know'd from her. It was the old way of quiltin', the way Grandma learned from her mother who'd come to America from the 'motherland'. They was made of soft heavy homespun yarn and filled with lambs' wool. They was real warm on cold nights or when you took fever. We all slept under 'em durin' the cold time.

I slipped through the cook room and eased one side of the quilt back just enough to see. The room's heat hit me square in the face as it crept through past the quilt. Cain was still tied in the rocker straight in front of the fireplace. Small yellow and blue flames heated a tea kettle hangin' center of the fire. Momma was rockin' in her rocker close to his left side, legs crossed, her head laid back on a small pillow and her hand on his arm. She had her eyes closed and was restin'. Granddad was on Cain's right with his back to me, rockin'. He had his pipe goin'. I could see the blue tobacco smoke risin' above his thick head of gray hair. One thing a true Collins didn't have to worry 'bout was his hair fallen out, as they was no slick-headed Collins men to be found around Choestoe. Black, brown, or red and thick as a beaver pelt grew our hair, 'cept for Cain. His was yellow.

Rose and Dancing Bear were gone, and there was a light in the loft. Grandma was lyin' on the visitor's bed back in the corner, her arms folded across her chest and her legs covered with a quilt. She was restin', so I walked real quiet-like to where Momma was rockin'. Cain was breathin' in hard. It sounded kinda like the butter sloppin' on top of the milk when I'd churn it. I stood on her side away from Cain and looked up into her smilin' face. She know'd I was there. She uncrossed her legs and lifted me up into her lap. I gave her a big hug, then turned around and settled my back against her front and stared into the fire. She wrapped her long slender arms around me and laid the left side of her face on top of my head. My world was right again.

"I missed you so much while you and Thompie were off visitin' Wolf and his family. I prayed every night for you and fasted for your safety. You were in God's hands, which gave me comfort." She was whisperin' so as to not wake Cain, who was sound asleep.

Granddad grunted, makin' me think he'd probably done the same. He'd fought in the war, sidin' with General Washington. I'd heard folks make mention that when he come home, he didn't say as much as he did 'fore the war. He stayed kinda quiet most of the time, although I'd heard him get riled up at camp meetin' and such. He and Grandma live down in the valley. He worked in the mill with the log sawin' and lumber makin' for their keep. Dad said he liked the more level ground, which he found in the valley close to the mill. The mill owner's folks was Irish, too. They could talk in the old country speak and understand each other fine. Sounded like music to me when I heard 'em talk. I learned it some, but weren't allowed to speak it at home. We was to learn and speak English like the

Americans we was bein' raised to be, though we added a little mountain to it. It was 'highland talk', as Momma called it. Our folks was from the old country. They talked different after learnin' the English, so that's how we talk, too. The Indians talked different than us 'cause of the Methodist and Morvians and their missionaries.

"I missed you every day, Momma," I said. "I loved bein' on the trail with Dad, but I wished you was there most all the time. I got lonely for you at night. Dad would tell me stories 'bout you and him courtin' and how y'all hunted the woods. It kept me from bein' sad so I could sleep. I loved sleepin' out in the woods with all the nighttime critters and their callin', hearin' the rain on the night cover in the late dark, or fallin' asleep listenin' to the fire poppin'. I liked it somethin' special, Momma. I want to do all that with you, too, and with Dad, Anne, and...Cain." It was a lonely word, his name, just then.

Momma squeezed me a little harder and said, "I am glad you had a good time travelin' with your dad. He is at home in the woods and knows the mountains he loves. It was good that you went to visit Wolf. We have been friends with Dancing Bear and his family for many years. They are as dear to me as my own. Still, I can't figure why Rose would come alone like that. It's not proper for a Cherokee maiden to travel through the mountains without protection."

She doesn't know! Cain and Rose was courtin' and Momma doesn't know! Rose a maiden? Although I still didn't know what that was, I know'd for sure Rose had it. George called her a maiden and now Momma was, too. What was so bad about bein' a maiden? What I was hearin' was that they was ways to livin' with it; sounded like a hard life. I prayed I'd never catch it.

"She come to see Cain, Momma," I near whispered, so as not to let him know I was tellin'. "She told her momma, but Dancing Bear had come here, so he didn't know. She caught up to us on the path just before dinner and told us she'd been followin' all mornin'. George weren't real happy, but he had no choice but to bring her on. She weren't gonna have it no other way and that was for sure."

"Well, I know she's here to see Cain, son," Momma explained. "She's worried. But why would she leave her folks behind and travel most of the way by herself? The woods can be dangerous to a maiden out alone. She knows Dancing Bear is on council now. She has to watch what she does and—"

Momma's words stopped dead center of the trail. She seemed to quit the thought she was on. Her tight hug around me let off some; felt her face lift as she looked over at a sleepin' Cain.

"Oh my," whispered Momma. "She loves him."

I never moved or said a word. I just laid there in her warm lap and watched the flames jumpin', wonderin' what she was thinkin'. It never set with me that she really wouldn't see what was goin' on; kinda sounded like she weren't none too happy 'bout all of it. There must be somethin' outa square about him takin' a shine to Rose. He bein' white could make things outa sorts, but I didn't see it botherin' most folk. They was a bait of white men in the mountains married to Indians, most of 'em Cherokee, so they ought not be any fuss made over what Cain might do. *Was it that we was like family and it made a difference that a way, or was it that my folks didn't want an Indian in the direct family? Surely, that weren't it. Dad liked the Indians and was friends to many, but would he like Cain lovin' on one of 'em? Would he mind havin' her for a daughter? If all that was good, then what was it that was givin' Momma worry?* She should be happy they was close like they was, but somethin' was there, I could feel it.

"What are you thinkin', Momma," I asked. "Are you happy for them?

"It's just that I never realized this had happened. I mean, sure, Cain and Rose—that finishes many questions I've had for a while. The travelin' he's done in the last several moons has been curious, but now those things all make reason. He was visitin' her and not tellin' us the whole truth about his goin'. I knew he was bein' crooked, but I didn't want to believe he would lie. Yet, if he loves her, then he would have no choice but to keep this secret. Dancing Bear would not approve of this before her season's harvest moon, durin' the time of the fallin' leaves. She has brought trouble for him because she is still honored as a maiden. Her clan will not like her takin' fondness for Cain before the time of her becomin' of age," she explained, though it were still a might confusin' to me.

"Momma, what does all this about bein' a maiden mean? I can't understand what all the fuss is over. George was worryin' on it, now you. What is a maiden? And how do you get rid of it? Can it poison folks or stop chickens from layin' eggs, or dry up our milk cow 'fore she freshens? It sounds plumb awful. I hate she's got it. I like her. You need to make it go away. We should call the old medicine woman," I said, clearly bothered by it all.

"Don't be silly, Jeb" she said with a laugh. "Bein' a maiden is not somethin' that's bad. It has to do with the age of a young Cherokee girl. She must first be made available by her father after her fifteenth summer. Then she can have visitors. Young bucks will come callin'. She will be of age this fall season, but not till then. Cain is already callin'. It's up to Dancing Bear to allow it or not. This is why there is concern, because it is not the custom of a Cherokee father to allow any such a thing. A maiden must wait until the time of her comin' of age. Dancing Bear and Rose spoke before he left for home, but I know not what was said. Rose went to the loft and did not speak to me after his leavin'. They are a quiet bunch at times."

"Momma? Do you like it that Cain and Rose are courtin'? Reckon Dad's gonna have it, or is he gonna put a stop to it? And why does Cain have different colored hair than all the rest of us?"

"Cain is a grown man, Jeb. He's goin' on eighteen summers. He makes his own mind now, as I can tell. He's a good son and he works hard. He respects Thompie and me, and he lives by the rules of this house. He's big and tough and God knows he can take care of himself. We've all seen that, so you quit your worryin' and know that all is well," she said, makin' sure I understood.

We both were silent for a while 'fore she spoke again, listenin' to Cain struggle for every breath.

"As for this with Cain, he's in the Father's hands now. We put our trust in the Lord and believe His will done. I believe it the Lord's will to see him through this darkness and out the other side. He's alive and some better, so we will have faith and pray."

"Some better?" I asked, leanin' my head over and lookin' at his gray face. He still seemed near dead to me, so it was hard to think on him lookin' worse. She never did answer my question about his hair.

Sleep took me sometime in the night. I woke 'fore daylight in my bed. I shared a bed with Cain, but his side was empty. He still had to sleep sittin' up tied to the rocker. It was time for me to make my mornin' trip to the outhouse, so I dressed in some homespun, laced up my foot skins and slipped downstairs. It was all quiet in the house and not a soul was stirrin'. Cain was still in front of the fireplace. I was thinkin' he was gonna get cold, 'cause the fire had burned down where only hot coals covered in ash lay glowin' kinda red. The tea kettle had been moved to the hearth. Momma and Granddad's rockers sat still and ghostly while Cain looked asleep. All three rockers sat in the same place as when I was sittin' with Momma earlier. I moved on to the back door. I really had to go.

I'd just finished my business and was walkin' back, when a feelin' come over me like they was somethin' outa place or somebody was near and watchin'. It was just one of those things that you feel and don't pay much mind to, but this one grabbed me hard. I stopped and looked around, expectin' to see George's big face, but he was nowhere to be seen. I wondered if he was still here or if he'd took off. Folks like him don't stay in one spot for long, so I figured he'd headed out. He reasoned Cain was in good hands. Dancing Bear left, so I was thinkin' he did, too. They was still some time left on Dancing Bear's new doin's with the election, and there was plenty of feastin' yet to be done. I would like to be there. I missed my new friend. Me and him could fuss over what to make of all this love mush. I'd much rather be huntin' the bottoms around Wolf Creek with Wolf than runnin' trails with some girl. Didn't make one bit of sense to me.

There weren't much light out yet, but I was plumb troubled by the sight I saw when I got close to the back door. Cain was out and leanin' against one of the locust posts that held up the porch roof. He had a touch of a smile on his face, and his eyes were closed as he drew in a huge breath of cool mountain air. His hands had a quilt drawn up around his throat, keepin' it hung over his shoulders and down nearly to the plank floor where he stood. His feet was wrapped in linen all the way up past his ankles. I knew inside them linens had to be Cherokee medicine herbs, or salve or pitch of some sort. Anne said it drawed up through the feet and helped with infection anywhere it needed.

I watched him take in several deep breaths of fresh air before I spoke.

"What are you doin' up, Cain? Are you feelin' some better, or have you just gone skunk drunk? You need help gettin' to the outhouse? Here, hold on to my shoulder and I will help you keep steady," I said, easin' over to stand by his side.

"Agh, that'd be fine," he said, strugglin' to speak as he leaned against me. "I find my legs are a little wormy with all this goin' on inside. Sometimes it feels like hell's fire inside my chest. I know it ain't right. But this ain't gonna whoop ole Cain, little brother, no, sir. Fever is a strong enemy. Me and him's a-goin' 'round somethin' fierce. Got the Holy Spirit on my side, though. That matters a right smart."

Cain was a whole lot Indian. Cherokee was kinda how he lived. He'd told me many times he weren't feared of the spirit world none; that he'd walked in it many times. He carried a pipe and tobacco everywhere he went. He was smart and figured things out. Dad depended on him a sight. He could do any work needed on mules, and knew the trade when it came time to sell. But Indian was in his blood. He cared little for farmin' crops, 'cept to make provisions.

It was a chore for him to work his way back to the main house. He was mostly makin' it on his own effort, but he was braced against my side near all the way. His arm was now over my shoulder, his quilt laid across my back and neck. I felt the ragin' heat from his body and could smell the musky herbs that were laid in the linens on his feet. He was stronger than he looked. That gave me hope. He walked up the back steps and into the house without me havin' to help him at all. The only thing he needed me to do was to help tie him back in the rocker. He'd grown quite tired from his short trip.

***

Five suns had risen since we got back from Wolf's. Dad and me was workin' on cleanin' up the place from all the damage the storm did. The barn was finished and all the fences were back up. The mules and stock were finally back in their proper pens. We were workin' on clearin' away the big trees what was blowed down. Dad was usin' Jim to drag the logs down to the wood shed, and we were layerin' the brush from the trees into a big pile to be burnt. Cain was some better and had gotten stronger. His color was more toward natural and his breathin' was more at ease. The infection had done its duty, though—he was weak. He had to spend most of his time sittin' on the porch, watchin' me and Dad, as Rose sat by his side. If he felt better, I know'd he'd be helpin'. He didn't look as near death as he had, so I weren't worried as much.

Momma was tendin' to the house and the porches. She'd already scraped what was left of them poor layin' hens off the logs, cleanin' and sweepin' all around the outside. She was inside fixin' dinner. We was all gettin' ready to go in to eat, when the sight of sudden danger filled my bones.

Less than a hundred paces from the house, three full-grown strange Cherokee warriors walked single file outa the woods and straight for the porch where Cain and Rose were sittin'. Each held a bow and had a full quiver of arrows laced across their backs. Dad grabbed a poleax and took off on a run to get between them and the house. Now I know'd what was outa place the other mornin' when me and Cain went to the outhouse.

These Cherokee weren't from Wolf's clan. Their paint was different. They wore their hair short and their clothes was all homespun, 'cept for their foot skins, which were made from cowhide or horsehide and were a dark color. Rose wanted to know their business, so she stood and walked off the porch to stand with my dad. You could tell by the way them Indians looked that this could be bad or good, but she didn't seem to fear.

They wore paint on their leggin's and carried more weapons than just their bows. They were dirty like they'd been travelin' and ain't had a chance to wash. I didn't like their look as they kept walkin' straight at Dad, never breakin' single file, their bows still hangin', but turned up. Two hawk feathers hung from the lead Indian's bow, with only one feather hangin' on the other two behind him. With motion unseen, the leader paused his bunch some twenty or thirty paces shy of where Dad and Rose stood, then walked on closer alone. He stopped dead in front of Rose and never let his eyes look away. It was her he come to see, Dad did not matter to him.

"You are Rose, daughter of Dancing Bear?" he asked.

"I don't know," she said. "I'm not sure who he is. Who is it that is askin' for him?"

"I am Two Suns Rising. I am what your white friends would call a general among our warriors in Yonah. We are from the valley of your mother. We are protectors of our chief and his family and the elders of the tribe. We have come to bring you a gift. We have been to Dancing Bear's. He sent this to let you know we are of no harm to you," Two Suns Rising said as he reached into a small pouch on his side and handed her an old bowl broken off one of Dancing Bears favorite pipes.

This was a pipe she knew her father would want returned for spiritual reasons, so she allowed we was safe with these Indians. She turned and looked at Cain, who somehow had Dad's gun pointed right at the heart of the Cherokee talkin' with Rose. I never saw him move, yet there he was, holdin' a big-bore rifle on these unwanted visitors. You could hardly tell he was ailin'. Made my skin crawl a little bit. I'd seen what that gun does to a deer, and from that range, it would've opened that Indian up like a gutted fish. Rose calmed it all down.

She handed the old pipe bowl back to Two Suns. It was up to him to return it.

"I am Rose, daughter of Dancing Bear. Why would you do this? What gift would allow you to come here to the home of my friends without being asked?" she said patiently.

"The son of our great chief, Coyote Is Wise, would like for you to know that when your father declares you, he would like for you to come to our valley for a visit. He has sent us to inform your father of his intentions." He then turned to the man now standin' next to him to receive a bundle wrapped in leather. He handed it to Rose. "And to inform you, of course, dear maiden," and he bowed.

She unwrapped the bundle and found herself lookin' at a most beautiful carving. She kinda stopped breathin' when the thing come outa the leather; never said a word. She just held it and looked at it, gently runnin' her fingers across the front of it. Slowly, she turned it for all of us to see, as I'd made my way to the center of things.

The carving was real-lookin', an exact look and size of her face, hair and all. Whittled out on a flat piece of split hemlock and rubbed slick, the split side was white that held her face. The outlines of her beauty were cut near perfect. Her eyes was lookin' clear right at you, and the lines on her face put her deep in thought. She was just as beautiful in the wood as she was standin' there with us. Carving was serious stuff in the mountains. Whoever did this one was powerful inspired. This would not be good. It meant somebody else was ruttin' over Rose, and just like old stubborn whitetail bucks, they could be some fightin' goin' on in the fall. Cain was gonna have to get healed up 'fore then.

Chapter Eighteen

The First Moon After the Second Frost

Rose was mindful of the meanin' of the carved face and took it to be respectful to the givers. To not accept it would've been rude of her. Gifts from Indians always had meanin', and not takin' it could've put her mother in a bad way with her folks back home. But she made clear her feelin's about its nature and meanin' to her, which was not favorable for the young Cherokee prince.

"I accept this gift from the son of your Chief, Coyote Is Wise. I am honored by his intentions. I will be traveling to your valley soon to be with my mother as she visits. I will thank him myself at that time," Rose said as the Indian's face grew hard. "But it will be because I wish to visit my family," she said, before puttin' her right palm to her chest. "My heart will still be here in the Choestoe Valley."

That Indian turned green-apple sour when he heard them words. The look on his face was anger mixed with curious. He looked up at Cain, then back at her.

"Maiden, have you given yourself to these settlers? You are not a white breed. You are Cherokee and the granddaughter of an elder. Your father is a leader of the whole Cherokee tribe, put there by the people. You belong to the nation. The Cherokee of the south are your people and you are of them. Your blood is not white. Neither should your sons and daughters be. You must come to your senses." He made his first mistake by movin' to grab Rose by the arm. Dad flinched a bit, but stopped when he heard a familiar noise.

The cockin' of a big bore rifle makes a bone-chillin' sound, and that was just the sound that come clear in the silence that followed the Indian's words. We all turned our heads and stared at Cain. He'd left the rocker this time and was braced up on a porch post, the barrel of the .52 caliber pointed right dead center of that Cherokee brave's chest. It was clear that he was serious 'bout what he was doin'. One bad move outa that Indian and Cain would've gutted him. I'd seen what that gun did to a deer when shot; know'd from that close range even Cain would not miss.

The Cherokee froze on the spot. He stared straight into Cain's eyes, saw what he was facin'. Cain not only growled real low when he meant business, but he had this look that was clear to anyone seein' it that a fight was on the way. The warrior had most likely seen that look before, which gave him warnin'. He raised his right palm and backed away slow and careful-like so as not to stumble or make any wrong moves, all the while watchin' Cain real close, not sayin' a word. He know'd by his look that Cain would drop the flint if he tried anything.

He backed near to where the other warriors stood, then turned on his heel and hightailed it to the woods. You could see him clearin' out through the trees before stoppin' just a few paces in. Two Suns Rising squared up toward us, plumb out in the middle of the trail, and raised his bow arm high over his head and hollered, "Coyote Is Wise will look forward to your visit, young maiden, and I look forward to meeting you again, sick one. Our paths shall cross when you are healed, and we will talk once more. Two Suns Rising will see this square because of your threat to his life this day. We will let the Great Spirit decide what—"

BOOM!

An explosion swapped places with the rest of that Indian's talk as the bow he held above his head splintered just north of the handle. Everyone turned to face the source of the blast. As the smoke cleared from the side porch, there stood Momma, her small bore rifle laid up against a locust porch post, the butt firmly braced against her right shoulder. Ole Two Suns, as I named him, had lit out, but he'd left his bow lyin' there on the ground, hawk feathers and all, cut clean in two by Momma's lead ball.

That was the first time I'd ever seen Momma shoot her gun, had proved all the talk right—she could shoot. It must've been at least fifty paces to where he was standin', and she hit his bow square on. That sure made me mighty proud, though it worried me, too. Indians like that didn't take kindly to gettin' shot at, even though they was talkin' killin'. Talk and burnt powder meant two different things to a warrior, and Momma had just burnt some powder. We'd be seein' these Indians again one day, I was sure of that. That bow was most likely sacred for Two Suns. I doubted he was gonna forget the time he visited Choestoe and met up with the Collins clan.

***

The team of mules I was followin' pulled a straight row, or I'd 'a-been throwed side down from the cuttin' plow they was pullin'. Dad learned his mules from early on how to follow the cut row. They made as straight a row as any mule could if the ground was good. For that, Dad got a sum for his plowin' mules when market time come. You had to take the mules to the farmers south of the mountains to a place called Gaines Town. The main path trailed right through the heart of it. Farmers would come there at different times of the year to buy mules, horses, oxen and such. Dad made most of his yearly poke at them markets. He hit the loggers in the late summer, too, with the mules he'd trained to log. He'd be short this year since Cain was laid up and couldn't help. I was too little to work trainin' the mules, but Dad rigged up a team and had me plowin'. I weren't but barely big enough for gentle mules.

Rose was gone. Dancing Bear and Wolf had come and got her. Nothin' seemed wrong, as they stayed a couple days before leavin'. Cain was doin' some better and his color was back to normal. He was eatin' now and could get out and walk, but that was about it. I was helpin' Dad all I could, but he was doin' most all that was needed to get the corn and syrup planted. Momma and Anne was a sight of help. They laid in the garden so we could eat durin' the cold time. It was most all Dad could do to get the corn in for the grain he'd need to feed the stock through the winter. George come some and helped, a *big* help, too, but you'd get up one mornin' and he'd be gone. That was just the way Indians was. He never left when he was needed, though, and he seemed to show up most when we really needed him to. Just how they know'd things was always strange to me.

Dad got it all planted thanks to George's help. The grain stores would be fine come fall. Cain was mostly better, too; should be full better by harvest unless he found some other way of gettin' hurt, which was always possible for Cain. He'd be healin' up just in time for Killin' Time. Boy, what a time folks had there! Me and Wolf loved that time most of almost any, 'cept for all the work we had to do skinnin' critters and loadin' guts.

Hog Killin' Time, or Killin' Time as folks called it, was a huge gatherin' time when folks from all around would meet up at the south end of Choestoe near Wolf Creek, just east of the England place, and butcher their meat stock for the year. Mrs. England got the word out that she would make sure all stayed the same, even though she'd lost her man. So folks come on and the weather was just right when we got there.

The first settlers had started workin' Killin' Time in the holler near Wolf Creek years before. Over time folks had made it bigger and more handy. It laid at the bottom of the valley, facin' the north side of Blood Mountain. The Englands' log home was no more than half a mile north on the top of the ridge above the camp, but they'd make camp just like the rest of everybody. I had a short wonder about the little chesnut haired girl and if she would be campin' with the widow England.

The place was perfect for meat makin' and laid down low outa the wind on Wolf Creek. It had plenty of flat ground and trees, and the creek ran less than twenty paces of the hangin' shed for fresh water. Burn pits was spread around for buildin' fires under iron pots to heat water for the oak barrels used to dunk hogs in. There was a long shed for killin', hangin' and skinnin' meat made from small, straight pine and poplar logs. It had a good-sized locust post holdin' up a solid log frame with a roof above that was covered in white oak boards, hand split and knot free. There were several heavy beams laid across the inside of the roof frame to hang whole meat critters on, with each havin' their own post under the ends. The flat ground around the creek was perfect for camp. Folks would be there for several days, comin' and goin'. Families would help other families and folks helped each other, which just made it better for all. It would happen durin' the first moon after the second frost of the season of the fallin' leaves. It was best if the families got together, 'cause it took a lot of work to make meat.

Hogs weren't the only meat to be had durin' Killin' Time, but beef and goat, too, and there was a lot of 'em. The effort took many. We had to get it all worked up timely 'fore any flies blowed the meat and set to makin' maggots after the meat was hung for curin'. Music-makin' folk would bring their guitars, fiddles and banjoes to make music every night. Killin' Time was a grand yearly doin'. They was no lack of jugs, neither—corn liquor, brandy, wine, and some folks had beer. Indians would come, too, to trade for pig and beef, though they didn't want much goat since they ate a lot of deer. Wolf and his family would come and help with the killin' in trade for meat and hides of the critters butchered.

Dancin' jigs was cut from the dances of the old country and the Cherokee. Indians would dance and teach folks. You know most of their dances meant somethin'. Singles would feel the spirit and take off on a one-man stomp dance, usually leadin' to the dancer fallin' or trippin' over his feet. Made me and Wolf laugh watchin' the liquor talk.

Mountain dancin' was always the favorite after the jugs got passed around. It would last most all night when the sky was clear and the moon was full. Meat roasted on campfires, where folks gathered, talkin' and tradin' and makin' music. Ideas and ways to do things passed from clan-to-clan, and likewise, stories about folks lettin' those curious know how their neighbor was. Tales of all kinds, good and bad, true and false, made the rounds. It was a time when folks come together, with it came many good memories, same way for me.

Me and Wolf got there almost at the same time. The second mornin' after the frost was when our dads made their minds to go. Most folks did similar 'cause it was the right time. There was a bait 'a folks there when we rode in that mornin', then Wolf's bunch came a while 'fore supper. We made camp not far from where George killed that sow bear what done Mr.

England in—me and Wolf was gonna have to slip up to the barn and check it out for blood and claw scratchin'.

Dancing Bear set his family up in the woods just a short stone's throw away from us. Cain was gonna like that. Rose was with 'em. I figured he'd be visitin' with her. Her time had come, after all, and she didn't have the maiden sickness no more.

Cain had spent the summer healin' and helpin' Dad and me what he could, not doin' no travelin' on account of bein' weak. Rose was helpin' her folks and never came back for a visit. Summers are terrible busy for mountain folk. He hadn't seen her since spring, and he was itchin', you could tell. His mind strayed away after they started settin' up so close by. He tied two knots wrong on mine and his night cover, so it fell in when we went to set the center pole. Before we knowed it, there we was, lyin' under a stinkin' heavy ole cover tryin' to get out. He dropped a load of sleepin' truck off one of the mules; near got kicked in the head when he went to pick it up, moved wrong, and that mule weren't waitin' on that. Then he near cut his own foot front to back splittin' kindlin'. He was lost. Big Jim and the other mules done had their truck took off and was stayin' away from him, too. They could smell the trouble he was makin'. Most of our mules respected Cain, so when he was nervous it made them nervous. Made me nervous, too.

Camp was set and we had a fire goin' when Wolf rounded the corner behind our wagon. The hog and calf we was gonna butcher was tied up to the rear of it. You had to be careful near 'em 'cause they was spiteful. Dad always fattened the meanest of the stock and sold the good ones, but these two was 'bout as bad as they'd come. I kinda felt a sorrow for 'em gettin' made into meat, but then didn't. I remembered how that hog bit plumb through the tail of one of Dad's coon dogs. Got it so Dad had to take his knife and finish cuttin' it off. He always trailed crooked after that. They's mean, but they sure was gonna taste good when the hunger come on. That's just the way things was by nature; a mountain boy took it no different.

Wolf come to our camp ready to get out and explore, and so was I. I looked over at my dad and he nodded, so I grabbed my possibles and we lit out. We ran to the creek first and started flippin' rocks around the edge, lookin' for crawdads and such. We found some small ones and throw'd 'em into the deeper water for the trout to eat, crossed the creek, then wandered up a big holler just east of our camp and found a deer trail that led toward the top of the ridge above the Englands'. It was late in the evenin' and near supper, so we figured to stay down low in our explorin'.

The trail forked after 'bout a half-mile up the holler. We turned south. Another half-mile led us to a place that was very different-lookin' than normal woods. It appeared to be a huge old mudslide with a lot 'a big rocks along the bottom of what looked like the whole end of a main ridge. The main ridges was the biggest of the mountains; would learn later that they was a path to many places and adventures. Wolf and me would travel miles along the tops of them big ridges. Every time was new and excitin'.

The boulders and all laid in a row way longer than a full-grow'd body could shoot an arrow from end-to-end. They looked like they'd just rolled down the mountain and piled up right where they lay. They was all sizes, with some bein' as big as a house, and all the cracks between the rocks was filled with earth. Them boulders was stacked one on another way up over our heads and looked real easy to climb. Moss grow'd most all over, with a few old logs pokin' out and scattered about, near rotted on the ends. Short, stubby ivy bushes had took root around the top edge and along the sides. There was a critter's main trail worn in the dirt that wandered through the huge rocks runnin' top to bottom, bein' higher in the east. It was an open door for Wolf.

"My friend, we need to climb up and see what is to be found here on these old stones. What say ye?" he asked.

I thought for a minute and then said, "Well, we're prob'ly a couple miles from camp. Seein' how it's gettin' on near dark and our folks will have food ready soon, we better save this for later and just head back to camp."

Wolf looked up at Old Man Sun and nodded, "Yes, that is true. For another time, then, since it is growing late. Supper will be ready soon. We will return to camp by the warrior's run. Later we will come and see this place and walk its trails."

We both checked our truck and made sure we had our knives tied on good for the run. This would be my first time to really use the run to travel from one place to another. Far as my knife went, I hadn't know'd till after George got me home from my first visit to Slaughter that Dad took my knife back with him without tellin' me. I never did see the skin house again. I remember thinkin' he would get my possibles, so I weren't really worried. I'd left out without 'em when Wolf grabbed me that first time. Dad was mindful when he saw it all lyin' there with my truck and didn't know where I was. He took me out to the woodshed for that. I got three lashes and a fussin' out 'bout how reckless I was for leavin' it lay around for anybody to get. He explained how special that blade was since it was a gift from a true Cherokee warrior and, most importantly, a friend. Made me feel terrible for a while after, but I did get my knife and possibles back. I promised him I'd never let it outa my sight again when I was carrin' it, and it never was. Good thing for my hide a few times, too. I never told him it was Wolf that caused me to do it or that I had no notion of where anything or anybody was when I woke up that mornin'. I was lucky Wolf thought to grab my foot skins the way he snatched me outa there and up the mountain, so it was no wonder I'd forgot my possibles.

The warrior's run is a true Indian way of travel, be it for battle or just to go from one place to another. Simple put, it's when a body runs at a steady trot for a long ways without stoppin' for no reason. Warriors can cover miles in a day, which durin' times of war it come in real handy. If needed, they could run all day and not stop. Dad said when he was a boy and the war was goin' on, he'd seen Indians run into camp from a long way off and not even be breathin' hard or sweatin' hardly any.

Once we'd checked and made sure our truck was good, Wolf turned to me and said, "I have never heard of this place in stories, Jeb. We will come back before Killing Time is over and walk its trails. It looks like a good place to camp on a walk or hide when the sky becomes angry or if danger is near. We will look for water and a place to shelter, but we must be very careful—the copper backed one and the rattle maker will be there, too. Many may still be prowling till cold time comes. The small ones are working quickly to gather food, and they become careless." He smiled. "Makes the fanged one fat before the cold time makes him sleep."

The trees in most of the woods were big, so small stuff didn't grow much underneath 'em. You could run all day and never scrape a tree, you just had to watch for chestnut burs and such. The trails up high was used most since the mind of the warrior's run is to travel fast from one place to the other. The big ridges are just right for that. They was places you could get caught up, like ivy or grapevines, or maybe a place where a bunch of trees died and grow'd back thick. Them kinda spots was good for deer, but you'd not walk through 'em. On your belly you'd be if you made it through at all, but the edges was good places to hunt.

We finished makin' ready, then he looked at me and said, "I will lead since I am wise to the run. We will trot. Breathe through your nose and stay close behind me. You will learn to lead when you have become a good runner. I am the best of all my family. Even Father follows me on ground near our home. If you become tired and need to stop, I will stop as well and wait for you."

He looked me in the eye for a second then turned and started off. I watched him for a little and then tried to do the same. I felt strange runnin' in the woods since Dad told me not to, but here was this young Cherokee who lived in the woods doin' just that. He didn't even really look like he was runnin'. I trusted Wolf to know what was proper, so I got goin', though it weren't much to doin' it, just trottin'. We was near home 'fore I ever needed to breathe through my mouth. Wolf never opened his that I saw.

We split trails once we crossed the creek and went to our own camps, but made plans to meet up later after supper. I noticed the hog and calf was gone from the back of our wagon when I got back; allowed they was most likely already hangin' on a single tree in the killin' shed, head down by their back legs. Their throats would be cut and the blood would be runnin' off their chins and into a catch pan for blood pie and mush. I never had a want for none of that. Momma only made it for Granddad.

The killin' happened first. The meat would need to hang overnight to get the blood out. George did most of the killin' on account of he wanted to have plenty 'a meat when his walk took him across the river. Made sense, too, since he was the strongest of all the folks there. It only took him one hard lick between the eyes with the back of a poleax.

Durin' supper, I remembered that Indians would start showin' up. They'd most likely start slippin' in durin' the night and would keep comin' and goin' for the next few days. They could smell the blood as the scent blew through the mountains, tellin'em Killin' Time had come. Painter cats and mountain cats would be smellin' it, too, and would be sneakin' around. Most Indians would camp out in the woods away from folks, but some like Wolf and his bunch didn't. Them camped in the woods took care of the cat danger.

They'd show up at daylight and help all day with the killin' and skinnin' and cuttin' up. After supper, they'd come back in their best skins and home spun to trade and gamble and celebrate. They'd stay a while. Most had friends among the settlers, just like we was friends with Dancing Bear and his family. Folks got to be with folks, as this was the only time many of these Indians would be near settlers the whole year, 'cept when they might run into one in the woods. They liked the things of the white man, their jugs, too. They would trade tobacco, Cherokee-made knives, pipes, jewelry and beads for brandy and such. Dad always brought extra mules and would trade with 'em for skins and guns and other things he could use or sell at market in the spring. It was a time of comin' together. There was never any trouble, even though fires stayed lit most of the night and the jugs kept movin'. It was a big time for the Cherokee, a bait of 'em would come. They got meat from raised hogs, and quarters of beef and hides. They met friends, made new trade and boys met girls. All other sorts of business went on at Killin' Time, too. Indians favored it for sure; depended on it for things they needed and wanted. It was a good happenin' for all the settlers and Indians of Choestoe.

Chapter Nineteen

The Spirit Cat

Wolf and me was awake at daylight the next day, seein' as it was our job to help pull skins. We weren't big enough to do much, but we was a lot of help when it come to pullin'. We was part of near two dozen young folk that was made to pull the ropes that were tied to hickory sticks rolled up in the hide of whatever it was we was skinnin'. We'd pull, and folks like Dad would work the knives and peel each critter like an apple without slicin' the good meat once. It was a trick to watch, as the settlers learned it from the Cherokee.

Some Cherokee brought raised stock to kill. Dad always tried to trade for some of their sausage, not that it was better than his, but it was different. He liked it. Nobody ever figured what'n all they used to make it so good, 'cause none of the Indians would let a body know. They kept it secret for some reason; it was just one 'a their ways. It was kinda like Mr. Weaver's tobacco and the secret he had for growin' it. Everybody know'd it come without seeds so he was the only one who could grow it, but somehow he always had seed himself.

Rose and Cain were together the whole time. They helped with the skinnin' by haulin' off the guts and heads and what not since Cain weren't quite done with all his healin' from that bucket hittin' him. All parts of each animal was used 'cept about half of the guts. But with this many animals bein' worked up at once, they was plenty of scraps to be left for the nighttime critters. They'd pull the mule team and the wagon up to the end of the skinnin' shed for folks to dump all the leftover in, and they'd take off. Strange how it took only a half an hour to make the trip for the other two wagons, but sometimes it took well over an hour for them to get back. The last trip they took must've been heavy, 'cause they didn't make it back till after supper, when all the skinnin' and guttin' was done. Momma never worried over it, though.

Wolf and me was the first pullers at the shed on skinnin' mornin'. We wanted to get it done so we could take off to the woods. It was a sight to the eyes to see the long skinnin' shed when they weren't nothin' there but meat critters hangin'. They was over a hundred critters kilt and ready to be skint hangin' in two long rows. Critters and Indians could smell the blood for miles. Everything would happen in its time now since all the killin' was done.

The first day of Killin' Time was when most of the animals was kilt and hung to bleed out. Some folks would come later, so we'd work them in, too. Me and Wolf went explorin' and found the rock ridge, while George done all the killin'. I didn't like bein' there for that. The second and third days was all skinnin' and guttin'. The next few days would be for hangin' before the cuttin' up and quarterin' got goin', which would take a good two days or maybe three. Those days in the middle, while the meat was curin', was for folks to do business and feast, to celebrate bein' together. It could get wild from time-to-time, with George seemin' to always be in the middle of things.

The weather was good and cool that fall, so the meat could hang a whole week. Me and Wolf hoped so, anyway. We got to hit the woods once all the skinnin' and guttin' was done. We weren't needed again till it was time to wash the meat down and pack it for travel.

It was over two miles to the rock ridge from the England place. It didn't take us long to walk, so the sun was barely up good when we made it. The ridge was still there, lookin' almost alive in the mornin' light. One could be tempted to think it could move on its own. The thick-leafed laurel that grew around the edges meant there was water somewhere, we'd just have to find it. We weren't carrin' water 'cause drinkin' springs is all over down low. We figured we'd find one here, too. I'd know'd that much 'bout the woods already. Bears would be usin' the ridge 'cause it was near perfect for the way they liked things. I didn't trust bears. I'd met a few.

Wolf moved around the base and I followed. He stopped when he found a good trail to follow, then raised his hands to shoulder height, palms up, leaned his head back and closed his eyes. He said a quiet prayer to somethin' I didn't know if I'd met yet. I felt the spirit, so I bowed my head and asked Jesus to watch after us. I knew my God was stronger than any of his, weren't worried, just in case he was prayin' to the other. I opened my eyes and he was starin' at me with a curious look.

"What are you doing, Jeb? Who is your prayer to, my friend? Do you know the Great Spirit, the maker of all things? If you do, then your prayer should be for guidance and protection, to show us the path our walk should take. He is our guiding star. He walks with us in the shadows when death is close. I trust Him to care for us in our journey in this world. Is that who your prayer is being heard by?"

"I prayed to Jesus," I answered. "I trust in Him, if that is who you mean."

"It is," he said, then turned to start up the trail. "I am glad we will be together across the river. Paradise will be much better with you there to run the trails with."

We wore home spun over our skins since the weather was cool. The air around the holler was damp as well as chillin', so the extra layer made things tolerable. The rocks had a shine to 'em. You could tell they were holdin' water. We didn't go far till we crossed a small branch and Wolf bent to taste the water.

"This is good water. Have some, Jeb, we may need it later."

I bent to scoop some in my hand when a yellow flash caught my eye. I reached to pick it up and found it to be heavier than most rocks. I allowed it to be a good piece for jewelry or to melt down for musket balls, so I put it in my possibles bag without sayin' anything to Wolf. They was a bunch more layin' there, so I stocked several to take back. I thought to put 'em back in the branch 'cause they weighed more than I cared to tote. But they was real pretty, so I got my back up and carried 'em with me. I saw a bunch more on up the trail in another little branch we crossed. Wolf kept goin' without drinkin' this time, but I stopped to take a minute to explore. He turned and come back to see if I'd seen somethin' he'd missed. I was a few steps up the branch back in some ivy bushes when he come to where I was.

"What do you see, Jeb? Did something catch your eyes, or are you just curious? Tell me, what is it you look for?"

I'd found a little catch 'a water no bigger than a wash tub, which was plumb full of yellow. There were small ones like the ones I'd picked up earlier, then there were some the size of chicken eggs. It was a beautiful sight, but for some reason I figured not to let Wolf know. I had no reason, really, just a gut feelin' that this should stay quiet. I was thinkin' this was gold.

"There is nothin' here. I had a mind to look around some, see the like. This is a strange place. I want to know what is here for when we come back. I feel it is a good place for us." I really did feel pulled by somethin'. Felt good, too.

"It does seem like it might be a good place. There is water and cover. I have also seen the tracks of bear, deer and turkey. Let us travel the trails here today and see what is to be seen. I know the ridges above this little valley. They are thick for the hunt," he said, makin' his way up the deer trail with me followin' behind.

***

Cain slept past daylight. When he come awake Rose was sittin' by his side watchin' him breathe. He was mostly better, but they still worried him 'bout bein' careful. Momma and Rose was makin' it a habit of comin' in durin' the night to make sure the pneumonia was stayin' gone. It set in while he was healin' back in the summer, but he was mostly fine now, they just worried over him. My momma didn't miss much when it come to her kids, so I reasoned Cain was hers for sure. He loved Momma, and him and Dad made sure she wanted for nothin'. Rose loved him, too. There was absolutely *no* doubt how he felt for *her*. It worried him all over. Trouble was, they was a Cherokee prince across the ridge feelin' for her as well. Cain was gonna have to face that one day. The thought made me grin 'bout how that prince did not want to cross blades with a healed up Cain. It would be bad for him when the time come, of that I had no worry. Cain weren't mean in any way, 'cept when he got his back up about somethin', and that prince pinin' for Rose would do it. Cain had only been whopped once, and that was from a mule strap by Dad. He'd never fought Black Oak or Dancing Bear, though.

"Good mornin', Ms. Rose," he whispered with a smile as he sat up in the tent. "You still worrin' over my healin' or are you just comin' over for a visit? Huh? Which is it? Come on, tell ole Cain." He tickled her tummy and she giggled.

"Don't get all high and mighty with me, Mr. Cain Collins. There are plenty of things I could be doing instead of worrying over you. Besides, you will probably just go and get yourself hurt or killed once you are well again, which would make any time spent worrying a waste," she said, tippin' her head back slightly and takin' his hands in hers.

"I ain't bein' all high and mighty, girl. I'm just lovin'," he said, squeezin' her hands right back, firm as he could, searchin' her eyes.

"Love? What do you know about love? Have you loved someone before me? Who was she? I will go and pay her a visit and cut off her hair. She is not welcome here to see you. You have been claimed," she said, grinnin' all the while. She kissed the back of his hand ever so faint as they looked deep into each other's souls.

She moved her face closer to his and said, "As I have told you before, I will be yours until we cross the Great River to be with Jesus and all our ancestors. Do not worry on things that happen across the ridge. My life is with you. Be it here in Choestoe or anyplace else, I will stay by your side, and you will be forever in my heart."

There it was, then. She'd already made her choice on beaus 'fore she ever laid eyes on the Prince. Her and Cain had been through somethin' that binds folks. If Cain had kilt them varmints, and I believe he did, he did it 'cause of the way he felt for Rose. He knew George and Dancing Bear would've took care of that threat, but he loved this person to the soul and felt obliged to render her safe. This I have never doubted.

***

We'd gone 'bout halfway up the pile when Wolf stopped dead in his tracks. He dropped his hand, palm backward facin' me, then crouched to one knee. I did not move 'cept to crouch like he'd done. He searched the ground with his eyes. I wanted to ask but stayed still and quiet. He weren't sayin' nothin', so 'a-course I weren't neither. This was his world, just like the farm was mine. I watched the way he walked the trails and worried on sign. I figured to try and do things the way he did. He know'd danger when it was near. The little we'd been together in the woods taught me that. He slipped back a few feet without ever risin' from his crouch.

"Panther," he whispered, studyin' the rocks above us.

Made me nervous, him actin' so. It was still a couple of years 'fore me and ole Jim tangled with that bobtailed cat on our trip home from the valley with Dad, so I weren't real feared, only just a little. I'd never seen no painter cat. I got to figurin'. I might be in for an awakenin' I weren't ready for. Panthers, 'painter cats' as the old-timers called 'em, could be devils for sure if you run into one that was sore about somethin'. The old Indian woman had told us stories 'bout 'em. They were bigger than the bobtailed cats; could kill a good-sized hog if they could catch one. Mountain hogs are hard to catch. Their tusks can rip right through the soft side of a cat, but the shoats was tender and got eat a right smart. The Indians would trail the big cats when they found their sign and kill 'em. The skins was soft when they cured and it weren't no good havin'em around. They was dangerous for sure.

"Come and see, Jeb," he said, as he looked down and pointed to the ground. "The tracks say this cat is in trouble. See how they move from side-to-side as she walks? Something is wrong. This cat is sick or maybe hurt. Let us follow the trail and see where it went. If it is dead, we can take its hide."

I studied the tracks left in places you wouldn't think to see 'em. The best ones to see was right in the middle of the trail and showed marks where the cat had dug in its claws, almost like it was in pain. Another track was in the soft edge of the trail and was heavy in the back and right side, as if it weren't walkin' right. I could see what Wolf was sayin'—for some reason this cat was most likely fightin' for its very life. Made a body wonder what happened to it since they weren't no blood on the trail.

Wolf took off after the cat with me behind, but we never left the trail till we got right near the top and the tracks was no more. Wolf moved to the north side of the trail and began lookin' for sign. He found nothin' that seemed likely, so he crossed back to the south. After a minute, he picked up where the cat had gone. I figured we were near its den bein' this high up.

"We are close to this cat. I believe it to be hurt or sick," Wolf said in a whisper. He grabbed the handle of his long knife. "Keep your knife pulled and ready. Stay close to me so it will think of us as one big danger. Keep an eye on our trail and listen to everything. I feel it has gone to its home to settle and rest. We must find this place."

I had some concern over lookin' for a painter cat that had somethin' wrong with it, but I figured this is what Indians did for fun, so I kept up while he did his best to follow its trail. I watched our rear and must've saw a dozen different painters slippin' up on us while we was trailin' that critter, but all turned out to be rocks or stumps or dark places. In my mind, from the stories I'd heard, painters was mostly black as they was about to eat you.

Black Death floatin' like a spirit through the woods, they'd say, 'bout how them cats moved. I would shiver as they told how they'd jump from tree-to-tree or rock-to-rock. Oh, and the sound they made when they cried sounded like a scared woman screamin', they'd say.

Oh, how the thought of them tales haunted me as we slipped along, tryin' to find the big cat. "Jesus protect me from claws and teeth," I prayed.

"We need to take different trails to find this cat," Wolf said after searchin' a while with no more sign. "You go around to the east and I will stay to the west. Be careful and keep your eyes open for any sign. We need to find the trail it took before we get too close. Keep your knife in the lead and be ready to fight in case it finds us before we find it. I have only seen a cat like this once before, so I do not know how it will act. I do know that it will be dangerous when we find it, if it still lives."

He headed west around the upper side of the rock ridge, leavin' me to go east. I was alone, they was a troubled mountain cat out here somewhere and I was to try and find where it went. If Momma know'd what I was up to just then she'd 'a-had me home in a minute, but weren't a body around to tell her 'cept me. I weren't comfortable with all this, but if Wolf was lookin', then so would I. Sure seemed a heap 'a trouble for a cat hide.

I tightened my grip on the knife George had give me and started around to the east, quiet as I could. The rocks was hard on my feet as I climbed some of the huge stones to get a better look at the surroundin's. I searched for that cat as hard as I could. After a few minutes, I come to notice how clear everything was. The sounds was all around, but one could only hear 'em if they was listenin' real close, kinda like if you were huntin', which I was.

The owl hoot was not right. The time of day was all wrong. It sounded like it had its head in a hole. I knew right away it was Wolf. When I looked up, he was standin' there wavin' for me to come to where he was. I obliged him. It was nice to not be alone anymore. I figured he'd found somethin'. When I got up to him, it was not what I expected.

The deer was less than half grow'd, its throat ripped open plumb all the way across and it was mostly eat. Some of the front half and all the hams was gone, and the bones was near cleaned. The gut pile was off to the side, like it'd been laid there. The head was gone all the way back to the ears; its jaws and teeth broke all to pieces and scattered about. The legs and hooves looked normal and was just lyin' there, almost like the deer was sleepin'. The kill was fresh, most likely caught durin' the night. But if the cat was hurt, how could it have got a half-grow'd deer? Got me to worrin' a right smart for sure.

"I believe this deer was supper for the cat we are looking for. No two big cats will live near the other unless it is the right time. She must have been hurt this morning or during the night. She is close. Stay quiet," he said, more as a warnin' than tellin' me what to do.

It kinda hit me again just what I was into. I wondered if I'd lost my senses, but then the pull of the hunt rode what it was that bothered me. Right then I started crouchin' and slippin', lookin' and listenin'. Wolf was in front and me in back, only a couple short steps between us. I was lookin' our trail when his fingers on my arm made me stop dead still. He never said a word, just hunkered low to the ground with his knife pointed down the trail. 'God be with us' was all I could set my mind to. I know'd he'd found it.

She looked asleep. Her hide was perfect with the wettest, darkest lookin' black coat you'd ever see. Made you feel like you could put your hand down in it and get black all over your fingers. Her eyes was closed, and her long slick tail was laid out and over her back legs. Her front legs and paws stretched side-by-side out on the ground, just kinda open with the soft pads a-showin'. There was no cuts or blood on her coat, which was thick and smooth like dark syrup. She was beautiful, but she was as dead as the deer we'd found back down the trail a ways. It near made me sad, till my mind come back and I reasoned it was still a mountain cat. They could kill for sure. I would not find it in my thinkin' to be sad for this cat.

I had no way 'a knowin' what Wolf was thinkin'. The look on his face was spiritual as he hit his knees and started singin' a soft quite song in Cherokee. I did not know one word of it, but I hit my knees, too, starin' at the fallen body on the ground in front of me. It was a strong feelin' what came over me, thinkin' on that cat. I never know'd there was such a critter in all the mountains. The old folks' stories made me see 'em like they was evil, but this cat was pure. You could feel that it was a piece of the woods, just like the trees and rocks and water. It had life. Wolf was right, her skin would be a proud thing.

Wolf finished singin' and walked around to the front end. He reached down to his right and picked up a small stick and tossed it on the head, but there was no movement. He poked its paw with the tip of his long knife and got no curl or quiver. The cat was dead. Sad again, as it kinda felt like a part of the woods just died and would now rot away. Made me curious to wonder what God needed with this painter cat, anyway.

He grabbed the front right foot and rolled the cat over. After he rubbed his hand over the side and rear of the cat, he motioned for me as he said, "Come to the head and help me take its hide. I am too small to do this proper without you. We will need to be very careful, because this is a special gift. The Creator does not let out such beauty very often. If you look close, there is no hole in this hide. To the old ones, that makes this spiritual. There are no rips or tears, which is also spiritual and has meaning. My grandmother will find this skin a special place. She will use it in her healing. Your name will be in the song together with mine as they sing of our bravery around the fire. My friend, you should have been born Cherokee, of that I am sure, but for some reason the Great One made you white. You got cheated, that is the way I see it."

Wolf made a sign with the first two fingers of his left hand and pointed at his eyes. That meant he was strong in what he was sayin'.

He told me to hold its legs apart as he started at the chin and worked his way down its throat with the back of his blade, slidin' along the meat under the skin. He slit it from chin to tail and then along the inside of each leg till he got to the spot where the leg bones and the feet come together. He stuck the point of his skinner into the leg joint and, with one firm flip of his wrist, cut the foot clean off the body. He laid his knife aside and started easin' the hide off with his hands, workin' his fingers 'tween the skin and the muscle. Took a while, but I could see how it come clean a lot better; there weren't a chance of cuttin' into the back of the hide and ruinin' it. Once we finally got the thing naked, I noticed the hide was a lot bigger when it come free of its body. It was gonna be a chore to carry back. We cut a couple of small oaks and used them to help tote it. Worked good, too, 'cept it made your shoulders sore. She was a full-grow'd cat, so we had to stop many times on the way back to camp. She was heavy.

We was 'bout halfway back to camp when Wolf and me just had to have some water. We stopped at a small branch under a shady place at the turn in the trail and dug us out a drinkin' hole, then sat back to let it clear. I was laid back on a good-sized laurel, and he was leaned up on a moss covered rock. I guess with the burdens of the trip bein' all it was, a body could give out a little, so we did. We flat fell asleep right there next to that branch without so much as a taste of its cool water.

It didn't seem like it while we was doin' it, but it'd been a chore to find and take that critter's hide. Totin' it back weren't no better; it was gettin' heavier as we went. It was past midday and nearin' supper, but we never bothered to eat, we was so worked up. We should've thought better of where our food was.

It was an eatin' sound what woke me. Wolf was awake and crouched on his haunches, lookin' back over toward the hide. I wanted to ask what was there he was starin' at, but he turned and motioned for me to be quiet. I had to know, so I eased up on my knees and kinda walked on 'em over to where he knelt, not makin' a sound while the small sticks on the forest floor dug into my knees.

My heart melted like butter on a hot biscuit as I looked on what had woke me. It was a panther cub. Not just any little ole barn cat kitten, but a full-born mountain cat cub. Supper was gonna taste extra good tonight, since it was workin' on the last of the deer jerky we'd packed. Wolf's food pouch was turned inside-outways, nothin' was in it. The cub had eatin' six big cuts. We'd just been robbed by what was most likely a three-month-old orphaned Black Panther. I hoped that was not gonna to be part of the story song.

It was black as night, just like its mother, pickin' our only food while we was asleep. It paid no mind to the skin we'd took, but it did take a shine to Wolf's pouch. I watched with a growl in my belly as it swallowed the last bite of our food for the day, then pounced on the pouch, near rippin' it apart wantin' more. Wolf weren't gonna have that, and told that cat so right then.

"Stop that cat," he near yelled, as he stood and walked out toward it. "I will not let you tear up my pouch and eat my food. I am sorry that you have lost your mother, but that is not my fault. Now, I want my pouch, so move away."

The cat did nothin'. It stood its ground and acted like it weren't gonna give nothin' back. Wolf kept walkin' toward it but it never moved. He stopped a few steps short, starin' at each other for what seemed like way too long. Finally, the cat started to move. I thought it was leavin', but all it did was ease closer to Wolf. I swear to this day it looked like that cat was wantin' more food. It sat back on its haunches, put its paw in the air, and looked up at Wolf like it was askin'. It opened its mouth, leaned its head back, and let out a sound that would freeze your blood if you ever heard it alone at night out in the woods. Wolf jumped back. This happenin' just weren't right.

It weren't afraid of us none; that's what made it mostly not right. This cat ought to 'a-run the minute it knew we was there. This would be a spiritual trip if ever we went on any. Wolf was born in Panther Cave, and here was this cat with no family to call its own—a painter cat born in the mountains—now left to try and make it without a mother to feed it. I reasoned without much thought what was comin' next. Wolf was gonna take this critter in, and I could think of nothin' better. Very few Indians ever had their spirit totem as a friend and family member. This could end up just like that by the way things was lookin'.

"If this cat follows us home, I will raise it until it is old enough to return to the place of the rocks. I will call her Spirit, as she has the spirit to survive and the courage and cunning to walk the trails. We will be family. We will run the trails together with our friend, Jeb Collins," he said, lookin' and pointin' at me like he was explainin' the way of things.

With that said, he moved up beside the cat and grabbed his pouch, then motioned for us to get goin'. The hide would need tendin' to and we was both hungry. We raised up the oak poles and put 'em back on our shoulders, then started down the trail back to camp. I was curious to see if the cat would follow us back. I was learnin' to believe in the ways of the Cherokee and the ways of their world livin' in the woods. I believed from what he'd said that if the cat followed us home, his words would hold true, the cub would become part of our lives. I liked that idea and kinda hoped it did, but I was worried about havin' a full grow'd panther comin' and goin' around folks and critters. That could be trouble for sure.

We was about to find out. After it sat there for a little bit tryin' to figure out where the food pouch went, it come to notice bein' left behind. The cat jumped up and ran to catch us, while stayin' back a ways. We was carrin' its momma's hide and it was followin' us back. Life was gonna get interestin' when we got to camp. Spirit was gonna cause a big-time pot-stirrin' if any of the folks learned of her, and my friend Wolf was gonna be in the middle of it, which meant I was gonna be in the middle of it. I was not gonna leave my friend and his panther. We know'd the truth. This would work out for the best, or so we hoped!

Chapter Twenty
_____

The Old Ones Danced

The smell of campfires was strong, bein' that the air was driftin' up the holler dead straight in our faces as we made our way back down the trail. The cub was gettin' a few whiffs of it, too, and weren't likin' it none. She was a ways behind and got a little farther and a little farther the closer we come to camp. That strong nose of hers worked good for her to be so young. Her instincts was those of a purebred mountain cat. Trouble was near for her and she know'd it. She didn't know what trouble was really, but she could feel the danger. By the time we crossed the creek to camp, she was hid. Wolf grinned as he turned to see her gone.

"She is cunning, that one. She hides and watches and learns. We will see her again, I feel it." He said this to his own self as much as to me.

I reached out, grabbed him by the shoulder, and asked, "My friend, what will Dancing Bear say on this? This may worry him and my dad a sight. Some will fear Spirit. Some are gonna want her skin. She must stay away."

"You are wise, Jeb. We will do what we can to help her, but Spirit's trail is her trail. We are only a part of the walk. We will watch and tell folks if the time comes, but for now we must keep this with us and protect her if we can by keeping a hawk's eye for her movements," said Wolf, knowin' much more 'bout what was goin' on than I did.

I was scared for the cat. Any Indian would love her hide, and keepin' it might be a chore for her and us. It would be up to her doin' to stay safe where she was now. Studyin' on it some, I come to realize it might not 'a-been right to let her follow us back, bein' that a whole mess of Cherokee was in the valley and all around for Killin' Time. Weren't a real safe valley for the likes of her. She would have to stay on her most cautious to survive the next few days. I was gonna be happy if she made it.

***

The fuss over that cat's hide was plumb wild. Once the word got around to folks, most just had to touch it. Dancing Bear and George had it stretched between two trees with a pole up the back to hold the head in place and the center flat, with the tail runnin' down the pole, its tip stoppin' just short of the ground. This hide was spiritual to the clan and had to be done just so. Dancing Bear took charge over it the second we carried it into camp. Wolf never said a word. I was just proud to be gettin' it off my shoulders. The two warriors that fetched it could've carried the whole thing alone, but they honored us by carrin' it like we did.

The old-timers of the Cherokee bunch stayed and prayed around the thing. They rubbed their knotty, leather-backed hands from the top of its head to the tip of the tail, speakin' Cherokee words I'd never know. They looked at its teeth and pulled its tongue out for a real close look. They checked its paws and tasted the dirt under its claws, opened its eyes and got closer still, like they was lookin' into its soul…maybe they was. Weren't long till one of 'em built a small fire and started a smoke. I figured when the tobacco pouches come out that they was stayin' a while. All their pokes must've been full of Weaver tobacco, too. It smelled different than normal-grow'd tobacco.

Near dark, folks was back to their own camps or settled in for a visit at other camps, and we was all done eatin'. The old ones still had a fire down in the trees where the hide was stretched. Dad and Dancing Bear went to sit by the main campfire to smoke. Me and Wolf went to see the hide—or whatever else was hangin' around there.

It was still light enough to see, so we found our way no trouble. It was what we found there that could be trouble. The cat was sittin' not five steps from the old-timers and their little smokin' fire. Wolf grabbed me by the arm and pulled me to the ground in behind some young maple trees still a ways from the hide. He stared hard at the strange happenin's goin' on right in front of us before sayin' anything.

"Spirit sits on her back legs," said Wolf. "This means she knows there is no danger for her. The old ones are talking to her. If I am right, soon they will dance. They are visiting the spirit world and speaking to those across the river through her. We must watch closely, for few ever see something like this."

I could not find a word to say. It was like the wind had gone from my lungs and I was weak. My legs was shakin', and I felt cold and kinda alone for some reason. I watched and could not believe what I was seein'. They was a purely wild critter sittin' with a bunch of old Cherokee men, and they was talkin'. The smoke from the pipes and the fire curled around her head, but she didn't care none. Seemed just so with them and Wolf, but for me it was plumb strange. Spirit would raise her head and lower her chin at different times in the talk, but she never left from sittin'. Once, she even scratched the back of her ear with her left rear paw, like nothin' was outa sort. We sat not makin' a sound and watched. This was a time we would remember always, and I wanted to miss none of it.

It was gettin' harder to see as the time hurried on, but we could still tell when they all rose and, one-by-one, walked over and bowed to Spirit. She was still in her sittin' stance, only now her head was bowed low. Each man moved to his right after bowin'. One began a soft chant as they circled the young cat and started dancin' real slow. They turned in little circles as they made a big circle plumb around her. Wolf know'd they was gonna do that.

The dancers had gone round her maybe a half dozen times when she stood and started goin' round in circles herself. She held her head high and was dancin' if I'm breathin'. There was no doubt she was dancin' right along with them old men. I was seein' it with my own eyes, for sure. She never left the inside of the circle. The dance went on for several minutes 'fore the old men finally hit their knees exhausted. They placed their hands on their legs and bowed their heads, while Spirit slipped outa the circle and started walkin' around 'em. She smelled each dancer and nosed her way through, stoppin' on about the third time 'round to put both her front paws on the back of each one she passed. It didn't seem real, but as soon as her paws landed solid on their backs, they fell over dead. What in this world was I watchin'? This cat had just killed four old men, and the last one was just squatted there a-waitin'. My look of shock must've let Wolf know I was scared near to death. He understood my worry and smiled.

"They are only sleeping, my friend. The world of the spirits lives in our dreams. What we just saw will be spoken of as if it was a dream. We can never let anyone know we saw this or it will show poor respect to the old ones. Stay calm, their dream is ending," he said, tryin' to make this straight for me. I was still worried a right smart.

She pawed the last old-timer and he fell over like a dead man. She then made another circle around the sleepin' old warriors, even crawlin' up on 'em and walkin' around a bit, stoppin' to smell each one again as she went. It was near the end of her visit to the last man that she stopped, eased back down on the ground, and turned to look straight at us. Did she know we was there? Had she known the whole time? What was goin' on? My heart was beatin' so hard it felt like it was gonna bust. I was wishin' Dad was with us.

She started walkin' toward Wolf, stoppin' maybe ten paces short. She stood up high on her back feet as she bent her head toward the sky and let out another of those screams like from before, her right paw reachin' toward the sky. I near wet my skins I was so scared. All five of the elders jumped up from the ground like they'd been kicked. Wolf was already talkin' in Cherokee, his left hand raised and his knife drawn in his right, blade up. I thought about prayin', but I didn't know if God wanted to hear this. It didn't seem like somethin' a body would want to worry Him over, critters actin' crazy and Indians fallin' asleep. 'Sides, I weren't sure God would believe me. I figured best not to waste His time. Likely as not, I'd scratch me up another sin mark if I did tell Him. I didn't figure to tell no folks, neither. They'd all figure me out of mind and scrambled like an egg. Who on this earth would believe me, anyhow? Best just kept quiet. Of course, Wolf saw it different, bein' Indian and all. I knowed a story would come outa this for sure. How could it not?

Spirit let down to all fours with her head high and her tail swishin' in slow, steady motions. She was ready for whatever come her way, and as of right then, it was silence. Me and Wolf was silent, the old ones were dead quiet. And in an empty way, even the woods had gone quiet. I never wanted to hear that scream again as long as I walked the trails of Choestoe, it truly was heart-knottin'. It come to me that she was only a few months old. I wondered what it would've sounded like if she'd been full grow'd and let out a cry such as that. They weren't a critter in the whole holler makin' noise—she'd scared 'em so at just her size. I would have to ask Wolf later why she needed to do all that hollerin'. She might've been scared, but she sure didn't look it. Looked plumb royal standin' there like that. Queen Spirit was what he should've named her.

The old ones made no motions or acted worried in any way. It was as though they were meetin' a friend on the trail. The cat turned from us and walked straight back toward where they was standin'. Just as she made by 'em, she jumped to a full-on run and headed up into the woods. She was gone so fast it was like she was never there, just a spirit blowin' through the trees. I looked at Wolf, who seemed to be studyin' what just took place, watchin' her back trail. The only thing she'd left behind was questions. I looked to see how the old ones were doin'. There was no sign of 'em. Even their little fire was cold.

We moved on to the hide without a word between us. It would take some time 'fore we'd thought enough on what just happened to talk it over. The spirit world the Cherokee lived in was a sight different than the spirit world I lived in. I'd seen their world come to life, just as I'd seen my world alive, too. Jesus was as real and alive to me as the sun comin' up in the east and the cool waters of the Notla flowin' north. I didn't think it possible for a young'un like me to come to mind over what we saw. I wondered if I was asleep, too. Seein' the beauty in the hide brought me back to the real world.

Wolf stared at the skin for a little bit, then ran his hand down each leg as he said, "My thoughts are about what killed this animal. She has no wounds on the outside, so I would think the inside is where the trouble was. We should go back there with the rising of the sun and back trail her until we find what caused her to cross the river. It is strange."

We were both tired, so we went back to our camps to sleep. Momma was sittin' in her rocker by the fire smokin'. Dad was nowhere around when I got back. He always brought her rocker when we had to camp. I went to sit by her bein' that I know'd she smoked. Dad knew it, too, and didn't really mind, but she didn't care to enjoy her smoke with folks about. I looked around, but Cain was nowhere in sight, neither.

She started talkin', the pipe never leavin' her teeth. "Well now, Jeb, I'd sure like to hear the story of how y'all come to have that hide. I was plenty worried for you bein' gone all day and then nearly late for supper. Cain, I knew was with Rose, your father with Dancing Bear, and Anne was with Old Mother. I was alone in camp, not knowin' where my little one had gone. Seems he forgot to tell his elders just what he was goin' to be doin' all day. It's okay, though, because I just talked with the Lord and told Him to look out for you. He allowed it'd be fine, so I ended my worry. I knew you'd be back when you got hungry."

The smoke from her pipe smelled sweet mixed with the smoke from the campfire. She would most likely sit right where she was till Anne made it home, but she'd not wait for Dad, of course. He might not come in for a day or so. Meat was just hangin' and they was Indians all about, so they was no tellin' what he'd get mixed up in or when he'd get back. She didn't worry over him like she did me and Anne. Cain and Rose was a different type of worry that I figured only mommas could understand. I left it at that. They could stay gone for a while, too, and it would not be a surprise to her. Momma said young love in the mountains was as close to Heaven as God would allow, but I was older 'fore I ever took thought with all that. Meant very little to me then, but for Cain it took hold and had meanin'. He'd been pointed toward Rose for several seasons. They was young, but their love was aged like good sharp cheese. You could see it when they was walkin' and talkin'. They'd get close and kinda stumble over one another's feet or sway back and forth, near runnin' into stuff like trees and porches. Foolishness to me, walkin' like that, when you can make it much better by your lonesome and be faster at it, too.

"I'm sorry I worried you, Momma. I swear to tell you 'fore me and Wolf go off anymore. We was just gone on a walk to see what there was to see. Well, Wolf crossed the trail of a painter cat just after daylight. He could tell it was hurt, so we spent the goodly part of the day tryin' to find her, and—"

"What?" she said, jerkin' the pipe from her teeth. "You went lookin' for a hurt panther? What in the world were you thinkin', Jeb? Hurt critters are dangerous if you get crossed up with them. That cat could've killed you if you'd walked up on it still alive. Would've happened quick, too. You promise me you'll not do that again, or I'll worry more next time you're gone. I figured you to have more notion than that, Jeb."

She was bein' very calm, but I could tell she was put-out a right smart, so I told her I'd mind better next time.

"I won't go after no injured critters till I get bigger, Momma, I promise." I thought that would settle it with her, but boy, I was wrong again.

"Bigger?" she asked, a little less calm now. "Not bigger, Jeb. Not ever is what I'm tellin' you. Cain should not even be doin' those things, you hear me? Why pull a lion's tail if it don't need pullin'? Use the smarts God gave you and don't mess with danger if it's where you don't have to. Life can end in many ways in the mountains. You've got to watch them all if you expect to make it. That's what we learned as we grew up here. Dad, taught by the Cherokee, made us learn the woods and how to stay clear of the things that can kill you. Injured critters and momma bears was some of the worst, he'd say. You mind me and always be careful of critters in the wild."

She stopped and looked at me real curious-like right in the middle of our talk, almost like she was rememberin' a thing from the past, "It may be time to teach you to shoot. Could save you before long if we did. I'll talk to your dad."

We sat up late talkin' 'fore Anne come back. Her and Old Mother had been workin' the creek and learnin' plants and what uses they all had. She was makin' a good healer, and her only fourteen-years-old. She'd be fifteen 'fore long, then I'd reckon the bucks would start comin' over to court. They'd already been over to help Dad with the mules and farm chores and stuff, just to get to stay for supper. I didn't like studyin' on that. Cain and Rose was all a body could figure on, bein' there was a Cherokee prince just across the main ridge of Choestoe waitin' for his time to come callin'. The visit durin' the last spring was still a visit. More would surely come. Weren't no laws against him comin' to call till Rose made her mind. Cain know'd the rules as good as any, as he was about the best at breakin' most of 'em when it come to Rose. He could only wait and see how she would do when the Prince comes to call. I figured it all for a fight, which would be bad for sure. A Cherokee prince raised for battle could make a good match for Cain, but I doubted it 'fore I really thought on it much. He was strong as Samson, tougher than a bear's hide and mean as a boar when riled. When and if that prince come callin', Cain would be riled no less than ever. We all know'd it, too.

Anne sat by me and chewed a weed that helped with sore muscles. Dog Hobble, she called it, after she said the Cherokee name, Du shu ga un sti ya. She was teachin' me the plants so I could help her gather. Old Mother was gettin' slow in her gatherin', so we'd help some, but Anne did most of it. It was nice to have her learnin' all the healin' ways, but it took up most of her time. Folks would be dependin' on her when Old Mother could no longer travel. She rode the mule Dad give 'em most all the time now; couldn't walk far enough to gather the right plants or bend over to take 'em if her eyes even let her see 'em. If it was the roots she needed, she got to where she left some in the ground 'cause they'd not be dug out proper. She was gettin' old, so Anne was doin' more and more. Anne weren't gonna do no different, though. She was called to it.

"Old Mother was glad to see the panther hide you and Wolf found. She said it is a gift from the Creator. If they give it to her, she will pass it on to me for healin' powers when she crosses over to where Jesus is. I want to hear the story of how you came to have it tomorrow, when I am not so tired. I have had no sleep in the last two days learnin' from her and helpin' with the healin', so I am gonna lay down in our tent and get what my body needs. Good night, Momma. I will help with breakfast in the mornin', if you will just wake me at first light. See you in the mornin', Jeb," Anne said.

"I am so proud of her," Momma whispered as Anne left the glow of the fire. "She has worked so hard and will be a most important woman to the folks of the mountains when she learns all Owl can teach her. All folks will come to know of her trade, both us and the Cherokee. She is touched by the spirits and knows the plants even better than I do. She will help lots of folks when her day comes, I know it. It's just who she is."

"Do you believe in the spirit world, Momma?" I asked. She looked at me with a wonder. "I mean the one the Indians walk around in and talk to animals in. The world only they seem to see; the world they talk about in their stories; the world where they see their folks that's died."

"I do believe in the Spirit world, Jeb, where Jesus is King and all other things are under His command. I do think the Indians believe in their spirit world, but to me it is a gathering of all that is throughout the mountains. The mountains have ways which are divine in nature. So yes, I do believe in their world if it includes my Savior."

Momma was headstrong over Jesus, 'bout how He walks with us all over. She'd not see it no other way. She know'd they's power in the Blood and it's there for the havin'. The love she said it took for Him to die for us all is greater than any bad this old world will lower on us; that the bad folks need to watch out. 'One day every knee will bow.' You didn't want to get her started if you didn't really want to hear it. She'd tell you straight up how she felt: "The Blood is what it's all about. You've gotta be washed in the Blood of the Lamb." Lot of times she'd burst into singin' after sayin' somethin' like that concernin' the Lamb.

Made sense what she said, so we left it at that. We was both tired, so we tucked in for the night without Dad. She'd learned durin' Killin' Time many years before not to wait up on him if he left the night the meat started hangin' or she might not sleep for a day or two. She figured he'd not be back, so she asked me to lay where he would've for the night. It was fall of the year, and the nights had grown cool. I'd long ago quit sleepin' with my momma, so it felt good to be back with her.

Wouldn't be long till I'd be too old, but for now it was real nice. Dad could just stay gone another day or two and I'd not mind. I didn't get to be with Momma as much as I used to back when I was little. She told me many times I was her favorite, but I heard her tell Anne and Cain the same thing. She loved me and them with all her life. After talkin' with her by the fire, I could see how the way I was learnin' to live could worry a body. I would need to be more careful about runnin' with Wolf. The Cherokee lived on the edge of danger, where normal folk tried to stand clear of. It was a life I was growin' to like, and I had no choice in the matter once I studied on it. I was learnin' from Wolf and his family that to live like a Cherokee, one had to be brave with pure thoughts from the heart. I prayed I would live it right.

***

I didn't wait for Wolf the next mornin'. I packed some food and my possibles 'fore first light and went to his camp to wake him this time. I'd told Momma 'fore sleep got us what we wanted to do, so she know'd where we'd be. He woke the second I touched his arm, know'd in a split thought what I was doin' there. He jumped up, grabbed his pouch and knife and we hit the trail to the rock ridge again. We was awful curious 'bout how that cat came to be dead. Wolf allowed it died from hurt to its insides. I figured he was right. Weren't no marks on the outside; we'd seen that hide all over and it was spotless and near perfect. Strange it bein' there though.

Wolf's oldest brother, Moon Shadow, stopped us 'fore we reached Wolf Creek and wanted to go, too, so they was three of us goin' back this time. He was a little older than us, but I liked him a sight. He was quiet and never said much, whereas his younger brother, Fox Running, was a talker. He was a good hunter and took his bow almost anyplace he went travelin' in the woods. He would go on a hunt and stay gone for days, takin' game for folks who couldn't hunt for themselves. The old Cherokee he took meat to gave him many gifts from the old times. He said he hunted for 'em 'cause Jesus wanted him to. I never doubted him with none of that.

The trail was easier to find this time since we'd wore it down some goin' in and out. The weather was the best it could be, clear and cool with a slight breeze sitrrin'. Wolf could smell the woods and sensed things I didn't. Shadow was doin' the same. Their noses would rise to the breeze; they could smell what was ahead. I figured I'd need to learn to do this, so I tried my stay at it. All I got was a cold burnin' inside my nose and frost in my lungs. Wolf was gonna have to teach me that trick for sure.

It was Moon Shadow that found the camp. He'd got to followin' behind a good ways and off the trail up high, hopin' we might jump a deer or such, then he'd get on its track. We knew it was a find, 'cause he hollered for us to come up to where he was and take a look. It was almost right above the place where Wolf had first found the cat's tracks crossin' the trail. Cherokee camp for sure, but not made by any of the clan from Choestoe. It was an overnight camp with seven in the bunch. They was one main sleepin' spot in the middle, with six spread out around it. The sleeper in the middle must be the most trouble, since his was near their little fire. They'd done nothin' to try and hide they was there, neither. The way they'd left the camp and the moccasin tracks around the fire clearly showed they was from a different bunch of Cherokee than what come from Choestoe.

Chills went down my spine as Moon Shadow said to Wolf, "Little brother, the valley has visitors. We must follow these tracks to see who it is that has entered our land. These Cherokee are not family nor of our clan. You will go back to camp and tell any warrior you find. I will wait here for them. Go now and do not come back with the warriors, as they will find me. I have a mind I know who this is. We must find them and ask them why they are here. Now go, and do not waste time," he ordered.

We left for camp without a word on his command. He would've took his bow to us if we'd 'a-said anything. He must've figured this could be bad. There was no doubt what we was lookin' at; we all know'd it. The story of Rose's visit by her momma's folks was told around many fires over the last few moons, and Cain was liked among the Cherokee clan in our part of the country. Some knew other secrets, too. My mind settled on a thought that raised the hair on the back of my neck and made my gut knot up. Cain was gonna need to get healed-up whole quick, now that the Prince had come to Choestoe.

Chapter Twenty-One

The Prince

Killin' Time was over and folks had gone their way once all the meat was cut up and packed for travel. Two warriors met Moon Shadow up at the rock ridge. They followed the visitors' trail east, but the trail left the valley after turnin' south, and no folks was ever seen. It was Cain's thought that it was the Prince lookin' in on Rose. Momma and Cain let the last bunch know how we felt about their type comin' for a visit without bein' wanted. Them bein' here made sense, though...and they'd be back.

Wolf weren't around when them Indians come to our place. But when I told him of it, he explained it all to me. The mask was meant to speak for the Prince. It was his way of lettin' Rose know he wanted to visit. Since she took it, he was now thinkin' she was expectin' him to call. The way the Prince was figurin' it, he was near courtin' Rose on account of her acceptin' his gift. Didn't matter that she took it outa respect, but took it she did, and that made him think she had a shine on for him. His bein' a prince and such wouldn't mean a thing to Cain. It was my thinkin' that the Prince ought'ta mind his trail and just let it go. I doubted he would.

It was nice to be home on the farm. The first thing I did after we stored the meat in the smokehouse was to look in on Peter, make sure all was good with him. Dad wouldn't let me take Peter to Killin' Time. He was teachin' me to work him, breakin' him to plow and pull. Peter was smart, so it wouldn't be long till he learned how to gee and haw, then he could go places with me again. That was somethin' I was waitin' on so I didn't have to walk everywhere. Dad still hadn't give him to me full, but I know'd he was. I'd be turnin' ten next winter. I needed me a mule for sure. Peter was from the same Jack as

Big Jim, so I reasoned they was brothers in a mule kinda way. He was gonna be big, too. His feet was already near as big as Jim's.

Weren't much to supper that night. We was ever last one of us tired. Momma, Anne and Rose all went to bed soon after we got home. For some reason, Rose had come with us rather than go to her place. Dad and Cain went out for a smoke. When they was done, Dad went to bed, too. Us kids never found out what he was into them nights away, but he sure was tired once we got home. My eyes was heavy and burnin', too, but still know'd sleep would not come for me for a while. I wanted to study on all that happened at Killin' Time, think more on what'n all me and Wolf did. The rock ridge would be a place I reasoned we'd be back to one day. Killin' Time would come next fall, so there we'd be.

Spirit was a question in my mind, one I knew Wolf was studyin' on, too. We'd seen her late the evenin' 'fore we left the England place. She seemed to be watchin'. I wondered if she followed Wolf home. Could be she might've had a lead to follow. Wolf was a sneaky one, that was certain. He wanted that cat to follow him home, then end up stayin' close by. Indians was just like that.

I was sittin' by the fire when Cain come back in. He wondered over and sat in Granddad's rocker next to me on the right, the healin' from the bucket still kinda showin'. He was better all the way around, though, and Anne said he was healed. Cain took it as gospel and walked all the way home from Killin' Time after we left with the meat, but he had to rest once home. He weren't able to help store the meat, but had to sit on the back porch and drink some cool water from the springhouse. Still, the walk had been good for his lungs. He was near white when we rolled into the backside of the house with Jim pullin' our wagon, but he made it.

He'd be back strong in a few days. His appetite had come back 'fore we ever left for Killin' Time. My, how that boy could eat. I swear he could eat a dozen eggs for breakfast if Momma would cook 'em. She wouldn't do it, though; said it'd make him sick. He'd still eat plenty, but that's 'cause Momma always had plenty cooked. You could never figure when a body would come by in need of a meal—Cherokee, mostly, either out on a walk or travelin', but white strangers and blacks, too. I was proud of them black folks comin' by, then I know'd they was free. Some of 'em lived with the Cherokee. Dad told me 'bout how some folks was greedy and they'd buy a body for money and work it near to death, beat 'em with horsewhips if they done wrong. I never could get my thoughts around a body ownin' another body, but it was legal and folks had 'em down south of the mountains. I never heard of or know'd of any in Choestoe, as folks did their own work to get by where I was raised. Dad taught us that Jesus died for everybody and all folks ought'ta be free to do as they wanted, but greed and lazy are a bad bunch, and some folks tend to give in to their weaknesses, he said.

"You alright, little brother?" Cain asked, pullin' the rocker up closer. "Everybody else left for sleep, and here you are by the fire alone. Somethin' worryin' on you?"

"No, nothin' really. I was just thinkin' on all me and Wolf did while we was at Killin' Time. I need to take you and show you the rock ridge we found up the holler from the England place. It's where the black painter lived and...died. I found these, too," I said. I reached to the hearth for some of the gold pieces I'd picked up outa the branches up there. I'd cleaned 'em up some and laid 'em out for Dad to look at. I was hopin' he could melt 'em to shoot in his guns.

"Jeb!" Cain said. "Do you know what that is? Do you have any idea what you've found? You must keep this very quiet and not tell a soul. This is gold!"

"Gold?" It didn't look like the gold coins I'd seen of Dad's, other than that strange color it had. "What is gold then, Cain? Can't Dad use it in his guns for shot?"

"Ah, of course he could, but don't be foolish, young'un. This here is what they make real coin from. It has value just like it is. Remember Dancing Bear tellin' us about it on our way home from fetchin' him for Dad when Lucky got killed? Don't you remember askin' me if gold was what we found up under the waterfalls? This is it, only these are much bigger than the little chips we find." Cain got up and walked around me over to the left side of the chimney. "Look here."

He reached around the edge and took one of the rocks out, then put his hand back in a ways, pullin' out an oiled rag that he laid out in his palm. He unfolded the rag to show a small stack of shiny gold coins. I realized then what gold was 'cause them was the same color as the chunks I'd found. I was goin' back for the rest just as soon as I got a chance. I snatched up the gold rocks layin' on the hearth and stuck 'em in the rag with the coins. I wanted Dad to have these, too. Cain just smiled and put the rock back.

"Never tell Dad I showed you where he hides them coins. He won't like it none if he knows you know his hidin' place. Keep this 'tween you and me, and I will cover for the nuggets you put in with his coin."

"I'm goin' back to get the rest, Cain. I want Dad to have it all," I said.

"Where did you find these, little brother?" Cain opened his hand to show me two of the nuggets, as he called 'em.

"I found 'em in the branches on the rock ridge. Not all water had the gold stones, but some places did. I found one waterhole where there are many, both big and small, like those," I said, pointin' to his hand.

"Did Wolf take any of the gold with him?"

"No. I did not show him or tell him of the ones I took. I think he saw some nuggets, but he said nothin' to me over 'em."

"When you go there, you will take me. We need to go soon. I know Wolf saw the gold stones. He will tell his family. They will go there and fetch it all if we don't go first. Gold has a meanin' to Indians. Gold is important to the Cherokee. They take it and hide it so the white man won't know it's here, and they stay quiet when they find it. I can tell you that you weren't the only one who took gold from the rock ridge. Wolf did, too. I know he did, him bein' Cherokee and knowin' how they figure gold. The Cherokee here in Choestoe wear very little and rarely talk of it."

What he was sayin' was strange to me. I figured Wolf would've told me, but Cain said he'd not. I was rememberin' that Indians had their ways and stayed the trail when they know'd they was right. I figured Wolf might tell me later, but me and Cain was goin' in the mornin' to get what I'd left. Sleep would most likely be real hard to come by for me now. I was goin' back to the rock ridge, this time with my brother.

It was after breakfast the next day when Cain and me finished up our chores and got goin'. George had come in durin' the night. He and Rose had left for Slaughter shortly after first light. Cain rode one of Dad's horses and I rode Jim. We got there a couple hours 'fore supper. I took Cain to the spot where I'd first found the nuggets. They weren't a single bit of gold nowhere. The Cherokee had been there, we found their tracks.

"I can't figure this, Cain," I said, confused. "They was plenty of them gold pieces in the branch when we come before. You were right about them Indians, they come got 'em all."

"Yep, kinda figured they would. I reckon they come by on their way home and cleaned it out. They may 'a-not got 'em all. Let's look around some and see."

They weren't hardly a piece nowhere. Even the little spot I'd looked at when me and Wolf was there before was cleaned out—nothin', no gold at all. I got to thinkin' I should've grabbed more the first time, but what I got was plenty heavy in my poke. We kept lookin'. I just know'd they couldn't 'a-got 'em all, but we found precious little. Two dozen tiny things that looked like small peas. We kept on lookin' till dark near come on us 'fore startin' back. Disappointed in what little stock we'd found, Cain did find one good-sized nugget 'bout the size of a chicken egg. He allowed he was gonna keep that rock for himself. Made me reckon they was more there. I thought to go back, but would need to start keepin' my eye out for this gold from now on. If I found any, I wouldn't be tellin' one body where it was or that I'd found a thing, ever.

The whole way back I was studyin' on why Wolf would act so one-sided on this gold findin'. He stayed the trail that day like he didn't notice at all. You couldn't help but see it layin' there in the water, all bright and shiny like it was. Made you wanna just sit there and look at it. But not him, he went on like it weren't nothin' he minded about. The whole time we was back and forth to the rock ridge he never said one word about seein' any, but then him and his family go there and take it all.

He had to have some thinkin' as to why they would do that and not leave any for other folks. This all seemed different than how I was growin' to know Wolf. Dad said Indians have their ways, so I just took it at that and left no worry over it. Wolf was my friend, and he'd done no wrong concernin' me. But still, it didn't settle all the way, really; left me in a fix on how to take what they'd done. I wanted some more of that gold and they got it all, so maybe that's what was stirrin' me. Thinkin' back on the way I was feelin' then, I know I'd just got me one more of them sin marks next to my name in Heaven's Book. I thanked God for the Blood.

Cain and me was 'bout halfway home when the faint smell of wood smoke caught our noses. We stopped in the trail and tried to figure out from where it was comin'. The breeze was from our left, so it had to be from that direction. Somebody was camped nearby.

We tied our rides and walked a ways facin' into the wind, tryin' to scent exactly where they was. We both hit our knees and got low to the ground, hearin' somethin' at the same time— voices. You could barely make 'em out. The words weren't clear, but it was folks. No way it was folks we know'd. They'd all be home after bein' gone so many days for Killin' Time. No doubt, these was strangers. Cain would have to look in on 'em, see who they were. I felt for my knife to make sure it was near, as he was already slippin' toward the camp, his right hand on the handle of his own knife. Cain was goin' to see who was in the valley.

The scent trailed up toward a small flat gap between two sharp ridges. It was full-on woods with huge chestnut, pine and oak growin' all through it. It weren't steep movin' up the holler in below where the smoke was comin' from. We hadn't gone far till we saw they was in the gap. Cain stopped and crouched on one knee while turnin' toward me to put his right hand on my shoulder.

"This is most likely Indians," he whispered. "White men would've camped down low where there's water, but Indians like bein' up high so they can be on the lookout for trouble. We will have to go in real quiet. We got the wind in our face so they won't smell us unless they got dogs. Follow me and don't make any noise. We will move up to our left so we can gain some ground, that way we can get up high and look in on 'em. I would leave you here, but I don't know how many there are nor if they're all in camp, so you gotta come with me. You steady with that?"

What was I to say? Go with Cain and run the risk of bein' found out, or stayin' where I was, alone, with strange Indians about. I figured my chances was better with Cain, so I nodded and started slippin' along behind after he seen I was good and moved on a little closer to their camp. He was better than Wolf at movin' quiet and still through the woods. I could tell if I was off a ways I'd have trouble seein' him. His legs kinda slid as he moved, and his head never raised or lowered, like a deer stayin' steady in its upper part while the lower part did the walkin'. Didn't take but a minute. We'd climbed a little, lookin' down on the gap. They was seven again—the Prince and his bunch. Cain started a soft growl way down deep in his throat as he saw the two standin' by the fire. Ole Two Suns was one of 'em. Standin' next to him was the Prince, Coyote Is Wise. I smiled as I remembered Momma shootin' that bow from Two Suns' hand. It was him what Cain was growlin' over.

Cain was mostly healed, felt like his old self ', cept for his wind. He couldn't go as long durin' the day as he could before the storm. He'd only work outside in the cool mornin' hours up till dinner; worked blacksmithin' or tendin' to the mules inside the barn durin' the hot time. He spent many hours in the hot water of the wooden tub. It was doin' him right. Old Mother left herbs for him to soak in. He was near back to normal 'cept for his breathin'. She said his lung might never get back to the way it was since she didn't know if the lung had been sliced long or just kinda poked through. Time would tell.

We kept movin' till we was perched within thirty paces of their camp, lookin' straight down on 'em. We could even hear their words. They looked like they had before, dirty and sweaty. Only the Prince was different. He was clean, his shoulder length hair was greased and tied back with small leather braids. He wore full skins with a home spun shirt, just like Dancing Bear's family. He wore beads and a solid gold band over his homespun around the upper right arm to show who he was. He carried no knife or pouches, and his foot skins were nice, unlike the ugly ones his bunch wore.

They spoke Cherokee mostly, but the one word we did know when they said it was Rose. The second time we heard her name it was followed by a laugh. That's when the growl started back as Cain rose to his feet. He would have none 'a that funnin'.

"Stay here, little brother," he said, pushin' me closer to the ground. "I'll be right back."

They stopped laughin' when they saw him stride outa the woods and join their company. He never said a word, but stared long and hard toward ole Two Suns. He waited for what would happen next, as did I.

The looks on their faces was pure shock. Indians held a lot 'a stock in courage and bravery. Cain walkin' into a strange camp 'a that many Cherokee was nothin' short of either true courage or scrambled thinkin'. They was about to find out which of the two it was, 'cause Cain was scared 'a nothin' I'd ever know'd of, and he didn't look scared at all now.

Two Suns showed no fear, neither, as Cain pointed at him and spoke.

"You came to my home uninvited and scared my family and future wife. My mother sent you away without the bow you raised over your head in a threat to me. Now you come here again, and you laugh when you say the name of the girl I love. I will have no more insults from you. As you can see, I am no longer the sick one. I think we should have that talk you promised me on your last visit," With that, Cain pulled his knife, meanin' to fight this seasoned warrior to the death, or close.

"I will answer you, my young enemy. I am Two Suns Rising, a warrior of the Yonah clan. This night I will take out your heart and roast it over the fire and eat it. My prince will marry this young Cherokee girl of the Notla River Valley, and you will be lost in stories," he said, pullin' his knife.

"It's called Choestoe Valley, you pumpkin-head, and she will have none other than me," growled Cain, as he gripped the handle of his knife harder and crouched into a fightin' stance, blade up.

They had started to square off when the Prince stepped between 'em. He held his hand back to Two Suns, faced Cain, and said, "Enough, Two Suns! We have come in peace and are doing nothing that is wrong among our clans. It is not against the tribal customs for either of our clans to venture into the land of the other. If you were not a white man, you would know these things, my light-haired friend. Let us sit and smoke, and we will decide what is best from this coming together between us. I wish only to visit and leave in peace, of this I promise you."

"Take your peace and go when Old Man Sun breaks the ridges at first light. There is bad blood between me and this heathen you call Two Suns. I mean to settle this with him," said Cain, spittin' on the ground at Two Suns' feet.

"There will be no fighting between our clans or with white men today," said the Prince. He turned to Two Suns and put his hands on both his shoulders to stop him from makin' a charge at Cain, as Two Suns' veins was near poppin' from his skin he was so mad. Cain'd got him good. I couldn't help but grin.

The Prince turned back to Cain and said, "We have come in peace to speak with the daughter of a tribal leader and the future chief of the Choestoe clan, the daughter of Dancing Bear and his wife, A-Ga-Li-Ha, who was a member of our clan in her growing up years and whose parents still live with us. They have given us permission by runner to be here. I heard your words to the leader of my warriors and I realize now that you are the one who claims her heart. You must know that I would like to own her heart as well; to join our two clans as I become chief of our clan across the ridge. I wish for the chance to present her with my feelings and let her decide which of us she wishes to spend her life with. That is only fair to her since she would become very important to all Cherokee. She must be given the opportunity to decide on this possible in her life. Would you not agree she should know of this?"

"You're wastin' your time, Ki'yote," Cain said. "She ain't leavin' Choestoe over the likes of you and your clan. You can talk to her all you feel you need, but it will be a waste of words. I will cause you no trouble since you are here under

Dancing Bears allowance, but I ain't no Cherokee, and my rules is different than his. So if I catch any of you on our place again, it will be a fight...and I mean any of ya'."

Cain put his knife away and looked right at ole Two Suns. "Me and you will have our talk one day, warrior, and it will be me who takes out your heart. I will feed it to my dogs and you will know no love across the river. Of this the spirits will sing, 'cause you are a coward who talks mean to women and in front of children. I will right you, and you will deserve it."

The Prince had to step in front of the warrior again as he jerked toward Cain. You could see that Two Suns felt what Cain was sayin' by the hate in his face. If these two lived, there would be a fight to the death, of that I was sure. Cain had made an enemy for life; it was as much his choosin' as it was the Indian's. Cain took insults just like any mountain man. This *would* be made right. It would not be today, but it would happen—their trails were set.

***

We got home plenty after dark. Supper was cold but still on the table. Momma know'd we'd be in 'fore too long, so she left it out just like she always did. Dad come in just as we sat down to eat. I could tell by the look on his face he was troubled. I figured Momma probably got worried, which would've throw'd Dad outa sorts. If that was so, then we was the cause, and he was gonna want to know where we was. It weren't normal for them to worry like that, though. Cain stayed gone for days sometimes, only not with me goin' along, so maybe that was it. But that thinkin' for them didn't make sense neither. Somethin' was stirrin'.

"Cain," Dad said as he laid his hands on the table. "Black Oak came here last night not only to get Rose but to deliver a message. He has brought word from Dancing Bear. The Prince is comin' to Slaughter."

"That I know, Dad," said Cain. "We crossed paths with the Prince and his bunch about two miles east of here. I trailed 'em to their camp, went to their fire and had a talk with that prince and explained how things was. He said he was in Choestoe as a guest of Dancing Bear, so I left it at that and we come home. Jeb stayed in the woods. They didn't even know he was around. The Prince said he was leavin' for Slaughter in the mornin' to have a visit with Rose. They should be goin' back over the ridge in a couple of days when she makes it right. She'll tell 'em me and her are joined, and that ain't never gonna change. I'm glad he's here. This will make things straight."

Dad looked like he'd took cold as he sat back in his chair and studied on what Cain had just told him. The worry in his face growin' even more strained. He never said a word but just sat there and stared at Cain. Momma must've been listenin' from the back. She come in after Cain had finished explainin' and sat across from us at the table, the oil lamp on the Lazy Susan coverin' some of the worry on her face.

The desire for food was leavin' me with the way she looked. I had to ask from concern, "What's wrong, Momma? Are you okay? You look like you seen a haint."

Momma dropped her head a little but never said a word. Dad sat up in his chair some, still watchin' Cain.

"Do you understand what this means, Cain? The Prince bein' here himself with guards and all? Has him comin' here made you understand that he is serious about what he thinks his future with Rose will be? Stop and think about what it would mean to the tribe as a whole if the Prince and Rose were to marry and join the two clans. The leaders of both would come together as one, and the combined clan would have the most strength in the whole tribe. It means that Rose will go with him to his home across the ridge, to Yonah. She'll stay there for two seasons and learn their ways and get used to his clan. Cain, the Prince and his bunch are not here just for a visit. No, they've come to escort Rose back across the main ridge and into their valley, a valley that you will be forbidden to trail 'cause you've made a claim for her. Dancing Bear has given his desire for her to go there and stay with her mother's family. Rose must honor his wishes. It's her duty as the daughter of the next chief of the Choestoe Valley clan. She is leavin' Choestoe, Cain. She may not be back. When the Great Creator washes the leaves in color this fall, she and the Prince could be ready to marry."

Cain was eatin' while Dad told him what was goin' on, never really stoppin' till after Dad was done tellin' what George had said. He washed it all down with half a mug of buttermilk. He chewed his last bite and wiped his face clean with a linen Momma kept on the table—them napkins was handmade and real soft.

He pushed his plate back and looked over at Momma for an uncomfortable amount of time, dropped his head a little, then finally said, kinda slow, "Momma, think close now, did Rose say anything that she wanted me to hear in them words from Black Oak? Did she say straight any words for me? A goodbye, maybe?"

Momma looked at Cain like it was the last time she'd be able to lay eyes on him, kinda struck he'd ask such, sayin', "Why, yes, she did, but it's hard for me to say. I felt I wouldn't speak of it now; that maybe I'd wait for later, or maybe, I thought, never. I don't want to hurt you. It grieves me for all this to be comin' on you. I just can't."

Cain went to Momma and picked her up from her chair. He put her in a full-armed bear hug, her feet danglin' inches above the plank floor of our log home, and spoke real close in her ear. "Go ahead and say, Momma, it won't sting. You're my favorite girl in the whole put-together. Ain't nothin' gonna hurt me as long as time is, 'cause me and you got forever. Please tell me, Momma, I need to hear it."

Momma and Cain hugged like that for a minute or two, with her head laid on his shoulder. He put her down and she looked up at him, a tear on her cheek.

"She wanted Black Oak to tell you to give up the trail and don't try and follow it out, that Sunshine will be watchin' for you. It burns to hear myself say such to you, Cain. Please forgive me."

"There's nothin' to forgive you for, Momma," Cain said softly. He placed his left hand on her back and looked over at Dad. "Thanks for tellin' me, Dad. I will thank Black Oak next time I see him. I will worry on this later. I am tired and need to sleep now. Come on, Jeb, it's late."

And with that he let Momma go, took me by the shoulder as he eased toward the door leadin' to the main room and the stairs to the loft where we slept. I looked at Dad. He and momma were mumblin' somethin' they didn't want me to hear, which was fine. After all this, I didn't feel like hearin', anyways.

Sleep was right for me, too, as I wandered off toward the main room, leavin' them to talk on things. It felt strange, Cain takin' the word and goin' on to bed—it just weren't like him. He was the type to walk into a strange camp without a second thought, so it didn't seem proper him takin' this so calm. My gut told me he weren't as laid down on all of it as he wanted our folks to think. I know'd Cain, and I was figurin' he was studyin' on all this right then, tryin' to settle with it. He loved Rose and she loved him, of that I was sure. No, he weren't done with this even a little bit. There was no doubt in my young mind. Cain would be gone soon.

Chapter Twenty-Two

Wolf and Spirit

I was right. Cain left within the week, and he weren't gonna be back for a while. I'd found he was gone when I woke that mornin', got up and looked around. He'd took jerky and all his possibles, a blanket and some warm clothes, his bow and a whole quiver full 'a huntin' arrows. Dad didn't say much when we found he was gone. He and Momma know'd he'd be goin', just like I did. Momma had thoughts on where he might be, but any of 'em or none of 'em could be a possible. Hard to think on what he might do. It was Cain. One thing was for sure, though, whatever he was doin' was account of Rose bein' on his mind.

"He's walkin' his own trail and will make his mind on how he carries on. We can pray for him. Right now, that's the most we can do, so we will leave it at that," Dad had said, which sounded straight to me. No more was said, and me and Dad went to the barn to start work.

Peter raised his head when I walked into the barn. I went over to him, and as soon as I laid his halter on, his tail started swishin' back and forth. He was true-mule stock. They weren't nothin' he liked better than a good day's work. We was a while back from Killin' Time. Since then he'd learned to log, plow and carry. Dad probably worked with him a month or more 'fore we'd left for Killin' Time. He was close to knowin' it all then, but now he was plumb knowledgeable. He know'd my voice and could turn and pull and stop on my word. He know'd Dad, too. I missed Cain.

I was leadin' him outa the barn when Dad hollered and told me to bring him to where he was. I couldn't see Dad, but I could tell from him hollerin' he was behind the barn in the mule pen. I walked around the corner and saw right off what he wanted. One of the mares was tied up short and havin' trouble birthin'. This would be a first for Peter and for me. We was fixin' to pull a new baby mule. Dad's Jacks were so big that sometimes the mare had trouble gettin' the new ones birthed, even these Draft horses. I was not gonna like this. Where was Wolf when you had this goin' on? *He* would like all this for sure.

"This mare has been at this all night. We gotta give her some help," Dad explained. "The next time she starts to push I'm gonna tie off the little one. Then we have to wait and pull it on the next push. Peter may be good for this, he's young and has good feel in his feet. Don't want to jerk it, just ease the pull and hold Peter steady. I've had to pull this mare before, so I'll prob'ly cull her after this one gets raised."

Dad had a thin braided rope that was slick with bear grease and soft to the touch. He backed Peter up and looped it around the base of his neck, then run it along his back and through the groove between the top of his hips. He kept him in a straight line with the back of the mare, 'bout two paces from her rump. This was gonna be a sight, I could tell.

"She's gonna start pushin' in just a bit. When she does, you will see the feet and nose start showin'. They'll be stacked up with the nose on top of the feet. I'm gonna wrap this rope around its feet, but I will have to cut the birthin' sack the foal's been livin' in to do it. If its head slips back after I've opened the sack, it could smother, so once its head starts showin', don't let Peter back up. Do you understand me, Jeb?" he said, gettin' his knife ready.

"Yes, sir, I got it," I mumbled. "Don't let Peter back up, and pull easy."

"That's right, don't let him pull quick. Listen to what I tell you now when things get goin', Jeb. I don't want to lose this little one."

He'd no sooner said that when the mare let out a painful moan, so I moved to my place in front of Peter and grabbed his lead up close to his jaw so that he'd know to pull slow. She was tired, and they would both die if we didn't help. She was standin' on all fours, and when the moan started, she hunkered down a little and raised her tail. It was the most natural thing I'd ever witnessed. The foal's nose and feet were startin' to show. You could see they was inside a thick, dingy somethin'—looked like creek water after a gentle rain.

Dad waited till the nose and feet was showin' good, then reached up real quick and sliced through the foggy creek water to let the little one taste its first outside air. He grabbed both the feet together and slipped the rope over 'em in one slick motion. By watchin' that, a body could tell he'd done it before. He then pulled the knot tight and signaled me to get Peter leanin'. All I had to do was tighten my grip on his halter, and he shifted his weight forward slowly. He must've felt the rope draw tight from the weight 'a his pull, 'cause he stopped pullin' and started to hold steady.

It is a strange happenin' to see one critter inside another like that. Right then, I understood why folks said birthin' was a miracle. It really is somethin', bein' a part of it and seein' it up close. My biggest wonder was how it stayed alive all sacked up in there like that. I made a thought to ask Dad later.

Peter held still until the mare started pushin' and the rope went a little slack, then he leaned into the pull with a little more effort. The baby mule began to inch its way toward life. Peter had it solid when that rope went taut; that thing was comin' out now for sure. The mare was in pain; him pullin' her baby weren't helpin' with that none. It was like they was havin' a pull against one another, but the mare soon realized that what strength she had left weren't near enough to match Peter's. 'Sides, he'd been workin' hard the last couple of moons, and he was strong. He weren't Big Jim strong yet, but he was close.

The mare kinda relaxed as Dad let off on her tie some and rubbed her head. Peter kept the pressure on for the final few minutes. After a bit the foal just eased on out and plopped on the ground like natural. Dad got the rope off as the mare started to try and tend to the slimy little thing wallerin' around on the hay-covered yard. She put her nose under Dad's backside as he was workin' the rope loose from the newborn female, nearly pushed him to the ground 'cause he weren't outa her way fast enough. That was a funny sight, seein' Dad near fall to the ground pushed by one of his old mares. The horse started lickin' and eaten at the bag wrapped around the foal and never stopped till the coverin' was layin' in one place and the foal was separate. She cleaned the baby off and licked it all over, leavin' it to flop around and find its legs while she went back and ate all the birthin' stuff what the foal came in. Dad said it kept the mountain cats and such away and made her baby safe. She was a good mother. I thought Dad ought to think again on cullin' her, but he said he would. That's that. There weren't no other way to study on it. When that foal was raised, this mare would go away. She'd be a good mare for a regular size stud, but these Jacks of Dad's were outa General Washington's own rake, who had the best of his day. They were topnotch and big.

It was a beauty and she must've weighed as much as a good size sack of ground meal. Long legs and a big head. Didn't take her but a little bit and she was walkin', shaky and wobbly, but walkin'. I couldn't really tell what her sure color was, she'd most likely change some when she got to growin', but she looked dark, so I was thinkin' she'd be black.

She wandered around till she found her momma and got the first meal of her life. She'd poked around on the wrong end of the mare for some time, but then she found the mare's springhouse. That thing got to stompin' around and swishin' its tail that milk was so good. She and her momma was bonded now; they'd know one another from now on, even though she'd be leavin'. If the foal ended up where she was goin' one day, they'd still know each other. Mules for the most part were mindful. Dad would cull the crazy ones or give 'em to the Indians, who could tame 'em down a right smart and use 'em. But it took more time than Dad could give, so he didn't fool with it.

***

Black Oak, George, would visit our home several times a year. You never know'd when him or some other friend would just come on in. You'd always kinda expect it and look out for folks comin' and goin, so him ridin' down the trail to our place later that day was no surprise. He was astraddle his mule and in full dress with his killin' possibles tied on, though that weren't normal travel for him, even this late in the fall. His favorite huntin' weapon was his adl-adl, which was in its place tied with leather straps on the side of his totin' pouch. He could make an arrow fly so fast with that thing you could hardly even see it. I watched him kill one of Momma's chickens with it; hit it square in the side of its head on a dead run for cover; rolled it end over end like a rock rollin' down a hill. He carried a blowgun, too, and a small pouch of darts along with his hatchet and knives. I figured he must be on a hunt showin' up like he was, but most times when he come he'd have meat throw'd over the rump of his mule for us to eat. He eat a right smart, but he had no fresh kill nor looked fresh washed, neither.

I waved to him excited-like, thinkin' maybe he was comin' to get me to go huntin'. My stomach jumped into a knot at the thought of gettin' out in the woods, but as he got up close I could see they was worry in his face. He may be goin' huntin', but I now figured it most likely weren't for critters. They was trouble again, and it could only be one thing—Cain!

George scattered the chickens as he rode into the barnyard and dismounted. He walked by me and put his huge hand on top of my head, his fingers runnin' down past my ears. It felt like somethin' warm and strong just swaller'd my head, but I was sure glad to see him, even though I know'd somethin' was wrong and he was most likely bringin' bad word concernin' trouble. He made me feel calm and safe, kinda like Dad did, but not quite as comforted. Sometimes, we talked 'bout Jesus and how He did what He did for Indians same as settlers and other folks. Black Oak understood the meanin' of the Lord's Blood, 'cause Indians were used to blood. He'd let you know where he stood on that fact, too. He, Dad and Momma were tight to the word.

George was one of the Cherokee that would go to the church house for meetin' when the preacher come to preach. He only come a few times a year, but ole George never missed. He even got baptized one Sunday. Took two men and the preacher to get him dunked, but the most funny part was when he stripped down to what he was born in to have it done. White folks in the church weren't ready for that; a couple of the older women fell plumb out at the sight of such a big man, naked and all. The rest of the Cherokee attendin' thought nothin' of it, as naked was natural to them. Some of the Indians were spooked, though, by the black clothes and big hats them preachers wore. They'd not draw near. Dad give the young preachers a mule when they'd first come, if they needed one, so that they could spread the word better. They was good mules, too, not none of 'em culls.

"Thompie," said George as he stopped in front of Dad. "We must sit and smoke and talk. I will go and build up the fire."

He never waited for Dad to say a word, he just moved on over to the fence and tied up his mule, then went to the main fire pit and started layin' on wood to the coals. Momma was boilin' soap most all the day before, and the coals under the ash was still hot. Dad gathered up the tools we was usin' and started totin'em to the toolshed, so I did likewise with what he left. He always left the light stuff for me.

Weren't but a few minutes that we had the tools back in the shed and was out sittin' by the fire with George. Momma's kettle that she used for soap was still hangin' over the pit, and it smelled like the dried flowers she'd been mixin' in the makin's. As the kettle got hot, the scent got stronger. Dad wouldn't let her use his cookin' kettle what he boiled meat and taters and such in. He claimed it fouled the meat with all that fancy smellin'. He once got her to mix some soap with the dirt from the forest floor to use 'fore he hunted to hide his scent, but he never did that again. George and Dad got out their smokin' pouches and each packed a full bowl. I know'd we was gonna be there a while 'cause it took some time to smoke a whole bowl. This was serious.

The warrior lit his pipe and leaned back on the stone-sittin' bench that him, Dad and Granddad built years before for sittin' and talkin' like we was doin'. I'd spend many nights right in that same spot, listenin' to stories and starin' at the stars, warmed by a hot fire. The smoke from their pipes was mixin' with the sweet scent from Momma's soap kettle, which made me feel even less worried.

George looked over at Dad and started searchin' for words. They finally come. "Cain is in the land of Yonah. A runner was sent during the night by the uncle of Ag-Ga-Li-Ha to tell Dancing Bear that the Yonah clan knows of his visit to their valley. He left from Dancing Bear's days ago because he was unsettled with the come-together the family made over Rose. Dancing Bear reasoned with him. I was there. He told Cain that Rose must honor her family and do what is right, but only if her true heart is the root to the tree of her decision. He told Cain that with a little time, this could end in his favor, but Cain has fear that the Yonah clan will try and hold her or sell her when her decision is against the Prince. Cain thinks they will feel it better for the tribe if she is gone from this land than for the daughter of Dancing Bear to marry a white man, especially one as white as Cain," George finished, then looked at me and winked.

Dad showed very little 'bout what he'd just heard, just stared into the fire as he asked, "Where is Dancing Bear now, Black Oak? Does he feel the same as Cain?"

"He is making ready for this trail to see with his own eyes and feel with his own heart. He wants to be there if Cain is right in his judgment. There will only be five in all when we join the trail. It will be a dangerous trail if they try and hold our daughter. Blood may be shed, but we must make sure Rose is returned. Cain is a man and knows his own way. He will watch for himself unless they find him, then he will need us to save his life. Dancing Bear thinks it best for you to ride your horse and for us to ride the mules to the low gap and trail in on foot. Wolf and Jeb will go and keep the stock while we slip into the valley of Yonah to talk to Rose. There is a chance we will need them to get home quickly, so the horse and mules are to be in the low gap waiting. This is what Dancing Bear has said concerning his worry for his daughter. He ask for your help," Black Oak said.

Dad just kept suckin' on his pipe stem and packin' the tobacco ever so often with his thumb for several minutes without sayin' a word. He finally leaned forward, put his elbows on the tops of his knees and took his pipe from his mouth.

"Dancing Bear is worried for his daughter, and I for my son. We will follow this trail and both of these young folks will be looked for equal. Rose is no less important to me than Cain is to Dancing Bear, and I will be concerned for his well-bein' just as I am for our dear Rose. I worry we are late; that Cain may be closer to trouble than he was yesterday. Also that Rose might've made her decision clear by now. Dancing Bear is prob'ly movin' toward the gap, so we should get stirrin'," said Dad, makin' things clear and knockin' the burnt tobacco outa his pipe against the stone.

"I understand your words. I, too, feel for Cain. We will find his trail once we have spoken to Rose. She cannot be sold away as a slave." Black Oak was firm.

"You are right, of course, wise one. Rose must be taken care of, but I will not let them hurt my son, neither. If he has been captured and is still alive, then I will free him and kill his enemy the same as I will if they've laid a hand on Rose. She is to be part of my family, and she will be treated as such."

Black Oak simply nodded and went off in the direction of the barn. Dad and me went inside the house to add a layer of homespun to the skins we was wearin' and to get what possibles we'd need. We packed some extra clothes and a couple of quilts that we rolled up in our sleepin' truck. I made sure I packed my bearskin Dancing Bear give me, too. It was cold and winter was on us. Dad told Momma what was goin' on. She packed us food and jerky. They hugged for the longest till she let him go and started in on me. She gave Dad a small pouch Anne had made up for travelin', with some medicine herbs for cuts, and bandages and leather straps for coverin' and stoppin' bleedin'. Old Mother was teachin' her well. Those simple things could save your life in the mountains. Dad was proud to have 'em, same as me.

We tied our gear on Jim's back, and I laid my bearskin over Peter's. 'Course, I had to double it up and run it long-ways, head to tail, or it would hang plumb to the ground on both sides. We didn't use saddles on the mules, just a wide leather strap run across their backs just behind their shoulders to put your feet in as you rode. They were made by the Cherokee, and white folks hardly used 'em. I liked mine. It was a lot less trouble to use than a saddle. Our mules' backs were so wide it was real comfortable ridin'. They didn't run unless they had to, so you really didn't need no saddle 'cept to get on and off easier.

Wolf was the first one to greet us when we rode in to the low gap. He ran to where we was, and in one smooth motion, he grabbed Peter's mane and threw himself in behind me to land sittin' square to my back. He wrapped his arms around my middle and near bear-hugged the breath right outa my lungs. I was proud to see him, too. I said so, once I got my wind back. Peter didn't even flinch when Wolf jumped up on him. He was a good mule, turnin' out to be a lot like Jim.

Wolf rode on in to the gap with me and then jumped off to go and see my dad, who eased from the back of his horse then bent down and shook his hand Indian-style before we led the mules and Dad's horse to the edge of the gap.

"Why did Thompie ride a horse instead of his mule?" asked Wolf.

"Dancing Bear feels they might need a fast ride when they get back from checkin' on Rose, so Dad brought the horse just for that if they need it," I said. "'Better to have it and not need it, than to not have it and need it,' Dad said."

"I see," said Wolf. "Come, we must see to the stock so our fathers can get going into the Yonah valley to make camp before they leave to check on Rose and Cain at daylight. Dancing Bear is worried over both."

We stretched a rope between two good sized oaks and pulled it tight, tyin' it off on both ends so we would have room to tether all the stock. Jim didn't like bein' on a rope, but he let us tie him off along with the rest. The one thing we had to make sure of was that our rides was there and ready when the men got back from the valley. That was our most important chore on this trail. It felt good knowin' our fathers trusted us with such an important task.

We weren't there for more than a minute when Dad and Dancing Bear walked off to have a talk. It was important for them to know exactly what this trail was about. They must've felt like they needed to talk it over, seein' how Dad was real concerned 'bout Cain, but this trip was mostly 'bout Rose. There had never been a hard word said between 'em, so they'd settle on this, too. They just had to talk a while.

"Dancing Bear, I know you worry over your daughter. You must know I worry for her, too. You know also that my son is in this valley and trouble is waitin' on him if the Yonah clan finds him. I know that Cain feels they will hold Rose or sell her if she goes against the Prince. That is the worry we both have. She will decide for Cain, so we must make sure she is able to leave as she wants. But Cain will be in more trouble once she makes her decision known, and that concerns me. I will help you find Rose. I will protect her with my life, but I want to find Cain as well. Do you understand my worry, Dancing Bear? Young love can make one do stupid things, like wrestle eagles for their feathers," said Dad, grinnin' a little at Dancing Bear.

"My friend," said Dancing Bear, "I am very concerned over the threat to my daughter, but I am also very concerned over the safety of my son, Cain. I know this clan and they are ruthless in their dealings with outsiders. They have killed some from our clan and we theirs, but I want this to be done with no bloodletting if that can happen. That said, though, I will kill all that lay a hand on my family, that includes your family as mine. I will give my life if need be for Cain. You are my brother, Thompie, and I yours. I tell you now so you know my heart on this: my children are your children, and yours mine. We will take care of this and all other needs as from one family."

Dad was taken to mind. As I watched them talk, a strange look come over his face. I didn't know it yet, but Dancing Bear had just made it clear to Dad how serious he felt over our family. As a leader of the Cherokee tribe, Dancing Bear had just made us a part of the Choestoe clan. He offered Dad his forearm in a sign he wanted to settle on an agreement, and Dad locked it with his. All was now clear between them on how they would go. Blood for blood and family for family. Me and Wolf didn't know, but Dad and Dancing Bear would become blood brothers when this trail ended, and not just by swappin' blood on the inside of their right forearm. Then all would know that our family was now a part of the Choestoe Cherokee clan.

As far as the leaders of our families was concerned, we were all one family now. Nothin' could change that, not even death. A bond like this with a Cherokee is somethin' very serious. For him to trust Dad so strongly told a body a lot on how he felt over us. My family was all of a sudden adopted by this great leader among his people. But for now, only him and Dad know'd. When the story song was sung over this trail, the whole Cherokee Nation would take us as family. Me and Cain had just become adopted Cherokee. Life would now be different.

Wolf and I was now more than friends. The Spirit would let us know that soon. But for now, our chore was to keep the mules and horse ready for travel. We was expected to stay in the low gap and not let our fathers down. We would be here when they returned. I prayed Rose and Cain would be with 'em.

Chapter Twenty-Three

First Blood

Wolf's brothers Fox Running and Moon Shadow trailed with Dancing Bear to the low gap, headin' into the valley, too. It was steep out the backside of the gap, so they stayed the main tops south till they could see the rock of the mountain Yonah. The songs said many warriors lost their lives there; that it was a haunted place where the spirits were restless. I thought it was beautiful the first time me and Wolf went there. We never seen no haints and we had much fun climbin' the rocks.

Dancing Bear decided it best to stay away from the main path and use the back trails made by warriors in years gone by. They made it easy to travel; trees were marked and bent to show the way. The Cherokee were clever and lived with the woods as one. Wolf's family taught him and me later on.

It was late in the afternoon, and the clouds was hidin' Old Man Sun. Me and Wolf was gettin' our heavy canvas night cover tied up and the bearskins laid out for sleepin'. I hoped that we'd be stayin' a while, but Dad said it'd pro'bly only be for a night or two. Dancing Bear wanted to go in and make camp and move in on the Yonah town 'fore daylight. Since the sky was lookin' like rain, we meant to make our fire small so we could put it under part of the cover tied overhead. It might smoke us up a little, but it would not go out if rain did come, which it did.

The woods was laid bare and all the trees was without leaves, 'cept some of the young birch that keep their leaves till the new ones come out in the spring. The men could see for a long ways in the woods, but also had to watch and be careful of bein' seen. It weren't near as dangerous for the Cherokee in the group as it was for Dad. The Yonah clan wouldn't mind Dancing Bear and his family, as Black Oak was kin, but they'd take mind to Dad bein' there 'cause 'a Cain, so they stayed outa sight. They made camp in a small holler surrounded by ivy to make sure their fire stayed hid and its smoke was hard to scent. Dancing Bear talked over his plan for the next mornin'. Nobody was smokin'.

"We will leave well before the sun rises, then split up and take watch from the higher ground," said Dancing Bear. "It is important to not be seen. If you are, make sure they think you alone. When we see Rose, we will watch to see that she is being treated with respect, then Black Oak and I will slip in and talk with her to make sure we hear the truth and not a forced word. One thing: do not go in the camp until we have talked over what we see. If things are not right, or if Rose or Cain is in danger, we come back here and make our plans. If one of us is taken, stay calm, we will come for you. We must work together for the sake of our children, brothers and cousins. Is this agreed among us?"

They all spent a minute thinkin' before anyone spoke.

"This is a good plan. I feel it's right," said Dad, breakin' the silence. "If things are not the way they should be in the camp, then we should come back here and talk over the best way to make it right. I will do as my brother has said and meet back here after we see how things are."

All there agreed.

They were all quiet after Dancing Bear made his words known. Black Oak was puttin' venison jerky on to boil with the dried apples and onions Momma sent. Moon Shadow found some winter ramps not far up the side of the ridge behind the camp and hung 'em over the fire to dry, the strong, stingin' odor of the onion kinda coverin' everything. Dad said they was strong 'cause they cooked the roots, but he found it good when mixed with the boiled jerky and apple mush. Me and Wolf had cold jerky and dried apples, which suited us just fine. Momma packed the last of her mornin' biscuits in my possibles pouch; told me them was for me and Wolf so not to let the men folk know nothin' of 'em. We gladly kept our mouths quiet on that. They sure was good when we split 'em open and laid in the dried apples.

Me and Wolf got our firewood in 'fore the rain come and we got a little campfire goin'. The heat felt good as it warmed the inside of our night cover. We'd formed our cover to three sides so that we had a good warm spot to stay the night and the cold rain couldn't get to us. We had Wolf's bearskin for our sleepin' cover and my bearskin and a quilt to lay on, which made it real warm and cozy. We talked a little 'bout how this was our first night campin' alone, but that didn't amount to much, as both of us had trouble keepin' our eyes open. Sleep come on us after dark. We both slept through the night like dead folk, never wakin' once.

Dad and all weren't near as comfortable as me and Wolf was. They had no sleepin' covers, and the rain had put their little fire out. They was usin' their blankets to try and shield the rain till it quit late, a couple hours 'fore daylight. They was all soaked through to the skin, with no sleep. They left camp cold and tired, but the wet ground made slippin' up on the sleepin' Cherokee a little easier. The air was gettin' colder. All five was in place and shiverin' before Old Man Sun ever woke. The Cold One would be hollerin' soon.

Yonah was a tradin' post that the clan took charge over. They lived in a village just to the north, so it made sense. It would all move to Enotah later on, but Yonah was a small place where the Cherokee from, Choestoe, Nachoochee, Yonah and all other Indians south of the great ridges would gather to trade and make business at special times. It was a flat, cleared, wide holler that was surrounded on all sides by mountains and small tops. It would be hard to shoot a deer with Dad's long rifle if you was on one end of the cleared place and it on the other. The width was near the same.

There was one log buildin' and it was kinda big. It had four doors and a dozen windows, with porches on two sides. There was a large board-covered area off to the side and out in the woods, kinda like the long shed we used at Killin' Time; long and wide and would hold a lot of folks. The land was cleared all around the log buildin' and out in front for gatherin', and two small branches trickled down either side for fresh water. There was a barn for stock with a corral that would hold a hundred animals if need be, with trails leadin' in from all directions. Many could camp there when folks come together. It served the Cherokee of the mountains and the surroundin' clans very well, what few times of the year it was needed. They played ball there, too. Now that was interestin' to watch.

The missionaries taught school there, but Cherokee was all that was allowed to come to the school. No white man went there durin' school times other than the missionaries to teach the Cherokee. Many of the Cherokee from Choestoe learned to read and write English proper while goin' there for schoolin'. Wolf and his family went there to learn the English. They'd gather three times a year for a couple of moons, and the family would be given books and *Bibles*. They'd take and give 'em to other folks, too, that never went to the school to try and help 'em learn to read and speak English, and the missionaries would talk to 'em 'bout the Blood.

Unlike most Cherokee clans in the mountains, the Yonah clan had a village. Most all the old folks and many others lived in the village, includin' A-Ga-Li-Ha's momma. That is where Rose was stayin' and hopefully would be where they found her. Dancing Bear wanted to make sure things were in order without the Yonah clan knowin' he was about. If all was found to be good, he planned on walkin' into the village below and visitin' with his daughter. If things were bad, then them not knowin' he was around would give him some time to think on what to do.

It was just light enough to see, and Dancing Bear was sittin' alone in the woods above the shed, thinkin'. Black Oak sat a few feet to his right, and my dad was several paces on further to Black Oak's right. They know'd daylight would be bringin' answers to questions—answers they may not like—and unfortunately, daylight was near, and with it, so were answers.

It was just light enough for the eyes of a warrior when the answer to at least one of Dancing Bear's questions was answered. As he looked on the long house—there was Cain, tied up, gagged, and hangin' by his arms from behind, his feet not touchin' the ground. They'd strung him up across one of the roof beams in the big covered place, his head hangin' low, blood stains down the front of his homespun shirt. Cain was their captive. It weren't but a minute, then there was light enough for Dad to see.

How dare they! Dad thought as he looked on him hangin' there. *What do they think gives them the right to do this to my boy? That prince is gonna pay with his blood.*

With revenge and savin' Cain in his head, Dad drew his knife and stood to go and get his boy. A huge hand grabbed his shoulder from behind and pulled him back to the ground. Black Oak and Dancing Bear had seen Cain hangin', so Black Oak come to get Dad on Dancing Bears orders. The clan would kill Dad and Cain if he went down there, and Black Oak and Dancing Bear weren't gonna let that happen.

"My friend," said Black Oak, still holdin' Dad in place. "This is a bad thing that is happening, but if you go down there now, they will kill you and Cain. Dancing Bear will see how many watch over him, then we will know the best way to free him. We will kill all who try to stop us, but until we know how many guard him, we must stay away. Trust me, brother, I know it is hard, but you must wait. Dancing Bear is watching to see. He will know soon."

The hate Black Oak saw in my dad's eyes was from deep in his soul. Dad was a mountain man through and through, with a whole lot of Cherokee mixed in. This was gonna be made right. First blood had been drawn, and it come from Cain. Dad would settle this proper. George know'd it.

Dad looked Black Oak right in the eye. Through gritted teeth in a kinda whisper growl, he said, "He's tortured my boy for lovin' one of his own, 'cause one of his own won't love him. He is a coward. I pray they've not been this unkind to Rose. I will see him bleed out from the blade of my knife, Black Oak, and slowly, like he has done to Cain. Forgive me, Father, forgive me, Jesus. Forgive me, Holy Spirit, for this I will do."

Black Oak walked with Dad a bit to give him a chance to settle himself. After a few minutes, he led the way as they returned to camp and met up with Dancing Bear. Fox Running and Moon Shadow was out lookin' for Rose. One of 'em would come back soon when they found out where she was, while the other stayed behind to watch. Dancing Bear was sittin' at a small fire, smokin', when they walked back into camp. They were hid good. You'd have to know the camp was there to find 'em.

"Thompie, my brother," Dancing Bear said, as he stood and walked to Dad then held him by the shoulders. "Your son is alive. I went to him and talked with him, but could not free him by myself. They did not see me. He knows we are here to get him. He is not hurt, but is in much pain. He is weak and could talk very little. He knows nothing of Rose, as they found him before he talked with her."

"Cain is still healin' from the lung wound, Dancing Bear," said Dad, the worry all over his face. "The pull on his chest from the way he's hangin' could force the lungs to move and rip open. He will die if that happens. We've got to get him down, and now!"

"Yes, of course, my friend," said Dancing Bear. "We will go and get our son. I have spotted only two guards, but they are warriors. You and Black Oak move to a place south of where he is tied. I will cross around where they watch and approach from behind. I will walk out to turn their eyes, then Cain can be freed. The Prince put warriors here for a reason. They will kill without heed, so be ready, because they will be ready. I was lucky to get so close this morning, but it was dark. We will need more luck to get him now without a fight. If we get divided, slip back to camp and we will gather here. Now, go quietly, Black Oak. I will see you and Thompie at the long house." And with that, he was gone like smoke in the trees.

It was slippery goin' down the ridge toward where Cain was hung. The rain had stopped for the time, but water kept drippin' off the leaves and had soaked through Dad's hat and down the back of his neck, drippin' off his nose and chin, but he felt none of it. The anger in his soul was hot; real live steam was leakin' out from the neck hole in his winter skins. He'd left his homespun at the camp since it didn't turn water like his deer skin did, but he was still soaked through.

Black Oak was huge, but he moved on the stalk like a cat. It weren't but a few minutes that he had 'em within forty paces of Cain. It would've been an easy shot with a bow if Cain was a big, fat doe. Black Oak stopped short of the edge of the wood line and squatted to the ground. Dad said his heart give on him and his knees went weak at the sight of the two warriors pullin' down on Cain to make more pain for him. The gag in Cain's mouth did not let out any sound from his screams. The two must've moved to the shed while Dad and Black Oak was slippin' down the mountain. The sight of him so close, just hangin there bein' tortured and nobody helpin', was more than Dad could stand. His vision became very narrow. Black Oak saw the look on his face.

"Thompie," Black Oak whispered. "Thompie, do you hear me? Listen." He grabbed Dad's arm and got him to look him in the eye.

"We wait. You heard, we wait. Dancing Bear will handle this. He will lead them off and then we will go and cut Cain down. I am going to the other side so that we have him surrounded. Stay still until you see them leave. Draw your knife, Thompie, just in case it is needed. These warriors may think themselves gods, I will show them God," he said, grinnin', as he drew his huge knife and left.

If he'd looked close at Dad 'fore he left, he would've seen Dad's knife shinin' sharp, locked in his right hand with the blade up. Dancing Bear was wantin' to lead 'em off and take Cain as quiet as possible; Dad know'd that. But when they got nearer that shed and he could see close his boy hangin' there with pain on his face, could hear him moanin', Dad made up his own mind on how he was gonna do. He was gonna get Cain, and if He, the good Lord, willed it, he was gonna kill some bad Indians what done this to him. His mind was settled and he breathed a short, short prayer. Two Indians weren't gonna do this to his family and get away with it, he would see to it. Thing was, he was gonna see to it right then.

Black Oak and Dancing Bear expected no less when Dad drew his knife and walked out in the clear openin' headed for Cain. His mind would not turn back. The nearest of the two warriors spotted Dad and grinned a smart little grin as he leaped toward Dad like a deer, tryin' to block his way to Cain. Dad dropped to a runnin' squat, and just as the two colided, he brought his right hand up from behind his right-side and sank the blade of his knife in the bottom of the Indian's center, just above his belt. He jerked the sharp blade up toward his heart with a hard pull, runnin' it plumb through his homespun shirt and out the bone in his chest, slicin' all—guts, heart and lung. The warm blood covered Dad's hand and arm, makin' the handle of the knife slick. He could smell the richness of its warmth, grippin' even tighter on the deer antler handle. Dad moved aside and kept his trail as the knife finished its chore and cleared the Cherokee's throat. The Indian fell in a bath of mud and blood behind him, but Dad never took his eyes off Cain as the Cherokee warrior curled up, holdin' his guts in place, and died.

The next warrior was runnin' full on and was on Dad in a second as Dad squared to meet his attack. They hit full-force. Black Oak said later he heard the steel in their knives as they come together. Dad spun and they hit the wet ground as the Indian tried to wrap his arms around Dad like a bear. It was the last move that Indian would ever make.

Dad's left arm was pushin' against the Indians chest, keepin' him from closin' him up, while his right arm stayed free and low. He fought hard till he was able to slide his blade under the arm of the warrior, findin' an openin' close to his chest. With strength found only in rage and revenge, Dad slowly slid the knife up, cuttin' through the Indian's lower jaw, through the tongue, through the roof of his mouth and into the brain, where Dad gave it a little twist just to add some pain, before the tip showed through the top of his head. Dad said later he felt the dyin' quiver as the Indian's body shut down.

Dad was up and jerkin' his knife free 'fore the Cherokee draw'd his last breath, never hardly takin' his eyes off his hangin' son. Hate filled his soul as he ran, worried at the sight of what they'd done to Cain. He weren't a half dozen steps away when he threw his blood- and brain-smeared knife over the top of Cain's head, cuttin' the rope in one easy slice. Cain came fallin' down into his Dad's arms at the same time an arrowhead shot through the front of Thompie's right shoulder, just below the top of his back. Dad turned as he fell so that Cain's body would land on him. This kept Cain from hittin' the hard, dirty ground, but shoved the arrow through near to the fletchin'. Once Cain was layin' free, Dad reached for his small knife with his left hand and cut Cain's hands loose.

The third warrior, who must've been hid in the tree line 'cause Dancing Bear never saw him, was comin' on 'em in a hurry. Dad was doin' all he could to stand and take the fight. But it was all for nothin'. The broadhead from Black Oak's adl-adl hit the warrior square in the hip. You never heard such a squeal! Sounded like a young boar when Dad took his nuts out. Black Oak hurried to him and stuck his foot in his mouth to shut him up. Dad was up and walked to where the wounded Indian was layin'. He reached for his last knife to cut the Cherokee's throat, but Black Oak grabbed his arm and would not let him do it.

"The place where Cain was hangin' looks empty. He will do just fine there," said Black Oak, smilin'.

Black Oak took the rope from Cain as Dad moved over to check on him, the arrow point still leakin' blood off its tip. Black Oak jerked the arrow outa the warrior's hip, but this time there was no squeal. His massive foot was in the wounded warrior's mouth, mud and all. He picked the Indian up and tied the rope around his wrists, his arms behind him, just as they'd done Cain. He throw'd the lead over the very beam Cain was hung on, then filled the warrior's mouth with mud so he couldn't holler. He turned and walked toward the nearest post, pullin' on the rope till the Indian was hangin' with his feet free of the ground. He looped it over another small beam and tied off to the post. He would hang till somebody freed him. He was in some serious pain, but neither my dad nor Black Oak cared. Cain had been there just minutes before. Dad remembered how the dead warrior had added pain to Cain while he was hangin', so he walked back to the hangin' warrior, lifted his foot, and started slowly pushin' down on the back of his legs. No one could hear his screams. Thompie smiled.

Dancing Bear already had Cain up and was headin' toward the trees near as fast as Cain could walk. The wounded warrior's squeal was sure to alert any of his clan that was close by. Black Oak helped Dad to his feet and took off followin', but Dad was in a lot of pain. Dancing Bear wanted to get Cain hid 'fore any of the Yonah clan came and found what had happened to the guards and the one Black Oak hung up in place of Cain. It weren't far into the woods till they found a chestnut log they could hide behind, but Dad was 'bout out, his eyes barely open now.

After gettin' Cain looked at, Dancing Bear turned to Dad.

"Thompie, can you hear me? You and Cain must go from this place. You are hurt and will need proper care. We will free this arrow, then you must find the strength to go to the low gap and take the horse home. Black Oak, my sons and I will take care of Rose, so do not worry. We will take her and follow you soon."

The arrow was black flint and sharp, drippin' red with Dad's blood. Cain said later it reminded him of the back of a black widow spider. Black Oak raised Dad up a little, which made him groan in pain, as the arrow was still in one piece. The turkey feather fletchin' still showed full and was stickin' outa Dad's back. Blood flowed outa his front and his back. The point had done its damage.

Black Oak took his small knife and cut two notches direct across and on either side of the arrow's shaft, 'bout six inches from Dad's back, makin' him hump up in pain. He squeezed his right hand around the shaft with the base of his palm tight on the back of Dad's shoulder. Usin' his left hand and two thumbs, he pinched them together with some strength and broke the shaft at the notches. Dad went out from the pain.

"It is good that he is out," said Black Oak. "It is better if he does not feel when we pull the rest of the shaft through the front of his shoulder. He would scream if he felt the burning pain, I know."

Dancing Bear put the palm of his left hand against the front of Dad's right shoulder next to the shaft behind where the point was tied. With the shaft held still between his thumb and forefinger, he grabbed the shaft next to the arrowhead with his right hand and gave it a quick, firm pull, removin' the shaft all the way clean from the way it was travelin'. That woke Dad up. Black Oak had to put his hand over Dad's mouth to quiet the scream, as Dancing Bear was busy stuffin' the hole with fallen oak leaves; that's all they had. Dad would be mad enough and hurtin' enough to walk now. He was awake enough to know he and Cain needed to get outa there 'fore they got found. It was a tough walk without dealin' with bleedin' or hangin' wounds, so it was gonna be real tough for them, bein' that both of 'em was hurt, Dad now worse than Cain.

The rain let up near daylight, but was back now, and footin' was terrible. Cain half walked, half carried Dad back toward the low gap, who was bleedin' out every time his heart beat. Cain was stiff as his body tried to put itself back right; his shoulders was weak and he was havin' trouble keepin' his arm around Dad. It was even hard to keep his fingers closed tight to Dad's buckskin as they climbed. The trail was uphill all the way out, and slick. Cain told me later they'd get two steps up the mountain and slide one back, climbin', goin' tree to tree one at a time.

The rain was makin' it easier for Dancing Bear to sneak into the village to get Rose. Fox Running come to camp not long after Dad and Cain left, said they'd found her and talked with her. She was at her grandmother's place and she was ready to leave, but the Prince would not let her leave to come home. She had to stay in the village with his warriors watchin' out for her. She'd asked to leave three days earlier, but he'd refused her.

It was most important now for her to leave, and for all of them to get back to the mules soon without any of the clan findin' out. Two dead Yonah Cherokee would get folks riled up, and they would be blamin' Cain and Dad. Black Oak didn't kill the third one, so no bad blood would go to him. He hung that heathen, though, and told him who he was, even though all Cherokee know'd George Black Oak.

It was too much. Cain nor Dad could make it on foot. The forest floor was slick, the trail they'd chose was gettin' steeper, and they were both weak—Dad from loss of blood and Cain from the torture and no food. Cain was thinkin' that if they stayed to the valley as long as they could, then maybe they would have enough strength to make it when the trail got steep. But it just weren't gonna happen. They needed Jim.

***

Me and Wolf had a long day ahead of us just sittin' around, waitin' on everybody to come back, tendin' to mules that didn't need no tendin', and watchin' it rain. We'd already walked back to a small branch we'd crossed comin' to the gap and got a store of water for 'em and tied their meal sacks on. We were told to make sure the mules was ready to go when they got back, which was what we'd done all mornin', but they was only so much of that a body could do. We wanted to go into the valley and find 'em, but we know'd we'd get the strap for leavin' the gap, so we stayed right where we was. No tellin' when they'd be back, neither. Still, Wolf bein' Wolf, he had to go out, said he'd bring me back a surprise. Turned out it was a real Wolf surprise, too. I near wet my skins. He did that to me a lot. I'd never really wet myself, it was just that he near made me many times. I liked bein' around him a right smart, though. Him and his family kept things interestin'. He was my friend, but you had to be ready for near anything with him. He was full of questions, which got him into most everything. Besides that, he was very brave. He weren't no different much than any other Cherokee, really, 'cept for the things that made him Wolf…like havin' a female black panther as a friend. A real friend.

He'd only been gone a little while when the mules and Dad's horse got kinda itchy and started movin' around a little. I laid some wood on the fire and went outside the cover for a look. The rain stayed steady, but not real hard, drippin' off my hat brim. I'd took to wearin' hats like big folks and I was growin' to like 'em.

I looked around the gap and up the sides of the ridges to see what was spookin' the critters, but I saw nothin'. I walked to each one and rubbed down their heads with an oiled homespun rag we kept on the tie rope. The oil helped 'em with all the water runnin' down their faces and over their eyes. They didn't mind the weather, though. Mules was tough as hickory nuts and loved bein' outside in the woods. At least Dad's did.

"Jeb," came the voice from up the side of the gap to my left. I looked, and of course it was Wolf, wavin' for me to come to him, but knowin' we was told to stay in the gap. I had no choice. He weren't gonna come to me if that was as close as he'd get 'fore he hollered. So, I went.

I checked the ties and made sure the stock had water. I was kinda sure I'd be back 'fore too long, but it'd likely be a

while. Nothin' Wolf did happened quick. I was surprised he
was back this soon.

The climb to get to where he was went across rocks and
was steep, so I got there in no hurry, leadin' him to tell me I
moved like Owl the Wise One.

"I will need to teach you how to run through the woods
like the deer, or almost like the deer, since you are not
Cherokee," he said, smilin'. That thinkin' would change when
we learned Dancing Bear and Dad had adopted us.

"What is it Wolf, that would make you have me leave the
gap and climb up here?" I questioned, near outa breath.

"Only a little ways further and you will see for yourself,"
he said as he motioned. "Follow me."

"We gotta get back to the gap, Wolf. What if they come
while we are gone?"

"It will be after dinner at least, Jeb. That is still a while
away. Old Man Sun is not high up yet. We have time and the
mules are fine. Come on, I want you to see."

I followed him for another quarter mile before he
stopped, turned to me, and said, "What do you see, Jeb?"

Lookin' hard, at first I saw nothin'. Then I caught a peak
of a sleek, black somethin' easin' through the trees. I know'd in
a second what that was.

"What is this, Wolf? What have you done, my friend?
Why is this cat here with us? This is not the way of things,
Wolf. Does your Dad know of this, her followin' you like she
is?"

"She does follow, Jeb. She stays near to where I am and
she comes when I call her. I can't explain it, but I can call her
to me if she is in reach of hearing, and she always is. She
followed us home from Killing Time and I fed her for several
days. Now she feeds herself, but she still stays near our home. I
have called her many times and have been very close to her two
times. Once I even rubbed the end of her tail, one stroke with
my finger, but she lit out before I got any closer. Watch, I will
call her now."

Wolf put his hand to his mouth and made a sound that
reminded me of a deer fawn bleatin', only it sounded crossed
with a goat. I didn't like goat, nor nothin' made from anything

that come out of 'em, but Spirit must've. She was there in a split second, stoppin' some twenty paces shy of where we stood. She would come no closer. I was a bit nervous watchin' her run toward us till she stopped and sat on her haunches. She looked at me and kinda raised her nose to the air, tryin' to get my scent. I now know'd what made the mules edgy. I wondered if she was rememberin' me.

"She is beautiful, Jeb," he said softly. "I see her all the time around our place. She never comes very close, but will not run off when I go to her. I take her meat scraps, but she hunts for her own meat to survive. I do not know where she sleeps. I believe this to be my ancestors watching over me from across the river."

We sat starin' at each other for several minutes 'fore she stood quick-like and looked back toward the gap. She swished her long black tail like a snake lookin' for mice, and her ears were standin' straight up. Her nose was in the air and her nostrils was movin' from side-to-side, her long, shiny whiskers twitchin' nervous-like while catchin' the air above her head. She'd smelled somethin'. With a sudden look of what a body would think was goodbye, she turned and trotted off, her ears turned back and listenin'.

I was somewhat woods savvy now. A tingle like I'd never felt before rose on the back of my neck. I know'd without a doubt we needed to hurry back to the gap, somethin' must be about the mules. Spirit let us know they was somethin' stirrin', and my guts was talkin' even more. One thing you pick up real quick in the woods is how the critters that live there carry on. The noises they make or the ones they don't will let a body know if other critters is movin' near. Her takin' off like that was no different than if she would've just stood up and spoke, 'Hey, go look in on the stock. They's somethin' there.' And we did.

I was leadin' now, not wastin' any time. Wolf followed. I was in a near full trot goin' down the side of the ridge. I had a feelin' that we should be in the gap, and for some reason I couldn't shake it. It was like a thought you couldn't loose from your thinkin', or like when Momma sings at breakfast and you hear the words all day in your head—you just can't help it.

The pull was strong and got stronger by the second. I was a good way ahead of Wolf, which weren't normal, and runnin' just about as hard as I could go. I know'd I'd messed up and I needed to be where I was told to be. I crossed the last bit of ground 'fore I could see full on to where the mules was on the west side of the gap. The sight stopped me in my tracks. I was standin', starin' and breathin' hard when Wolf come up beside me, his breath soft and even.

I'd learned even at my young age that there are times in our lives when the things you do make you know you are human. Dad always said, "Humans make mistakes, that's why God sent us Jesus. He knew we needed Him." This was one of those times for me.

I'd left where I know'd I was expected to be. If I'd stayed there like I was told to do and not gone wanderin' off, Cain might not be layin' dead in the south end of the low gap just now. Jim loose and standin' over him a ways from where he'd been tied. My head got to swimmin' and my heart twisted in a knot as Wolf and me stood starin'. All I could think was, *Please, God, don't let him be dead on account of me bein' stupid.*

Chapter Twenty-Four

Cain Digs Deep

Cain weren't dead, he was just give out, and it looked like he was by himself. We looked around some, but found nobody. We couldn't tell proper what happened to him or if he'd come from down in the valley, but it looked like he was in a lot of pain. He was laid up in a ball with his arms spread out funny and his head kinda tucked. They was blood and bruises on his face and he was dirty. His hands and wrists was bruised somethin' awful and was bleedin'. He'd been through a bad time, but just what it was we'd have to learn later, 'cause the jibberish he was speakin' weren't even a language. He couldn't hold his eyes open. I could tell his mind was very tired.

The rain started gettin' harder and colder, with small bits of ice now mixed with it. The cold was closin' in. Cain was very weak. Wolf was under one arm and me the other as we drug him up outa the gap and in under our cover to the bearskins. Wolf built up the fire while I stripped him naked so he could dry and warm. We hung his skins outside to wash in the rain. I emptied his possibles bag and there was nothin' in it. His pipe and smoke pouch was gone, as well as both the knives he carried. Somebody had took his truck.

He'd just whooped several months of fightin' death and the rain was doin' him no good, so that put us in a hurry. Momma had packed some rags. We used 'em to dry him good while checkin' him for holes and cuts as we went. We found none, but the places around his shoulders and neck was swole' up terrible, like he'd fell or somethin'. He had some explainin' to do when he come awake better.

We got a pair of homespun britches from Dad's pack and put 'em on him. They was near too tight but fit well enough. We eased him under the bearskin. He was startin' to warm a little when he got to mumblin' about Dad. Somethin' or another 'bout how he needed Jim, or get Jim, or somthin'—he just weren't makin' no sense. He'd tried to loose Jim when he first come to the gap and looked to be headed toward the valley. That put in my mind that he was probably goin' back to where he'd come from, but needed Jim for whatever it was he'd left.

It troubled me that I weren't where I was supposed to be when he'd showed up. Me and Wolf not bein' there left him with no choice but to have to try and muster the strength to go back by himself, as wore out as he was. If I'd minded Dad and stayed in the gap with the stock, I would've been there to talk to him 'fore he give out. That could mean Dad's life if things was that bad. I felt awful. Dad would make me hear 'bout it later on...if he was alive. I would have to worry on that later. Right now I was most worried 'bout Cain. Why was he goin' to all that trouble, him bein' hurt and wore out like he was. There was no way to really know what he was up to or if he was even worried over Dad. He could've just been spoutin' out words with Dad on his mind.

"His body is really cold and his brain is not working right," said Wolf. "We need to make him warmer. We will lay down on top of the bearskin real close with him. Our bodies will warm him faster. Hopefully he will talk to us soon. Your father is in his mind, so it sounds like he may be in need. It was hard to understand the words in Cain's sloppy talk, so we need him to wake and speak. Now, lay yourself down on his right and I will lay here on his left, and we will make him warm so his thoughts will clear."

We'd only laid a few minutes talkin' over why we figured Cain was takin' Jim, when he got to talkin' jibberish again. We must've been warmin' him some. He was comin' around real slow-like. His eyes were closed, but his breathin' was harder and he was tryin' his best to talk. They weren't no blood comin' from his mouth, so I figured his lung was still in place, which was a miracle seein' how his wrists showed he'd been hangin'—anybody could tell that once a body studied on it. Thinkin' on that kinda got my back up toward all Cherokee, even Wolf.

"Cain's been tortured," I said, kinda quick without thinkin' on it good. "I believe his wrists show signs of him bein' hung up by a rope. I don't cotton to that kinda behavior toward folk, Wolf. Do all Cherokee do this to people for so little a reason?"

"No. Forgive them. It is not normal among my clan or my tribe, but this has to do with things of the heart, which is more than just a normal fight between clans. We treat tribe members fairly if they do law-breaking like murder and hurting folks. We punish those who do wrong, and in our eyes this is very wrong. If this is what has happened, and I believe you to be true, my father and our clans will make it right, of that I am sure."

"Where do you think he was tryin' to get to when he took ole Jim?"

"That is still a worry to me. I have thought he may be running from something and the spirits brought him here, but the more I study over it, the more I believe he was trying to go down in the valley. He was far enough south in the gap to make me think that he was headed there. It seems he was in a hurry, and that is the steepest side and the quickest way in. He may be tangled up with the clan from Yonah over Rose. He will wake and we will know soon," Wolf said.

Wolf weren't exactly right about when ole Cain was gonna wake. It was daylight next mornin' before he ever stirred. Even then they weren't much to it. Me and Wolf had caught Jim and got the stock back right 'fore dark. We slept near all night, wakin' some to listen for Cain. Next mornin' the rain was still fallin' soft and steady. We was sittin' under our cover watchin' it, hopin' he'd wake, when a low groan and a little cough let us know he was stirrin'. I'd slept little thinkin' on Dad. Now I was hopin' to find out what all happened and hopefully where he was, if he'd been with Cain.

I moved up on his right side so he could hear me. Wolf squatted on his left. I bent down and put my mouth to his ear and spoke softly.

"Cain? Can you hear me, Cain? We need you to wake up and talk to us if you can. Why is it you needed Jim, Cain? Can you tell me that? Huh? Listen, Cain, have you seen Dad?"

When I mentioned Dad, his eyes popped opened and he drew in a hard breath that made a suckin' sound like when you was gettin' Momma's hot soup off a spoon.

"Dad...Jeb...get Dad," he said, near whisperin'. He spoke through a painful squint. "Valley...valley...hurt...Dad's hurt...go get him, Jeb."

He could hardly form the words so a body could make 'em out. I looked over at Wolf who was as lost in what Cain was sayin' as I was, and it showed on our faces. Cain must've seen our worry. He jerked straight up sudden-like, throwin' me and Wolf off to each side a little. He reached and grabbed Wolf by the collar with both hands and pulled his face to where their noses near touched.

"Follow my back trail to the bottom of the valley," he said through pain and gritted teeth, his eyes open but just. "Go east to the gap, then south to the small top back of the long ridge that runs north to south. Dad is there on the top, waitin'. He's hurt."

That was it. He went plumb out on us and we had to tuck him back in under the bearskin cover. He was just plain wore out. Whatever it was he'd been through had took most of what he had to give. Dad bein' hurt and needin' help gave him a poke of strength, but that had played out now. He'd mustered just enough muscle to reach and get Wolf and tell him where Dad was. That was smart that he grabbed him instead of me, 'cause Wolf could follow that trail Cain left for sure, and I most likely could not. He was exhausted; that little was all he had left. He could go no more.

Me and Wolf checked the stock and double-checked their ties since we know'd for sure they was a painter cat about. We untied Jim and headed straight outa the gap and down into the valley. Wolf leadin' after Cain's trail, with me behind on Jim. Wolf would have to pay mind to the way Cain had come, so me and Jim stayed back a ways. We had to go slow to make sure we had the right trail with the rain and all, but Wolf stayed to it. It weren't long till we'd made it all the way through the bottom of the valley and right up into the gap below the top where Dad was to be. I prayed he'd be there and that he was alive as we tied Jim off in the gap.

It was a small top covered in old, tall ivy risin' up outa the valley a little ways, kinda hid behind the big ridge runnin' north to south. I wondered why Cain would leave Dad here hid like this. Seems he'd 'a-left him out in the open 'case anybody come by and been able to help carry him on to the low gap. Cain never did nothin' without no reason, so he would've had one for why Dad was left in such a place this far off the trail. Then it come to me—Indians! He was keepin' Dad safe. I suddenly felt very small.

"Wolf," I said, as he turned to me.

"Yes, Jeb, what is it?"

"Have you give any thought as to why Cain would leave Dad hid up here like this and not down by the trail in the valley? Why would he lead him off up this little holler and hide him like this when it would mean a lot more movin' and roustin' on Dad?"

"I have thought of this and I believe there must have been trouble, Jeb. The Yonah clan could be searching for Cain and your dad. We must watch ourselves as we search this top for him, and be careful on our way back to the low gap."

The lead to the small top was covered with ivy thicket that was way up over our heads, with trails so faint a body could hardly see 'em. We had to use 'em, though. They was the only way you could get through. Once in the thicket you could only see a few paces in any direction. The most visible of the deer trails followed the ridge back outa the gap south, just like Cain said. Bein' that Cain was hurt, he most likely stayed to the easiest trail, at least Wolf was thinkin' so, 'cause he was followin' it. It was hard goin' so we had to bend over as we walked, but it weren't far to the top.

The ivy cleared out some the higher we got, and Cain's trail got harder to follow. Wolf had to stop many times on our way up to the top to search for their sign. I don't think he ever really did find it again 'fore we got to the top. Didn't really matter, the top weren't real big. Dad was there somewhere, we just had to find him.

He'd be hid and may not be awake, so we looked real good all over. There was some rocks just off the top to the north. When Wolf caught sight of those, he took off in hurry.

He felt somethin' or saw the trail, 'cause he was there in a couple of jumps. He squatted to his heels and started lookin' off the backside. After takin' a quick look, he stood and turned to me. I'd already seen that face on Wolf before. I know'd he'd found my dad. I prayed that he was alive as I ran to where Wolf was standin'.

Dad was sittin' on the ground leaned up against a big rock, just past where Wolf was. His head was laid back on the rock behind his left shoulder and his eyes were shut. He was out, and looked dead. There was a bloody hole in the front of his right shoulder and a trail of blood leakin' down from it. His color was that of the mornin' fog. If he was breathin', he was gettin' very little air. He weren't movin' and his chest was layin' flat. I got kinda weak in my legs at the sight of him.

"I saw blood on the stones here," Wolf said as he pointed to the edge of the rock face in front of him. "It looked like he had leaned against the cold stone and the blood was runnin' down, but where is it? I know I saw it."

I saw no blood, and I was walkin' by right where he was pointin'.

"Where did you see blood, Wolf?" I asked as I moved by him toward Dad. "I looked, but I saw no blood on those stones. It must've been the rain playin' a fool on your eyes. Now move and lets' get to tendin' Dad."

"You are wise, Jeb," he said as he jumped down into the rocks by Dad. "I trust you with my life, but I know what I saw. There was blood on those stones that led me here. I do not know why there is no blood there now, but there was."

Dad was breathin' but just a little. It was gonna be real hard to get him out by ourselves. He was so big, but it had to happen. Us two young'uns had to get him outa them rocks and back to the low gap. We had to do it now, somehow, without killin' him or lettin' any of the Yonah clan know we was here. I really wished George was with us.

It was rainin' on Dad's face and he was out, so they weren't no wakin' him. We was gonna have to figure how to move him, even though he was too big for us to carry. It didn't take Wolf long till he had it in his mind how to move Dad, which of course was the Cherokee way.

"There is only one way we are going to move him, and that is to use drag poles and make a travois. That is how the people moved wounded folks during the war. We will cut a couple of hickory saplings the size of our arms and strap him down so we can move him. We must move quickly, but pay mind to your dad's wound. He has bled much and is very weak. Now, we need to find some small hickory while keeping our eyes on the woods." The look I saw in his eyes made me glad to have him as my friend.

Weren't no hickory nearby, so we took a couple of white oaks a little bigger than my arm. It took us a while to cut 'em with our knives, but we did it and fetched 'em back to where Dad was laid out. He weren't no trouble to get on the poles once we laced some ivy limbs across to put him on. We both took off our shirts and laid 'em on the limbs to make it softer 'fore we rolled him on. We moved him real steady-like, and thankfully he come awake a little. He looked and know'd we was there, but that was 'bout it 'fore he closed his eyes again.

I thought it was tough goin' up to get Dad, but I started thinkin' that was easy compared to bringin' him down the way we was. The trails in the thicket was barely big enough for a deer, weren't near big enough for two boys and a big grown man laced to poles. We fought the limbs and tried to keep Dad from gettin' banged against 'em, but it weren't no use—he was sufferin' from our efforts. The way we was goin' it'd be dark 'fore we ever got him clear and off the top. We was gonna have to crawl.

It was easier once we hit our bellies. We went down feet first and pulled Dad as we went, inches at a time. The goin' was slow, but we was movin', and it was easier on Dad for sure, slidin' instead of bouncin'.

Jim was anxious when we finally made it back to the gap. Dad seemed no worse than before, which was a miracle the way the trip down went. We covered him in a blanket we'd brought, and Wolf tucked it in around the edges. We was just gonna tie a leather strap from pole-to-pole at the ends and let the strap lay across Jim's back in front of his hips so it wouldn't slide off. That would be comfortable for ole Jim, then we could work him back to the gap pullin' Dad. At least that was what we hoped was gonna happen, good Lord willin' and the Indians didn't get us. *God help us! Please don't let Dad die,* I prayed. Folks in the valley depended on God. It was just the way our faith guided.

Wolf had come ready. He had leather straps and the rags from Momma, and of course Anne's medicine pouch she'd made for us. He bent and started diggin' leaves from the hole in Dad's shoulder. You could tell somebody must've poked 'em in to try and slow the bleedin'. If we could get him home alive, them leaves might prove to be one of the things that saved him.

Wolf took up the medicine pouch and dug around till he found a twist of inner bark from a hickory tree tied with a small piece of homespun cloth. He cut some ends off with his small knife, then stuck the bunch in his mouth and started chewin'. He made an awful face while he was chewin', but he kept at it till the lump was softer and chewed up some. He then bent over Dad and spit out the nasty tastin' juice right in the middle of the hole in Dad's shoulder, droppin' the wad in his hand. He rolled it between his palms till it was the size of the hole, then stuck it in with his left hand and thumped it with the palm of his right, stuffin' the front hole full. Dad grunted but did not wake.

"This wound was made by an arrowhead, be it from a bow or an adl-adl. The inside bark of the nut hickory helps with arrow wounds and fights the evil spirit that makes the wound angry. It was good Anne thought to put some in the pouch. The juice from the bark is not enough to heal him, so we must keep moving to get him back home, for his blood will soon be gone."

I looked at Dad who was an awful sight. The arrow that made the hole may've been tipped with somethin', 'cause he looked near dead. He would not wake even for pain, a bad sign. He was near spent and Wolf know'd it, just as I did. It was gonna take the help of the Almighty to get Dad home and safe without him dyin' first, but we was gonna do all we could not to let him down.

The rain had stopped some, and Jim couldn't 'a-been no better. He tracked as smooth a trail as a mule was able. We had Dad back down low in just a short time. We weren't able to hide from nobody, so we figured it best to just make a straight shot of it right back to the low gap.

We followed deer trails when we got down to the very bottom of the valley, and tracked past several small branches and some really old rocks that had moss growin' all over 'em, thick like Momma's pound cakes. The valley went up on both sides. They weren't many trees, but the ones around was tall and shady, and there was many big rocks. It was dark and damp like our root cellar; the air felt thick as you breathed it in, tastin' the earth across my tounge. We was down at the bottom of the bottom. You could feel the pull of Mother Earth as we walked what felt like the lowest part of the whole put-together. Wolf said he could feel the old ones who'd crossed the Great River walkin' with us, but it just felt spooky to me, like haints lived there. I didn't want to come back to this place without havin' to.

We stopped a little ways on to check Dad, and Wolf spoke of the way he saw things.

"We will need to be very careful when we take Thompie up the ridge and out of this low place. Jim will have a tough time with his footing, so we will go side-to-side up the main holler that leads to the gap. We will have to hold your Dad steady from the low side each time we switch back till we reach flat ground. Do you think we can do this, Jeb? Do you think you can walk Jim steady enough to make it out without killing your father?"

I was shakin' so with scared and cold that it was hard to talk, but I mustered up enough to say, "I know for sure Jim's able. I'll lead." And with that, we took back to the trail, me leadin' and Wolf watchin' Dad from behind.

I swore I kept seein' little peaks of slick black in the woods followin' us when I looked over our back trail, which reminded me that I was in the world of the Cherokee. If not, how was it then that Wolf saw the blood on the rock when there was none to see, but it leadin' us straight to Dad, helpin' to save his life? Where did the old ones and their fire go when they were conversin' with Spirit? How did the old medicine woman know when folks needed her, and how many times had she needed to show up and did in just my short life? I believed Dad, he allowed it was the work of the Holy Spirit.

It was hard goin', and that's sayin' it soft. The ground was plumb slick. I could tell that Jim was gettin' fed up with it all. He didn't want to make them turns 'cause Dad was slidin' around and he could feel it. I'd done had to tie his lead off short and lay the reins across his back to handle him, which turned out to be a blessin'. We'd switched back maybe twice, with Wolf watchin' the low side, when on the third turn, Jim'd had enough. He jerked that lead from my hand so fast it burned my wet, wrinkled skin. There weren't gonna be no more crisscrossin'. Jim know'd right where to go, and it was obvious he was gonna go there and take Dad. He made a hard turn north toward the top, slingin' Wolf sideways up against a poplar tree, so hard it bruised the ribs on his right side. It happened so fast that Dad stayed plumb still and never quivered a bit in the travois.

I watched as Jim's new trail was gun-barrel straight, right at the gap. He weren't makin' no more turns, no, sir. It was to the top for him, and Dad, me and Wolf weren't gonna be able to stop him now. His mind was made. We followed as best we could, but Jim was in a hurry. A mule like him climbin' a mountain with somethin' as light as Dad and the travois weren't no slow thing. Mountain mules was tough. They loved nothin' better than to get with it and go. Jim weren't no different. I swear he know'd it was Dad on the pull, and that somethin' was wrong. He surely smelled the blood, seein' as Dad's right side was covered in it.

The travois bounced very little as we lost sight of it headin' toward Cain and the rest of the stock in the low gap. I just hoped none of the Yonah clan crossed trails with Jim 'fore he could get Dad out. He was 'a wonder of a mule for sure, a gift from God,' Dad always said.

Chapter Twenty-Five

A Tragic Event

We followed Jim's track, which wandered through the high and low places headed toward the tops but always in line with the low gap. He'd found the smoothest path to make a trail from and worked that holler proper, never drug Dad over a rough spot nor through no ivy thickets nor over no rocks. It was still a rough ride. They was spots in the trail where we'd see Dad's blood. I tried to reason that if he was still bleedin', then the death spirit had not found him yet. My heart near stopped at one spot there was so much. I felt so helpless. I honestly did not know if my dad was gonna live or die. My knees gave out and I hit the earth and cried. I wanted my dad. I was not hopeless though. I know'd it was all in the palm of the Almighty. He would take care of Dad whichever way it went. Knowin' that give me comfort.

Wolf hit his knees beside me and said, "My friend, I have known the sting of death and it is very painful. You must see that if he crosses the Great River he will be in a much better place. A place where there is family and the trails are safe, no enemies hunt you, and the deer are as big as Jim. It is away from us for now, but one day all those who know the Christ will be there, and no one will die and leave again because of the Blood. We will be there with them one day, too, Jeb. I know the thought of that will help with the hurt."

It did.

We tracked north for a long ways thinkin' we might catch up to Jim, but it weren't gonna happen. That mule was strong, and he would be in the low gap 'fore me and Wolf could even see it. The mountain was steep to the south side, but it was nothin' we weren't used to, 'cept that this time we was in a hurry. That changed things. Wolf was leadin' and I was back a-ways. We was goin' faster than normal, just about to run outa

effort, when the rounded south side of the low gap come in
sight. I realized we was almost back. I near cried again when I
saw Jim was standin' and waitin' on us with his head down
where the steep ground broke to the gap and started gettin'
level. Seemed like it took a long time after we seen Jim to get
to Dad. He looked no worse than when we'd last seen him. Jim
did good. The rain was still softly fallin', givin' Dad's face a
shine that was not real against his gray color; had only stopped
a few times since we'd first got to the gap.

Jim was foamed up good. You could tell he'd worked a
hard pull gettin' Dad back safe. We was lucky none of the
Yonah bunch caught up to him. If they'd had we'd a-not been
seein' Dad right then. I gathered Jim's lead and got him to
movin' while Wolf went to rouse Cain. We was gonna need his
help gettin' Dad the rest of the way home. Jim had a bloody
place on his back from the strap holdin' the travois poles. It
weren't bad, but he was done pullin'. That kinda spot can get
bad in a hurry if not tended. Peter would need to pull Dad on
home, which made me proud. He was a good mule.

Wolf and Cain was sittin' up by a small warmin' fire
under our sleepin' cover. It looked like Cain was talkin' to him.
I led Jim to a stoppin' point a few paces short of the fire. Cain,
who weren't movin' normal, but was movin', walked out to
check on Dad—not much different from when he left him, 'cept
he'd lost more blood. I couldn't look on him...he looked dead
to me.

The rain had cut back to a drizzle you wouldn't even
notice but for it hittin' you in the face. Cain reached and
checked Dad on the neck with his fingers and gave me a bad
look.

"You and Wolf done good goin' and gettin' Dad. We got
a lot to talk about later, but for now we need to head on home.
Wolf will have to stay here for the others. They will need the
mules and the horse 'cause Rose will be comin' back with 'em.
I've talked to him and explained it all. He said he'd be fine with
it for us to get Dad on. Now go get Peter, and let's get movin'
before Dad goes across the river," Cain said with a hard effort.

"You alright, Cain?" I asked. "You gonna be able to make it back home with me and Dad, or do you think Wolf should go with me and you stay back for them with the stock?"

"That's rightful thinkin', Jeb. It could be better, but I need to be with Dad while he's travelin'."

Cain always had his reasons for doin' things, so me and Wolf minded. We both got warm homespun shirts on and sat by the fire while Cain got himself ready. The soft, warm clothes Momma packed was made of lamb's wool, which would turn water. We all had one shirt of pure lamb's wool, as we didn't have enough lambs every year to make but one. Dad got the 'one' this year, and Cain had it on, so Wolf got Cain's to wear since Dad was layin' on our skin shirts.

The rain was done and the sky had started showin' some blue as soon as we got the travois rested on Peter's back. The young mule was a little short with it for a minute, but then settled in and got comfortable. A mule had to be comfortable with what it was they was supposed to be pullin' or they'd get their back up and not move. Folks called it stubborn.

The trail in and outa the low gap was used a right smart and was easy to follow. I was leadin' Peter, and Cain was followin' along behind, watchin' out for Dad. He weren't walkin' like his old self; you could tell he was sore. He weren't talkin' like his old self, neither.

Fact was, he weren't his old self. His mind was on whatever it was that went on in the valley, of that I was sure. Nothin' made him get quiet like matters concernin' family and his beloved. Rose was on his mind; the look in his face was of worry mixed with pain mixed with mad. There was somethin' to be settled. I was thinkin' it was gonna be settled Cain's way this time.

The trail home was wet and slick, and water would drop on us from overhangin' limbs, but the sun's rays through the trees was Heaven-like, all crisp, bright, yellow and orange light that showed us the trail clear. Peter was doin' just fine and all was goin' the way we needed it, but the light was fadin' fast. We needed to step it up some to make it in 'fore dark, so I gave Peter a slight tighten on the lead and he quickened his pace. Cain never said a word, he just picked his walk up some and went on, hardly raisin' his head any. He looked to be walkin' some better, and my worry for him let off some. At least he weren't spittin' up blood. Even I know'd to be on the lookout for that.

I led Jim outa the woods and up the lower trail to our home. It'd been a long trip and I sure was glad to be back. Dad hadn't opened his eyes that I'd seen since we left the little top where Cain hid him. Cain weren't no good, neither. His color had gone back to gray and he was bent over, strugglin' for air with his hands on his knees, as we stopped near the back porch steps leadin' to the cook room door. His hair was long now and hung down near to the ground bent over like he was; was wavin' back and forth as he kinda gasped in short breaths. Directly, he laid down in the wet grass of our backyard on his side, restin' his head on his arm. I thought silently that I hoped they weren't no chicken piles where he'd laid down. He looked like he didn't care if the whole ground was covered in it. He was wore out again. I was gonna have the farm to myself for a few days the way it was lookin'.

I climbed the back steps to the porch and walked kinda slow over to the back door. The latch string was out, so I reached to grab it, but didn't pull on it yet. It was gonna be hard to look on Momma's face when she first seen Dad and then looked on Cain, too. I'd been with 'em both for a while and know'd what they looked like, but now it was just gonna be throw'd on her. This was gonna be bad for her and a shock, but she would stand strong. She always did.

I must've stood there thinkin' a minute, 'cause the next thing I know'd the string went loose in my hand and the door swung open. I was not ready for what I came to be facin'. The face was wrinkled and dark, its skin saggin' like leather britches dryin' in the sun while waitin' on the boilin' pot. The hair looked like the mane of a white horse, combed, and she was smilin' a slight grin. The old medicine woman was lookin' at me like she was sizin' me up for how big a pot she'd need to boil me in. Her look was that of worry; had a stare in her eyes that made me wonder even more why she was there. She reached and put her hand on my shoulder.

"You have made strong roots with the spirits young one, Wolf as well. What you have done is right with the Creator. He smiles down on you. Tell me now, where is Thompie, and is he still alive?"

I was not shocked at her showin' up the way she done, but for her to know that Dad was the one hurt and near death was hard to chew. I couldn't get a hold on it. She know'd when things happened and come ready every time, always had the right medicines for the sickness or hurt she'd be tendin'. She weren't always there, meanin' we'd have to go and get her on occasion, but she was there mostly.

I didn't answer her fast enough, so she pushed me aside and walked on out to check Dad. I looked around in the house, which appeared empty. I turned and went back out. Momma and Anne was there, both of 'em tendin' Dad and Cain. They'd been in the barn gettin' the critters settled for the night. Momma was with Cain while Anne and now Owl was seein' to Dad. It had been a long trip for me and I was tired, so I just sat down on the back steps and watched the women folk gettin' busy. I put my elbows on my knees and bowed my head some and thanked God for helpin' me and Wolf make it back, and for keepin' us from meetin' any of them Yonahs. He walked with us in that valley of death. I know'd it, as sure as I was sittin' there.

***

Dancing Bear walked into the village like the important man he actually was, his two sons and Black Oak trailin'. None had weapons. It was more for show of trust than anything since he was on shaky ground with his neighborin' brethren. They'd found the dead warriors, and the whole village was angry and on edge.

No warriors was in sight. It was an insult to Dancing Bear to only have women and little ones to meet him. He know'd the warriors had been watchin' him for a while and would not bother him without cause. He had done no wrong, but his friend had. If that friend had been Cherokee instead of white, then Dancing Bear would be held to blame. He must get Rose quickly and leave.

Dancing Bear stopped near the well in the center of the village and was surrounded by children and women, but not one warrior stood in the crowd of Cherokee. He got the message.

"Brothers from Yonah," Dancing Bear yelled, slowly circlin' the well and watchin' the woods. "Hear my words and know that I feel your loss. Two wives are without their husbands. Two families have lost their keepers. That is very sad for the family and loved ones. I, too, know the pain of the death spirit, as we all know the stories of the war times. Let us not walk that trail again. Ask the Great Spirit who created us all to mend our pain and anger. I have come for my daughter. I have been told she was kept from coming home. I hope this is not true. Her heart is in my valley and will stay in my valley. That is her decision. I did not help her to decide, your prince did.

"Thompie Collins killed your warriors while saving his son from Two Suns Rising's torture. I saw my white son hanging from the timbers of the long shed. I, too, welcomed blood revenge for this act of cowards. The time now is for mourning, but this will be talked about through the smoke of council when the leaves fall. Torture for no reason will not be tolerated against tribe members or blood brothers of the tribe. There is a time when we must act to keep our families safe, but matters of the heart call for compassion, not hatred and pain. Another may lose his life this night. But hear me, I will not seek due if he does. There has been enough death. I go now with my family. I will return after council meets during the time of new leaves."

Rose had come from her grandmother's home and walked to Black Oak's side. Her aunt and uncle, cousins and grandmother all came with her, their pouches packed for travel. That did not surprise Black Oak, who stayed still and calm, his eyes was watchin' close every movement he could catch. They was renegades in this bunch; he know'd it, as did Dancing Bear.

"The family of my wife, A-Ga-Li-Ha, is leaving with us. They will return with me if they so choose. We will leave this valley. No talk of what happened here will have place around our fires. When the pain is gone, we welcome all visitors. I hope you will want to come," said Dancing Bear as he and his group made its way slowly north outa the village.

They cleared the village and made it to the woods. All felt like they was past any danger. The men had left their weapons hid in the woods not far north of the village in case they was forced to make a run for it. Black Oak was leadin' and Dancing Bear was followin'. They was just a few paces shy of their truck when an arrow centered a white oak not two paces in front of Moon Shadow's nose.

Everyone froze.

The Indian was tall, lean and strong, two feathers hangin' to his left side. His pace was slow and quiet. He was in no hurry—he had a captive bunch. A simple look only Black Oak had seen caused seven battle-hardened warriors to appear and circle Dancing Bear and his family. Things had just got bad. All wore paint, and they had bows with sharp flint-tipped arrows that could break bone.

Two Suns Rising moved on slowly as his trail took him past Black Oak, though he never took his eyes off him as he went by. He know'd Black Oak could kill him with one blow from the back of his hand or closed fist. His aim was to face Dancing Bear, and that is where he stopped, face on, noses nearly touchin'.

He stared Dancing Bear in the eye for what seemed like a minute, then moved toward Fox Running. With the motion of a snake, Two Suns drew his long knife and slit Fox's throat. 'Fore he know'd what'd happened, his blood started to flow. Fox Running felt the sting and reached up as the warmth flowed over his hands and down his arms. He looked at Two Suns in shock, then over to Dancing Bear. Almost like he was sayin' goodbye to his father in his final moments, as he sank to his knees, gaspin' for air, the crimson runnin' down his front. Rose ran to him and tried to stop the blood, but there'd be no way. Warriors kill when they want.

Dancing Bear went wild as he lunged for his son. It took three of the warriors just to hold him back as the blood drained outa Fox's life. Black Oak was on Two Suns in a second, would've had him, but Two Suns jerked Rose up by the hair and held his bloody blade to her throat. The look in his face made it clear he did not care if he killed a second time.

Two Suns moved Rose in front of Dancing Bear, still keepin' the knife at her throat while he spoke.

"The first man the white devil killed was my brother. His blood is on you for this daughter's trouble. Now you and I are straight, a life for a life. I hope they can be friends across the river. Listen to my words now, sad family: the next blood to run will be the blood of your daughter's chosen. I will hunt him down and he will die, slowly. I will cook his heart over my fire and share it with my family. A white man's heart is weak, but still the heart of my enemy. He will know no peace across the river."

The warriors had all gathered in close, as Two Suns released Rose. Another slight motion and the whole bunch disappeared into the woods, war cries trailin' behind. Dancing Bear rushed to his son and did all he could to stop death from comin', but there was just no way. The blade had done its owners work.

Fox Running was dead.

The family started softly singin' his death song. Dancing Bear sat and hugged his dead son and cried, his blood stainin' Dancing Bear's skins. The killin' happened so fast that it was hard for them to believe what they saw. Fox Running was alive and beautiful just a few minutes before, now he was gone to be with those across the river. It left a body cold inside thinkin' on it.

***

Wolf was by himself and sittin' by the fire late in the day when Spirit showed up, unexpected-like. She laid down on her haunches across the gap and just kinda stared his way. She came from downwind, had not made a sound slippin' in that Wolf or the stock had heard. It was a surprise her showin' up close as she did. The rain had quit, but Wolf was still chillin' from the wet, so he stayed by the fire and watched her. He really weren't thinkin' on much, just kinda sittin', when somethin' from inside reached up and grabbed him at the same time Spirit let out one of her hair-raisin' screams. He said later it was like one of Dad's mules kicked him in the guts while lightnin' struck overhead. He lost all his wind and near lost his supper. It was a pain he'd never felt and it worried him. He figured it from the spirit world, lettin' him know somethin' bad had happened, but just what it was he couldn't know. He never would've thought it was as bad as it turned out to be. He told me later he reasoned it to do with my dad; that he was worried Dad might've died. He'd not know until they all returned to the low gap that it was his brother who'd died, that he'd been murdered. Killed by a coward, Cain would say.

***

Dad was laid in the guest bed, near dead as a body can get and still be breathin'. It was my turn to sit with him. It seemed lookin' on him that he weren't there. Momma had already got the little mirror out and put it under his nose a couple times to make sure he was still pushin' air. Anne, Owl and Momma was sleepin' since it was late at night and they'd worked on him all day. The hole was as clean and cared for as could be. Old Mother and Anne had mixed a batch of medicine, and the wound was full of it. Nasty-lookin' stuff was leakin' outa the hole now 'stead of blood, but Anne said it was proper. Cain was sittin' with me, rockin' in front of the fire with his pipe goin'. Granddad and Grandma got word Dad was back and hurt near about the time we got him home, and they'd come just after supper. The Indians know'd. We'd met a couple on the trail. All the Cherokee of the Choestoe clan know'd my dad and respected him. They got the word on down the trail. They was already folks settin' up camp around our home so they could be with us and pray and help Momma. It was what folks did. It's what Jesus would've done. One of their own was hurt, and they was gonna see to it that all was done that could be done.

I'd checked Dad 'fore I went and sat with Cain by the fire. There weren't no change—barely any breath and no movement. Anne said the evil spirit of infection had got in and was rottin' his blood. Old Mother had done all there was that could be done. God would need to do His blessin' now, if that would be His will.

Cain's hands and wrists had a salve mix Anne had made and smeared on 'em, and Old Mother had given him a tea for the pain in his shoulders. He was just sittin' and smokin'. We'd not had a chance to talk gettin' Dad back and all, so naturally, I had to give in to my bein' curious.

"How'd you come by them wounds on your hands and wrists, Cain? Did somebody do that to you? Are you gonna be okay?"

He never said nothin', yet I know'd he heard me. We just sat there not sayin' a word for a bit till he finally spoke.

"You don't need to worry none 'bout what happened to me, little brother. It ain't for young'uns like you to think on. Just know they's folks out there that'll do a body harm when it don't seem right. But in time, they end up gettin' what's comin' to 'em. I can tell you sure the folks what done this to me and Rose will get what's comin' to 'em. Season that and know that taste is the truth."

"Is Rose hurt, too?" I asked, not thinkin' they'd do anything to Rose.

"I never got to talk to her 'fore they caught up to me, but from what I saw, they was keepin her from leavin'," he said, starin' into the fire. "I made my mind that weren't gonna happen if I could help it. I'd come up with a way to go about gettin' her, but I got riled goin' in and made a mistake. They found me 'fore I could get her gone from there. Ole Two Suns and his bunch, they was. Warriors, all of 'em, same ones we saw at their camp. They done this to me." He raised his arms to show me his wounds.

"Dancing Bear will bring Rose home and all this will be over soon. Me and you will need to work the farm and tend the mules till Dad gets healed up, so you will need to stay around and see to it. Right, Cain?" I asked, hopin' he would answer right.

"That's right, little brother, but don't worry over it. Things got a way of workin' out, you'll see. Dad'll whoop this and we'll all gather meal corn together in the time when the leaves fall. Ole Cain ain't goin' nowhere. I need to heal up, and we got to get Dad back on his feet and the farm squared up. Rose will be along in time, and we'll get goin' on makin' us a family and have some young'uns like you," he said, a slight smile showin'.

Well, that was a bunch of mule-nasty he was speakin'. I know'd it. It weren't what he said or the words he spoke, but the mad in his voice that told me he was talkin' backwards. He'd be around, but it would be once this was all settled his way. Rose was comin' home with Dancing Bear and Cain know'd it, so he had no worries over her. It was what happened to him while he was in the valley and the things he went through at the hands of them heathens what caught him. Cain would heal up alright, and then he'd be gone, most likely by himself. There would be a chance he would not come back at all once he got goin', but that would be in the hands of the Great Spirit. There was no doubt in my young mind what Cain was thinkin'. Revenge. He was meanin' to kill Two Suns.

Chapter Twenty-Six

Cain's Revenge

A cold spell had set in, and Dad was still asleep the day after we'd found out about Fox Running. Black Oak and Rose left Dancing Bear and Moon Shadow at the low gap to take Fox's body home. The family had just made it outa the Yonah Valley when Dancing Bear sent them to check on Dad and bring word of what happened to Fox Running. They told of how the renegade called Two Suns had murdered him as they was leavin'. There was fresh cuts on both of George's arms. Dancing Bear and Sunshine would take Fox into the woods and bury him on the east side of the Rattlesnake so he will see Old Man Sun's first light early in the mornin's. The place was just south of where Dancing Bear had captured the eagle feathers, a spiritual place for his family. They was all beginnin' mournin'. Rose would cut off her long, beautiful hair, and Cain would cut his, too. Fox Running and Cain was blood brothers. Cain always saw Fox like a brother and looked after him; the two was close huntin' brothers and would go on hunts and walks for days durin' the cold time.

Now, Cain was growin' a real hate for ole Two Suns as the sadness tore at his heart. He was alone to figure things out since Rose went back with Black Oak at daylight. She and Wolf was expected to be home while the family was in mournin'. I think it was better for Cain that she be gone, 'cause he had some hard thinkin' to do. Killin' was a serious chore. There'd be no honor in this'un. This killin' just needed to be a killin', like huntin' an outlaw bear—get the critter dead and be done with it.

Two Suns was a renegade, as Black Oak named him, and renegades was outlaws to the white man. It was gonna get bad for him and his outlaw bunch when they was found. They'd all hit the woods and hardly a sign of 'em would be showin' after the murder of Fox Running. Black Oak told Cain and Momma that him and Dancing Bear was goin' back to the Yonah Valley as soon as Fox was buried to find 'em, even though they was still in mournin'. Cain never let on he'd be goin' with 'em, but he weren't sayin' much 'a nothin'. He was healed up some from the torture, but his mind was in Yonah, and on Rose. Their future was in his hands now, and he was near ready to take its trail. 'Fore all that, though, chores had to be done. Cain was goin' renegade huntin'.

Moon Shadow was at the murder and he was eager to make it all square. Fox's death had changed him and he had mean in him now mixed with hate. He made ready to go with Dancing Bear and Black Oak but was told to stay with several other young warriors and keep Two Feathers from tryin' at Dad and our family. Weren't no goin' back when one was told by Dancing Bear, so Moon Shadow would only have the hope that the evil one would show up lookin' for a fight. Most folks figured Cain would stay, too. As Black Oak told it, them heathens would be movin' and not put down in one place for fear of gettin' found. Bein' on the run like they was meant they could go most anywhere, and that made 'em even more dangerous. They know'd they'd crossed-up with both clans when Two Suns slit Fox's throat, and all would pay with their lives if they was caught. But Cherokee warriors are a tough bunch to track, even by other Cherokee who live to track and hunt. They spread out to travel, then pack back up at night for camp. Black Oak was the best tracker in the Choestoe clan, meanin' they'd need to watch real close to not leave sign he would find.

***

Old Man Winter had laid in on the Choestoe Valley the mornin' after Dancing Bear and Black Oak left to go back into the valley, two days followin' the killin' of Fox Running, and cold was all around, makin' it a poor time to be trackin' in the woods. Snow could come at any time. We'd get a few good lays every winter, but it was the cold north and west wind that

could kill a body. The wind could blow hard and cold enough
to burn your skin red if it touched it. We wore hats mostly
through the year, but in the coldest of times we wore skin with
the hair turned in to cover our heads. Mine was made from
bear, which seemed natural to me, and it could cover my whole
face and neck if I wanted. All I had to do was just loose the
knots holdin' the cold flaps up and they'd fall down to the tops
of my shoulders. I could use the same straps to tie 'em under
my chin and back of my head to cover my face if I needed, so it
kept my head warm if I had to be out.

Cain had his whole set of winter skins on, Dad's favorite
.52 caliber Kentucky long rifle, powder and ball, his adl-adl
with sharp flint on the arrows, his possibles and some 'a Dad's
knives, as he slipped through the low gap at daylight the
mornin' after Rose and Black Oak left to go back to
Slaughter—the second mornin' after Fox's murder. He was
packed to hunt long. Nobody know'd where he'd gone for sure,
but it was no surprise to Momma when she found he was gone.

He was movin' slow and watchin' every movement of
every place he could as he made his way to the Yonah Valley.
Cain worked to keep his mind on the trail and fought to keep
Rose from his worry. Had he held her for the last time and not
even realized it? Was Two Suns gonna kill him 'fore he could
lay eyes on her again in this life? He laid it in God's hands as to
whether or not he would cross back through the gap after he'd
met up with Two Suns. One of the commandments was "thou
shalt not kill", but that one was gonna be forgot by a few for
now. He hoped God would understand his need for forgiveness
after all was made right. Him or Two Suns, one was gonna
cross the Great River soon. Cain know'd it could likely be him
if he was not watched over. He stopped before leavin' the gap
and bent to his knees to pray; needed to speak for himself to
make sure that Jesus know'd what was goin' on. It was terrible
worrisome on a body. He was facin' the fight of his life, for his
life, and all he wanted to do was go and be with Rose. He
know'd he had to keep his thoughts straight or it would be his
heart that got cut out. Fox Running was his friend, and his
sister, Rose, was to be his wife. The murderer Two Suns Rising
had done enough. Cain allowed he was not gonna hurt no more

folks. Cain got his back up and set his mind straight, started thinkin' only 'bout the fight ahead. It would be Two Suns who crossed the Great River, and Cain was gonna see to it.

***

Dancing Bear and Black Oak had been on the trail hard the whole day, yet still hadn't found a true sign as to where the outlaws had gone. Their trails all split up after the place of the killin', and it was near impossible to figure which trail they ended up takin'. They was battle-scarred warriors that know'd how to hide and keep hid. They also know'd when and how to kill. Now was a time to hide and keep outa sight till they got all the evil they needed to do finished with, then leave and hope folks forgot. The only problem was, it weren't gonna be forgot. Two Suns would pay the price for what he done sooner or later. Now that Cain's mind was right and he was on his trail, that debt was gonna be paid.

***

The knock on the door was soft, not hard like Black Oak or Granddad would do. I lifted the latch and eased the door open. Standin' in front of me was the most beautiful sight, 'cept for their hair—Rose and Wolf, with full beads on. I always loved seein' Rose. I reckon I loved her as much as any, and Wolf bein' here opened up a whole 'nother world for me. We'd be in the woods soon! My heart near jumped from my chest when the thought come to mind. It was always good when folks you liked come to visit.

"Rose, Wolf, welcome back to our home," I said. I didn't get the door much when folks come, as one of the big folks got it most times. "It's powerful good to see y'all. Come on in where it's warm."

"How is Thompie?" Rose asked.

"He's still sleepin', ain't opened his eyes yet. We talk to him and hold his hands and rub on him. He's still breathin', so he's still walkin' in this world," I said, tryin' to answer like a

Cherokee as best I could. I really didn't know how he was for sure, just near dead-lookin' was all.

Rose bent down on her knee and looked me in the eye.

"He is going to be fine, Jeb. He is strong. If the death spirit was here for him he would be across the river now. Stay strong, Jeb. Pray long and talk to Jesus for his life." She grabbed me and hugged me real hard, cryin'. I felt the tears drip and run down the back of my neck. They felt warm. She was still very sad, mournin' Fox.

As Wolf and me locked forearms and smiled at each other, I said, "Hello, my friend. I hope you're figurin' on stayin'. Will y'all be here for a while?"

"If it is by your mother's permission, then we can stay. Rose must ask her out of respect, because of Thompie and his healing. I know Rose can help take care of him, and if it is good with your family, I will stay, too," said Wolf, keepin' to the rules of respect and honor. He was Cherokee, pure Cherokee.

They know'd they could stay 'fore they ever left Slaughter Mountain, and that the two older warriors who come with 'em could stay as well. Moon Shadow welcomed the more experienced warriors, 'cause his thoughts was tellin' him the fight might cross the ridge and come to our place from the Yonah Valley. It only made sense they'd want to get to Dad 'fore the mountains on both sides of the big ridges got full of warriors who'd be huntin'em. The Cherokee didn't welcome killin' and torture unless they was a reason. Two Suns killed Fox Running to settle a debt, but in the eyes of the Cherokee, the debt was owed to my dad, a white man. All Cherokee would see it this way. Two Suns know'd that. To the tribe and to the family, this was plain ole murder. The Cherokee warriors of Dancing Bear's and A-Ga-Li-Ha's blood would see to it that things was made right to bring life on the ridges back to square, if they found 'em 'fore Cain did. If Cain found 'em first, mountain justice would be served. Either way Two Suns Rising and his murderin' warriors would only live if they left the valley...most likely they would not. They still needed Dad dead to square the life of Two Suns' brother. If they got Cain, that would make it even sweeter.

Rose was fully beaded when she come back to our place, so was Wolf. They wore necklaces and armbands with full beadwork on 'em. Wolf's knife sheath and pouches was covered in 'em, hangin' and wove into leather braids strung from the handles. They believed the ones across the river would come to get Fox Running soon, and they wanted to look their best for the visit. That weren't hardly how the *Bible* said it happened, but that's the way they saw it, so I didn't study over it. Wolf and his family didn't wear full on beads much, only for special times, so it was a sight when they had 'em all on. Momma had some fine stuff she wore on occasion, too, made mostly by A-Ga-Li-Ha. Indians was a givin' bunch but they liked to trade, too. She and Momma would trade her bead work for Momma's sewin' work. Momma got beautiful hand-made jewelry and Sunshine and her family got fresh homespun clothes. Folks traded. That's how they bought things in the mountains, mostly.

***

The leaves on the ground was frozen as Cain slipped through the woods. The sky was gray and looked like it might start snowin', but he never really noticed. A body could see deep in the woods when it was gray like it was, and he was movin' slow, watchin' through the trees—he know'd he was close. A faint track of a skin-covered foot caught his eye as he was followin' a deer trail down a ridgetop not far from the low gap. His skins matched the trunks of the trees, so he was near crawlin' from the base of one huge tree to the other. He'd found two more tracks just a short way back. Now he was trackin' what he thought to be three of the renegades. Cain hoped that Two Feathers, as we called him, was in with 'em. Trouble was, they was headed back north across the main ridge, north, toward Choestoe.

***

Dancing Bear and Black Oak covered a lot of ground near where the devils first split up by walkin' the hollers and ridges in all directions, but found very little sign. They'd searched every trail around where the killing happened that a man could travel and found nothin' to tell a story. It'd been hard trackin' since they'd crossed into the valley in search of revenge, but their work had grow'd no fruit and it was cold. From the lack of sign, both men know'd the heathens was gone, *and* in what direction they was most likely headed. Weren't been enough time yet for word to get out much 'bout the murder of Fox Running, so the outlaws would figure it safe enough to try and slip in, kill Thompie and get out 'fore any warriors got on their trails. God could only know where they'd go from there. Every Cherokee warrior in Choestoe would be tryin' to catch their trail and hunt 'em once word did get out. Folks loved Dad and Fox Running, and all would believe it murder.

As they sat and smoked over the first fire they'd built all day, Dancing Bear began to speak. "The trail is cold, Black Oak. Our enemy has gone from this valley. I fear we know where he goes. His debt has not been paid to the one who did the killing, even though my son was made to cross the Great River. Thompie is in danger, if he still lives, and Moon Shadow and the young men of our family will soon have visitors, I fear—warriors on a trail of murder. We must eat and rest. Then go at first light to the home of my brother. I pray to the Almighty that we will not be too late. My heart will not hold with the loss of another member of my family."

"No, we are not too late," said Black Oak. "They will need time to move and not leave sign or be seen, so they will not hurry. We can go straight through the low gap at daylight and pass by them, staying to the main trail. We can run and will make it back long before they reach Thompie's place. This is so, Dancing Bear."

"You are wise, my brother. Like a warrior, you keep your thoughts on what is at hand. Like a fool, I am confused by a broken heart. We will travel at first light. If Thompie still lives, we will fight for him and his family. Two Suns Rising will see justice done."

***

The tracks was fresh. Cain was followin' back a ways so he could stay hid. The trail was more sightful now, as two more sets of tracks had joined the one he'd been followin' a quarter mile back. Dark was comin' on them outlaw Indians, and they would bunch up soon for night camp. They was headed down into the valley, and there was no doubt in Cain's mind now what their minds was set on. This was the same bunch that hung him up and tortured him for nearly two days. He had it out for any of 'em, but would wait and watch for now. He figured they'd be eight left since they was eleven 'fore Dad ended two of 'em and Black Oak wounded a third.

It was a dark night and the shortage of moonlight played in Cain's favor. He'd followed the murderers to their night camp and waited till it was way past last light to slip within fifty paces downwind of 'em. He could smell their stench. He'd not be fool enough to walk in on 'em this night. They was after blood and his would do for sure. He know'd these Indians and where they was most likely headed, so he figured to wait his time and follow close behind till they split up, then work on makin' things square with ole Two Suns.

***

Black Oak was right when he told Dancing Bear they could beat the renegades to our place. The warrior's trot had put them through the low gap, back down into the valley and over to our place in just a few hours. All seemed the same to Dancing Bear as when he'd left a few days before, except for Rose and Wolf now bein' there, and Moon Shadow and the guard he was with. Dad still hadn't woke that anybody had seen, but Momma hadn't had to use the mirror for a while since he was breathin' some better.

There was one thing that had changed, although Dancing Bear couldn't see it. Word of Fox Running's murder had got out, and the Cherokee warriors of the Choestoe clan was makin' their way to the low gap. They would find the sign of those who'd passed along the ridges east and west of the gap, then make their way in packs of two, each takin' a different trail. They was gonna see to it murder was paid blood-for-blood. Luck was soon gonna run out on Two Suns and his heathen bunch, they just didn't know it yet. Once the warriors of the Choestoe clan struck their trails outa the low gap, they would not let a single one of them murderers leave Choestoe. And since that Yonah bunch was warriors, they would not be taken for slaves—it would be death for all those who followed Two Suns and his killin' trail.

***

Cain made a cold camp on the east side of Rattlesnake Mountain after watchin' Two Suns' camp for an hour or more. He tracked back a good half a mile from their camp 'fore stoppin' for the night. He wanted no chance those renegades would find him. He'd made the mistake of thinkin' them careless once before and got caught. This time, it was certain to him he would not let that happen again. A quick death may be the only mercy he showed any of 'em.

His mind had cleared straight when he got close to their camp earlier in the day; now he had nothin' in his thoughts 'cept the comin' fight. His plan was to slip up close again a couple hours 'fore daylight, then follow Two Suns when the bunch split up for the day. It was him that was the head of the snake. Cain know'd enough about snake-killin' to know you had to take off the head to end the danger. He figured once Two Suns was dead that the rest of the bunch would get gone. It was him Cain wanted anyhow, so all should work out for the best if he could just kill him. It all sounded good in his mind and he figured it to work, but he know'd enough about plannin' a fight to know things hardly ever went as figured. He would trust God to guide him and give him courage. Fox Running was his friend.

Daylight was slow comin', with it a feeling like it was gonna rain anytime. Cain's legs was growin' numb from sittin' so long and watchin', but he'd not move for worry he'd be spotted. He'd been watchin' the camp for a good hour. Dad's gun primed and loaded lyin' in his lap. It seemed the warriors weren't in no hurry to get goin'. He hoped they'd split up soon.

Somethin' was not right. Two Suns Rising weren't with 'em. It was light good. Cain could clearly see seven warriors and no leader. He'd made sure they was all there the night before. Now there was only seven.

Cain wondered where he'd gone to and why. Then he figured it. His skin grow'd cold and wet—Two Suns was in the woods on the hunt. He'd be circlin' the camp lookin' for folks just like him. It was an old warrior's habit; he'd find Cain if he didn't keep a sharp eye. Cain got his legs out from under his backside and stretched 'em out on the hill to get the blood flowin' good. He needed to move, to join the hunt. Two Suns was in the woods, and Cain weren't gonna be caught again. It was his time to do the catchin'.

He'd been sittin' in an ivy thicket on a small hill overlookin' the camp, but now he found himself easin' to the backside of it and stalkin' off to the west. The ground was wet and he could move real quiet. He made sure not to break any hidden sticks that ended up underfoot. Two Suns would be doin' the same thing. It was gonna end up bein' who saw who first when the fight come. Cain's heart was racin'. A cold shiver run down his back like the Death Angel had flew across him. It'd been kinda like this down in the Yonah Valley when they slipped in behind him and knocked him plumb out with a blow to the back of the head. He'd woke up tied and hung like a meat pig; they laughed at him over it. The thought of all they did to him come back, with it his anger, makin' his muscles tighten up. He reached for his knife to have a grip at the handle. He thought he could feel the blade slippin' through the soft skin of ole Two Suns, straight to the heart. He longed for revenge and know'd it was near—Cain could feel him.

***

Two Suns had near finished his circle of the camp and had not found any sign of his enemy. He felt comfortable that his bunch was safe and nobody know'd they was anywhere around. He would soon reach the home of the one who had killed his brother. He would make sure to send the white man walkin' on the other side of the River. He know'd the wound made by the arrow days before might have done him in, but he had to make sure 'fore he left the country. He and the renegade warriors who'd chose this trail would no longer be welcome in the mountains once folks found out about Fox Running, and they know'd it. They would go and kill the white man and his yellow-haired son, take his weapons and his stock, rape his women, steal his family and take them away to sell as slaves. White slaves was rare and fetched a lot of money in the right market. He know'd that market and how to sell. He and his bunch had sold there many times. He smiled at the thought of how the white man would feel about what he was gonna do to his family.

***

It was just a glimpse, a split second of movement, but it caught Cain's eye. A dark, shiny motion that was most likely not a bear. He lowered himself some and kept his eye on the spot where he'd seen...what? Another slight eyeful told him it was an Indian, but which Indian? A feather, white and brown, wavin' slightly with the breeze as he stalked. Could be Dancing Bear's eagle feather—he'd be wearin' it, certain. Another glimpse, and—no, not Dancing Bear, hair was too short. Another movement told more. Stalkin', huntin', movin' so as not to be found, a warrior, learned in the ways of war and slippin' through the trees hardly seen. He was smooth like deep river water flowin', movin' toward the camp with a watchful eye. But was he friend, or enemy? He crouched some as he stalked out from behind a small white pine, lookin' in all directions to make sure he'd not missed seein' anybody. It was Two Suns!

Cain could see him clear as the sun itself, now. He must've felt safe, 'cause he just all of a sudden stood right up and walked into camp, stoppin' on the other side of the campfire from Cain. He reached out with both arms and warmed his hands over the flames. The anger in Cain boiled at the sight of him standin' there, talkin' without worry to his killin' brothers. He was taller than they was.

Cain told me later that it had all seemed like a dream. The gun was against his shoulder and the bead from the .52 caliber laid square on Two Suns' chest 'fore he even realized he'd raised it. Cain couldn't have stopped now if he'd tried. It was almost like a spirit took hold of Cain's arms, makin' him near helpless to stop even if he'd wanted to. The evil was gonna die now, and he held the bead steady just like he'd been practicing.

BOOM!!!

***

Black Oak and Dancing Bear was on the hunt and near the bunch when Black Oak heard the shot, so he turned and started movin' toward it, cautious-like. He watched and listened close as he went. Even though the ground was wet, he could hear the thumpin' of footsteps runnin' near straight at him. He know'd when he heard 'em that it weren't no critter, as he'd heard this noise in battle. A warrior was pickin'em up and puttin'em down, runnin' for his life and headed right at him. He froze as he watched. Within a few seconds he saw the Indian comin' on a dead run. Black Oak know'd when he saw him that he was one of the murderin' bunch, and his blood rushed to his heart and into his arms. As the Indian come on, Black Oak stepped out from where he'd been watchin' and slapped that Indian square in the mouth, landin' him on his back with a thud. The knife was already drawn. In it the warrior saw, reflected off the huge blade of George Black Oak's knfe, his last ray of sunshine this side of the River. He wished, as the edge found his heart and the light started to fade, that he'd never met Two Suns Rising.

His world went dark.

***

As the smoke from the burnt powder was risin', Cain made his way east and moved to the other side of the camp and reloaded. He was mad at himself for takin' Two Suns the way he'd done, but he was just so ready to see him dead. It was near cowardly to do what he did, but when things got the way they were and folks was gettin' hurt and killed the way they was, things was sometimes done different. It didn't matter how the murderer died, just that he was dead and would hurt no more folks. That would be all anybody cared about. That was the way Cain felt, too. He just wanted the devil dead and the killin' to stop. There was no honor in courage when evil like him walked the earth. Cain know'd everyone would feel the same—just send him on and let's be done with it. Cain obliged 'em.

There was no movement in camp, so Cain moved on in. He wanted to know for sure the murderer was dead. There was a good-sized puddle of blood where the lead ball had knocked Two Suns flat down on the ground. He was gone but would not be far. The blood was dark. Cain could tell it was flowin' from vitals. It would now only be a matter of a short time till the lead ball would finish its chore. The crimson trail tracked south into an ivy thicket. Cain leaned his gun against a tree and drawed his knife to go and finish his work. He know'd from the sight of blood that ole Two Suns would be very weak, so he walked faster than he would if he was blood-trailin' a deer or bear. He'd been right, it weren't far-in till he found what he know'd he'd find. Two Suns had gone as far as he would go in this life, but still, he had life.

He was leaned back against the base of a maple tree, strugglin' to breathe. His right hand tryin' to stop the flow of life from his wound, but the hole in the left side of his chest was from a square hit by a .52 caliber Kentucky long rifle. The blood was leakin' out between his fingers, thick in front and puddlin' up to run behind him in the back. The ball had gone plumb through. Cain found it near unbelievable he'd gone as far as he did. Cain moved up in front of him and squatted on his heels to look evil right in the eye. He felt no sympathy as he put the point of his knife under the dyin' warriors chin, makin' it hard for Two Suns to draw air.

"You should not have taken an innocent life with your evil ways, heathen," Cain said, as the dyin' warrior struggled to breathe. "I have killed you with no honor, 'cause there is no honor in killin' cowards like you. You will not be known in any songs. I will stay here and watch you suffer while you die, like the ones you made to suffer here in Choestoe with your yellow-backed killin'. You are a fool. I will marry the Cherokee girl your prince wants. We will have a long life here and make many children to carry on my name. This you will never have. I will cut out your heart, and you will feel no love across the River. Know when you get there and see my ancestors that it was Cain Collins, son of Thompie Collins of Choestoe that sent you there."

Chapter Twenty-Seven

Life Goes On

The murderer's body was stiff by the time Dancing Bear and Black Oak found the camp. His heart had been tore from his chest, gone, and his right hand was cut clean off, layin' in his lap. Black Oak found the heart stuck to a small broke Hemlock limb not far from the camp just like he know'd he would, the blood dried and no longer drippin' to the ground. There was no sign of who was there and done the killin'. No Cherokee with any honor would claim this.

Dancing Bear was leavin' the place just like he and Black Oak found it. They would not touch anything, would wash themselves as soon as they found proper water. The evil that was in that murderer was loose and stalkin' about; his ancestors needed a few days' to gather and cross the river to come and fetch the soul. Gave a body the shivers just thinkin' on it. The dead one would never have love on the other side without his heart, and he could not hunt without his hand. His soul would be blind from the Hemlock limb piercing his heart. He was doomed to suffer there for what he caused on Mother Earth, and all the songs and stories about him would cease to be spoken around Cherokee fires. To speak the name could bring back the evil; that was to be guarded against forever.

Dancing Bear and Black Oak built a fire after they washed, and smoked over all the things that had happened. It had been a terrible thing for him to lose Fox Running, but now his son would know peace on the other side. His killer had been made to pay by somebody who'd made sure he would not find peace among his ancestors. Dancing Bear smiled as he thought about how he'd be seein' his son again with Jesus, but would never have to lay eyes on the murderin' coward that made his son go away. There was a special place for folks like him. Once he got there, he would bother nobody else. Those thoughts was comfort enough for the heart-broken father.

Dancing Bear was at peace.

***

Cain had washed in the same little creek that Dancing Bear and Black Oak washed, but left no sign he'd been there. It had been at least two hours since the killin' shot, and he wanted no livin' soul to know it had been him that pulled the trigger. He was not proud of what he'd done, killin' that way, but it was done. It was a good thing to be rid of the worry. His next concern was Dad and he set his new trail for home. His plan was to stay the night with Dad and then move on to Slaughter the followin' mornin' to find Rose, not knowin' he would see her much sooner than that at our place. He was gonna walk with her and explain things to her; how he loved her and wanted to spend the rest of his life by her side. He was gonna talk with Dancing Bear and ask that he be allowed to visit in a courtin' way and if he'd oblige him by letting him marry his daughter. It was a good trail and he walked it many times in his mind as he made his way home. He didn't understand what he was feelin'. For the first time in his natural born life...Cain was scared.

***

Rose was waitin' on Cain. She just had no notion of when he might return or if he would return. A simple walk to the barn. A look to the trail he'd be comin' in on. A want for his warm body she hoped was still on her side of life. She felt the danger in her soul as the one she needed was facin' certain death if he made a mistake. She prayed he wouldn't. As the tears wet her cheeks and fell to the dirt, her prayers came for her as her beloved limped from the woods. A pause for a look and then an exhausted, painful trot to her arms. The one was now complete. His heart was now complete. His life was now complete. God was good.

***

Wolf missed his brother. It was several moons later 'fore he ever really got the loss outa his day-to-day livin'. The time of mournin' was over and he was home, but he just kept on hurtin'. I stayed with him a lot durin' the rest of that season. He finally got to where he wanted to get back out in the woods and do the things we liked to do. He'd lost some of the spark in his eyes that winter. Truth be told, I don't think he ever got all of it back. It was like a part of him left with Fox Running. They'd been very close brothers. Him dyin' would bother Wolf for the rest of his whole put-together. Yes sir, that killin' changed Wolf.

Dad was better. He'd woke up some time durin' all the goin's on, but Momma didn't tell him nothin' till he was up takin' soup. Fox Running's killin' struck him hard. He kinda blamed himself, but it weren't his fault at all. He was lookin' out for his family—evil had to be dealt with—and the killin' just become part of it. Justice was had and the thing was now behind all the folks it touched. Life went on.

We plowed and we planted, and when the time for harvest come, we would harvest. Wolf and me would start huntin' deer and bear and hog in the fall. I would soon learn how to shoot Momma's small bore rifle. Wolf had already taught me the bow. Dancing Bear had made me one of my own. I could take squirrels and rabbits and turkeys for supper with it. That made Dad proud and filled his belly. He loved squirrel dumplin's.

I'd found me a place Momma called a prayin' place. I would go there and pray and think in the quiet. It weren't far up in the mountains; took me 'bout half an hour to walk there takin' my time. The view out over the valley was a comfort when the leaves was off. I would spend a lot of time there just by myself, if I didn't have chores or weren't out huntin'. I could see the tub Dad built from there, and the iron kettle, too. I liked goin' to my prayin' place. I could talk to God and hear Him better 'cause it was quiet. I'd go there a right smart.

It was there not long after all had settled that I found myself sittin' and restin' and just lookin' out over the valley through what holes in the leaves I could see through. The colors in the leaves would blind a body; the beauty was more than one could take in. Harvest was comin' on, then the late fall with Killin' Time just a while off. I prayed for my family, I prayed for Wolf, and I prayed for all the folks that lived in the valley, White and Indian. I prayed for the Cherokee in Yonah and I prayed a prayer of thanks for the peace the two clans now shared, with no more killin' than what'd been done already. Them renegades was never seen in the mountains again. Folks was happy. I was happy. My family was happy. The Cherokee for the most part was happy. Even Dad's mules was happy. God had blessed our lives by lettin' us live and grow in Choestoe. As I made it from a child to an old man, I learned to depend on Him for the things I needed; to trust Him as a guide through this life. I trusted in Him and know'd He'd take care of me. And He did. That's the way it was for me and my family and for most of the folks that lived in Choestoe. A most beautiful valley. The land where the rabbits dance.

Meet Our Author

J. R. Collins

J. R. Collins was raised in the valley he so passionately writes about. A descendant of the first pilgrims to the area, he proudly claims heritage and roots through the people of the Appalachian Mountains that settled in the Choestoe Valley sometime in the latter part of the 1700's. Born and raised in North Georgia, he grew up like Jeb, hunting and running the ridges of Choestoe.

Collins is a graduate of Young Harris College in the North Georgia Mountains. As of 2013, he has been Director of Advertising for *The North Georgia News*, after having worked as staff writer for sports stories and special events.

He is in the process of publishing *Tips from the Range - Ten Things All Golfers Must Know*, and is currently writing Jeb's sequel, *Living in the Land Where Rabbits Dance*.

Made in the USA
Columbia, SC
25 June 2021

40521292R00163